OTHER BOOKS BY LARRY COLLINS AND DOMINIQUE LAPIERRE

Freedom at Midnight
O Jerusalem!
Or I'll Dress You in Mourning
Is Paris Burning?

THE

FIFTH HORSEMAN

A NOVEL

LARRY COLLINS

AND

DOMINIQUE LAPIERRE

SIMON AND SCHUSTER · NEW YORK

COPYRIGHT © 1980 BY LARRY COLLINS AND DOMINIQUE LAPIERRE
ALL RIGHTS RESERVED
INCLUDING THE RIGHT OF REPRODUCTION
IN WHOLE OR IN PART IN ANY FORM
PUBLISHED BY SIMON AND SCHUSTER
A DIVISION OF GULF & WESTERN CORPORATION
SIMON & SCHUSTER BUILDING
ROCKEFELLER CENTER
1230 AVENUE OF THE AMERICAS
NEW YORK, NEW YORK 10020
SIMON AND SCHUSTER AND COLOPHON ARE TRADEMARKS OF SIMON
& SCHUSTER
DESIGNED BY EVE METZ

MANUFACTURED IN THE UNITED STATES OF AMERICA

1 2 3 4 5 6 7 8 9 10

LIBRARY OF CONGRESS CATALOGING IN PUBLICATION DATA
COLLINS, LARRY.
    THE FIFTH HORSEMAN.
    I. LAPIERRE, DOMINIQUE, JOINT AUTHOR.   II. TITLE.
PZ4.C7123FI   [PS3553.047487]   813'.54   80-14643
ISBN 0-671-24316-0

CONTENTS

And I looked and behold a pale horse:
and his name that sat on him was Death,
and Hell followed with him. And power
was given unto them over the fourth
part of the earth, to kill with
sword, and with hunger, and with death,
and with the beasts of the earth.

REVELATION, 6:8

PROLOGUE

WEDNESDAY, DECEMBER 9

THE RAIN, THE BITTER RAIN OF WINTER, FLAYED THE window with its silken lash, sending jagged rivulets coursing down its plate-glass surface. The man peered out, across the empty canyons, into the black recesses of the night. He shuddered. No night to be on the water. His eyes strained for a glimpse of the familiar outlines of the harbor at his feet, the low-lying lights of the Jersey docks, the tip of Governor's Island, the distant blink of West Bank Light out beyond the Verrazano Bridge.

Behind him a Teleprinter clacked. He glanced at his watch. It was a few seconds after midnight. Twenty miles out to sea, the first incoming freighter to enter the Port of New York on this Wednesday, December 9, had just arrived off Ambrose Light, passing as she did into U.S. Customs control. The man turned to his desk. He was, from his command post in Room 2158 of the World Trade Center, responsible for the Customs control of the harbor for the next eight hours. He opened the logbook on his desk to a fresh page and entered at its head the date of the new day beginning in the records of the Port of New York. Then he tore off the piece of paper spewed out by the Teleprinter and diligently entered the scanty information it provided on the 7,422nd ship to enter the harbor that year: her name, the *Dionysos;* the flag she flew, Panamanian; her destination, Pier 3 of the Brooklyn Ocean Terminal.

When he had finished, he flicked the *Dionysos'* name onto the keyboard of the computer terminal beside his desk. The terminal was linked to the NCIC, the National Crime Information Center. The record of any criminal violation in the history of the *Dionysos* from the seizure of a kilo of heroin in her hull to the brawling of one of her seamen in a Galveston, Texas, bar would be reproduced in seconds on the screen above his keyboard. He noted the lime-green column of light forming there: "No Record of Violation."

He grunted and marked the letters "N.R." beside the *Dionysos'* name in the space his log provided, evidence there was no reason for the U.S. Customs to be concerned with the aged freighter riding the heavy swell of the Ambrose–Barnegat Channel.

For generations a little red ship tossing on the edge of the Atlantic's angry tides had been the sentry post before the New World, the harbinger to millions of men and women of the Promised Land. The old Ambrose Lightship was gone now, a museum piece moored to a pier in lower Manhattan. The Ambrose Light off which the *Dionysos* waited in the predawn darkness was a Texas oil-drilling platform, a dull-gray structure topped by a cluster of radar antennas and a helicopter pad. Beyond the steel piles that held it to the ocean floor, the bottomless gray seas rolled down to the Bay of Biscay and all the shores of Europe. Behind it, a pale glow stained the horizon, the reflected lights of the great city to which Ambrose was the gateway.

On his bridge the master of the *Dionysos* stared impatiently at those beckoning lights. The rain had eased now, softening to a cold spray that stung his bearded face. Beneath his feet he could feel his vessel's aging plates creak with each toss of the Atlantic's waves. She was one of the few Liberty ships, the DC-3s of the oceans, still in commission. From the Anzio beachhead through a score of owners and half a dozen flags, she had hauled cargo and contraband around the world for almost forty years.

The company under whose registry she now sailed, Transocean Shippers, had been incorporated six months earlier under public deed 5671 issued by Notary Public Three of the Circuit of the City of Panama. The address given on its registry certificate was that of a small law firm in Panama's Calle Mercado. In the law firm's files, the company's headquarters was carried as a post-office box in Lucerne, Switzerland. As was the case with most of the world's shipping, from supertankers to obscure fishing vessels, all trace of the *Dionysos'* owners ended there at an anonymous post-office box.

The Sandy Hook pilot on the bridge beside the master grunted and tossed his cigar overboard. The time had come to start the *Dionysos* up the Ambrose Channel to port.

The master watched as off to starboard the low silhouette of Jones Beach gave way to the outlines of Coney Island and the squat shadows of the tenements of the Rockaways. There was no sound on the bridge except the intermittent clang of the buoy bells rocking in the darkness on the Atlantic's swell and, rising from below, the slap of sea on steel.

Then, suddenly, the master knew that the man was there. Without even looking he sensed his brooding presence on the bridge. He glanced sideways and saw him, the *Dionysos'* only passenger. He was hunched over the starboard rail, his back to the master and the pilot, his black leather jacket's collar turned up to ward off the rain, a checked tweed cap jammed tight over his ears. Silently, he stared at the oncoming shore. The master moved to his side.

"Not cold?" he murmured.

There was no reply.

The man drew a cigarette from the pocket of his leather jacket. He did not offer the master one. He struck a match, cupping its flame with the cradle of his palm as he did—the swift, practical reflex of a man long accustomed to lighting cigarettes in the open, in defiance of the wind. In its brief glow the master saw again the uneven welt of the flesh of the scar that ran from the passenger's left ear down to his shirt collar.

The passenger was in his early thirties. He was not tall; barely an inch or two taller than the stubby master. He was lean; but even there in the darkness on the bridge the master could sense the heavy roll of his shoulders, the bulge of an upper chest so muscled that it was out of proportion with the rest of his body. Probably a weight lifter, the master had thought when he saw him first, sitting on the edge of his bed in the cabin the ship's owners had ordered the master to turn over to him.

His hands were wrapped tightly around the railing of the bridge, his knuckles seeming to emit a whitish glow, as if, driven by some inner strain, he was trying to rip the rail from its moorings. They were frightening, those hands, crude blocks of flesh. The passenger had spent hours during the voyage hardening them, hammering them against the ship's bulkheads in karatelike blows.

"Been to New York before?" the master asked.

The passenger turned his eyes to him. They were pale blue, a blue as fragile, as delicate as the bule of old Wedgwood procelain; the only fragile aspect, the master had often thought, of the passenger's being. There was no hint of feeling in them now. They were as cold and as remote as the sea around them. He looked at the master, studying him for a long moment. Then, wordlessly, he returned to his silent contemplation of the shoreline.

Ahead a blinking beacon beckoned to the *Dionysos,* West Bank Light. She hove to starboard around the light, leaving off to port the most dangerous spot in the harbor, Roman Shoals. On her new course, she pointed up the Narrows, her prow bearing straight for Verrazano Bridge. Suddenly, there in the light of breaking day was the prodigious spectacle that had brought joy and hope to so many millions: the towers of Manhattan emerging from the mists, dark tree trunks of a petrified forest of glass and steel, tips brushed by the scudding clouds.

The *Dionysos* sailed straight ahead toward the skyline rising before her prow. The master could distinguish the buildings of lower Manhattan now. He pointed them out to his passenger, the twin towers of the World Trade Center, Chase Manhattan Plaza, the Bell Telephone Building. Finally, he waved toward the familiar figure in her greenish robes of bronze, lost almost against the imposing backdrop.

"Statue of Liberty," he announced. "Recognize her? You must've seen pictures of her."

The passenger gazed at him. Again his face was expressionless, as void of emotion as a pharaonic mask.

"No," he said.

Then he turned away and spat down at the dirty green water sliding along the hull.

The *Dionysos'* horn shuddered the air. Shifting her course away from Manhattan's beckoning skyscrapers, she swung east to the low-lying piers of Brooklyn, toward three long piers pushing out to sea on wooden piles, their surfaces darkened to the color of dried blood by seaweed and algae.

Two generations of GIs had sailed away from those decaying piers of the old Brooklyn Army Terminal, off to the trenches of Belleau Wood or the beaches of Normandy. Along the roof of the middle pier was a last reminder of the great crusades that had begun and ended here. The words painted there to greet millions of GIs returning from Europe had been a bright blue once, as bright and fresh as the hopes they had stirred. Now they were a lusterless gray, a fitting match to Brooklyn's drab, decaying docks. The passenger strained to read them in the early light.

"WELCOME HOME," they said.

Shortly after the *Dionysos* had moored, an inspector of the U.S. Customs and an officer of the Immigration and Naturalization Service appeared at the top of her gangplank. The master escorted them to the ship's small wardroom, where he signed before the Customs inspector four copies of one of the oldest and most traditional documents of the world's sea lanes, a ship's manifest.

"Report and Manifest of the cargo laden on board the S.S. *Dionysos* whereof Mr. Saltaferro is master, sailing from Piraeus and bound to New York," it began. Below was listed and described every piece of cargo the *Dionysos* carried, the shipper and consignee, the port at which she had taken it on and the port for which it was destined. Because of the letters "N.R." entered next to her name in the port's log the night before, her Customs inspection ended there with the master's signature.

Meanwhile, the mate had mustered the crew before the INS officer. Each seaman presented his seaman's book to the officer and was issued an I-95, a crewman's landing permit, which would allow him to come and go freely while the ship was in port. The INS officer handed the crew list to the master for his signature.

"No passengers?" he asked.

The master laughed. He gestured at his ship's tawdry wardroom, littered with old Greek newspapers, faded pinups, its wood panels reeking with the odor of rancid olive oil.

"Does she look like the *QE2*?"

The INS officer laughed, too.

The passenger watched the officials leaving the ship from the porthole of the master's cabin. When they had left, he removed his belt and unzipped the zipper which ran along its interior. From the pocket inside he removed a pile of hundred-dollar bills. He counted out five and fitted the rest back into his money belt.

He stepped into the next room, the master's office, and looked around. An old copy of *Playboy* lay on the master's desk. He opened it to the centerfold, carefully inserted the money, then closed the magazine, went back to the cabin, shut the door and lay down on the bed.

Roughly thirty minutes later, there was a knock on the cabin's main door.

"Who is it?" the man called out from the bedroom.

"I have something here for you. From Laila," a voice answered from the office.

"Put it in the middle of the *Playboy* on the desk. There's something there for you. Take it and go."

A tall gangly youth, his head totally shaven in response to some bizarre urge, entered the office and picked up the *Playboy*.

The man in the bedroom waited a few seconds after hearing the door slam behind the departing messenger. Then he rushed to the office to open the envelope that had been left behind. It contained a Social Security card and a piece of paper with an address and a telephone number. Below them was scrawled one word: "Welcome." The man smiled. This time, he thought, the word meant what it said. Suddenly he went taut. The door was opening behind him. The bald young messenger was back at the door. He stared for an instant at the passenger. "I'm sorry," he murmured, "I forgot my hat." He moved to pick it up and leave.

The man looked at him, his eyes as expressionless as they had been earlier on the bridge of the *Dionysos*. Then he relaxed.

"Hey," he said, his voice soft and gentle. "Come in. Have a drink. I've got to celebrate my arrival with someone."

An hour after sunset, his checked hat pulled tightly down over his ears, the collar of his leather jacket turned up against the cutting wind off the harbor, the passenger drifted out of the Brooklyn Ocean Terminal in the midst of a cluster of the *Dionysos'* crewmen heading for a night's drinking on the Brooklyn waterfront. No one made any effort to verify the identity of any of the seamen leaving the docks. He walked off alone down the ill-lit streets, past the burned-out tenements and barred windows of one of America's worst slums, disappearing into the Brooklyn night.

The following morning, several hours after the *Dionysos* had sailed, a pair of bums cooking a fish-scrap stew by the Fulton Fish Market noticed a body bobbing in the East River. Forty-eight hours later, a DD13, missing-person or unidentified-DOA form, recorded the incident in the archives of the New York City Police Department. The deceased was described as a Caucasian male, six feet two inches tall, weighing 172 pounds, between twenty-seven and thirty years of age, with brown eyes and a shaved skull. Cause of death was listed, according to the coroner's report, as a ruptured trachea provoked by a severe karatelike blow to the windpipe.

PART I

SUNDAY, DECEMBER 13:
7 P.M. TO MIDNIGHT

"This will change the world."

THE UNSEASONABLY COLD DECEMBER DAY DREW TO a close. Mounds of still-fresh snow, the heritage of the unexpected storm which had swept up the eastern seaboard seventy two hours before, lined the streets of the nation's capital. That snow, and the freezing weather which had followed it, had kept most of the city's 726,000 inhabitants indoors this Sunday afternoon, December 13.

The family dwelling behind the familiar façade of 1600 Pennsylvania Avenue had left their living quarters only once, to walk the eight blocks separating the White House and Washington's First Baptist Church. There, as he often did, the President had taught Sunday school, offering his fellow worshipers his own definition of the Bible: a constant interchange between God and man in which we struggle to justify ourselves. Now the somber strains of Sibelius' *Finlandia* filled the White House living quarters, a reminder of the pleasure the President of the United States found in the works of classical composers like Bach, Vivaldi and Wagner. In the dining-room fireplace a birch log fire crackled, giving the room a cozy, almost snug air. It also served the practical purpose of driving the chill from a room whose thermostat was set at sixty-five degrees, one more reflection of the President's determination to set an example of energy consciousness to his profligate countrymen.

Precisely at seven o'clock, the President and his family sat down to supper. On this December evening that family included his wife and two of their three children. Theirs could not have been a more informal group nor, appropriately enough, one more typical of a certain image of the two hundred and thirty million Americans over whom the man at the head of the table presided. Both he and his wife were wearing well-washed jeans. As always on Sundays she had, to the consternation of her staff, prepared supper herself, black-bean soup, cornbread, country ham and collards. The President invited his daughter to offer grace, and the four people joined hands around the table while she asked the Lord's blessing on the simple meal they were about to eat. Then, with a smile for his wife, the President attacked his black-bean soup.

The Presidency of the United States is a cruel burden, one to age any man, and the energetic glow of strength and purpose the President had brought to the White House had long ago begun to dim under the trials of his office. The lines that crinkled the corners of his sad blue eyes were deeper and far move evident now than they had been when he entered this house, and his once sandy hair had turned pale.

Still, the nation led by the man dining in the White House this December evening remained the most powerful, the richest, the most wasteful, the most envied and imitated nation on earth, the world's first producer of coal, steel, uranium, copper and natural gas. Her farmlands were a wonder of productivity. Nine tenths of the world's computers, almost all its microprocessors, three quarters of its civil aircraft, a third of its automobiles came out of American factories.

All that was safeguarded by a military establishment which possessed a destructive capacity unique in human history; the most sophisticated network of satellites that technology could produce; by seven layers of electronic warning systems and radar installations so sensitive they would detect a migrating flight of ducks hundreds of miles from the U.S. coastline. Indeed, the countrymen of the President could, that December evening, consider themselves a privileged caste, the people on earth least likely to be exposed to the horror of an enemy's assault.

The President had just finished the last of his soup when the phone rang in the sitting room next door. The sound was seldom heard in the living quarters of the White House. Unlike most of his predecessors, he preferred working off tightly worded pieces of paper, and his staff was trained to restrict his phone calls to only the most urgent messages. His wife rose to take it. A frown clouded her usually composed features when she came back.

"I'm sorry. It was Jack Eastman. He says he has to see you right away." Jack Eastman was the President's Assistant for National Security Affairs, a former Air Force major general who had taken the place of Zbigniew Brzezinski in the corner office of the White House's West Wing made famous by Henry Kissinger.

The President dabbed his lips with his napkin and excused himself. Two minutes later he opened the door of the living quarters himself. Eastman was a lean, youthful-looking fifty-three years old, all bone and muscle, one of those men to whom an old classmate, an old Army buddy, an old mistress can exclaim after twenty years of separation, "You haven't changed a bit" and, for once, mean it. One glance at Eastman told the President that this was not a routine interruption of his Sunday evening. He waved him to a seat and settled himself in a comfortable apricot wing chair beside the television set.

Two kinds of men had occupied the high office Eastman now held, presiding over the flow of documents that was the great trunk artery upon which the security of the United States depended. There were those like Kissinger and Eastman's predecessor, ambitious men determined to run the world for the President of the United States from their seat beside the throne; or those like Al Haig, who had served Richard Nixon, products of the military, brilliant chiefs of staff, sorting out the options, honing the recommendations down to a fine point, but always careful to leave the real decision-making in the President's hands.

Eastman belonged to the latter group. He was all business. Calculated flamboyance, the need for attention, an obsessive preoccupation with the media were as abhorrent to him as anonymity would have been to Henry Kissinger.

He handed the President a white folder. "Sir, I think you should begin by reading this. It's the translation of a document that was delivered to the Madison Gate at lunchtime in the form of a tape recording in Arabic."

The President opened the folder and took out the two typewritten pages it contained.

NATIONAL SECURITY COUNCIL

File Number: 12471–136281
CONTENTS: One envelope, manila, containing one blueprint, thirty-minute BASF tape cassette, four pages of mathematical formulas. Package delivered to EPS Sergeant K. R. Mabuchi, Madison Gate, 1531, Sunday, December 13, by a female, blond, estimated age, middle thirties, wearing a beige cloth coat, identity unknown. Translation of tape prepared by E. F. Sheehan, Department of State:

25

"6th Jumad Al Awal, 1,401 Year of the Hegira.

"To the President of the American Republic, may this message find you, thanks to the Grace of Allah, savoring the blessing of good health. Greetings and Respectful Tidings.

"I write to you as a man of compassion concerned with justice and the sufferings of the innocent and oppressed peoples. No people has suffered more from the oppression of the world this century than my Palestinian Arab brothers. They were driven from half of their ancestral home by an alien people, forced onto our Arab lands by your imperialistic Western powers. Then that same alien people occupied the other half of my brothers' lands in defiance of the Charter of the United Nations in their aggressive war in 1967.

"Now that alien people systematically attempts to dispossess my Palestinian Arab brothers from the last half of their homeland by placing upon it in ever-increasing numbers their illegal settlements, settlements which even you have condemned. The ultimate aim of this Zionist conspiracy is to occupy all that land, to uproot my brothers, to banish forever from our Arab soil the Arabs who were born upon it.

"You said you wish to establish peace in the Middle East and I beg God's Favor upon you for that, for I too am a man of peace. But there can be no peace without justice and there will be no justice for my Palestinian brothers while the Israeli, with your nation's blessing, continues to take away their lands with their illegal settlements.

"There will be no justice for my Palestinian Arab brothers while the Israeli refuses, with your nation's blessing, to allow them to return to their ancient home. There will be no justice for my Palestinian Arab brothers while the Israeli occupies the site of our sacred mosque in Jerusalem.

"By the grace of God, I now possess the ultimate weapon on earth. I have sent with this letter the scientific proof of my words. With a heavy heart but conscious of my responsibilities to my Palestinian Arab brothers and all the Arab peoples, I have ordered my weapon placed on New York Island. I shall cause it to explode in sixty-three hours from midnight this night, at 2100 Greenwich Mean Time, 1500 Eastern Standard Time, Tuesday, December 15, if, in the intervening time, you have not obliged your Israeli ally to:

1. Withdraw all of the illegal settlers and settlements he has established on the lands seized from the Arab nation in his 1967 War.
2. Withdraw his people from East Jerusalem and the site of the Holy Mosque.
3. Announce to the world his willingness to allow my Palestinian Arab brothers who wish to do so to return immediately to the

lands taken from them in 1967 and to enjoy there their full national rights as a sovereign people.

"I must further inform you that, should you make this communication public or begin in any way to evacuate New York City, I shall feel obliged to instantly explode my weapon.

"I pray God will deliver upon you the blessings of His Compassion and Wisdom at this difficult hour.

> MUAMMAR AL-QADDAFI
> President
> Socialist People's Republic
> of Libya"

The President looked up at his adviser, consternation and astonishment on his face. "Jack, what in God's name is this all about?"

"Sir, we just don't know. We haven't been able to determine whether this is really from Qaddafi or whether it's just another hoax of some sort. But what's of real concern is the fact that the nuclear-emergency command post at the Department of Energy out in Germantown tells us the design that came in with this thing is a very, very sophisticated piece of work. They've sent it on to Los Alamos for analysis. We're waiting to hear from them now. I've convened a Crisis Committee to deal with it for eight o'clock in the West Wing, and I thought you should know about it."

The President pressed the index finger of his left hand to his lips, thinking hard.

"How about the Libyans?" he softly inquired. "Surely they don't confirm the authenticity of this?"

"We haven't been able to raise any of their people either here or in New York, Mr. President. But they have so few people stationed here it could just be a coincidence."

"And our people in Tripoli?"

"State's onto them. But it's in the middle of the night over there, and getting hold of someone in authority in Tripoli in a hurry is always a problem."

"Has someone run a voice analysis on the tape?"

"The Agency has, sir. Unfortunately, the result was inconclusive. There seems to be too much background noise on their comparison tapes."

The President knotted his eyebrows in displeasure. The shortcomings of the CIA were one of his constant concerns.

27

"Jack." His mind was moving forward now. "It seems to me highly unlikely that this is from Qaddafi. No head of a sovereign nation is going to try to blackmail us by hiding an atomic bomb in New York. At the very worst it would kill twenty, thirty thousand people. A man like Qaddafi has got to know we have the capacity to utterly destroy him and his entire nation in retaliation. He'd be mad to do something like that."

Behind the President, through the room's graceful windows, Eastman could see the lights of the White House Christmas tree, bright golden sparks flung against the December night.

"I agree, sir. I'm inclined to think it's a hoax of some sort or, at the worst, a terrorist group masquerading behind Qaddafi for some reason."

The President nodded. He had reread not so long ago the FBI's 1977 study on the menace of nuclear terrorism and remembered clearly its conclusions: there was no danger of such an act from any of the identified and localized terrorist groups with one exception, the Palestinians. In the event of an Arab–Israeli peace settlement which left the Palestinian movement embittered and desperate, there were, the report warned, elements among them with the sophistication required for acts of nuclear terror.

The telephone rang. "Excuse me," Eastman said. "It's probably for me. I told the switchboard I was with you."

As his National Security Assistant moved to the telephone, the President stared moodily out the window. He was not, he knew, the first American President to face the possibility that terrorists had hidden a nuclear device in an American city. That had been Gerald Ford. The year had been 1974, the city Boston, and that threat too had involved the intransigent Palestinian problem. It had come from a group of Palestinian terrorists who threatened to detonate an atomic device in the Massachusetts capital if eleven of their fellows held in Israeli jails were not released. Like all of the fifty-odd nuclear threats made against U.S. cities or institutions in the decade of the seventies, that one had turned out to be a hoax. Before it had, however, his predecessors in the White House had to ask themselves whether they should—or could—evacuate the city—and not a word had ever leaked to the Bostonians whose lives might have been at stake.

"Sir?"

The President started as he turned to look at his adviser. He had paled noticeably. He was holding the telephone with one hand cupped over its mouthpiece. "Los Alamos just called in a preliminary analysis of the blueprint. They say it's a viable weapons design."

Across the Potomac River from the White House an elegant auburn-haired young woman in her middle thirties hurried through the waiting room of National Airport and down the stairs leading toward the Eastern Airlines shuttle terminal. She stopped in front of a bank of gray metallic left-luggage lockers and chose one at random. She placed a small white envelope inside, rolled two quarters into the slot commanding its lock and removed the key. Then she opened a second and deposited a bulky shopping bag inside. It contained a blond wig and a tan polo coat. This time she did not remove the key. Her task completed, she crossed the hall to a telephone booth and swiftly dialed a number. When her party replied, she mumbled only two words into the receiver, the number of the key she held up before her: "K six-oh-two."

Seconds later, she was rushing toward the terminal and the eight-o'clock shuttle to New York.

The man who had taken her telephone call carefully noted the numerals K602 on a slip of paper on which a telephone number, 202-456-1414, was already written. It was the number of the White House switchboard. He tucked the paper into the side pocket of his sheepskin coat and stepped out of his public telephone booth into the early-evening crowd flowing through New York's Pennsylvania Station. He was in his late thirties, a florid-faced man with a thin black moustache and a tendency to corpulence that his bulky coat effectively concealed.

He sauntered through the waiting room, then hurried up the station steps and out into the cold. A few moments later he was at the corner of Broadway and Forty-second Street, the edge of Times Square, savoring once again the torrents of light that had so impressed him years ago on his first visit to New York. No energy crisis here, he thought, staring at the glowing marquees, the garishly lit store windows, the advertising panels, sparkling carpets of color stretched out along the walls of night.

With the deliberate pace of a man who is looking for something, he crossed the street and started up Broadway. The spectacle on those sidewalks was even more grotesque, more Breughelian, than he had remembered. At Forty-third, a Salvation Army band and chorus, shivering in their blue uniforms, struggled through "O Come All Ye Faithful," only a few yards away from a gaggle of whores in satin hot pants, the shiny fabrics of their trousers clinging so tightly to their hips and upper thighs that every detail of the wares they offered was available for inspection.

You found every face in the world in that crowd, he mused. Gawking tourists; well-dressed theatergoers indifferent to the throngs around them; black pimps in leather greatcoats and high-heeled shoes; slum kids down from uptown screeching at each other like migrating starlings; shuffling winos, hats held out for a couple of coins; potbellied cops, pickpockets scanning the crowd for a victim, soldiers and sailors, their faces so young, so trusting.

At Forty-sixth Street a Santa Claus so emaciated no amount of padding could disguise him adequately for his role listlessly tolled his bell before an empty alms bucket. Just behind him, a pair of black transvestites in hip-high leather boots and peroxided wigs called out from a doorway, the timbre of their falsettos leaving no doubt about their sex.

Crossing the street, sensing the vibrancy, the palpable, dynamic human dimension of those throngs, he felt a sharp twinge of pain cramp his stomach. The ulcer. He turned into a Howard Johnson and ordered a glass of milk. Then he renewed his march up Broadway.

Suddenly, the sound of Frank Sinatra singing "Regrets, I've had a few, too few to mention" told him he had found what he was looking for. He entered a brightly lit radio and record shop, walked down its lines of albums and tapes to the banks of empty cassettes. Anxiously, nervously, he picked through them, looking for the one he wanted.

"Say, my friend," the clerk announced, "we got a special on Sonys. Three for four ninety-nine."

"No," he replied. "I need a BASF, a thirty-minute BASF."

The clerk shrugged and reached for a box on the shelf behind him. He threw three BASF tapes on the counter. "There you go. Three for five ninety-five."

His customer picked one up. "Thanks," he said, a hesitant, almost forced smile on his face, "but I only need one."

A few blocks away from Times Square, at the Kennedy Child Study Center on East Sixty-seventh Street, the Daughters of Charity of the Order of Saint Vincent de Paul prepared to open a spectacle of a vastly different sort. Gently, as unobtrusively as possible, they shepherded their children toward the tinseled brilliance of the Christmas tree beckoning to them like a lighthouse of hope from the center of the auditorium.

The spastic uncertainty of the children's movements, the slant of their eyes, the heavy tongues that rolled around their half-open mouths, all bore witness to the curse which lay upon their little bodies. They were mongoloids.

The mother superior motioned to the children to sit down, took an electric cord and plugged it into a socket. At the sight of the sparkling tissue of light inflaming the tree, a pathetic babble of discordant sound rose from the wondering faces around it.

The mother superior stepped toward their parents gathered around the room. "Maria Rocchia," she announced, "is going to open our program by singing for us the first lines of 'O Little Town of Bethlehem.'"

She reached into the circle of uplifted faces and took the hand of a ten-year-old with black hair tied in pigtails that tumbled to her shoulder blades. Gently, the superior coaxed her toward the center of the circle.

The child stood there a moment, terrified. Finally she opened her mouth. The only sound which escaped was a raucous bleat. Her head began to shake violently, sending her pigtails swirling about her. She stamped her feet in fury and frustration.

In the first row, a middle-aged man, his heavy torso wrapped in a well-pressed gray suit, reached a hand upward and plucked nervously at the collar of his white shirt. Each gesture of the child, each incoherent sound she emitted, sent a tremor of anguish through his heavy body. She was his only child. Since his wife had died of lymphatic cancer three years before, she had been in the nuns' care.

Angelo Rocchia stared at his daughter as though somehow the intensity of the love radiating from his ruddy face might calm the

31

tempest shaking her frail figure. Finally she stopped. A first hesitant sound, then another and another flowed from her mouth. The tone was harsh, yet the rhythm underlying it was perfect.

"O little town of Bethlehem,
How still we see thee lie . . ."

Angelo Rocchia dabbed with relief at the sweat sparkling on his temple just where the retreating skin of his forehead met the mass of his wavy gray hair. He unbuttoned the jacket of his suit and let his chest sag. As he did, one of the attributes of his calling became visible on his right hip. It was a Smith and Wesson .38 heavy-barrel service revolver. He was a detective first grade of the New York Police Department.

Twenty-three miles from the White House, deep in the Maryland countryside, a man in an underground cocoon reached for a telephone at the same time the little girl in New York was concluding her carol. He was the duty officer of the Department of Energy's Germantown, Maryland, nuclear-emergency command post, one of the dozens of steel-and-concrete moleholes, some secret, some not so secret, from which the United States would be run in an emergency or a nuclear war.

On the order flashed to him by Jack Eastman in the White House, minutes after Los Alamos' preliminary analysis of the weapons design had come in, he was about to set into motion the most effective response the U.S. government had been able to devise to the menace of nuclear terrorism. His gray telephone gave him access to the U.S. government's "Autodin-Autovon" closed military communications circuit, a global network whose five-digit numbers were listed in a seventy-four-page green volume that was probably the most secret telephone book in the world.

"National Military Command Center, Major Evans," came a voice answering his call from another underground command post, this one far below the Pentagon.

"Department of Energy, Emergency Operations Center," the warrant officer continued. He had no need to corroborate his identity or the source of his call since he was talking over a direct, secure line. "We have a nuclear emergency, code priority 'Broken Arrow.'"

He suppressed a shiver speaking those words. They were the code for the highest priority assigned to a peacetime nuclear crisis by the Department of Energy.

"Emergency site New York City. We require airlift facilities for a full mobilization of our dedicated personnel and equipment."

Those words were sending into action one of the most secret organizations under the control of the U.S. government, a collection of scientists and technicians kept on twenty-four-hour alert at the Department of Energy's Germantown headquarters, at the nuclear-weapons laboratories in Los Alamos and in Livermore, California, and at the old nuclear testing ranges north of Las Vegas.

Inevitably the group was known officially by an acronym, "NEST" for "Nuclear Explosives Search Teams." With their ultrasensitive neutron and gamma-ray detectors, their carefully refined and highly secret search techniques, the NEST teams represented the best scientific answer the United States had for the threat posed by the envelope delivered earlier in the day to the White House gate.

At the Pentagon, Major Evans pushed a series of code numbers onto the computer terminal at his communications console. In a second, the essential details of the emergency he had been requested to handle appeared on the television screen in front of him. He saw he would have to stage an airlift of two hundred men and their equipment out of Kirkland Air Force Base in Albuquerque and Travis Air Force Base in Oakland, California. The screen also showed him that the Military Air Command at Scott Air Force Base outside St. Louis had orders to assign an emergency of this sort top priority.

The major's computer console provided a last injunction: the planes must be routed to the Air Force base nearest the emergency site to allow the government to run the coming operation in strict secrecy, as far from civilian eyes as possible. He flicked another query onto his computer terminal.

"Your assembly area," he told the warrant officer in Germantown, "will be McGuire Air Force Base, New Jersey." Eighteen miles southeast of Trenton, an hour's fast driving from the Lincoln Tunnel, McGuire was the closest base to New York that could handle Starlifters. The Pentagon major looked at the clock overhead. As he was talking, his deputy beside him had already been in contact with the Scott Air Force Base operations desk.

"I mark nineteen fifty-nine Eastern," he told Germantown. "Your first designated aircraft will reach Kirkland at eighteen-thirty Mountain."

High in the night sky over Kansas, a C-141 carrying a load of spare engines to Lackland Air Force Base in Texas had just shifted course and was droning southwest to Albuquerque. Hunched over his chart table, its navigator was already working out the details of the flight plan he would follow on his trip back to New York.

It was precisely eight o'clock when the President of the United States entered the National Security Council conference room in the West Wing of the White House. The men and women in the room rose the instant his familiar figure appeared in the doorway. To even his most sophisticated advisers, there was always a special aura about the personage of the President, some intimation of the crushing dimensions of the problems he bore, of the awesome power that was his, of the responsibilities which made the holder of his office unique among men. He motioned to them to sit, while he remained standing, biting his lower lip as he often did when he was trying to concentrate, appearing, in his faded jeans, his rumpled cardigan, even smaller, even more vulnerable, than usual.

"I want to thank you all for being here tonight," he said in that soft, almost apologetic tone of his, "and ask you to pray with me that what's brought us here is just a hoax because . . ." his voice trailed off ". . . because if it's not, we've got a long, long night ahead of us."

He took his place in one of the inexpensive chairs upholstered in rust fabric ringing the oval conference table. The room was as unprepossessing, as unimaginative a place as the board room of a medium-sized Middle Western manufacturer of cardboard containers. Yet it was here that the thermonuclear Armageddon had been envisaged during the Cuban Missile Crisis; that the decisions which sent half a million Americans to fight and die in Vietnam had been debated; the plight of the fifty U.S. hostages seized by followers of the Ayatollah Khomeini pondered.

Its banal appearance was deceptive. At the touch of a button a massive screen came down from one wall. Another button swept aside a set of curtains to reveal an electronic mapboard. Beside each seat was a drawer containing a secure red telephone. Most important were the facilities of the White House Communications Center just beyond, holding the room in an L-shaped embrace. There, banks of communications consoles with televisionlike screens linked the room and the White House to every vital nerve center of the U.S. government: the Pentagon, the CIA, State, the National Security Agency, the Strategic Air Command, NORAD's National Command Center in Colorado Springs. A call coming out of that conference room could be dispatched to any U.S. military base in the world, to the gunnery officer of a guided-missile destroyer cruising off Guantánamo Bay in Cuba, to most U.S. military aircraft in flight.

The President glanced at the two dozen people filling the room. The principals, seated at the conference table itself, constituted the inner core of the U.S. government, the same kind of ad-hoc emergency committee that had guided the government debates in the Iranian hostage crisis: the directors of the Central Intelligence Agency and the Federal Bureau of Investigation, the Chairman of the Joint Chiefs, the Secretaries of Defense and Energy and the Deputy Secretary of State, sitting in for the Secretary, who was on a tour of Latin America.

The President turned first to William Webster, the soft-spoken Missouri jurist who led the 8,400 agents of the FBI. Since the Boston incident, his Bureau had had the primary responsibility for handling nuclear extortion threats. "Bill," he asked, "what have you got on this?"

"We've reason to believe, Mr. President, the extortion package was assembled outside the United States," Webster began. "Our lab has established that the typewriter used for the note was Swiss made. An Olympic. Manufactured between 1965 and 1970 and never sold, as far as we've been able to determine, in this country. The blueprint paper is French. Available only over there. The cassette was a standard thirty-minute West German BASF. The complete lack of background noise would indicate it was made in a studio under at least semiprofessional conditions. Unfortunately, there were no identifiable fingerprints on any of the material."

The President's next question was to a lean bald man in a Harris tweed sports jacket and gray flannels sucking a pipe, on his right. Gardiner "Tap" Bennington, the heir to a Massachusetts textile fortune, had replaced Stansfield Turner as the head of the CIA six months earlier. The Yankee patrician was one of the last of the Agency's old boys, a veteran of the OSS days when "Wild Bill" Donovan had plucked the nice young men off the playing fields of Yale and Harvard and inspired them with the unseemly vocation of spying for their country.

"Do we have any intelligence to indicate a Palestinian terrorist group might be ready to try something like this, Tap?"

"Not really, sir. It's something they've talked about for years. But it's always sounded more like hashish talk to us than anything else. We did have one report in the intelligence community in 1978 that a bunch of them were being trained by the Libyans to pull an armed raid on a nuclear power plant. Hijack it, so to speak. But we were never able to confirm it.

"We've been pulsing all our Palestinian assets since this came in. There are people out there capable of making a nuclear device. And there's material around. But so far we've had no indication that any of the groups we're watching have married the two up."

"How about the Israelis?" the President queried. "Have you been onto them?"

"Not yet, sir. It's our feeling it's still a bit early for that. For the moment we recommend holding this as tight as possible."

"And the Libyans?" The President turned to address his question to Warren Christopher, the Deputy Secretary of State. "Have we had any answer from Tripoli?"

"No, sir. The chargé went personally to the army barracks at Bab Azizza where Qaddafi and most of his ministers live, saying he had an urgent communication from the government of the United States. The guards wouldn't give him the time of day. Told him they had orders not to admit anyone before eight A.M." Christopher glanced at the clock on the conference room wall. "That's five hours from now."

The President drummed the tabletop with his fingertips. That would seem to confirm his suspicion there was little likelihood that Qaddafi was behind this. "Tell me, Tap," he said to his CIA director, "would Qaddafi even have the capacity to do something like this? Where's his nuclear program at these days?"

Bennington struck a match and noisily lit his pipe, a ploy he had learned from his second boss, Allan Dulles. "Well, sir, as you know, he's never made any secret of his intention to get atomic bombs." Bennington picked up a file stamped "Top Secret" from

36

the table in front of him. "We've been keeping a close eye on him and he's done a number of things that concern us very much. He's been literally flooding this country with students taking nuclear courses. Over a fifth of the Libyans who've studied here since 1973 have been enrolled in some kind of nuclear program or another."

The President shook his head. If Qaddafi gave away his oil as cheaply as we give away our knowledge, he reflected, we wouldn't have an energy crisis on our hands.

"All that, of course, is ostensibly for peaceful purposes," Benningtom continued. "What really worries us are the secret initiatives he's undertaken to get hold of plutonium or uranium for military purposes, the business in Chad, the link with the Paks which you're aware of."

The President was growing impatient. "Okay, Tap, but where is he right now? Can he or can he not make a bomb?"

Bennington leaned back in his chair. "In our judgment, he's at least five years away from it. He still has only one source of potential fissile material on Libyan soil, and that's that nine-hundred-megawatt light-water reactor the French have just set up for him."

The director of intelligence's words struck a responsive note around the room. Pressed by the staggering deficits left in France's balance of payments by the oil price rises of 1979, President Giscard d'Estaing had finally agreed to sell Libya a nuclear reactor, ostensibly to be employed to desalinize water.

Bennington leaned toward the President. "The reactor, as you know, is under International Atomic Energy Agency safeguards. They have inspectors down there regularly from Vienna. We've seen their reports and we see no evidence the Libyans have diverted fuel from the reactor."

A loud honking noise seemed to explode in the room. It was the Secretary of Energy blowing his nose. Delbert Crandell had a face that was stained the roseate hue of the overfed and underexercised. He was a Texan, crass, outspoken, and at the same time a knowledgeable physicist. With a dab of his handkerchief he cleaned up a stray splotch of mucus from the conference table and returned it to his vest pocket.

"If the only thing that stands between us and Qaddafi's making an atomic bomb from that French reactor of his," he noted in his rasping voice, "is those UN people over there in Vienna, we'd best head for the bomb shelters right now. They're like all those

UN agencies. They're so choked up by their Third World politics they couldn't fart if they spent all night eating red beans and ham hocks. They've got inspectors over there who can't tell a screwdriver from a monkey wrench. Some South American dictator's son who got the job because it was Argentina's turn to fill the slot."

It appeared for an instant that Crandell was through, but he was not. Almost angrily, he turned on Bennington.

"I'll tell you something else. Your own CIA nuclear inspection program isn't worth a shit, either. You've spent five years trying to figure out what the South Africans are up to, and you still don't know. The Indians blew up a bomb under your nose and you didn't have a clue they were going to do it. Hell, you people didn't even know the Israelis had a bomb until Ed Teller came back and told you they'd built one—with our goddamn uranium smuggled out of that plant up there in Pennsylvania."

The President rapped the table with his knuckles. "Gentlemen, we're wandering. Could Qaddafi have gotten the plutonium he'd need to make nuclear weapons out of that French reactor if he had cheated on it?"

His glance addressed the question to Harold Brown. The Secretary of Defense was one of the few men the President had retained from the previous administration. No one in the room was better qualified to answer it than he was. Brown was a former director of the Livermore, California, weapons laboratory, ex-president of Cal Tech and a brilliant nuclear physicist.

"Of course he could," he answered. "The French and the Germans have been going around the world for years trying to tell people you can't get nuclear weapons out of a nuclear power plant, so that they can sell more of them. Well, the fact is you can. We blew off a bomb made with plutonium that came from a reactor's burned-out fuel rods fifteen years ago. They know that. We gave them the results."

"Well, he'd still have to reprocess the plutonium, wouldn't he? Find a way to get it out of those fuel rods?"

"Mr. President, there's a common misconception in the world that reprocessing plutonium is a very complex, costly technique," Brown replied. "It isn't. It's nothing but straightforward chemistry and it's all out there in the books. If you want to do it on an amateurish basis, you don't need any of those complicated choppers or cold rooms. All you need is time, money and people and not all that much of any of them.''

The President's skeptical regard told Brown that he wasn't convinced.

''You know how the Russians clear a minefield, don't you? They march a company of men through it, right? If Qaddafi used the same technique here, got himself twenty Palestinian commandos willing to expose themselves to more radiation than was good for them for the cause, then the whole thing would become almost terrifyingly simple. In six months they could extract enough plutonium from the used fuel rods of a reactor like that to make twenty bombs. In a couple of cow barns where a satellite would never spot them.''

The Defense Secretary sighed. ''The PLO gets plenty of commandos to volunteer for suicide raids. Why wouldn't they be able to get twenty of them to volunteer to die of cancer to make a weapon that could destroy Israel?''

Two thirds of the way across the United States, Harold Agnew, the director of Los Alamos Scientific Laboratories, stared anxiously out of his office window to the blinking lights of the lovely little community nestling at his feet on the Pajarito Plateau, seven thousand feet into the mountains of New Mexico. It was a quintessentially upper-middle-class American town of adobe homes and ranch-style houses, well-watered lawns and neat gardens; with the red-and-yellow beacon of its McDonald's, a Holiday Inn and, on the Municipal Building's lawn, a red-painted thermometer measuring the community's progress toward its United Way Fund goal.

And yet the sole reason for the existence of Los Alamos was the creation of the means of mass destruction. It was here thirty-six years before that man had designed and produced his first nuclear weapon. The office of Harold Agnew was a museum to that achievement. Oppenheimer, Fermi, Einstein, Bohr, ghosts of geniuses long dead, stared down from portraits on the wall at the man who was now the guardian of their great enterprise. The primitive lab at Berkeley where the first submicroscopic particle of plutonium had been produced, the world's first atomic pile, the crew of the *Enola Gay* on the eve of their terrible voyage to Hiroshima—

every milestone along that historic route was recorded by a photograph on Agnew's wall.

Harold Agnew himself was one of the few men still alive of the score of scientists who had been present at the birth of the Atomic Age in a converted squash court under the west stands of the University of Chicago's Stagg Field on a bitter cold November day in 1942. He was a big, burly blond man with sloping shoulders and heavy arms, a man who looked as if he should have been a second-generation Swede running a gas station in northern Minnesota rather than the director of one of the most sophisticated scientific institutions in the world.

When he had marched up the mesa sprawled below him with Oppenheimer and Groves to build the first atomic bomb, all the plutonium on planet Earth could have fit on the head of a pin with room left over for a flight of angels to dance. And now? Agnew thought moodily, contemplating those blinking lights. That was a question which had come naturally during the trials of the last hour while a team of his weapons designers had labored over the blueprint delivered to the White House gate. They had broken the blueprint down into its components, picking it apart, hunting the one fatal flaw, the one violation of the very precise rules of nuclear weaponry which would render the design meaningless. Outside his office, on the huge Los Alamos computer banks, other men had run off the formulas that had come in with the design, checking neutron densities, heating factors, lens curvatures against the figures stored on the computer.

As the minutes had gone by, Agnew's thoughts had frequently gone back to that exalting morning in Chicago almost forty years ago. He'd been down on the atomic pile with two friends and an ax that day, ready to cut a rope and flood the pile with a cadmium solution if the reaction ran away—and if they were still alive to cut it.

Enrico Fermi, the great Italian physicist, had been up on the balcony calmly giving orders in his rich tenor voice. The counter had started to go wild, running faster and faster like a heart fibrillating. Nothing had shaken the Italian's composure. Finally he had taken out his slide rule, made a series of quick movements, then nodded his head and said, "It's self-sustaining." With those words, mankind had entered the era of the atom.

For Agnew, the exaltation, the exhilaration of that great moment were as alive now as they had been then. They had known at that instant they could beat the Germans to their terrible goal. But, above all, they had shared the conviction that man had mastered at last the elements of his globe, harnessed to his own ends its most primeval force.

The rasp of his buzzer interrupted him just as the last pale light of day was fleeing the mountainscape of New Mexico.

"We have your call to the White House," his deputy announced. The scientist sighed and picked up the phone.

The incoming call was switched to the small white squawk box in the center of the oval table so that everyone in the National Security Council conference room could hear and address the scientist at Los Alamos.

"Mr. Agnew," Jack Eastman declared, "have your people completed their appraisal of the atomic bomb on those blueprints?"

The voice filtering into the room through the white plastic holes in reply seemed strangely hesitant.

"Mr. Eastman, the drawing on the blueprint which you submitted to us is not for an atomic bomb."

The men in the White House emitted what seemed an almost collective sigh of relief. The distant scientist did not hear them. He continued. "It's my very sad duty to inform you that the design on the blueprint is for something a hundred times worse."

A quick, nervous gasp in the distant scientist's voice was audible to each of the men and women in the White House basement. "The blueprint is for a thermonuclear device, Mr. President, a three-megaton hydrogen bomb."

Every time his bare fingertips touched the metal of the television antenna, the passenger of the *Dionysos* felt a numbing flash of pain spurt down his fingers to his wrists. Beneath him his feet, unaccustomed to snow and ice, slipped and skidded on the half-frozen mounds left on the exposed rooftop by Friday's snowstorm.

Warily, he glanced at the buildings around him. There was no light burning in any window from which someone could see what he was doing.

Off to his right was the river. With a compass, he fixed his television antenna at a very precise angle pointing toward its black expanse. She had followed her instructions perfectly in picking the building. There were no rooftops higher then his along the antenna's carefully calculated line of vision, nothing that could block an incoming radio signal.

He took the six-foot needle of phosphorated bronze, smaller than an automobile aerial but capable of discerning the weakest burst of electronic noise, and fitted it carefully into the socket prepared for it in the television antenna. Every few seconds he had to stop to blow on his numbed fingertips, to give them the sense of precision they needed to make the connection he had practiced a hundred times between the aerial and the antenna.

When he had finished, he straightened up, stiff with cold, rubbing the aching scar on his neck as he did. Suddenly, from the street below, the clatter of voices drifted up to his rooftop. He peered down. Half a dozen people spilled out of the artist's loft across the street. Impassively, he watched them glide off through the shadows, his ears following the crystalline ripple of the girls' laughter as it faded in the night.

The President was the first person in the National Security Council conference room to break the shocked silence that had followed Harold Agnew's revelation.

"My God!" he gasped. "Is this really possible? That Qaddafi could have done this without our finding out what he was up to?"

This time it was Agnew who hesitated. The hydrogen bomb represented the ultimate refinement in man's search for the means of self-destruction. Unlike the atomic bomb, which depended on converting to reality a widely understood scientific theory, it depended on the most potent secret unlocked by man's brain since the cavemen of antiquity had harnessed fire. It involved the one precisely perfect interweaving of the bomb's key elements. There was only one. There was no "almost." There was no margin whatsoever for error. That relationship was probably the most ferociously guarded secret on earth. Thousands, hundreds of thousands, of qualified physicists understood the theory of the atomic bomb. Barely three hundred people, perhaps fewer, were privy to the secret of the hydrogen bomb.

42

"I admit it strains credibility, sir," Agnew replied, "but the blunt fact is that this is a viable weapons design. Whether it's from Qaddafi or someone else, someone, somewhere out there, has gotten hold of the secret of the hydrogen bomb."

Exploding a hydrogen bomb was a task so complex it was often compared to setting a wet log ablaze with a single match. It required putting three competing processes into perfect balance under conditions of temperature and pressure so extreme they rivaled those at the core of the sun. Essentially what was involved were two atomic "triggers" on either side of a mass of thermonuclear fuel enclosed in a liquid membrane of tritium. Their explosion allowed for the perfectly symmetrical compression of the fuel which the tritium helped to drive up to the incredible temperatures needed for ignition. The entire assembly was wrapped in a cylinder of uranium 238 which turned some of the neutrons fleeing the atomic explosion back into the device, delaying its disintegration for the microsecond required to allow the whole process to take place.

"The device is meant to be contained in a cylinder roughly the size of an ordinary oil drum," Agnew continued. "The length is about half again as long as a drum. We calculate it would weigh almost fifteen hundred pounds. There are connecting wires meant, I presume, to be hitched up to some kind of separate control panel, probably a device that could receive an incoming radio burst and release an electrical impulse into the high-explosive charge."

For several seconds there was not a sound in the conference room. The President cleared his throat.

"Where in God's name would someone like Qaddafi have gotten the information to build something like this? Could he have gotten it from those articles that were published in Wisconsin in 1979?"

"No." This time Agnew did not hesitate. "Those articles set out the theory behind the H bomb very completely. But they didn't come to grips with the precise formula behind it, which is that absolutely perfect quantitive and qualitative interrelationship between its three competing elements. Without that, you've got no explosion."

"And this design has that?"

"Yes, Mr. President, I'm sorry to have to tell you the configuration here is exact."

Jack Eastman leaned forward toward the squawk box. "Mr.

Agnew, I want to be very precise. What we're dealing with here is a design, a blueprint, not a device in being. Are there still imponderables in here we haven't talked about that could prevent this from going off?''

"Of course there are," Agnew replied. "Everything depends, for example, on those atomic triggers exploding with perfect synchronization, and that in turn depends on detonating with absolute precision the high explosives that set them off. It's a very, very complicated process.''

The President coughed. "Mr. Agnew," he asked, "assuming for the moment this device really existed and really was in New York and really was exploded, what would its effect be?''

For a long moment, the little squawk box in the center of the table was silent. Then, almost as though they came from some disembodied voice speaking from another world, Agnew's words again filled the room.

"It would mean, sir, that, for all practical purposes, New York City would be wiped off the face of the earth.''

"Hey, lady, got room in there for me?''

The woman couldn't help smiling at the speaker. He was a young Marine waiting to board the Eastern Airlines nine-o'clock shuttle from New York to Washington. Lasciviously, he eyed her figure swathed in her ankle-length red fox fur coat as she swept past him. Laila Dajani was used to men's passes. With her long auburn hair, her black prominent eyes, the slight sensual pout of her well-fleshed lips, she had been attracting them since she was eighteen. She gave a casual toss to her hair and continued on to the shuttle terminal from the plane that had just flown her into the city from the nation's capital. Her beauty, the way she invariably stood out in a crowd, was, she knew, a risk. To deliver her letter to the White House, she had worn the blond wig and an old polo coat which she had left in the second locker she had opened at National Airport.

She moved casually to the exit, spotting at the door the dark-coated driver of the limousine service she had used regularly since she arrived in New York.

"Nice trip, ma'am?''

"Lovely, thank you.''

Laila settled into the car's comfortable upholstery. As they pulled away, she took out her compact and, pretending to adjust her makeup, scrutinized the traffic behind them in the mirror. They were not, as far as she could tell, being followed, She sank back into the seat and lit a cigarette. The car and the driver were a reflection of one of Carlos's golden rules: a smart terrorist always travels first class. The best way to slip undetected about the world, the Venezuelan master terrorist maintained, was in that upper-middle-class spectrum which lay just below the level of the ostentatious rich, at the very heart of the society he meant to destroy.

The cover he had invented for Laila's two visits to the United States was ideally designed to accomplish just that. She was on a buying trip for La Rive Gauche, a boutique for wealthy Lebanese on Beirut's Hamra Street, an institution which had survived, as such places inevitably do, all the convulsions of the Lebanese civil war.

The shop's elegant proprietor, the widow of a famous Druze chieftain, was a passionate supporter of the cause, an engaging woman who saw no contradiction in selling Dior, Yves Saint-Laurent and Courreges dresses by day and preaching violent revolution by night. Getting a fake Lebanese passport had been simple. Procuring stolen Lebanese passports for Palestinian terrorists was as easy in Beirut as buying postage stamps. Nor did she have the slightest difficulty in getting one of the 200,000 U.S. visas issued annually in the Middle East. The overworked consul who had given her her visa hadn't even bothered to make a phone call to check on her assumed identity; the Rive Gauche letter supporting her application had been enough for him.

And so, as Linda Nahar, a Lebanese Christian, she had haunted the showrooms of Bill Blass, Calvin Klein and Oscar de la Renta on her two trips to New York, the first in August, the second beginning in November. She had quickly become one of the newest ornaments of a certain New York world, weekending on Long Island, lunching at the Caravelle, disco dancing in the garish splendor of Studio 54.

The driver braked to a stop in front of the Hampshire House on Central Park South. She dismissed the car, picked up three messages at the reception desk and two minutes later stepped into the charming disorder of the suite she rented by the month on the thirty-second floor. It was littered with the impedimenta of her assumed calling: fashion brochures, copies of *Vogue, Harper's Bazaar, Glamour, Women's Wear Daily*. Indeed, her photograph in *Women's Wear* at Diana Vreeland's Pageant of Chinese Dress for the Met had caused Laila a moment of anguish. Fortunately for her, *Women's Wear* was not a journal scrutinized with any intensity by the CIA's Office of Palestinian Affairs.

She tossed her coat on a chair and mixed herself a drink. Moodily, she stepped to the window onto Central Park that constituted one of the sitting-room walls. Looking at the park in its pristine mantle of new snow, at the skaters gliding over the shell to her right, at all those proud façades crawling with blinking pinholes of light, Laila shuddered unavoidably.

She took a long swallow of her whiskey and thought of Carlos. He was right. Never think of the consequences of your mission, he warned, only of the unexpected problems that could prevent you from carrying it out. She drained her glass with two thirsty gulps and walked to her bathroom to draw a bath.

Before stepping into the tub, she gave herself an approving glance in the mirror: the taut, flat stomach, her firm buttocks, the defiant thrust of her breasts. For a long moment she lay there, luxuriating in the bath, caressing her skin with the bath oil's thick, bubbly film, rubbing it through her earlobes, along the passage-ways of her neck, massaging it playfully over her breasts until her nipples stood erect. Lazily, she lifted one leg from the bath water and rubbed the foam along her thighs and inner legs. At the sight of her crimson toenails, she smiled. Imagine, she mused, a terrorist who paints her toenails.

She was brushing out the long mane of her hair when the phone rang. Picking it up, she heard the din of voices in the background.

"Where the devil are you?" she asked, a flashing undertone of anger in her voice.

"We're having dinner at Elaine's." Her expression changed the instant she heard the caller's voice. "We're going on to the Fifty-four. Why don't you join us?"

What better cover could she ask for? "Can you give me an hour?" Laila asked with a husky voice.

"An hour?" the voice answered. "I'd give you a lifetime if you'd take it."

His usually bland features shrouded with concern, the President of the United States stared at the circle of advisers surrounding him. The last great crisis his nation had faced when the fanatical supporters of the Ayatollah Khomeini had seized the U.S. Embassy in Teheran paled beside this threat. This was the ultimate act of political terrorism, the almost too inevitable conclusion to a decade of escalating terrorism. And, he reflected bitterly, if this really was true, a nation whose citizens were living in nomad tents barely a generation ago now possessed the power to destroy the most important city on the planet. Millions of people are being held hostage, he thought, to the extravagant demands of a zealous despot. He turned to Jack Eastman. "Jack, what contingency plans do we have to handle something like this?"

It was a question Eastman had anticipated. Locked in a safe in the West Wing were the contingency plans of the U.S. government, all constantly updated, each wrapped in its black imitation-leather jacket with gold lettering. They covered everything: the speed with which the U.S. and the Soviets could reach comparable firepower thresholds, possible Chinese reactions, NATO disagreements, the security of the sea lanes, right down to how many C rations were necessary to deploy the 82nd Airborne Division into the Panama Canal Zone or land a division of Marines on Cyprus. Their origins went back to Henry Kissinger's days. Eastman had reviewed them an hour ago. They dealt with every imaginable world crisis—every one, that is, except the one which now confronted the President of the United States.

"I'm sorry, sir," Eastman replied, "we don't have any."

Eastman noted the flicker his words produced in the President's blue eyes, the "laser look," the familiar warning that he was angry. He had folded his hands on the table before him. "All right," he said. "In any event, whether this is from Qaddafi, whether it's from some terrorist group, some crazy scientist, or someone else, I wish to make one thing clear to you all: the fact that this threat, real or not, exists is to be kept an absolute secret."

The President's words reflected a U.S. government decision, taken during the Nixon administration and consistently adhered to since then, to avoid at all costs going public with nuclear threats. The knowledge that a threat existed in a given city could provoke a panicked reaction more devastating than the threatened explosion itself. Discrediting each nuclear hoax cost at least a million dollars, and no one wanted to see the government deluged by such threats. There was the danger that an irrational, semihysterical public opinion could paralyze the government's ability to act in such a crisis. And in this case, the President was well aware, there was yet another reason: the ominous injunction to secrecy in the threat note.

"Well, if this really is from Qaddafi our answer's simple." It was Delbert Crandell, the Secretary of Energy. "Lather those bastards from one end of Libya to the other. That's all. Wipe them out. Lay the Trident missiles on the subs we have on patrol in the Med on them. That'll turn the damn place into a sea of glass in thirty seconds. There won't be a goat left alive over there."

Crandell sank back, satisfied. His words had a cathartic effect on the room. It was as though the outspoken Energy Secretary had given voice to a thought all had had but no one else had been prepared to express, the brutal but reassuring affirmation that, in the final analysis, the United States possessed the power to squash a menace such as this.

"Mr. Christopher." The President's tone was soft, sad almost, as he addressed the Deputy Secretary of State. "What is the population of Libya?"

"Two million, sir, give or take a hundred thousand. Census figures over there aren't very reliable."

The President turned down the table toward the Chairman of the Joint Chiefs. "Harry, how many people would we lose if a three-megaton device went off in New York? Without evacuation?"

"Sir, it would be difficult to give you an accurate figure on that without looking at some numbers."

"I realize that, but give me your best estimate."

The Chairman reflected a moment. "Between four and five million, sir."

There was dead silence as the awful mathematics of Fuller's figures registered on everyone in the room. The President sat back, lost for just a minute in a private thought no one in the room dared to interrupt. The giants of the world, the United States and the USSR, held each other in strategic checkmate because they shared a parity of horror, an equilibrium once described with almost too perfect irony by the acronym for the philosophy on which the U.S.'s thermonuclear strategy had been based—MAD, for "Mutual Assured Destruction." I kill you, you kill me. It was the old Russian comedy, everybody dies.

48

But this, if it was true, was the terrible alteration in the rules of the game that had haunted responsible world leaders for years, the end game in the struggle against nuclear proliferation for which he had fought so hard—and with so little success.

Detective First Grade Angelo Rocchia watched with pride the woman advancing through the restaurant, noting approvingly each head that turned for a second glimpse at the lithe movements of her figure. Men always had a second look at Grace Knowland. Her fluffy black hair was clipped in a pageboy bob that set off her high-arched cheekbones, her dark eyes and her pert mouth. She was not quite medium height, but she was so well proportioned, so finely muscled, that her clothes, like the simple white blouse and beige skirt she was wearing tonight, always seemed molded to her body. Above all, Grace radiated a fresh, engaging vitality that belied the fact that she was thirty-five, the mother of a fourteen-year-old boy, and had led a life not noteworthy for its placidity.

"Hi, darling," she said, brushing his forehead with a quick, moist kiss. "Not late, am I?"

She slid onto the red velvet seat beside him, right under his favorite oil of the Bay of Naples and Vesuvius. Forlini's was, as Angelo liked to say, "the kind of place where things transpire." A few blocks away from City Hall, it had been for years a favorite hangout of top cops, judges, politicians, men from the DA's office and minor Mafiosi.

He handed Grace a Campari and soda and raised his Black Label on the rocks to her. Angelo Rocchia drank very little, but he was fastidious about what he drank: "sipping scotch" and good wines, preferably the little-known Chianti classicos of Tuscany.

"Cheers."

"Cheers. I hope it wasn't too difficult."

Angelo lowered his glass and gave a slight move to his shoulders. "Each time, it's the same thing. You think it can't possibly hurt any more and it always does."

Grace gently folded her hand over his. She had a pianist's fingers, long, slender and strong, her almond-shaped nails trimmed short.

"What's hard is making yourself understand there's no hope."

Grace saw a flicker of despair cross his face. "Let's order." She smiled. "I'm famished." Her gaiety was a forced effort to ease Angelo from the depression that inevitably gripped him on Sunday evenings.

"Evening, Inspector. Try the linguine. Terrific."

Angelo looked up from his menu. Standing before his table was Salvatore "Twenty Percent Sal" Danatello, his corpulent figure bursting out of a pale-blue double-knit at least three sizes too small for him. The detective looked at him, a sneer of contempt easing over his face.

"How's the family, Sal? Keeping your nose clean?"

The change in Angelo's tone, the abrupt switch from the soft, intimate half-growl he used with her to this inquisitor's voice, its timbre as cold, as cutting as a knife's blade, always disturbed Grace.

"Sure thing, Inspector. You know me. Running a legitimate business. Payin' my tax."

"Terrific, Sally. You're just the kind of decent, upright citizen this city needs."

Sally hesitated a moment, hoping for the introduction Angelo had no intention whatsoever of making, then shuffled off.

"Who's that?" Grace asked.

"A wise guy."

Grace understood the jargon of the New York Police Department. She watched the Mafioso's disappearing figure with curiosity. "So it wasn't his wife and kids you were asking about. What does he do?"

"Knows good lawyers. Been busted three times for loan sharking and walked every time." Angelo snapped a breadstick in half and jabbed one jagged end into the butter dish before him. A sly grin crossed his face.

"Of course, *The New York Times* would say it was just another example of how we waste our resources prosecuting nonviolent crimes."

Grace pressed her finger to her lips like a schoolteacher trying to hush an unruly classroom. "Truce?" It was a little sign between them, a convention they employed whenever the deeply held convictions inspired by their different vocations, hers as a City Hall reporter for the *Times,* his as a detective, clashed.

"Yeah, sure," growled Angelo. "Truce. What the hell, *The New York Times* is probably right anyway. Sally's collectors got a special, nonviolent way they clean up his bad debts."

Despite herself, Grace fell for his ploy with an inquiring tilt of her head.

"They put your fingers in a car door. Then they close the door."

Angelo savored the horror sweeping her face just an instant. "It's like the ad says. The man runs a full service bank."

She couldn't help laughing. He was a born actor, this detective of hers, with his Roman emperor's profile, and his wavy gray hair that always made her think of Vittorio de Sica; hair she knew he had styled once a month to conceal the bald spot emerging at the back of his head.

They had met two years ago in his Homicide Squad office at 1 Police Plaza when Grace was doing a major takeout on violent crime in the city. With his dark suit, his white-on-white tie and shirt, the way he rolled his *r*s like a tenor at the Met, he had seemed closer to her idea of what a Mafia don should look like than a detective. She had noted the old-fashioned black mourning button in the lapel of his jacket, the nervous way he kept picking peanuts from his pocket. To stop smoking, he had explained.

For almost a year they had met for an occasional dinner every couple of weeks, nothing more binding between them then their deepening friendship. Then, one steaming night in August, it had happened. They'd gone that evening to a little seafood restaurant in Sheepshead Bay. The bluefish were running and they had each ordered one broiled with sage and rosemary. For a long time they had lingered on the terrace, sipping espresso and the last of their Frascati in the fresh Atlantic breeze. Suddenly, there on the terrace, Grace had sensed a barely disguised yearning in the way Angelo's eyes kept returning to the blouse she had partially unbuttoned in the warm night air. She'd been through three affairs since they met, each begun in promise and ended in pain. Angelo was not a handsome man; yet there was an undeniable appeal in his battered, craggy face. Above all, there was a solidity about him, a promise of strength like that of the old oak that has survived many an autumn storm. Walking out the door, Grace reached for his hand.

"Angelo, take me home with you," she whispered.

Now, beside her, Angelo gave a soft groan as he contemplated the menu. They were after him, every time he took his Department physical, to lose a little weight. "Watch the blood pressure," they'd say. Tomorrow, he thought, and ordered cannelloni, a *bistecca Fiorentina,* and a bottle of Castello Gabbiano Riserva 1975.

Grace gave him a disapproving glance, then asked for a veal pic-
cata and a green salad.

"Hey," he mumbled, "I'm the policeman, remember?"

As the waiter moved away, they lapsed into silence. Grace
seemed suddenly distant, absorbed in some private world of her
own.

"What's the matter?"

"I got some news yesterday."

"Good or bad?"

"Bad, I guess. I'm pregnant."

Angelo set his whiskey down with a slow, deliberate movement.
"You sure?"

She slipped her hand over his. "I'm sorry, darling. I wasn't
going to tell you. Not yet, anyway. Your question caught me while
I was thinking about it." She reached for her glass and took a
measured sip. "It's one of those things that should never happen
anymore, I know. I was careless. You see, after I had Tommy I
had some trouble. They told me it was very, very unlikely I'd ever
conceive again." She giggled and the corners of her dark eyes
crinkled with her laughter. "And until you came along, I never
did."

"I guess I should take that as a compliment." Angelo slid his
heavy arm along the top of their seat so that his fingers rested
lightly on her shoulders. "I'm sorry. I suppose it's my fault. I
should have been watching out. I guess I'm out of practice."

"Sure. I guess so."

Grace studied the detective an instant, an appraising coolness in
her eyes, waiting for another word, another phrase. It did not
come. She twisted and stretched her long fingers on the tablecloth.
"It's strange carrying a life inside you. I don't think a man can
ever understand just what that means to a woman. I've spent the
last thirteen years living with the idea it would never happen to me
again." She took another drink. Her eyes were downcast, her
voice suddenly plaintive. "And now it has."

Angelo let his regard travel around the crowded restaurant a
moment, taking in the heads leaning conspiratorily together, making, unmaking deals. As he did, he tried to puzzle out the mood of
the woman beside him.

"Grace, tell me something. You're not thinking about keeping
it, are you?"

"Would that be so terrible?"

Angelo paled slightly. He took his drink, swallowed the last of his whiskey, then stared moodily at the glass clasped between his fingers.

"You know, I never told you, Grace, about Catherine and me. She had troubles, too. We tried for years to have a baby. She kept miscarrying and miscarrying. We didn't know why."

He lowered his glass to the table. "We couldn't figure out what God or nature or whatever the hell you want to call it was trying to tell us. Until Maria was born." Angelo was a long way from their crowded Italian restaurant. "I'll never forget going into the delivery room that morning. I was so proud, so happy. I wanted a boy, sure, but a child, that's what mattered. And there she was, this little tiny thing all red and shriveled, the nurse holding her up there by the ankles. Those hands, those little, tiny hands, were moving, kind of picking at the air like, and she was crying."

He paused a moment. "And then I noticed her head. It didn't seem quite right, you know? It wasn't round. The nurse looked at me. They know right away. 'I'm sorry, Mr. Rocchia,' she said, 'your daughter's mongoloid.' "

Angelo turned to Grace, the sorrow of that instant, of all the painful instants that followed it, on his face. "Believe me, Grace, I'd die before I'd hear those words again."

"I understand you, darling." Her hand closed over his. "But they have a test now. It's called amniocentesis. They can tell if a child's going to be a mongoloid before it's born."

"How did you find that out?"

"I checked with my doctor."

Angelo made no effort to conceal his astonishment. "So you've been thinking a lot about this?"

The waiter appeared with their dinner. They watched in awkward silence as he set their plates before them, then drifted off.

"I suppose I have. It's caught me so much by surprise." Grace picked at her veal. "You see, I know it's the last chance for me, Angelo. I'm thirty-five."

"How about me?" There was an edge of petulance in his voice. "Do you really think a man is anxious to become a father at my age?"

Grace laid down her fork and meticulously dabbed at her lips with her napkin. "What I'm going to say sounds selfish, I know.

And I guess it is. But if I decide to have the child, it will be because I want it. Because I want something to help me fill the years I see ahead. Because this is a last chance and you don't let go of last chances in life easily. But I'll promise you one thing, Angelo. If I do decide to keep it, it'll be my responsibility. I won't burden you with the problems my decision causes. I won't lay any responsibilities you don't want on you."

Angelo felt a sudden chill. "What do you mean? You'd want to bring it up like that, by yourself? Alone?"

"Yes, I think perhaps I would." Again Grace rested her hand on his. "Let's not talk about it anymore. Not now at least." She smiled. "Guess what? Our beloved Mayor's giving a press conference at nine tomorrow to explain why he hasn't been able to get the snow off the streets. Because of my piece in this morning's paper."

Much farther up Manhattan, on Central Park South, Laila Dajani stepped out of the Hampshire House, shiny black satin disco pants flashing beneath her fur jacket.

"Studio Fifty-four," the doorman ordered her cabdriver.

The driver looked at her appreciatively in his rearview mirror.

"Hey, you must know people, lady."

"I have friends." Laila smiled. Then, as they approached Fifty-seventh Street, she leaned forward. "You know, I'm going to change my mind. Take me to the corner of Thirty-second and Park."

"Got friends there too?"

"Something like that."

Laila stared out the window to stop the conversation. When they reached Thirty-second and Park she paid the fare, smiled at the driver and began to stroll casually along the avenue. Her eyes remained fixed on the taillights of the cab, following them until they disappeared from sight. Then she quickly turned and hailed another cab. This time, she told the driver to take her where she really wanted to go.

In Washington, D.C., the FBI's fortresslike headquarters at Tenth Street and Pennsylvania Avenue, seven blocks from the White House, blazed with lights. On the sixth floor of that headquarters the Bureau maintained a nuclear-emergency desk manned twenty-four hours a day by a trio of specially trained agents. It had been there since 1974 when the FBI assigned nuclear extortion a priority so urgent it was reserved for only a handful of major incidents headed by the most dreaded occurrence of all, Presidential assassination.

Fifty times in the years since, the agents at that desk had been confronted with nuclear threats. Most had been the work of cranks or demented ideologues, the "don't touch the Alaskan tundra or we'll put a bomb in Chicago" sort of thing. But a significant number of those threats had seemed deadly serious. They had included threats to blow up bundles of radioactive waste in Spokane, Washington, and New York City; warnings of nuclear bombs alleged to be hidden in Boston, Detroit, Washington, D.C., and four other American cities, and in a Long Beach, California, oil refinery. Some had been accompanied by designs of nuclear devices that had also been deemed "nuclear capable" by the weapons analysts of Los Alamos. The Bureau's response to those threats had, on occasion, included the deployment of hundreds of agents and technicians to the threatened cities. Yet no word of their activities had ever reached the public.

Within half an hour of receiving the first alert from the White House, two teams of agents were onto the problem, a Crisis Assessment Team whose task was to determine whether the threat was real or not, and a Crisis Management Team responsible for dealing with it if it was. The fact that the extortion message was in a foreign language had immensely complicated their job. The first rule in an extortion case is to look at the extortion note or telephone call for clues. The Bureau employed a Georgetown University linguistic psychiatrist whose computers had proven to be remarkably accurate in providing a thumbnail description of an extortioner based on the language he had used in his threat note or phone call. In this case, however, his talents had been useless.

As soon as the first warning had come in, a team of agents had gone to the Carriage House Apartments, a four-story yellow stone apartment house at the junction of L and New Hampshire, abutting the building housing the Libyan Embassy. Two of its occupants had been relodged in the Washington Hilton, and listening devices trained on the embassy next door had been placed in the walls of their apartments. The same thing had been done to the Libyan UN embassy in New York. Taps had also been installed on the phones of all Libyan diplomats accredited to either the United States or the United Nations.

That operation had provided its first fruit while the NSC was discussing the consequences of Agnew's report. Two Libyan diplomats, the ambassador to the United Nations and the first secretary of the Washington embassy, had been located. Both had vehemently denied that their nation could be involved in such an operation.

At 2031, just after Agnew had given his conclusive determination that the design was for a viable thermonuclear device, an "All Bureaus Alert" had been flashed out of the Bureau's sixth-floor communications center. It ordered every FBI office in the United States and overseas to stand by for "emergency action demanding highest priority and allocation of all available manpower."

FBI liaison agents to Israel's Mossad, France's SDECE, Britain's MI5 and West Germany's Landswehr were ordered to go through files, pulling out descriptions and, where available, fingerprint records and photographs of every known Palestinian terrorist in the world.

One floor above the communications center, Quentin Dewing, the FBI assistant director for investigation, was in the midst of organizing the mobilization of five thousand agents. Agents shoeing horses in Fargo, South Dakota, catching the last of the day's sun on Malibu Beach, walking out of Denver's Mile High Stadium, washing up the supper dishes in Bangor, Maine, were being ordered to leave immediately for New York, each order accompanied by a vital closing injunction: "Extreme, repeat, extreme discretion must be employed to conceal your movements from the public."

Dewing concentrated his efforts in three areas. The nation's bureaus were ordered to locate and take under permanent surveillance every known or suspected Palestinian radical.

In New York and in half a dozen cities on the Atlantic seaboard, FBI agents were in action in every ghetto, every high-crime area, "pulsing" informers, querying pimps, pushers, petty crooks, forgers, fences, hunting for anything on Arabs: Arabs looking for fake papers; Arabs looking for guns; Arabs trying to borrow somebody's safe house; anything, just as long as it had an Arab association.

His second effort was to lay the groundwork for a massive search for the device, if it existed, and those who might have brought it into the country. Twenty agents were already installed at the computers of the Immigration and Naturalization Service offices on I Street, methodically going through the I94 forms for every Arab who had entered the United States in the past six months. The U.S. address listed on each card was Telexed to the bureau concerned. The FBI intended to locate, within forty-eight hours, each of these visitors and clear them, one by one, of any suspected involvement in the threat.

Other agents were going through the files of the Maritime Association of the Port of New York looking for ships that had called at Tripoli, Benghazi, Latakia, Beirut, Basra or Aden in the past six months and subsequently dropped off cargo on the Atlantic seaboard. A similar operation was under way at the air freight terminal of every international airport beteen Maine and Washington, D.C.

Finally, Dewing had ordered a check run on every American who held, or had ever held, a "cosmic top secret" clearance for access to the secret of the hydrogen bomb. It was typical of the thoroughness with which Dewing's bureau worked that shortly after 8 P.M. Mountain Time an FBI car turned into 1822 Old Santa Fe Trail, a twisting highway leading northeast out of the capital of New Mexico along the route over which the wagon trains of the old Santa Fe Trail had once rolled. With its silver RFD mailbox, the yellow metallic newspaper tube with the words *New Mexican* on its side, the one-story adobe house at the end of the drive was a supremely average American home.

There was nothing average about the Polish-American mathematician who lived inside. Stanley Ulham was the man whose brain had unlocked the secret of the hydrogen bomb. It was one of the supreme ironies in history that on the spring morning in 1951 when he had made his fateful discovery, Stanley Ulham was trying to demonstrate with mathematical certainty that it was impossible to make that bomb based on the premise that had underlain years of scientific effort. He did. But in doing so, he uncovered the glimmering of an alternative approach that just might work.

He could have wiped that terrible knowledge from his blackboard with a swipe of his eraser, but he would not have been the scientist he was if he had. Chain-smoking Pall Malls, flailing feverishly at his blackboard with stubs of chalk, he laid bare the secret of the H bomb in one frantic hour of thought.

The FBI agent did not require even that much time to clear the father of the H bomb of any possible complicity in the threat to New York. Standing in his doorway, watching the agent drive away, Ulham couldn't help remembering the words he had uttered to his wife on that fateful morning when he had made his discovery: "This will change the world."

A gray veil of cigarette smoke hung over the National Security Council conference room despite the continuous functioning of the building's intensive air-circulation system. It was a few minutes past ten; not quite two hours remained before the ultimatum period contained in the threat message was due to begin. Paper cups and plates littered with the remains of the cheese sandwiches and black-bean soup the President had ordered the White House kitchen to send in to the conferees were scattered along the table and by the base of the room's paneled walls.

At the far end of the room, three Air Force colonels finished assembling a group of charts and maps. The senior officer, a youthful-looking colonel with a tapestry of freckles covering his face, stepped forward.

"Mr. President, gentlemen, we've been asked how Qaddafi or a terrorist group could transmit a radio signal from Tripoli to New York to detonate the device on the blueprint we've been shown, and what technological resources we possess to prevent such a signal from coming in.

"Basically, there are three ways you can detonate this. The first is a kamikaze volunteer who baby-sits the bomb with orders to set it off at a certain time if he doesn't get a counterorder."

"Colonel," Bennington interjected, "if this threat is really from Qaddafi, that is very much the last method he'd use. He'd want absolute control over this himself."

"Right, sir," the colonel replied. "In that case, there are two ways to do it, by telephone or radio." The room was still, all eyes fixed on the speaker. "To attach the power pack you'd require for this to the ordinary telephone is a very simple matter. Just a question of opening the telephone and connecting a couple of wires. That way the pulse of an incoming call is routed into a preprogrammed signature detector. The pulse opens a circuit into a microprocessor in which a preprogrammed code has been stored. The microprocessor automatically compares it with the code, and if the two match it releases a five-volt charge of electricity into the bomb.

"The beauty of this is a wrong number can't set it off by mistake; and all a man has to do to explode the bomb is call that number from anywhere in the world and feed it his signal."

"It's as easy as that?" the President, jarred, asked.

"Yes, sir, I'm afraid it is."

"Can New York be isolated, absolutely sealed off from all incoming telephone calls?" the President asked.

"No, sir," the Colonel replied. "I'm afraid that's a technological impossibility."

He turned authoritatively back to his briefing charts. "It is our judgment, however, that in a situation such as the one we've been given, Qaddafi or a terrorist group would choose radio to detonate the device. It would offer more flexibility and is completely independent of existing communications systems. For a transmission over this distance, he'd have to use long waves which bounce off the ionosphere and come back down to earth. That means low frequencies."

"How many frequencies would be available to him for something like this?" the President asked.

"From Tripoli to New York, a megahertz. One million cycles."

"One million!" The President rubbed the stub of his chin between his thumb and forefinger. "Could we jam all one million of those frequencies?"

"Sir, if you did that you'd wipe out all our own communications. We'd close down the police, the FBI, the military, the fire departments, everything we'd need in an emergency."

"Never mind. Suppose I gave the order, could we do it?"

"No, sir."

"Why?"

"We simply don't have the transmitter capacity."

"How about all our jamming devices in Europe?"

"They're useless in this case. Too far away."

"He's going to need something to receive this radio signal in New York," Bennington remarked. "Some kind of directional antenna."

"Yes, sir. the easiest thing would be to put one in a standard television antenna on a rooftop and connect it to a pre-amplifier.

Then the signal could be picked up and transmitted to his bomb wherever it is in the building over the television antenna cable."

"Surely you could put a fleet of helicopters over Manhattan and scan the frequencies he might use. Get his device to answer back, then pick it up by direction finders, triangulation?"

"Yes, sir, we have the capacity to do that. But it would work only if his system is programmed to respond. If it's only programmed to receive, we'd get no reply."

"Well, there's another way to do it if it turns out to be from Qaddafi," Bennington said. His pipe was out and everyone in the room had to hang attendant on his words while he struck a match. "Explode half a dozen nukes in the atmosphere over Libya. That'll set up an electromagnetic blanket that will smother any radio communications out of there for at least two hours. Shut them down completely."

"Mr. President." It was Eastman. "For my part I don't believe this threat is really from Qaddafi; but in the unlikely event that it is, we're going to have to make some assumptions, and the first one I would make is that he's not going to expose himself to such evident retaliation. He'll have a fail-safe system like a ship hidden somewhere out there in the Atlantic"—he waved at the vast blue stain on the map behind the colonel—"from which he or someone else can always detonate the bomb if we lay a preventive strike on Libya."

The President nodded in agreement and looked back at the briefing officer. "The basic question to which we need an answer, Colonel, is this: Do we or do we not have any technological devices, systems or whatever which can guarantee that we can prevent a radio signal from being beamed into New York to detonate this thing if, in fact, it actually exists and it's really in New York?"

The colonel tensed nervously at his question. "No, sir," he replied. "I'm afraid that given the present state of the art, trying to intercept or stop an incoming signal like this is scientifically impossible. It's like trying to catch the right snowflake in the middle of a blizzard."

As he was speaking, the red light on the telephone at Eastman's elbow flashed. It was the Army Signal Corps warrant officer in charge of the White House switchboard. Eastman stiffened listening to him.

"Mr. President," he announced, "the switchboard's just received a telephone message from an anonymous caller. He hung up before they could trace the call. He said there was a message for you of the utmost importance in locker K602 in the luggage containers next to the Eastern Airlines shuttle terminal at National Airport.''

One fly-specked light bulb dangling from an overhead cord lit the garage. Its pale cone of light left pools of untouched shadow clinging to the garage's walls and corners. At the back of the garage, a six-foot-wide cement loading dock rose above the black curds of oil and grease staining the floor. The dock's back wall was a thin partition separating the garage from the abandoned warehousing area to the rear. Through it, a faint scraping sound drifted into the garage. Laila Dajani shuddered listening to it. It was the sound of rats scurrying through the deserted warehouse.

Her brother Kamal sat on a cot set up at the end of the platform, near a forklift truck. The passenger of the *Dionysos* twisted an air pistol in one hand. To his right, against the wall, were his latest victims, a pair of dead rats.

Laila's second brother, the eldest of the trio, had just entered the garage. Whalid Dajani was in agony. His face was pale; specks of sweat sparkled at his temples.

"Why don't you take another pill?" Laila demanded, her tone almost peevish.

"I've already taken five. That's all I'm supposed to take." He showed his sister the package of Tagamet pills she had gotten for him to ease the pain of the ulcer for which he'd earlier gulped his glass of milk on Broadway. "It says so on here." His eyes turned away to the far end of the platform. It was there, just inside the shadows, a long, dark form like that of a shark lurking below the surface of the water. It was painted black. Stenciled in white around the barrel's waist were the name and address of the import-export firm to which it had been destined. Cords kept it firmly lashed to the pallet on which it had arrived.

He dabbed at his damp brow. Don't think, they had told him. Don't think of anything but your mission. But how did you not think? How did you force from your mind what you'd seen: the faces, the seas and seas of faces, old faces, young faces, faces of misery and indifference, faces of laughter and happiness? The faces of little girls on their sleds in Central Park, of the black policeman telling him where to get off the subway; of the news-stand vendor, half snarling, half laughing "Good morning," selling him his paper. How could he not see the crowds, the buildings, the rushing cars, the lights that represented so many lives?

Behind him, Whalid heard the cot creak as his brother got up. "I'm thirsty," he mumbled. "Anyone want a Coke?"

Dazed, Whalid shook his head. Kamal stepped to a carton by the wall and pulled out a bottle of Chivas Regal whiskey. "Maybe this is the medicine you need."

"God, no." Whalid grimaced. "Not while my ulcer's bothering me like this."

Laila stirred impatiently. "How much time do we have left?"

"Enough," Kamal answered. He picked a piece of cold pizza from a flat cardboard box by his cot. As he did, his sister noticed the name and address of the restaurant where he'd bought it printed on the carton.

"Are you sure no one's going to be able to identify you in those places?" she asked.

Kamal gave her an angry glance. The constant boss. "Let's set up our firing circuits," he said.

"Why?" Whalid protested. "We still have plenty of time."

"Because I don't want anything to go wrong."

Whalid sighed and walked over to a gray metal case the size of a large attaché case resting on the floor beside his bomb. Nothing could have looked more innocent, more benign, than that case. Decals from TWA, Lufthansa, half a dozen of Europe's best hotels were stuck to it. Indeed, the Customs officer at JFK had stopped Whalid as he was entering the country with it on Thursday bearing a Lebanese passport identifying him as Ibrahim Abboud, an electrical engineer.

"It's a microprocessor tester," Whalid had explained, "to check to see if computers are working properly."

"Ah," the Customs officer had remarked admiringly, closing the case that was designed to help destroy his city, "complicated, isn't it?"

Just how complicated he could not have imagined. The case had indeed been adapted from a microprocessor tester, a U.S.-made Testline Adit 1000. One blazing summer's day in July, the technical director of the Libyan telephone system had showed a Testline

1000 to Ishui Kamaguchi, the resident director of Nippon Electric, the Japanese firm which had installed Libya's telephones. What he wanted, he had explained, was an adaptation of the device which would offer a means of remote radio control of an electrical discharge, a system that would be both infallible and absolutely inviolable.

Six weeks later, Kamaguchi had presented the Libyans the case now on the garage floor and a bill for $165,000. Only the genius of the Japanese for miniaturization could have produced the array of fail-safe devices built into the case to frustrate any attempt to tamper with its functioning. It was equipped with a magnetic-field detector that would order it to detonate instantly if it picked up any indication of an attempt to burn out its electronic circuitry with a magnetic field. There were static filters to counter any efforts to jam its radio receiver. Three tiny tubes sensitive to pressure changes protected it against the danger of gunfire or an explosion. Once it was hooked up, the pressure change caused by a New York telephone book falling toward the case would be sufficient to activate its circuits.

While his brother watched intently, Whalid opened its triple locking system and folded back the case cover to reveal a pale-blue control panel. On it was a cathode-tube screen, a keyboard and five keys bearing specific commands: END, AUTO, INIT, DATA, TEST. There was also a locked cassette player. Fixed into it was a thirty-minute BASF tape, a small red crescent in its upper-right-hand corner. Programmed in Tripoli, it contained instructions for the case's minicomputer.

Two connecting cords were neatly coiled inside the cover. One was designed to be hooked up to Whalid's bomb, the other to the cable running up to the antenna Kamal had installed on the roof. Each was equipped with a "dead man control." If any effort was made to disengage them once they had been hooked up they would automatically activate the firing system. Hidden below the panel's blue surface was a radio receiver, a microprocessor, the minicomputer and a brace of powerful, long-lasting lithium batteries.

As the two brothers watched, the cathode-tube screen lit up with a green glow. The words "STAND BY" formed on the screen. Whalid glanced at them, then punched the key marked INIT. The word "IDENTIFICATION" appeared on the screen.

Carefully, Whalid punched the code 01C2 onto the keyboard.

63

The word "CORRECT" appeared on the screen. Had his code been wrong, "INCORRECT" would have appeared there and Whalid would have had exactly thirty seconds to correct his mistake or the case would have autodestructed.

On the screen, the words "STORAGE DATA" appeared. Whalid looked at the checklist in his sister's hands, then punched F19A onto his keyboard. Through the tape player's window he could see the BASF cassette begin to spin. It turned for just under a minute, transmitting its program to the minicomputer's memory bank. The tape stopped and the words "STORAGE DATA: OK" arose on the screen.

Whalid methodically punched three successive code numbers onto the keyboard, following each by tapping the key TEST. There was a pause after each code, then a phrase appeared on the screen: "COMPUTER CONTROL: OK"; "MICRO-PROCESSOR: OK"; "RADIO FREQUENCY SIMULATION: OK."

"All right," Whalid said, "everything's working properly. Now we'll test the manual firing system."

Fundamentally, the case had been designed to fire the bomb in response to a radio signal. It contained, however, a manually operated backup firing capability which any one of the three could operate if something went wrong. Whalid carefully formed the number 0636 on the keyboard. Those numbers had been chosen for their firing code because none of the Dajanis would ever forget them. They represented the date of the Battle of Yarmuk when the Arab warriors of Omar, the successor to the Prophet, defeated the Byzantines by the Sea of Galilee and established Arab domain over their lost homeland. As Whalid's finger tapped the second "6," the green light on the screen blinked off. For two seconds, it was replaced by a bright-red glow.

"It works." Whalid shuddered. "We can detonate from here if we have to." He glanced at his watch, then up at the ceiling. "We've got seventeen minutes to go."

In Washington, D.C.'s, National Airport, a tight police cordon screened off several dozen late-evening travelers stretching and straining to follow the progress of the FBI's capital Bomb Squad. Cautiously, the agents scanned the bank of gray metal luggage lockers with Geiger counters, looking for radioactivity. They

64

found none. Then three German shepherds trained to detect the scent of high explosives were led along the locker ranks. Finally, a pair of agents employing a touch as delicate, as precise as that of Japanese women assembling the circuitry of a computer chip unscrewed the door to locker K602 and gently eased it from its hinges.

To their relief, the only thing the agents found in the locker was an envelope leaning against the back of the compartment. Typed on it were the words "For the President of the United States."

The message it contained was brief. It said that at midnight Washington time, 6 A.M. Libyan time, at a spot 153 miles due east of the junction of the twenty-fifth parallel and the tenth longitude, at the southern tip of the Awbari Sand Sea in the southwestern corner of Libya, Muammar al-Qaddafi would provide the United States with a conclusive demonstration of his ability to carry out the threat enunciated in his earlier communication. To facilitate aerial observation of the demonstration, the Libyan dictator proposed a carefully defined air corridor running south to the site from the Mediterranean Sea through which U.S. observation planes would be allowed to fly unmolested.

There was not a sound except for the dry rustle of the rats in the darkened warehouse. The three Dajanis squatted on the cold cement loading dock, waiting. Whalid held his watch in his hand, mesmerized by the sweep of its second hand. Again, he turned his regard upwards. Somewhere up there in the infinity of space, a tiny ball of metal tumbled through the canopy of night. It was a forgotten satellite, its existence known only to a handful of amateur radio operators around the world. Among them was the head of the Libyan state. Softly Whalid began to count off the passing seconds: "Three . . . two . . . one . . . zero."

The sound of the last syllable hadn't faded when it happeved: the green light glowing on the screen of their control case blinked off. In a split second, another color replaced it in almost instantaneous response to the gesture of a man burning with hatred and fanaticism halfway around the world. It was the same ominous red glow that had appeared there a quarter of an hour ago.

Laila gasped. Whalid slumped forward, half relieved, half horror-stricken. Kamal looked on in silence. The red glow faded and

65

the words "RADIO FREQUENCY GLOBAL CONTROL: OK" appeared on the screen. Then they too faded and were replaced by the word "CONNECTION." It was as though now that all their tests had been successfully run, the blue case before them was taking over, eliminating from the carefully elaborated chain of command any further need for the frail and uncertain intervention of human hands.

Whalid fitted the cable running from his bomb to the olive-drab circular plug an inch in diameter that connected it to the case. The next time the light on the screen glowed red, a flash of electricity from the case's lithium batteries would pour through those pins to detonate the thermonuclear device lying on the platform.

Whalid stared at that black object he had created. Oh God, oh God, he thought, why did you ever give men such power?

"What's the matter?" his brother asked.

Whalid started like a child in a classroom caught daydreaming by a teacher. His watch was still in his hand.

"The red light didn't glow a full two seconds," he replied. "Are you sure you connected the rod up on the roof to the cable tightly?"

"Of course."

"I think we better check it." Whalid took the pencil flashlight. "I'll go up with you and hold this while you check it."

The two men started for the door. Before they could get to it, Whalid doubled up in agony from the pain of his ulcer. "I can't go," he whispered, handing the flashlight to Laila. "You go and hold it for him."

By the time Laila and Kamal returned, his spasm had passed. He was sitting on the dock, anguish no longer contorting his face.

"It's all right," Kamal said.

Whalid reached over and punched a final tap onto his keyboard, striking the word "END." The control case was now locked. Only a code known to the three Dajanis could open it again.

"Whalid," Kamal said, "you better spend the night here in case they're looking for you. How about you, Laila?"

"Don't worry about me, Kamal," she replied. "No one will look for me where I'm going."

Shortly after eleven-thirty, the President, riding in the front seat of an unmarked Secret Service car, rode up to the river

66

entrance of the Pentagon. The members of the Crisis Committee, moving at irregular intervals to avoid drawing attention, had preceded him. An MP saluted the Chief Executive and led him to a plain white door under an archway bearing the words "JOINT CHIEFS OF STAFF." Its only identification was a set of figures, 2B890. A pair of guards, armed with sidearms, verify both visually and electronically the identity of each visitor, even that of the President of the United States, passing through that door. In addition, a closed-circuit television system records on videotape the face of everyone who enters, the hour and the day he came in, and his reason for being there.

There is good reason for that rigid security. Beyond that door lies an Ali Baba's cave of the electronic age, the most mind-boggling display of technological wizardry of which twentieth-century man is capable, the National Military Command Center of the United States.

Seated in a leather armchair at the oval conference table dominating Room 2B890, the President can, quite literally, watch the world go by. Every communication system the United States possesses, every electronic-surveillance network, all the vast electronic gadgetry at the disposition of the CIA, the National Security Agency, the Defense Intelligence Agency, all ultimately funnel into that immaculately white room not much larger than a small movie theater.

The network of KH-11 satellites girdling the globe can flash onto any one of its six movie-sized screens a live television picture of any quarter of the planet. So fine is the resolution those satellite cameras provide from ninety miles into space that the President, sitting in his armchair, can tell the difference between a Jersey and a Guernsey cow in a pasture in Nottingham, England, or note the color and make of an automobile leaving the gates of the Kremlin. He can talk to a Marine Corps lieutenant leading a platoon on a patrol in Korea or eavesdrop on, and have instantly translated, a conversation between an airborne Russian MIG-23 fighter pilot and his air controller in Sebastapol. He could listen, thanks to the CIA, to the sound of men's footsteps walking in certain offices in Moscow, Potsdam and Prague, overhear their most intimate conversations, the clink of their vodka glasses, or count the clicks on their telephones as they dial a number.

And, from that leather armchair, the President could be both a spectator and a participant in the ultimate tragedy. He could order a Minuteman missile launched from its site in South Dakota, then, like a spectator in a movie house, watch on one of the screens before him as the thermonuclear horror he had wrought devastated the people, the streets, the tenements of some Soviet city.

Still wearing his blue jeans and his old cardigan, the President settled into that armchair and indicated he was ready to begin. On the wall opposite him, enclosed in a huge black frame to give contrast to the pictures they held, were six large screens used for displays.

The rear admiral in charge of the center, one of the five flag officers in command of the shifts that manned it twenty-four hours a day, seven days a week, moved behind his console. He began by flashing onto his six screens, with almost bewildering speed, a portrait of the military forces of the Soviet Union as they were deployed at that very moment: nuclear submarines, every one at sea pinpointed by a blinking red light on a world map; missile sites caught in a resolution so fine the men in the conference room could watch their Soviet sentries pacing their beats; Backfire bombers on the Black Sea Coast; SS-20 missiles along the Oder.

The Admiral plunged the screens into darkness with a button. There was nothing, he said, in the Soviet's military posture to indicate that the Soviet's armed forces were in an alert status beyond their normal readiness state. It was unlikely that the Soviets were involved in what was happening in Libya.

He turned back to his console and flicked a series of controls. Now a stretch of desolate sands reddening in the first light of morning appeared on the screen. At its center, barely visible, was a tower.

"There, Mr. President, is the location we were given on the note that was found in National Airport."

A second screen lit up. On this one was a detailed resolution of the tower on the first. It was a spindly metal assembly resembling an old-fashioned oil-drilling rig, and at its top the men in the conference room could make out the outlines of a large cylindrical object looking like a barrel and resembling very closely the description of the device on the blueprint given to them by Harold Agnew three and a half hours earlier.

The Admiral turned again to his console. There had been, he noted, no satellites in position over Libya at the time the threat

68

had been delivered to the White House. The precious satellites, whose orbits were set once each month by the NSC, were for the most part employed over the Soviet Union and Eastern Europe. Since the first alert, however, three KH-11s had been shifted into fixed orbits over Libya, and the images delivered by a second satellite rose on one of the six screens. It was a cluster of buildings, the barracks compound of Bab Azizza to which the U.S. chargé d'affaires had earlier been refused admission. Watching the screen, the men around the President could see the paratroopers who had turned the chargé away stomping their feet in the morning chill.

The image moved as it was adjusted and stopped again, this time on a series of small buildings. A white circle popped up around one of them, indistinguishable from the others, a roof inside a little walled compound.

"Sir," the Admiral said, "we believe this to be Qaddafi's residence. We've had it under surveillance since shortly after Los Alamos' first alert. We've seen no evidence of any activity whatsoever or any sign that the building's even occupied."

"What makes you think that's Qaddafi's residence?"

The Admiral adjusted the focus of the satellite picture so that the walled compound enclosed in the white circle filled the screen. Clearly visible, in the compound yard, was a black tent and, apparently tethered to it, a camel.

"Sir, Intelligence informs us Qaddafi keeps a tent and a camel in his yard because he likes fresh camel's milk for breakfast. This is the only residence at Bab Azizza that meets that description."

The Admiral turned back to his display and called up a map of Libya's Mediterranean Sea coast. On it, in the Gulf of Sidra, midway between Tripoli and Benghazi, was a spot of white light. Northwest of the light, not far from the island of Malta, was a blinking red light.

The blinking red light, the Admiral explained, was the U.S.S. *Allen,* an electronic-surveillance ship. It was crammed with sophisticated listening devices, like those with which the CIA had peered into the heart of the Soviet Union for years from its listening posts in Iran. The white light indicated the listening station to which the *Allen* was steaming at twenty-seven knots. Once there, she would be able to eavesdrop on every radio communication made in Libya and all of the telephone calls carried by her modern microwave communications system. Virtually every phone call made in Libya, from a man ordering a radio for his Toyota to a mistress arguing with a jealous lover, to any call made by Qaddafi himself on anything other than a buried, secure line would be intercepted, copied and stored on shipboard computers.

NSA headquarters outside Washington had already sent to the *Allen* voice samples of Qaddafi and five key Libyan leaders. Every intercepted call would be run past those samples by the computer so that calls made by any of the six men could be culled instantly from the hundreds of thousands of other calls being made across the country.

The Mediterranean coast disappeared, to be replaced by a map of Libya. Down its western edge ran two closely parallel red lines, the air corridor laid down by Qaddafi in his message. Two thirds of the way down the corridor a naked eye could follow the progress of a flashing red light.

"Sir, we ordered a Blackbird out of Adana to provide us secondary observation as soon as we received word," commented the Admiral. A Blackbird was an SR-71, a vastly improved version of the old U-2 spy plane, this one capable of flying over two thousand mph at 85,000 feet. They carried supersensitive heat and radiation sensors developed to monitor in minute detail China's and France's nuclear tests.

The President turned his attention back to the site identified in the National Airport note. Underneath the tower, in the quickening sunlight, the crisscross tracings of dozens of tire tracks were now clearly visible.

"Harold," the President asked his Defense Secretary, "what do you make of it?"

"It looks a lot like the pictures I've seen of the old Trinity test site." "Trinity" was the code name for the test of the first atomic bomb in the New Mexico desert in July 1945. "Simple. Primitive. But efficient."

Brown looked at the screen like a professor studying a student's design, hunting for its flaws. "Somewhere around there we should be picking up some sign of the command post he'd use to set this thing off."

"We've swept the area for it, sir," the Admiral answered. "Unfortunately, we haven't been able to spot anything."

"Of course you haven't." The voice was Crandell's, a rasp almost as harsh on the ears as the sound of gravel spilling down a

70

metal chute. "Because there isn't any. That Arab son of a bitch is jerking us off, that's what he's doing. Two million people. That's all he's got in his country, two million people. They're so goddamned backward, most of 'em, they can't even drive a car without stripping the gears. Know what a Frenchman told me once? He caught one of their pilots looking into the gas tank of one of those Mirage planes they sold 'em to see if there was any gas left —with a match!"

Crandell roared with laughter, savoring the image of the ignorant Arab blowing himself and his aircraft to pieces in his search for gasoline. "And you really believe those people could do something like this?"

The President ignored him. "Harold," he said, "he's going to be letting the world in on his secret if this works, isn't he?"

"Not necessarily. That's about as remote a part of the world as you can find down there. Only a few Bedouin tribes running around. Nearest town's well over a hundred and fifty miles away. They'll see a hell of a flash of light all right, but not much else."

"What about fallout?"

The Admiral overheard the President. On one of the screens, superimposed over a map of northeast Africa, there appeared a sausage-shaped arc thrusting across southern Libya, northern Chad, the Sudan and into the southern corner of Saudi Arabia.

"Sir, this is the fallout pattern we're predicting based on the strength and direction of the upper air winds over the site."

"No radiation monitoring devices there," Brown noted. "They'll be reading a four or a five on their Richter scales in Europe. Probably put it down to an earthquake if it goes off."

It was four minutes to midnight. There was little to do now but wait. On the clocks suspended on one wall of the room, the white numbers silently clicked off each passing sound.

The President's eyes concentrated not on the test site but on the screen on which Qaddafi's bungalow lay trapped in its circle of white. The details of the house and garden were clearly visible, the reddish tiles on the roof, the purplish splash of flowers beside the house. In the garden there was what looked like a child's playground.

Is it really possible, he asked himself, that a man living in a pleasant little house like that, a man with children, a man who believes in his God as devoutly as I believe in mine, could propose

71

something as mad, as senseless, as this? What is there, he wondered, what hatred, what lust for power, what drive for revenge for a wrong that didn't even affect him or his own people directly, that could drive him to so irrational an act? He shuddered.

Harold Brown sensed the President's anguish. "Well, sir," he said, in a voice so soft only the Chief Executive beside him could hear it, "either we have a terrible problem on our hands or the cruelist hoax anyone's ever played on a U.S. government."

The President nodded. He said nothing. He continued to gaze straight ahead, concentrating totally on the screens before him.

The numbers rolled away toward the last zero, droplets falling rhythmically to an instant past. There was no sound in the room except the whir of the ventilation system. Even the lieutenant colonels manning the consoles, as used to tension as runners are to cramps, were pale with the strain.

Eleven fifty-nine. Four precisely aligned zeroes appeared on the clocks' panels. No one saw them. Every eye was on the screen along the room's far wall, on the emptiness of the desert, on the frail tower planted on its sands like a withered tree trunk that had somehow survived there despite the ravages of time and nature.

Five seconds, ten seconds. Nothing happened. Fifteen seconds. Thirty seconds. The first creak of twisting armchairs indicated that the tension pent up in the room was easing. Forty-five seconds. Nothing, not even the eddying currents of a passing gust of wind, moved on the screen.

One minute. Men at last sat back in their armchairs. A relief so intense it was almost a physical presence enveloped the room.

"I told you the son of a bitch didn't have it." Satisfaction seemed to mix with the sweat sparkling on Crandell's face.

Tap Bennington chewed on his pipe stem. "Mr. President, we've now got to decide what our response to the threat should be. I think we should review immediately the range of military options we can address against Libya."

"Tap, just a minute, for God's sake." Warren Christopher of State was pleading. "We still have no confirmation whatsoever that Qaddafi is behind this."

"You mean," a furious Crandell demanded, "you propose to let that son of a bitch get off scot free just because his goddamn bomb—"

He never finished. A white wall of light seemed to explode from the screens of Room 2B890. So blindingly luminous was its flash, so painfully intense its glare, the men in the room flinched and shielded their eyes. Then, from ninety miles into space and a quarter of the way around the planet, the satellite cameras sucked up the fireball soaring over the Awbari Sand Sea and sent it hurtling onto the screens of the Pentagon, a roiling caldron of exploding gases: whites, reds, yellows and oranges, arranged in a dazzling kaleidoscope of light and fire.

For seconds, too stunned to react or speak, the two dozen men in the room stared, thanks to those cameras, at a sight no human eye had ever beheld, the bowels of hell, the incandescent heart of a thermonuclear explosion.

The first sound to intrude on the room came from seventy thousand feet over the site, from the pilot of the SR-71. Mechanically, indifferent to the spectacle below him, he read off the swiftly changing measurements of his instrument panels: a tide of thermal X rays, gamma rays, beta particles rushing past his detectors. His figures meant nothing to most of the men in the room. It did not matter. Everything they needed to know was right there on the screen before them, in the unsurpassable beauty and horror of a fireball rising from the desert floor.

The President squeezed Harold Brown's forearm in his fingers. He had paled and his mouth hung half open, his lower lip curling downward with dismay. Watching, mesmerized, he could think of only one thing: John the Divine's Revelation of the Apocalypse: ". . . behold a pale horse: and his name that sat on him was Death, and Hell followed with him."

Now, he thought, a Fifth Horseman has emerged from the entrails of hell to scourge humanity with terror, with arms so terrible even John's hallucinating imagination could not have conceived them.

"My God," he whispered to the man beside him. "Oh my God, Harold, how did he ever do it?"

PART II

". . . at last we shall make justice prevail."

THE ANSWER TO AN ANGUISHED PRESIDENT'S QUES-
tion could be traced back to a November afternoon in Paris not
quite one year before the Libyan's threat message had been delivered to the White House gate.

France's President Valéry Giscard d'Estaing, punctual as usual,
entered the Cabinet Room of his Élysée Palace precisely at four
o'clock that afternoon. He circled the table to greet first the Prime
Minister, then the Ministers of Finance, Industry, Foreign Affairs,
the Interior and Defense. When he got to Pierre Foucault, Chairman of France's Atomic Energy Commission, a broad smile broke
out on his composed features.

"Bravo, *mon cher,*" he said to his old friend and schoolmate.

Foucault's reply was a glance at the empty chair beside his. The
scientist he had summoned to this restricted and secret meeting
was late.

A slight flaring of his nostrils betrayed Giscard's irritation. "We
shall proceed as planned," he said. He took his seat at the head of
the table and, in that slow, precise enunciation he reserved for
particularly solemn occasions, began.

"Messieurs," he declared, "I have asked you here today to
inform you of an event that is certain to have an overwhelming
impact on the destiny of our nation. A team of French scientists
working at our laser fusion research center at Fontenay-aux-Roses
has succeeded within the past week in solving one of the most
formidable scientific challenges in man's history. Indeed, they
have done something scientists around the world have been trying
to do for thirty years—produce energy from fusion. The results of
their work will ultimately permit this country, and indeed the entire
world, to resolve the most intransigent problem we all face, the
global energy crisis."

He paused to allow the impact of his words to register. "We

have asked the man responsible for our success, Monsieur Alain Prévost, to join us, but he has apparently been held up in traffic, so I shall ask Monsieur Foucault to begin.''

The President nodded to his Atomic Energy Chairman, who picked up the carafe in front of him and filled his water glass. He took a sip. Then he held up the glass as though he were about to propose a toast.

''Messieurs,'' he began, ''the meaning of our breakthrough is that the water in this glass . . .'' he paused an instant for dramatic effect, swirling the water in his upraised glass, allowing it to glisten in the pale sunlight, ''is now a source of energy capable of lighting the lamps of mankind. It means that there is now in this glass of water alone enough energy to meet the power requirements of the entire city of Paris and all its inhabitants for forty-eight hours.''

Foucault brought the glass back to the ministerial table with a sharp crash. The men around him gasped. He paused, savoring the shock his words had produced. Then he began again, his voice softer. ''Until now, man has met his energy needs by exploiting the heritage of the past, the coal, oil, gas and uranium buried in the earth's crust. His long-term survival on this planet has depended, however, on finding a new source of energy, one that is by its very nature virtually inexhaustible. There are only two, the sun—and water.

''With water,'' he said, ''we begin with the most abundant resource on the planet. It is, after all, everywhere. All water contains one of the simplest atoms on earth—deuterium, or, as we say, 'heavy hydrogen.' This water glass is full of them. If we can bang two of these atoms together hard enough so that they meld—that is, fuse—the result is a release of energy so enormous it staggers the mind.

''Let me give you an example. One kilogram of the petroleum we now purchase at such an exorbitant cost in the Persian Gulf releases thirteen kilowatt hours of energy when it burns. One kilogram of heavy hydrogen, properly fused, will release . . .'' again Foucault paused, measuring each word for dramatic effect, ''ninety-one million kilowatt hours of energy.''

The ministers let out what was nearly a collective gasp.

''The search for this energy form,'' he told his now spellbound audience, ''goes back to the 1930s when the English astrophysicists at the Cavendish Laboratories realized that this was the process which explained the unaccountable energy releases of the sun and the stars. If it could be done in the stars, they asked, why couldn't it be done on earth?''

Foucault leaned forward, savoring for an instant the role of a pedagogue. ''It meant, messieurs, dealing with time in billionths of seconds. A billionth of a second is to one second as one second is to three hundred and thirty-two years. It meant creating conditions of temperature and pressure that are equivalent to hell on earth.

''The Soviets made the first great leap forward in 1958 with the ingenious use of magnetic force to produce the effect we sought. In the late sixties when the scientific community introduced the power of the laser beam into our work, real progress began. As you all know, we here in France have been at the forefront of laser technology. Our stunning and quite unexpected breakthrough of a fortnight ago comes as a result of the scientific advances we made in the late seventies developing our new carbon-dioxide laser.

''I must caution you all,'' the Minister warned, ''on the need for the utmost secrecy about our advance. What we have done is to demonstrate for the first time the scientific feasibility of the fusion process. Applying it commercially will require years and years of work. The potential commercial benefits to this country of our head start, however, are incalculable. We must not allow the premature disclosure of our discovery to deprive France of the just— and immeasurable—rewards of our scientists' work.''

So mesmerized were the men around the table, no one noticed a *hussier* slip into the council chamber and discreetly hand an envelope to the Minister of the Interior. The Minister glanced at its contents, then, his face a register of the gravity of the message he had just read, turned to Valéry Giscard d'Estaing.

''Monsieur le Président,'' he said, interrupting Foucault's speech, ''the Brigade Criminelle of the Prefecture of Police has just informed me they have discovered a car with a corpse in it abandoned in the Allée de Longchamps in the Bois de Boulogne. The corpse has been tentatively identified through a laissez-passer issued to attend this meeting. It appears to belong to this scientist we are waiting for—'' he glanced at his paper—''Alain Prévost.''

Three blue police vans, yellow roof lights blinking, marked the scene. A cordon of policemen screened off passersby, prostitutes and poodle walkers gawking in morbid curiosity at the Renault and the shrouded figure laid out on the ground beside it. Ignoring his policemen's salutes, the Minister of the Interior, trailed by Pierre Foucault, swept through the cordon up to Maurice Lemuel, head of the Police Judiciaire, France's top police investigatory force.

"*Alors?*" barked the Minister.

Lemuel turned to a plastic sheet laid out on the Bois de Boulogne grass. On it were two items, a wallet and a slide rule, its white lacquer surface yellowed by age and use.

"That's all?" the Minister asked. "No sign of the documents he was carrying?"

"That's all, sir," Lemuel replied. "That and the pass we identified him with."

The Minister turned to the Atomic Energy Chairman. "It's perfectly incredible," he said, his voice full of barely controlled anger. "You let these people go walking about Paris carrying secret papers as though they were taking shirts to the laundry."

"Olivier," Foucault protested, "these men are scientists. They just don't think about security the way you do."

"Maybe they don't," the Minister said. "But you're supposed to. You're personally responsible for the security of your agency. Which has been appallingly bad in this case." He turned back to Lemuel. "What have you learned?"

"Very little," the policeman answered. "We'll need an autopsy to be sure of the cause of death. I would guess from the expression on his face that he was either smothered or had his windpipe broken by a very forceful, expert karate blow."

Shortly after 4:30 A.M. the following day a telephone's harsh summons jarred the stillness of the Minister of the Interior's private apartment above the Place Beauvau. He groaned. From under the covers, his hand flayed uncertainly at the darkness, searching out the sound.

His caller was the Atomic Energy Chairman. "They called," Foucault gasped. "The people who killed Prévost. They want a million francs for the attaché case. They just got through to our director of research at Fontenay, Pierre Lebrun. They told him if we want it back he has to be at the Cintra Bar on the Vieux-Port in

Marseilles at exactly twelve noon today with one million francs in hundred-franc notes in a plastic shopping bag of the Bazaar d'Hôtel de Ville. He's supposed to wear a dark-blue suit, black shoes, a white shirt and tie and a felt hat."

Despite the seriousness of his caller's words, the Minister could not help laughing. "Dressed like that, your poor Monsieur Lebrun is going to stand out like a nun in a whorehouse down there."

He rose from his bed, looking about for his clothes. "Have Monsieur Lebrun at my office at eight o'clock," he ordered. "I'm going to convene a meeting of my top people immediately."

The four senior police officials of the French Republic sat respectfully in front of the Interior Minister's desk, a gift from Napoleon to one of his distant predecessors. They were Paul-Robert de Villeprieux, the director of the DST, France's counter-espionage service; his bald, slightly stoop-shouldered colleague General Henri Bertrand, head of what was familiarly known in the Ministry as La Piscine ("The Pool"), the SDECE, France's intelligence service; Maurice Fraguier, the forty-five-year-old director general of the National Police; and General Marcel Piqueton, commander of the forty-thousand-man Gendarmerie Nationale. The Minister quickly summarized the details of the extortionist's call.

"Gentlemen," he said, sipping at the black coffee he had ordered for them all, "what are your views?"

Fraguier, chief of the Police Nationale, began. "Quite frankly, Monsieur le Ministre, I had suspected we were dealing with an affair of state here, a theft of industrial secrets by a foreign intelligence service, the CIA probably, or the KGB. This message makes it quite clear it's a banal case of extortion organized by the Corsican *milieu*. This is characteristic of the way the Corsicans behave in payoff delivery situations." Fraguier lit a cigarette and sat back in his chair. "It doesn't require a great deal of imagination to predict how it's going to work. Right near the Cintra Bar down there in Marseilles they've got the biggest Corsican neighborhood in France, the 'Bread Basket.' They'll use it for the payoff, because they feel safe in there.

"They'll let Monsieur Lebrun sit and marinate for a while in the Cintra while they study the neighborhood to make sure we're not around. Then he'll get a telephone call. He'll be told to leave immediately for another address up in the Bread Basket by a very precise route. They've picked *l'heure du pastis,* so they'll probably send him to another bar and they'll give him a pseudonym, Jean Dupont. Once he's in the bar he'll get another call with the instructions as to where to leave the money. It will be very nearby, but out of sight of the bar. The trashcan in front of 17 Rue Belles Écuelles. Or they'll say, 'Hang it on the handlebars of the blue bicycle leaning against the door of 10 Rue des Trois-Lucs. Do it immediately and come back to the bar.' When they've picked up the payoff, he'll get a last call telling him where the papers are.''

The Minister placed his hands before him as though in prayer, lightly tapping his fingertips together, contemplating the scenario his police chief had outlined. He turned to the head of the SDECE. Eyes half closed like a monk in meditation, a Gauloise cigarette that never seemed to move dangling from his mouth, General Henri Bertrand sat motionless on his spindly chair. The perfect stillness of the man was attested to by the inch-and-a-half-long ash dangling at the end of his cigarette. He spoke and it spilled over the lapels of his gray suit.

''Since when have your Corsican friends been so interested in science?'' he asked Fraguier.

''When the Russians wanted to get hold of our designs for the Concorde, what did they do?'' Fraguier replied. ''They went down to Marseilles and knocked on the right Corsican's door, did they not? Perhaps that experience taught our Corsican friends the value of industrial secrets.''

Bertrand brushed the ashes from his suit. ''Their asking price seems low,'' he suggested in his quiet voice.

''Yes,'' Fraguier agreed. ''But remember, for them it's a lot of money. They may not realize just how valuable those papers are.''

''What guarantee do we have,'' asked the Minister, ''that they haven't photostated those documents and won't try to hold us up again?''

''None whatsoever,'' Fraguier answered. He paused. ''But they won't. Corsicans are honorable people. They only cheat you once.''

For a moment, the only sound in the office was the creaking of the Minister's chair as he slowly rocked back and forth. In a sense, they had been fortunate. If they made the payoff, it would all be over. The incident would never get to the public and the secret of the scientific advance would be kept safe.

"All right, do it," he ordered his police chief. "I'll arrange with the Treasury for the million francs."

A gray stain seeped along the edges of night. Dawn was about to break over the barren immensity of the desert. That period immediately preceding the emergence of the solar disc on the horizon was known to the followers of the Prophet as El Fedji, the first dawn. It lasted only minutes, just the time required by the Faithful to recite the first of their five *sourates,* the daily prayers prescribed by the Koran.

Dressed in a crude shepherd's cloak of brown and white stripes, a flowing white kaffiyeh held in place by one cord on his head, a man in his late thirties emerged from his goatskin tent and spread a prayer rug on the sand. Turning east, he began to invoke the name of Allah, Master of the World, the All-Merciful and All-Compassionate, the Supreme Sovereign of the Last Judgment.

He prostrated himself three times, touching his forehead to the earth each time, glorifying as he did the name of God and His Prophet. His prayer finished, Muammar al-Qaddafi, the undisputed ruler of the Libyan nation, sat back on his rug and watched the rising sun flame the desert sky. He was a son of the desert. He had entered the world in a goatskin tent similar to the one in which he had just passed the night. His birth had been heralded by the rumble of the artillery duel fought that evening between the gunners of Rommel's Afrika Korps and Montgomery's Eighth Army. He had spent his boyhood wandering the desert with his tribe, maturing to the searing gusts of the siroccos, the blessings of the winter rains, the quick flowering of the pastures. From the sand seas below Cyrenaica southwest to the palm trees of Fezzan, there was not a prickly bush, a sweep of grass or a dried-out riverbed that had escaped his predator's gaze in the nomad's quest for pasturage for his flock.

Regularly, when he felt overwhelmed by the frustrations and disappointments of the power that was now his, he retreated back here to his desert to immerse himself again in the wellsprings of his being. Now, as he meditated on his prayer rug, his eye caught the gleam of a pair of headlights on the horizon. A white Peugeot 504 drew toward the small military encampment half a mile from his tent where his visitors were screened and the communications which tied him to Tripoli were installed. The three sentries on duty waved it to a halt and meticulously scrutinized first its driver, then his papers. When they had finished they ordered the driver out of his car. They ran a metal detector over his body. Finally, satisfied, they allowed him to set out alone, on foot, toward the Libyan dictator.

Qaddafi followed his progress across the sands. When he was a hundred yards away Qaddafi stood and walked out to meet him. "*Salaam alaikum!*" he called out.

"*Alaikum salaam,*" the visitor replied.

Qaddafi advanced a few steps and embraced him on both cheeks. "Welcome, my brother," he said. He drew back and looked at him, amused. Whalid Dajani was red-faced from the unaccustomed exertion of his half-mile walk in the desert.

"I have . . ." he began in an excited gasp.

Qaddafi raised his hand to interrupt him. "First, coffee, my friend," he said. "Afterward, *insh' Allah,* we will talk."

He took Dajani by the arm and led him into the tent, where he picked up a brass coffee pot from the fire glowing in his brazier. He poured the pale Bedouin coffee into handleless porcelain cups shaped like oversized thimbles and offered the first one to his guest. They drank. Then Qaddafi lay back on the Oriental rugs thrown around the floor of his tent. The suspicion of a smile crossed his handsome face. "Now, my brother," he said, "tell me your news."

"The package arrived," the visitor replied, "last night." He took a deep breath and held it trapped in his lungs as though trying to hold back with it the rush of words ready to spill from his mouth. Finally he exhaled a breath that reeked of the dozens of peppermint Lifesavers he had gulped to kill the odor of the Chivas Regal whiskey he had been sipping all night long. Alcohol was totally banned in Qaddafi's domain.

"I can't believe it yet," he said. "It's all there. I studied it all night." He shook his head in disbelief. Once again he saw the columns of figures plunging toward an infinity of power such as few minds had ever been privileged to contemplate.

His vision, however, was not that of the limitless reserves of energy that had enfevered the mind of the French scientist who had first looked at them barely a week before. What Dajani had glimpsed was a vision of hell, the dark underside of the dream of fusion, the terms of a Faustian compact Alain Prévost and others pursuing his dream around the world had had to strike with the capricious gods of science. For, in opening to man the vista of unlimited energy for as long as he and his planet might endure, they had also exposed the keys to a force so destructive it could set a premature end to his, and his environment's, existence. Frozen into the endless rows of figures in the computer printout Prévost had been taking to his meeting at the Élysée Palace was the secret of the hydrogen bomb.

"Carlos and his people worked quickly," Qaddafi observed. "You're sure there's no way this can be traced back here? Our relations with the French are vital."

Dajani shook his head. "They copied the papers right away. Then they called the French as though they were Corsican gangsters looking for a ransom."

"And the French believed them?"

"Apparently."

Qaddafi rose from his carpet and moodily stirred the coals glowing in his brazier. "My brother," he said, "when we started this operation you said the Frenchman was working on a new kind of energy."

His visitor nodded.

"Why is it," Qaddafi continued, "you were able to get the secret of the hydrogen bomb from what he was doing?"

"Essentially," Dajani replied, "what they were trying to do in Paris was to make a mini-mini-hydrogen-bomb explosion. A controlled one so that they could use the energy it released. People have been trying to do that for thirty years, since the Americans exploded the first hydrogen bomb."

He paused, then reached to his temple and with a dramatic gesture plucked a single strand of hair from his balding head. He held it up before Qaddafi's intrigued eyes. "What they were trying to do was to make a bubble no thicker than this hair explode. To do it, they had to squeeze it to one thousand times its normal density with a laser beam in a time so short the mind can't imagine it."

Qaddafi's eyes widened. "But why did the secret of the hydrogen bomb come out of that?"

"Because with all experiments like this, the evolution of every ingredient is being constantly recorded by computer. For one tiny, tiny instant just before that little bubble exploded, it took on the one perfect configuration of a hydrogen bomb. Its secret, the exact

85

relationship between its ingredients, is detailed here in the computer printout.''

Qaddafi rose and walked in silence to the entrance of the tent. He stood there scrutinizing the horizon, incarnadined now by the fast-rising sun. For an instant he forgot what the scientist had just told him. Instinctively, as he had every dawn in the desert since he was a boy, he studied the sky for some precursor foretelling the arrival of the Bedouin's timeless enemy, the *guebli,* the searing wind that rose in the desolate expanse of the Sahara. When the *guebli* blew, death rode its wings, and man and beast huddled together, as often he had with his father's herd, seeking protection against the onrushing clouds of sand under which whole tribes had been known to vanish.

This morning, though, the sky was a violent blue, not the silvery gray that heralded the *guebli.* He looked at it reassured, at the oneness of the vast canopy of sky and the endless horizons of his desert. The world stretching away from his tent was a cruel, harsh world; but it was a simple one in which choices and their consequences were clear: You crossed the sands in search of the well. You found the well and you survived. You did not and you died.

Perhaps now with what his visitor had brought him, he had reached his well, the one for which he had been searching for so many years. For a moment, standing there in the morning sunlight before reentering his tent, Qaddafi thought of the story his father had told him of the *kettate,* the tattooed fortuneteller, who had appeared at their campsite as his mother screamed in the pain that preceded his birth. She had gone to the tent in which the men of the tribe sipped tea waiting for the birth and shook out on a carpet the twenty-three rigidly prescribed oddments of her trade, an old coin, a shard of glass, a dried date kernel, a bone from a camel's hoof. Then she proclaimed it would be a boy. He would be an anointed of God, she announced, a man destined to stand out from all the others, to perform God's work in the service of his people. She had barely finished when the first part of her prophecy was confirmed. The scream of the midwife rang out from the woman's tent calling out the ritual phrase that greeted a newborn male: "*Allah akhbar*—God is great.''

Qaddafi turned back into the tent. From a copper pot he took a thick, creamy bowlful of *leben,* goat's curd, and a black wad of dates, the Bedouin's traditional breakfast. He set them on the carpet and bade his guest eat.

86

Dipping a date into his curds, Qaddafi pondered, as he often did, on the old woman's prophecy and how favored indeed he was in Allah's eyes. Allah had given him a mission, to bring His peoples back to God's way, to reawaken the Arab people to their true destiny, to right the wrongs that had been done to his brothers. And He had given him the means to accomplish it, the oil without which those who had so long exploited his people could not survive. To get it from him, the others had had to offer him the means to his vision: wealth, the arms he had bought, the technology he had acquired, the science his people had learned, and now this prospect his visitor had laid before him—the prospect of the ultimate power on earth.

"And, my brother," he said to Dajani, "we can build this from these documents they brought you last night?"

"It's a long, hard road with many, many problems. First we must finish our atomic program. There will be difficulties and risks —the danger the Israelis will find out what we are doing and destroy us before we can succeed."

Qaddafi looked out to the desert stretching away from the tent, a distant gaze in his dark, brooding eyes. "My friend, there has never been greatness without danger. There has never been a great victory without great risks."

He rose, indicating to Dajani that the conversation was over. "You have done well, my brother," he said, his voice almost reverent, "ever since Allah sent you here to help us. Now, thanks to you, at last we shall make justice prevail."

This time he walked his visitor back across the sands to his car. Gently he placed a hand on Whalid's elbow. A faint, ironic smile crossed his features. "My brother," he murmured, "perhaps you should not eat so many peppermints. Such things are bad for the good health God gave you."

The vista laid bare to Muammar al-Qaddafi in his desert retreat was only the last, terrifying consequence of an enterprise the Libyan had pursued from the moment, almost, that he had seized power. Power was something the Bedouin dictator understood instinctively, and what better way to assert his claim to the leadership of a resurgent Arab world than to be the first Arab leader to arm his nation with the ultimate weapon?

Qaddafi had taken his first step on the road to his desert rendezvous in 1969, shortly after he had consolidated his revolution. He sent his Prime Minister, Abdul Salam Jalloud, to Peking with an offer to buy half a dozen atomic bombs from China's nuclear arsenal. Rebuffed by the Chinese, Qaddafi turned to Westinghouse with a proposal to purchase a 600-megawatt nuclear reactor to desalinize sea water for irrigating his desert. Since no one in the world knew how to do that at anything remotely approaching an economically justifiable cost, the implication that Qaddafi had other uses in mind for the plant was clear. The State Department refused to authorize the sale despite the protests of Westinghouse and its congressional lobby. The Libyan then sought to buy an experimental reactor from Gulf General Atomic of San Diego. The reactor itself could not have been used to make an atomic bomb, but the fuel that Gulf General was ready to sell Qaddafi along with it—fully enriched uranium—was ideal bomb material. Henry Kissinger's personal intervention was required to block that initiative.

Qaddafi's program got into high gear after the 1973 war and his realization that Israel possessed atomic weapons. He himself picked the program's code name, Seif al Islam—"The Sword of Islam"—and placed it under the direct control of Prime Minister Jalloud's office. Three principles were to guide it. First, the weapons program would be carried out under the cover of a peaceful nuclear-energy program. Second, Libya would look primarily to Europe for its technology. Third, every effort would be made to staff the program with Arab scientists, men either recruited from universities and nuclear programs or trained at Libyan expense in the best universities in the world.

By the midseventies, the CIA began picking up indications that Libya was trying to recruit European nuclear engineers by dangling large Swiss-banked sums of money in front of them. One indication of how far the program's tentacles could reach was the dismissal of Dr. Klaus Traube, manager of Germany's Interatom Company responsible for research on the fast breeder reactor. Traube was revealed to have had a close relationship with Hans Joachim Klein, a young Libyan-trained terrorist who participated along with "Carlos" in the Vienna kidnapping of the OPEC oil ministers in December 1975.

It was, however, to the explosion of India's atomic "device" in the Rajasthan desert on May 19, 1974, that the Libyan owed his access to the secret of the atom. Pakistan's Zulficar Ali Bhutto vowed that night that his countrymen would one day possess nuclear weapons to rival his neighbors' even if they had "to eat grass" to get them. Given the impoverished state of Pakistan's treasury, his might have been an idle boast had it not been for a secret deal Bhutto negotiated with Qaddafi. Its terms were simple: in return for Libya's financing Pakistan's purchase of a plutonium-reprocessing plant and several reactors from France, Qaddafi would receive some of the plutonium the Pakistanis intended to divert from the plant and access to their advanced nuclear technology.

That arrangement ultimately collapsed when the French, under pressure from the United States, agreed to abandon the sale. In the meantime, Bhutto's overthrow and subsequent execution had brought a brief chill to Libyan–Pakistani relations. The combination of Libyan financing and Pakistani technology was too promising, however, to be lost in a clash of personalities, and the original collaboration was renewed in General Mohammad Zia-ul-Haq's pursuit of the "Islamic Bomb."

While his cooperative effort with Pakistan continued, Qaddafi also pursued his attempts to set up a purely national program. In 1976 he persuaded Jacques Chirac, then France's Prime Minister, to sell him the nuclear reactor for desalinizing sea water the Americans had earlier refused him. President Giscard d'Estaing quietly let the project fade until, under the pressures on France's balance of payments created by the 1979–80 oil price rises, he reluctantly authorized the reactor's sale.

The most dramatic confrontation in Qaddafi's long pursuit of the atomic bomb, however, had for its setting a place as remote from the goatskin tents in which he enjoyed resting as could be imagined. It was an ornate salon in the Palace of the Czars, the Kremlin. Qaddafi's interlocutor that December day in 1976 was not a Russian but the proudest industrial baron of the nation that had once colonized Qaddafi's people. Who could have better symbolized the unsettled and indulgent world whose way of life was menaced by the austere visionary emerging from his deserts than Gianni Agnelli: aristocrat, playboy, heir to a technological complex as sophisticated and as powerful as any in the world, the Fiat Motor Company.

Agnelli was the supplicant that day. He had come to Moscow in secret because he needed something Qaddafi had to offer, money.

89

Qaddafi already owned ten percent of his firm, purchased a few months before for $415 million, more than triple the market value of the shares. To an astonished Agnelli, he proposed to buy even more or release to him large investment sums if Agnelli could convert part of his company, with Soviet help, into an advanced weapons industry, including a major branch devoted to nuclear research and development.

It was a diabolical proposition. Agnelli was being asked to set an unstable nation just across the Mediterranean from his homeland on the road to weapons of mass destruction in return for the funds that might save his industrial giant from collapse. The Italian's readiness to consider the proposition, however briefly, was one more confirmation of the premise underlying Qaddafi's enterprise: that the day would come when, under the pressure of the energy crisis, there would be nothing in the West that was not for sale.

Whalid Dajani drove along the eucalyptus- and laurel-lined highway leading to the Libyan capital, sweating profusely, his mind still back in the desert, on the harrowing hours he'd lived since they'd brought him the transcript of Prévost's phone call a week ago. He could feel in his stomach the ache of the ulcer his doctor had warned him he was developing.

A man is dead because of me, he thought. A man like me, who had the ideals I once had. My God, he reflected, how far I've come, how far away I am from what I set out to be. He saw ahead, not the highway into Tripoli, but the other terrible road on which he was embarked.

"Since Allah sent you here to help us," Qaddafi had said. Whalid smiled bitterly. Allah had had nothing to do with it. It had been his brother Kamal and it had all begun that morning in January 1977 when Kamal had arrived in Paris.

The debarking passengers of Austrian Airlines Flight 705 from Vienna to Paris mounted the futuristic walkway of Charles de Gaulle Airport and clustered around the passport-control desk of Gate 26. Kamal Dajani was wearing a beige suede jacket and blue jeans, an Austrian Airlines carry-on bag hanging from his shoulder. A dark suntan, the product, presumably, of the ski slopes of the

90

Tyrol, burnished his lean face and emphasized the delicate blue of his eyes.

He presented the passport officer at the desk an Austrian passport identifying him as Fredi Mueller, an agricultural-machinery salesman from Linz, then strolled casually into the lobby and on to the nearest men's room.

He hesitated a moment before entering the last stall in line. He locked the door and set his airline bag on the floor. An instant later, a hand pulled it into the adjacent stall, then slid an absolutely identical bag back to his feet.

Kamal opened it up and methodically checked its contents: a Walther P-38 automatic; three magazines of 9mm. ammunition; two U.S. Army fragmentation grenades; a switchblade knife; a red guide, *Paris par Arrondissement,* on which he could locate his destination and the safe house whose address he had committed to memory; another set of identity papers, these French, identifying him as Mohammed Yaacef, an Algerian postgraduate student studying in France; a small vial of liquid; and, finally, five thousand French francs in assorted notes and coins. As he passed the toilet attendant on the way out, he sent a one-franc coin clattering into the saucer beside her. No need, he thought, to give her any reason to glare at him.

Forty minutes later, he got out of a taxicab at the junction of the Boulevard St.-Michel and the Boulevard St.-Germain at the heart of Paris's Latin Quarter. He crossed the Place du Luxembourg and strolled along the iron fence of the Luxembourg Gardens down to the Rue d'Assas. There he turned left until he reached number 89 at the corner of the Rue Tavard opposite the Tarnier Maternity Clinic. The building's ground floor was occupied by a bakery, and as Kamal climbed to the first floor he savored the odor of warm bread and fresh croissants that seemed to impregnate the dark stairwell.

He knocked at the first door on the left. Inside, he heard the thump of bare feet on wood, then felt someone staring at him through the door's peephole. "It's me," he whispered in Arabic, "Kamal."

His sister Laila opened the door. For an instant brother and sister looked at each other. Then, with half-stifled cries, they fell into each other's arms.

"Five years," Laila whispered. "Why so long?"

"I had no choice," Kamal replied.

She beckoned him inside. Before closing the door, she glanced down the stairwell, making sure he had not been followed. Then she fixed the door with a double lock.

"Show me what they did to you," Laila demanded as soon as they reached the sitting room. She was a year younger than Kamal, yet she had always managed to treat him with an air of superiority as though somehow the mere fact of having been born a female had given her a head start in life.

Grudgingly, Kamal removed his jacket and shirt. The scar along his neck ran down to an ugly tangle of scar tissue planted like the imprint of a tiger's claw below his left shoulder blade.

Laila gasped at the sight of that most visible heritage of the career her brother had begun crawling under a screen of machine-gun fire at a training camp for commandos of the Refusal Front on a windswept plateau above Damascus.

"They told me you were dead."

"That's what the bastards thought when they ran away and left me," her brother noted. Six times Kamal had taken a squad of fedayeen out of Fatah Land in Southern Lebanon to rocket a kibbutz, mine a road or ambush a passing car. On the seventh, an unsuccessful effort to fire a Katushka rocket into the Haifa oil refineries, his squad had been intercepted by an Israeli patrol. A cluster of well-placed grenades had wounded Kamal and scattered his men.

"You were lucky the Israelis didn't finish you off when they found you," Laila remarked.

"Luck has nothing to do with it. It's because you can't interrogate a dead fedayeen." The Israeli patrol had rushed Kamal to the prisoners' ward of Tel Aviv's Tal Hashomer Hospital. There he had lain in a coma for a week until the medical skill of his captors and the vitality of his own constitution had combined to save him.

He picked up his beige jacket and drew from its pocket the pendant-shaped vial three inches long that had been in his second airline bag. Laila gasped at the sight of the pale-yellow fluid in its bulbous base.

"My jasmine!"

Kamal nodded. His sister grabbed the vial, plucked out its stopper and thrust it to her nostrils. She gulped its odor the way a suffocating man might gasp at the first rush of air flowing from an

92

oxygen mask. Laila closed her eyes. A world, a forgotten world, swam back at her as the pungent scent invaded her senses. Abdul's perfume shop in the souk of Old Jerusalem, a dark cavern of olfactory miracles, its air so heavy with musky smells it seemed she could almost caress it between her fingertips.

"How did you—" she started.

"One of our people who was in Jerusalem on a mission brought it out," Kamal explained. Illicit traffic across the Israeli–Jordanian border was something Kamal understood. He had been an illegal export himself, hidden at the bottom of a truckload of oranges after his escape from the prisoners' ward at Tal Hashomer Hospital.

Laila clutched the vial to her breast. "Dear, sweet Abdul," she said.

Her brother started at her phrase. Those blue eyes of his, the eyes that, the family had always joked, were the legacy of an errant Crusader knight's dalliance with a member of the Dajani clan, seemed to protrude from their sockets, their delicate robin's-egg cast darkened by some interior storm.

"Don't be in a rush to use up that jasmine," he said. "It happens to be the last your dear, sweet Abdul ever sold. He's dead."

Laila gasped.

"He was executed for treason."

His sister looked unbelievingly at the vial in her hands, then at her brother who had brought it for her.

"May I have some tea?" he asked.

Too stunned to speak, Laila turned to the kitchen alcove behind her and prepared to light the gas stove.

Her brother continued. "I've come to see you because I need your help."

Laila spun, the match still sputtering in her hand. She had found her voice. "Why? Is there some poor grocer down the street you want killed?"

The tone of her brother's reply was as sharp as the snap of a breaking bone. "Laila, we never kill without a reason. He sold two of our people to the Jews." He paused, throttling down his anger before he continued. "I want you to convince Whalid to help us in a very important operation."

"Why me? Why don't you talk to him? He's your brother, too, isn't he?"

"Because Whalid and I don't talk to each other. We only argue.

93

And I'm interested in getting his help, not winning an argument.'' Kamal got up and moved to the window overlooking the clinic across the street.

"Whalid would never understand what I've been doing.'' Kamal looked out the window, almost melancholy, groping for a phrase, for a thought to explain himself to his sister. ''The end justifies the means.'' He uttered the words as though they were an original thought he had just discovered, the absolution of a new age designed to be pronounced before rather than after confession. ''For me they do. Not for him. Except in those laboratories of his where everything's an abstraction.'' He gestured with his head to the crowded street below. ''Never down there where it matters. He'd call me a criminal,'' he said softly. ''I'd call him a coward. After five minutes we wouldn't have anything left to say to each other.''

"You never did have much to say to each other,'' Laila remarked. ''Long before he went into those laboratories of his and you . . .'' She paused, searching for a word.

Kamal provided it. ''Became a terrorist. Or a patriot. The line between them is sometimes thin.'' Kamal walked back across the room, gesturing as he did to the kitchen. ''You were going to make me a cup of tea, remember?''

Laila set the kettle on her stove and came back to the sitting room. ''He's changed, you know. He's more French than the French are now. What happened to us, our parents, Palestine—all that just seems to have faded away like it was a part of a life he lived in another incarnation. He's like everyone else. The car. The house. The cleaning woman on Thursdays. His work. His wife. A happily married man, no?''

"We're not going to ask him to give up all that, Laila,'' Kamal's voice was calm, almost serene. ''But he's not like everyone else. Not for us at least.''

His words sent a tremor of apprehension through Laila, confirming what she had suspected from the moment Kamal had mentioned their elder brother.

"It's about his work—what you're after?''

Kamal nodded.

The kettle whistled. Laila rose. She walked to the alcove, her steps paced off in the slowed rhythm of someone whose mind is lost in thought. So that's what it is, she told herself. After all the

94

years, after all the rumors, the angry late-night discussions, they were going to do it now.

She set the cups on the table beside Kamal's chair, the noonday sun highlighting as she did the rich rolls of auburn hair cascading down to her shoulders. She shivered inadvertently as the enormity of what her brother contemplated overwhelmed her.

"How in God's name will we ever get him to help us?" she asked.

Outside, the harsh bleat of an ambulance rushing toward the clinic across the street pierced the noonday quiet.

Laila Dajani's face lit up at the sight of the familiar figure advancing toward her through the crowded waiting room of the Marseilles airport. Her brother Whalid still walked with his splay-footed gait. John Wayne, she had always thought, ambling away from his horse in an old Western. As he drew closer, something else struck Laila about her elder brother. My God, she thought, he's put on weight!

"Françoise feeds you well," she laughed.

Self-consciously her brother drew in his stomach. "You're right," he said.

Smiling broadly, Whalid led Laila out of the airport to his Renault 16 parked in the airport's reserved parking area, opposite the arrival lounge. He owed that privilege to a yellow-and-green sticker in one corner of his windshield. It was a security pass to the Nuclear Research Center at Cadarache, the heart of France's atomic-energy program and, above all, the developmental work on the Super-Phénix, the breeder reactor which France counted on to replace the world's first generation of nuclear reactors. Whalid Dajani was an expert on the bizarre behavior patterns of one of the most precious and dangerous elements on earth, plutonium. His doctorate thesis for the University of California's Department of Nuclear Engineering, "A Revised Projection of Neutron Release Across the Plutonium Isotope Spectrum," had been published in the March 1970 *Bulletin of the American Society of Mechanical Engineers* and stamped him as one of the most brilliant young physicists of his generation. A paper he had delivered on the same subject at a Paris forum in November 1973 had prompted the French to offer him a key position in the Phénix program.

Whalid steered the car out of the parking lot, away from the flashing traffic of the autoroute toward the narrow country road leading to the Provençal inn in which he'd told his wife, Françoise, to meet them for lunch. After the spontaneous emotion of their greeting, a strained silence fell between brother and sister.

Smoking nervously, Laila watched the rolling fields of vineyards, vines pruned down to gaunt skeletons, fleeing past her window. As they entered a small village, Whalid glanced at his sister. Her eyes were fixed on the square ahead, its dirt surface baked hard by the sun and the tramping of generations of boules players like the half-dozen men gathered there now, casting their lead balls on it in the pale winter sunshine.

"You said in your telegram you had something urgent to talk to me about."

A moving car is not a place for a serious conversation, Laila thought. You talk in a car when you want to say something without having to look at the person you're saying it to. End an affair. Give an order. Announce unpleasant news. But for what she had to say to her brother, she had to be able to watch him, to fix her eyes on his.

"What a lovely square!" she said. "So calm. Let's stop for a drink."

Whalid parked the car, and brother and sister walked to one of the three cafés whose terraces gave onto the square. Whalid ordered a *pastis*.

Laila hesitated. "No alcohol," she said.

"Try a nice mint tea, *ma petite*," the proprietress proposed. She turned and gave Whalid a friendly leer. "Very aphrodisiac."

As she bustled away, Whalid turned to his sister. "What was it you wanted to talk about?" he prodded gently. "Is it about Kamal?"

Laila's fingers plucked nervously over the clutter in her handbag until they came on her Gitanes cigarettes. She lit one and inhaled several times.

"No, Whalid, it's about you."

"Me?"

"You. The Brothers need your help."

Whalid felt a twinge of nervous tension cramp his stomach. "Laila, all that's behind me now. I have a life here, a life I've worked hard to build. I've got a wife I love. And I'm doing some-

96

thing that I love and that I know is important. I'm not going to jeopardize that. Not for the Brothers. Not for anyone.''

Whalid could not help thinking of the lithe blond French girl who would be waiting for them at lunch. He had met Françoise in the Cadarache senior employees' restaurant. Passing her a mustard pot, they liked to joke. She had given him so much: a sense of place at last, a meaning to his existence that gave dimension to the work in which he so passionately believed. Their seventeenth-century dwelling in the little medieval city of Meyrargues was for Whalid a citadel, a citadel his beautiful wife was helping to build against the encroaching tides of his past.

Beside him, Laila sipped her tea. ''Whalid, you can never escape your past. Palestine is your home. Jerusalem. Not here.''

Whalid did not answer. Brother and sister sat side by side a moment, united in silence by the bond of the suffering they had once shared. Neither had ever known the horror of life in a Palestinian refugee camp, but the pain of their exile from their native land had been nonetheless real for that. They represented a face of the Palestinian problem that a world used to the stereotyped miseries of the camps rarely saw: a Palestine that had once produced the Arab world's elite, a proud flow of scholars, doctors, businessmen, scientists. Forty-five successive generations of Dajanis had dwelt upon the hillsides of Jerusalem, deeding the city an unending flow of Arab leaders and thinkers, until 1947. Twice since then, in 1948 and again in 1967, Israeli gunfire had driven them from their homes. Israeli bulldozers had reduced their graceful ancestral dwelling to rubble in 1968 to make way for a new apartment complex. Three months later, their father had died of a broken heart in his Beirut exile.

Whalid took his sister's hand in his and softly caressed it. ''My heart screams out against what happened to us, just as loudly as yours or anyone else's,'' he said. ''But it's not the only thing it screams out for. I suppose now Palestine is the only cause in your life. It's not in mine.''

Laila fell silent, reflecting on what her brother had just said. ''Whalid,'' she asked after a long sip of her tea, ''do you remember the last time we were all together?''

Whalid nodded. It was the evening after his father's funeral.

''You said something that night I've always remembered. Kamal was leaving for Damascus to join the Brothers to get vengeance for our people. He wanted you to go with him and you said no. The Israelis were so strong, you said, because they understood what education meant. You'd been accepted to do your doctorate in California. Berkeley was going to be your Damascus, you told us. Getting the best scientific education in the world was going to be your way of helping your people and the cause."

"I remember. And so?"

Laila glanced at the square, at the boules players, at the dark-robed women gossiping in front of the Prisunic, cord shopping bags bulging in their hands. "Where is the cause, where are your people, in all this?"

"Right here," Whalid replied, tapping his chest. "Where it always was, in my heart."

"Please, Whalid," his sister entreated, "don't get angry. I wanted to say you were right that night. Each of us has to help the cause in his own way. With what he has. Maybe carrying messages to Beirut in my bra isn't much of a contribution. But it's what I can do. Kamal fights. That's his way. But you're special, Whalid. There are thousands, hundreds of thousands, of us who can carry a Kalishnikov. But there's only one Palestinian in the world who can do for his people what you can."

Whalid sipped his *pastis* and turned a cold, appraising regard to Laila. "And just what is this special thing the Brothers expect me to do for our people?"

"Help them to steal plutonium. But not for themselves, Whalid, for Qaddafi."

Whalid exhaled slowly, softly. He lowered his *pastis* to the table. Instinctively, he looked around to see if there was anyone in earshot who could overhear them. He ran his fingers across his forehead, feeling as he did the little beads of sweat that had formed there.

"I suppose the Brothers think I can just put a few kilos of plutonium in the back seat of my car some Sunday afternoon and drive out of Cadarache with it?"

"Whalid," Laila replied, "the Brothers are many things, but they are not crazy. The whole thing has already been thought over and studied in great detail. All the Brothers want from you is information. Where the plutonium is stored. How it's guarded. How many people protect it. Some idea of how they can get in and out of Cadarache without getting caught."

She opened her purse and picked through its contents until she

98

came upon a thick white envelope. "What the Brothers need to know is all set out here. And I'm authorized to promise you one thing. No one will ever know where it came from. No one will ever be able to trace it back to you."

"And suppose I refuse?"

"You won't."

His sister's smug reply, the presumptuousness of those who had sent her to him, infuriated her brother.

"I won't?" he said in a hoarse whisper. "Well, I do! Right now! And I'm going to tell you why."

He grabbed for her pack of cigarettes. His gesture prevented him from seeing the expression sweeping across his sister's face. It remained there just an instant, a strange, distant glance full of compassion and horror, fear and respect.

"I believe in what I do, Laila. I believe in it as passionately as I ever believed in Palestine." He paused, inhaling slowly. Despite the passion of his words, his tone was grave and measured. "Florence Nightingale once said, 'The first thing a hospital should *not* do is spread germs.' Well, the first thing a nuclear physicist should *not* do is spread this terrifying knowledge he has so man kills himself with it instead of using it to build a better world."

This time it was his sister's turn to erupt. "A better world!" she said scornfully. "Why does Qaddafi want the bomb? Because the Israelis have it. You know damn well they do. Do you think they got it to build a better world with? Like hell! To use on us if they have to."

Her brother remained impassive. "Yes, I know they have it."

"And you can sit here beside me, admit the Israelis have it, and still tell me you won't help your own people, your own people who've been trampled on like no other people in the world, to get it?"

"I can. And I am, because I feel a commitment to something higher than Palestine. Or the cause. Or whatever you want to call it."

"Higher than to your own flesh and blood? Your own dead father?"

Brother and sister were silent for a moment, each spent by the intensity of their argument. The midday sun was warm now and the stucco houses across the square seemed to radiate a terra-rosa glow in the bright light. The knot of hangers-on around the boules game had thickened, and the sound of their muttered comments lapped at the edge of the square, wavelets of a gentle sea sliding along a beach.

"The answer is no, Laila. I'm not going to do it."

A sense of emptiness, of despair filled Laila. For a second she felt physically ill.

A pair of boys, perhaps twelve years old, set their skateboards onto the hard-packed square. In an instant, they were swinging through it with the gentle grace of birds cruising a summer sky. Laila glanced at her brother's forearm. On the inside of his wrist, just above the steel band of his Rolex Submariner watch, was a tattoo, a blue serpent entwined around a heart pierced by a dagger. Laila leaned over to her brother and slowly, almost sensually, scratched the surface of the tattoo with her crimson fingernail.

"And this?" she asked.

He looked at her, furious. That tattoo was a souvenir of the most painful moment of his life, the death of his father after their exile from Jerusalem in 1968. The day of his funeral, he and Kamal had gone to a Saudi Arabian tattoo artist in the souks of Beirut. The Saudi had fixed that design on the flesh of each brother's forearm: a pierced heart for their lost father, a serpent for the hatred they bore those responsible for his death, a dagger for the vengeance they had sworn to obtain. Then they had sworn together a vow from the fourth chapter of the Koran to use their lives to avenge their father's death under pain of losing them if they faltered in their pursuit.

Laila saw his muscles twitching. At least, she thought, I've given a face to the people, to the cause, I'm pleading for.

"You got out, Whalid," she said. Her voice was tender; there was no hint of reproach in its tone. "You've been able to forget here with your new life, your wife. But how about the ones who didn't? Are they to be a people without a home foreever? Without an address? Is our own father's body never to go home again?"

Whalid looked at the tattoo under his watchband, glowering at it as though somehow his glare might erase its stigmata from his flesh.

"What am I supposed to be?" His voice was an angry, sibilant hiss. "A prisoner of this skin because I was born with it? Do I have to go against my reason, against the things I believe in, just because I was born in a place called Palestine thirty-eight years ago?"

100

Laila waited a long and thoughtful moment before answering. "Yes, Whalid," she said. "You do. I do. We all do."

After lunch with Whalid's wife, Françoise, brother and sister drove back to the airport in silence. Laila went immediately to the check-in counter to register for her return flight to Paris. When she had finished, she walked across the airport lounge toward the newsstand where Whalid scanned the headlines of the evening papers. His dark eyes seemed distant and melancholy, shutters turning his vision back into some interior world of his own. He's understood, Laila thought. He's miserable, but he knows he has no choice. She laid a hand on his elbow. "I'll tell them it's all right. You'll do it."

Whalid flicked the pages of a magazine on the kiosk before him, an unconscious effort to postpone a few seconds the terrible decision his sister's words had thrust on him.

"No, Laila," he said finally. "Tell them I won't do it."

His sister felt her legs tremble. She thought for an instant she would retch on the airport floor.

"Whalid," she whispered. "You've got to. You have to."

Whalid shook his head. The sound of his own voice saying "No" had dispelled his lingering indecision. "I said 'No,' Laila, and I meant it."

Laila was pale, her eyes blinking, unfocused. He doesn't understand, she thought. Or if he does, he doesn't give a damn. "Whalid, you must. You must."

He shook his head. Laila understood. There was no appealing his decision now. To her horror, she realized that she had failed. Fingers trembling, she opened her pocketbook and took out a second envelope, this one much smaller. "They told me to give you this if you said no," she said, pressing the envelope into her brother's hands.

Whalid began to open it. Her fingers closed over his. "Wait until I've left." Laila pressed her cheek, damp with tears, against her brother's. "*Ma salaam,*" she whispered. Then she was gone.

Whalid watched from the terrace of the airport as his sister crossed the tarmac to her waiting flight. She did not turn back. As she disappeared into the 727's rear hatch, he opened the envelope clutched in his hands. Glancing at the single sheet of paper it contained, he staggered. He had recognized instantly both the verse from the fourth chapter of the Koran and the handwriting in which it was written.

"And if they turn back from their vow," it read, *"take them and kill them, wherever ye find them."*

On Sunday, March 3, 1977, explaining to Françoise that he had family business in Paris, Whalid Dajani boarded the Mistral, the French railroad's crack express, for the French capital. Shortly before midnight that evening, the doorbell's raw screech shattered the quiet of Françoise Dajani's darkened bedroom. At the sight of the three shadowy figures gathered on her doorstep, the identification card with its official tricolor slashes thrust sharply at her half-closed eyes, Françoise gasped. Oh my God, she thought. There's been an accident. He's dead.

The three agents of the Direction de la Surveillance du Territoire pushed abruptly past her into the living room.

"What is it?" she cried. "Has something happened to my husband?"

Ignoring her, two of the agents headed upstairs toward her bedroom.

"Where are you going? What do you think you're doing?" she shrieked after them.

The leader of the trio, a stout florid man, grabbed her by the shoulders. "Get dressed," he ordered. "Immediately. Pack a bag with whatever toilet articles you will need for the next seventy-two hours."

Françoise protested. The agent reached into his pocket for the only explanation he was prepared to offer her, a brief typewritten order from a *juge d'instruction,* authorizing the DST to detain her for seventy-two hours.

Françoise moved toward the telephone. "I'm going to call my father," she announced angrily.

The agent reached the phone first. He locked the receiver into its cradle with his hand. "No, madame, no calls."

Not quite an hour later, Françoise Dajani was led into the office of the regional director of the DST, located on the twelfth floor of a commercial office building overlooking the Vieux-Port of Marseilles. Outside, the mistral moaned through the deserted streets, tearing at the wooden shutters of the old buildings nearby, its violent gusts rattling the plate-glass windows of the director's office.

The regional director, studiously ignoring her presence, scrutinized a report on his desk. Finally he pushed it aside and looked up at her with the cold, appraising air of an insurance adjuster trying to downgrade a claim. "We arrested your husband in Paris this afternoon. Together with his brother and sister."

"Arrested him?" Françoise gasped. "For what?"

"For planning to steal plutonium from the nuclear installations at Cadarache for the benefit of the Palestine Liberation Organization."

The slender blond woman tightened the muscles around her eyes, fighting a flow of tears. "I don't believe you."

"Madame, I'm not concerned whether you believe me or not. They were traced through an Israeli agent who saw your brother-in-law arriving at Charles de Gaulle Airport. They were arrested with the evidence of their guilt on them. All three have confessed. My only concern is whether or not you were involved in their crime."

There was not even a hint of sympathy for her in the middle-aged DST agent, only the professional interrogator's search for the revealing flicker of the eyes, the subtle shift in vocal tone, that would expose his quarry.

"Where are you holding my husband?"

The director glanced at his watch. "We're not. He'll be landing in Beirut in two hours. And he will not return to France—ever. The government has declared him *persona non grata,* although, in the circumstances, he has every reason to consider himself fortunate. It has been so decided by higher authority."

Just how high even the DST agent did not realize. Developing the Super-Phénix breeder reactor for overseas sale was a cornerstone of France's export program for the decade of the 1980s. The public revelation in a trial that a group of Palestinians had formulated a plan to steal plutonium from Cadarache could have been a devastating blow to the program in a Europe already alive with antinuclear sentiments. Rather than run that risk, the Minister of the Interior, with the President's concurrence, had ordered the three Dajanis deported.

Françoise sagged in her chair. Instinctively, her fingers went to the wafer-thin gold medallion around her neck. It was a representation of the fish which, on the walls of ancient Rome's catacombs, had symbolized the early Christians. She was a Pisces, and her father had given it to her on the eve of their marriage. She adored her father as she had never adored anyone else, even her husband. She had been a sickly child, and it was he who had nursed her, given her the strength to live. What had happened would leak out one day and then the gossip would start, the vile, vicious gossip. It would kill her father as surely, as cruelly, as a cancer slowly ravaging a vital organ. Beyond the director's window, twelve stories below, Françoise could see the blink of the Jardin du Pharo at the throat of the Vieux-Port. She listened to the desolate wail of the mistral, the sad music of her childhood, and saw herself as a young girl standing on the quay of the Vieux-Port with her father watching the fishing dories bobbing in the choppy blue sea. Despair, a bitter unreasoning despair at what her husband's act would do to him, sickened her.

"I'm sorry," she said. "I feel ill. May I have a glass of water?"

The DST official was only a few strides from his office on his way to the toilet down the hall when he heard the shattering of his plate-glass windows.

For just an instant there on his mother's balcony, his eyes idly roving the long and gentle swell of the Mediterranean, Kamal Dajani was at peace. To his left were the familiar crags of Pigeon Rock, the landmark which had pointed seamen the way to Beirut harbor since the Phoenicians had first planted their venturing triremes on the outgoing tide. Below Kamal's perch, along the coastal road, sweeping up the seashore from Al Maza Airport, was a gigantic open-air market: thousands of merchants, driven from the city center by the Lebanese civil war, hawking everything from eggs to transistor radios and Dior dresses off blankets tossed on the roadside, folding camp tables, out of automobile trunks.

The Lebanese, Kamal thought contemptuously—the only thing they prefer to killing each other is making money. That scornful observation brought Kamal back to reality. Failure did not sit well with him, and the failure of his operation could not have been more complete. He had only one minor consolation: they had managed, thanks to his muttered Arabic injunction to the others, to conceal their Libyan connection from the French. The DST had been only too ready to accept the idea that they were in the employ of the PLO.

Kamal's only concern at the moment was salvaging what he could from the disaster of their failed operation. If he could not deliver to Muammar al-Qaddafi the plutonium he wanted, perhaps he could deliver something else, something which in the long run might prove far more valuable: the scientific genius of his brother.

"À table!"

Kamal turned at his mother's words. Whatever their diverse accomplishments, their violent careers, her three children still instinctively obeyed the imperious commands of Sulafa Dajani. Small wonder. She was an imposing figure, the very antithesis of the stereotyped image of the Arab woman. No veil had ever shrouded her face. Her tall, lithe figure was clothed in a black Saint-Laurent suit, its beautifully tailored lines clinging to each indentation of a body that could still command lovers closer to her children's age than hers. A single strand of pearls set off the pale skin of her long graceful neck and the haughty cast of her chin. Her hair was black, close-cropped and curly, a few defiant streaks of gray illuminating it like flashes of light.

To her, her children's summary ejection from France was a reason for rejoicing. She did not need to know what their crime was. It had been committed for the cause and that was enough. Spread out on her living-room table was a huge Arabic *mezze,* a tapestry of hors d'oeuvres. She poured each child a glass of arak, crystal-clear licorice-flavored liquid, and raised her own in a toast.

"To the memory of your father; to the freedom of your people; to the liberation of your land," she said and swallowed the burning alcohol in one gulp. Not all the injunctions of Islam were to her liking.

Laila and Kamal turned hungrily on the food. The mother thrust a *samboussac,* a delicate meat pastry, at her disconsolate elder son.

"Eat," she commanded.

Whalid listlessly nibbled at its crust.

"What do you intend to do?"

He shrugged. "I don't know. It depends on what Françoise wants to do when she gets here. If she comes. If she can forgive me for what I did."

"She will come," his mother stated emphatically. "It is her duty."

"Whalid." Kamal's tone was wary. He did not know how much of his brother's bitterness at what had happened was directed at him. "Why don't you come to Libya with me?"

"Waste my life in that Godforsaken place?"

"That Godforsaken place may surprise you." Kamal continued. "There is more happening there than you know. Or most people know." Kamal stretched his heavy torso. "A man like you should never have a closed mind. At least come. Take a look. And then decide."

A telephone rang. Sulafa Dajani rose to answer it. None of her children noticed the faint glistening in her eyes when she returned and sat next to her elder son. Gently, she reached for his hand and pressed it to her lips. "My son, I'm so sorry. It was an officer of the French Embassy. Françoise is dead."

"Dead!" Whalid gasped.

Sulafa Dajani caressed his shaking head. "She jumped from a very high building while the police were questioning her."

Whalid slumped against his mother's shoulder. "Oh my God," he sobbed. "Françoise, my poor Françoise."

Kamal got up and lit a cigarette. He stared at his weeping brother.

"I did it," Whalid cried. "I killed her."

Kamal circled behind him and squeezed his shoulders with his powerful fingers. If there was any pity in his gesture it was not so much for his brother's grief as for his stupidity.

"Whalid, you didn't kill her. They did."

Whalid looked at him, uncomprehending.

"You don't believe that she jumped from that window, do you?"

Alarm and horror swept his brother's grief-ravaged face. "The French police wouldn't . . ."

"Don't be a poor fool! They threw her out of that window, for God's sake. Those French you loved so much. You wanted to be so damn loyal to. What do you think happened?" Kamal was flinging his words in short, bitter bursts. "And God knows what they did to her first."

Whalid turned to his mother, blinking through tears of sorrow and disbelief, searching for knowledge, for consolation.

Sulafa Dajani shrugged her graceful shoulders. "It is the way of all our enemies." She kissed her first son's forehead. "Go to Libya with your brother. You belong there now. *B'is Allah*—it is God's will."

PART III

MONDAY, DECEMBER 14:
MIDNIGHT TO 3:27 A.M.

"Destroy Libya."

THE ONLY SOUND REACHING MUAMMAR AL-QAD-dafi's ears was the low and mournful sigh of a distant wind. No Teleprinter's hum, no radio's cackle, no jangling telephone marred the perfect quiet of his desert. As was only natural, he had chosen to pass the critical hours preceding the test of his hydrogen bomb in the solitude of the spaces in which he had found his faith and nurtured his dreams.

His command post was the symbol of that vanishing race by whose precepts he strove to reorder the future, his ever present Bedouin tent. Not a single manifestation of the technology he sought to harness intruded on its spartan precincts. There were no television screens here parading the world before his eyes, no smartly uniformed aides laying out the options available to him, no blinking panels of light to remind him of the strength of his massed armies. Qaddafi was alone with the oneness of the desert and the stillness of his soul.

Here, he knew, there was neither the time nor the place for the useless or the complex. As the oncoming light of day stripped away the illusions of the night, so the emptiness of these expanses stripped life to its fundamentals. All here gave way to the inexorable struggle to survive.

Since time immemorial the intensity of that struggle had made the desert the incubator of the spiritual, its inhuman solitude the catalyst that had driven men to the extreme. Moses in the Sinai, Christ in the wilderness, the Prophet on his Hegira: each, in turn, had thrust on mankind the visions engendered by their desert retreats. Others had, too: visionaries and zealots, fanatics and spiritualists, part of the unending parade of austere and alarming men that through the centuries had emerged from those trackless wastes to trouble the settled world around them.

Immersed now in the reassuring familiarity of his desert, the latest of that long and troubling line awaited the results of his test in perfect calm. If it had worked, it was now, he reasoned, in their first flash of anger, that the Americans would lash out against him. If that was God's will, then he was ready to perish here in the surroundings that had formed him. If it had failed, he would have one course open: he would condemn the "plot" fomented within his borders, arrest a few Palestinians and stage a mock trial to mollify the anger of the Americans and the world.

His alert ears picked up the flutter of a helicopter coming to announce the result, to return him to his capital in triumph or shame. He watched unmoved as it drew up, then fluttered to rest fifty yards from his tent. A man leaped out.

"Ya sidi!" he shouted. "It worked!"

His first reaction to the news was to bow his head in prayer, a prayer of awe and gratitude for the power that now rested in his hands. Woven into the multicolored strands of the prayer rug on which he bowed his head were the outlines of the Islamic sanctuary which with that power he would now claim in the name of his faith and his people, Jerusalem's Mosque of Omar.

The President of the United States sat motionless at the head of the conference table in the National Military Command Center. He too had greeted the desert explosion with a prayer, a prayer for help in what he had instantly understood was the gravest crisis his nation had ever faced. Now he was staring straight ahead, his index finger pressed to his lips, every fiber of his being concentrated on the dilemma before him.

"The first thing I would like to say," he announced finally, "is all our actions must be based on the assumption that there is a hydrogen bomb hidden in New York," the President continued. "And we have also got to assume that Qaddafi is deadly serious when he threatens to detonate it if any word of this gets to the public."

In a strange way, the President thought, he may have done us a service. If word of this ever got out, we'd probably have an outburst of public opinion that would close down every option we have except forcing the Israelis out of the West Bank. He leaned forward and folded his hands on the table, letting his glance travel over his advisers ranged around the table, then the military men at their command consoles. "I don't think I need remind any of you of the moral obligation this places on everyone here. There are certainly some of us who have persons very close to us who may be threatened by this. But each of us has got to remember that the lives of five million of our countrymen may depend on keeping it a secret."

"Jack—" he glanced at his National Security Assistant—"do you have any specifics to recommend on that?"

"Well, sir, it goes without saying, only use secure telephones when talking about it." It was well known in Washington that the Soviets intercepted microwave calls in and out of the White House —just as the United States monitored those going to the Kremlin. "And no secretaries. If anyone has to write anything, write it by hand. With no carbons."

"How do we keep this from the press?" Bennington asked.

It was a vital question. There were two thousand journalists accredited to the White House. Forty or fifty of them were in almost constant attendance on its grounds during the day, the most able among them convinced on arising each morning that the government would lie to them at least once before sundown. Leaks were a way of life in the capital, and gossip on government secrets the main topics of conversation at its cocktail parties and dinners and the lunches at Duke Zeibert's and Jean Pierre's where its luminaries picked each other's brains as assiduously as they picked their Maryland soft-shelled crab.

"Should we tell the press secretary?" the President asked.

"I'm not sure," Eastman replied. "If we don't, his reaction will be more natural if he gets any queries on it. But if we do tell him, he'd damn well better be prepared to lie, stonewall and deny this damn thing right into the ground."

"If we do tell him," William Webster of the FBI drawled, "he can tell us right away if anyone in the media's focusing in on it."

"Don't worry," Eastman said, "if anyone in the media starts to focus in, we'll hear about it fast enough. The most important thing is to hold this as close as possible. The Kennedy people held on to the Missile Crisis for a week because only fifteen people in the government knew about it. You're also going to have to maintain the façade of a normal existence. That's the best way to keep the press off the track."

The President indicated his agreement, then shifted his attention to the admiral commanding the center. He ordered him to begin their stock-taking with the traditional appraisal of the military situation and the options open to the U.S. armed forces.

The Admiral stepped back to the speaker's stand. Eastman could not suppress a smile. Even at a moment like this, the Admiral moved automatically into his Pentagon "briefer's stance," feet a rigid six inches apart, left hand in the small of his back, his right wielding the absolute end in briefer's sex, a collapsible aluminum pointer with a glowing light on its tip with which he once again reviewed the Soviet's military posture. Nothing had changed. Noting that, Harold Brown, the Secretary of Defense, intervened.

"Mr. President, I would suggest our first action should be to alert the Soviets to what has happened. However strained our relations are, I think that in this we can count on their help in bringing Qaddafi to ground. Furthermore, they should be made aware that any military moves we make are not being directed against them."

The President agreed. "Open up the Red Line," he commanded Eastman, "and inform the Soviets I'd like to speak with the Chairman."

"Sir," Warren Christopher, the Deputy Secretary of State, said, "I think it's also essential we coordinate with our allies any actions we take and keep them informed of this at the highest level. I'd like authorization to get off 'Eyes Only' messages to Mrs. Thatcher, Helmut Schmidt and, above all, President Giscard. We've got to assume the source of Qaddafi's plutonium for the atomic trigger of that bomb was his French reactor. The French may be able to turn up information for us on the people Qaddafi has involved in this that will help the Bureau run them down."

The President gave his approval, then ordered the Admiral to resume his briefing. This time a series of bright-red lights on the semidarkened screen indicated the positions of all the ships of the Sixth Fleet, most of them gathered off Crete on an anti–submarine-warfare exercise. They represented the U.S. forces closest to Libya, and, the Admiral told the assembly, they could be ordered to start southwest immediately.

Harry Fuller, the Chairman of the Joint Chiefs, broke into his briefing. "Mr. President, I think there's one point that needs to be clarified right away. There is no viable military solution to this crisis. Sure, we can destroy Libya. Instantly. But that's not going to give us any guarantee whatsoever that his bomb—if it's in New

York—won't explode. And that, in my judgment, precludes our taking any military action against Qaddafi for the time being."

"I'm afraid I have to agree with that," the President noted grimly. "What do you recommend we do, then?"

"Every move we make," the Admiral declared in a voice that boomed through the room like a Navy klaxon sounding general quarters, "has got to be designed to remind Qaddafi of the potential consequences of his action. He's got to be kept aware every hour, every minute, every second of this damned crisis that we can thermonuclearize him in the blink of an eye. Let him live, eat and breathe that and see how he likes it."

The Admiral waved a hand at the red lights flashing on the screen. "I agree we should send the Sixth Fleet hell for leather for the Libyan coast. If they've got any liberty parties ashore, they'll just have to leave them on the beach. Once they get there, I'd put them right up against his coastline where his radar's sure to pick them up. Run a high-altitude aerial screen up and down the coastline from the carriers and tell the pilots to talk in the clear so he's constantly reminded they're carrying enough missiles to turn that goddamn country of his into an instant ruin." A dour smile appeared on the Admiral's face. "The deployment of force in a situation like this is designed to alter your enemy's perception of his actions. Maybe this will alter his."

"Mr. President." There it was again, that rasping drawl of Crandell's. "You're not going to like what I'm going to say, but I'm going to say it anyway. Destroy Qaddafi. Right now."

The Chief Executive gave his Energy Secretary a look of ill-concealed exasperation. It did nothing to staunch the flow of his unsolicited advice.

"The great mistake we made in Iran was not acting the very first day they took those hostages. The whole world would have understood us if we had. We waited and what happened? Everybody was holding us by the coattails. 'Don't do anything rash. Think about our oil. Think about the Russians.' "

"Mr. Crandell, we're not talking about fifty hostages in an embassy." The President almost spat the words at his Energy Secretary. Despite the placid surface he turned to the public, he was, in private, a man of considerable temper, capable, when angered, of lacerating meanness. "We're talking about five million people and New York City."

"We're talking about this country, Mr. President, and a man

who's declared war on us. We've got to show him and everybody else on this globe that there's a limit beyond which we aren't going to be pushed. Mark my words, if you don't respond to this man, challenge right now, tell him he's got five minutes to tell you where that bomb's hidden or he and his country are dead''—Crandell was waving a pudgy finger across the table—''then before this night is over you'll be ready to betray this nation's friends to satisfy a blackmailer.''

''Crandell.'' The President had paled under his efforts to rein in his temper. ''When I want military advice from you I'll call for it. I'm not going to put the lives of five million of our people at risk until I've exhausted every possible avenue of saving them and this world from an unspeakable catastrophe.''

''By talking, Mr. President, and once you've started talking you'll start compromising. Everybody always does.''

The President turned angrily away from his Energy Secretary. To lose his temper, whatever the provocation, in front of his advisers at this moment would be a disaster. Crandell looked at him, slowly shaking his head. Just like that good old boy, he thought, so nice, a guy spits in his face he thinks it's raining.

At the far end of the table, Bennington had just picked up his telephone. The CIA head listened for a moment. ''Excuse me, sir, but it looks like we've got another problem on our hands.''

Every eye in the room turned to the New Englander. ''Mossad's just got onto the Agency. They picked up the explosion on their seismographs. They're very suspicious that it was a nuclear shot and want to know what we've got on it.''

''Christ!'' someone groaned from the end of the table. ''If they find out what Qaddafi's done, they'll take him out on their own and we may lose New York.''

The President frowned. It had been almost inevitable that the Israelis would pick up the shock waves. As long as they didn't spot the fallout, though, they'd have doubts, and none of the fallout was heading their way. Right now what he needed was time, time to get the planning in order, time to get a grip on the problem before them.

''Stall,'' he ordered Bennington. ''Tell them it looks like an earthquake. Tell them we're checking it out and we'll keep them informed.''

On the wall opposite the President, the bank of clocks showed it was 12:30 A.M., 7:30 in Jerusalem and Tripoli. They had thirty-eight and a half hours left, and every minute of them had to be made to count.

"Gentlemen," he said, "let's try to define the areas we've got to address ourselves to in order of their importance. First is New York: what do we do about it?"

He twisted in his chair to face Harold Brown. Civil defense fell under his sprawling Defense Department umbrella. "Do we have a plan to get these people out of New York in an emergency?"

"Mr. President, Jack Kennedy asked that question about Miami on the second day of the Cuban Missile Crisis." Brown sighed. "It took two hours to get the answer then, and it was no. Well, I can answer you this time in two seconds. It's still no."

"Don't forget," Eastman warned, "he's threatening to detonate that thing if we start an evacuation. He considers those people his hostages."

The President looked at his adviser. There was an infinity of sadness in his pale-blue eyes.

"Do we take him at his word on that, Jack?"

"I'm afraid we have to, Mr. President."

"Even though it might mean five million lives?"

"It could mean five million lives if we call his bluff and he's not bluffing."

The helicopter bearing Muammar al-Qaddafi back to his capital settled down on a landing pad concealed in a grove of Aleppo pines nineteen miles southeast of Tripoli at 7:52 Libyan time. The dictator leaped out and slid into the driver's seat of a sky-blue Volkswagen hidden in the midst of the trees.

Four minutes later, followed by a jeepload of his red-bereted Praetorian Guard, he passed through a barrier of electrified barbed wire and headed down a long alley of cypress trees leading to the Mediterranean shore. No foreign diplomat, no distinguished visitor, none of Qaddafi's fellow Arab leaders had ever been invited into the elegant old dwelling set at the end of the drive.

With its finely wrought balustrade, the Doric columns supporting its portico, the Villa Pietri looked like a Roman nobleman's villa that had somehow been misplaced on the edge of the African continent. It had, indeed, been built by a Roman, a member of the

nobility of the textile trade, who had left his name on it. In the
years following his death, the Villa Pietri had served as the palace
of Mussolini's Fascist Governor General of Libya, as the residence
of the brother of Libya's King Idris, and later of the commanding
general of the U.S. Air Force's Wheelus Base outside Tripoli. The
first chief of state in modern times to employ terrorism as an instrument of national policy had taken over the noble old dwelling in
1971. It was the headquarters from which Qaddafi directed the
global activities of his terrorist network.

The Munich Olympic Massacre had been planned in its gracious
sitting room; so, too, had the assault on the Rome Airport meant
to kill Henry Kissinger in December 1973, the kidnapping of the
OPEC oil ministers, the Entebbe skyjacking. The eucalyptus trees
of the villa's gardens concealed the antennas that radioed Qaddafi's orders to IRA provos, West German students, Red Brigade
dissidents, even Islamic zealots infiltrated into Tashkent and Tur-
kestan. Its wine cellars which had once housed the finest Chianti
classicos of the Tuscan hills had been turned into an ultramodern
communications center, hooked into, among other things, Libya's
radar installations; one of its bedrooms housed a complete mock-
up of the control panels of a Boeing 747 and 707 on which many of
the hijackers of the early and mid-seventies had been trained. The
Libyan leader himself had assigned those who went out from the
villa to do his bidding their leitmotif: "Everything that puts an
infected thorn in the foot of our enemies is good."

Qaddafi was radiant with triumph as he drew up to the villa.
"Now," he announced to a handful of aides waiting to greet him at
the villa's doorstep, "I shall no longer have to endure being an
Arab President who stands by while my Palestinian brothers are
stripped of the last shreds of their homeland."

He embraced each in turn, his Prime Minister Salam Jalloud,
one of the few members of his original junta still with Qaddafi, his
chief of intelligence, the commanders of his army and his air force.
Then he led them into his study.

"They are criminals, these Israelis," he declared. "The whole
world has stood by watching them stealing our brothers' lands with
these settlements of theirs. Watching while a people is being systematically deprived of its homeland. This so-called peace of that
coward Sadat. What a mockery! A peace, for what? To allow the
Israelis to go on and on stealing our brothers' lands. Autonomy,

118

they said." Qaddafi laughed. "Autonomy for what? To let the foreigner take away your home!"

Qaddafi sighed. "I dreamt of leading a people that did not sleep at night; that spent its days in the djebels training for the reconquest of its Palestinian brothers' lands; that respects God's Holy Law and obeys the Koran because it wants to be an example to the rest.

"And what do I lead? A people that sleeps at night. A people that doesn't care what happens to its brothers in Palestine. A people that dreams only of buying a Mercedes and three television sets. We trained our best young men to fly Mirage jets in the battle and what did they do? They went down to the souks to open a shop and sell Japanese air-conditioners."

The intensity on the Libyan dictator's face mesmerized the men around him.

"Now," he went on, "with our bomb, why do we care if we are only a small power? Let the people go on dreaming of their Mercedes. I don't need the millions now, only the few who are ready to pay the price I ask. Did the Caliph conquer the world with the millions? No! With the few, because the few were strong and believed."

Qaddafi contemplated the tabletop a moment, staring at the watery circles left upon it by the bottles of soda his aides had drunk waiting for the test. Although he did not say it, he knew that success would make him, overnight, the hero of the Arab world, the idol of its masses. It would secure the larger goal which lay behind his much-proclaimed hatred of the Jewish state, bringing the Arab world with its vast oil resources and the power they represented under his command.

Salam Jalloud, the Prime Minister, shifted nervously in his chair. He was the one man in the room who had opposed Qaddafi's scheme from the outset. "I still say, Sidi, the Americans will destroy us. Or they will plot with the Israelis to trick us, to make us think they are going to do what we ask, then strike when our guard is down."

"Our guard must never be down." Qaddafi indicated a small black device on his desk. It looked like a miniature dictating machine. "From now on, this is our guard." The device, another contribution of the engineers of Nippon Electric, resembled the remote-control boxes which can open a garage door from a moving car. By tapping it with his finger, Qaddafi could send an electronic pulse to a room deep in a specially reinforced cellar of the villa. There, protected by three red-bereted paratroopers of his bodyguard, was the terminal which, in response to that gesture, would send his detonation code to Oscar and the bomb hidden in New York.

"The Americans are not fools," he continued. "Do you think five million Americans are going to die for Israel? For those settlements even they oppose? Never! They are going to force Israel to give us everything we want."

"Besides," he said, "we need no longer be afraid of the Americans. Until now they have been able to ignore our rights, to help the Israelis trample on the nationhood of our Palestinian brothers because they were a superpower. They were immune. Well, my friends," a thin, drawn smile appeared on his features, "they are still a superpower, but they are no longer immune."

In Washington, the President had left the Crisis Committee's meeting at the National Military Command Center to confer with Moscow on the red telephone line. While he was out of the room, his advisers gathered in anxious knots discussing the emergency. As unobtrusively as possible, white-jacketed Navy stewards slipped among them passing out steaming cups of freshly brewed coffee. Only Jack Eastman remained seated at the conference table, skimming through a stack of documents, most of them stamped "Top Secret."

He had to call on every resource of the discipline acquired in a lifetime of military service to concentrate on the material before him, to drive from his mind the ghastly spectacle they had all witnessed. His job was to sort out the dimensions of this crisis, to lay the options the United States had before the President as concisely and as clearly as possible—even if those options were only variations of the unthinkable.

He picked up a four-volume blue plan labeled "Federal Response to Peacetime Nuclear Emergencies." Millions of dollars of taxpayers' money, thousands of man-hours of effort had gone into preparing that plan. After one quick perusal, Eastman tossed it aside in disgust. New York would have been reduced to a charred graveyard before he or anyone else had been able to make sense of its bureaucratic jargon.

"The President, gentlemen," the lieutenant colonel at the NMCC command console announced. The Chief Executive strode briskly back into the chamber and was addressing the men in it before they had had time to sit down.

"I've spoken with the Chairman," he announced. "He assures me that the Soviet Union condemns Qaddafi's threat without reserve, and has offered to cooperate with us in any way he can. He is personally addressing a message to Qaddafi through his ambassador in Tripoli condemning what he's done and warning him of the consequences of his action."

"Mr. President?" It was the Deputy Secretary of State. "As a corollary of that I'd recommend we orchestrate along with Moscow, Peking and Paris a worldwide diplomatic assault on Qaddafi to show him that he's absolutely isolated. Cut off from any vestige of support anywhere in the world."

"Do it, Warren," the President ordered, "although I'm afraid we're not dealing here with a man who'll be responsive to pressures of that sort. You also had better call the Secretary back from South America." The President remembered how effectively John F. Kennedy had used a cold to cover his return to Washington from Chicago at the beginning of the Missile Crisis. "Tell him to pretext some health reason."

"We've also, Mr. President," Eastman said, "got the constitutional aspects of this thing to consider. We have to bring in the Governor and, much more important because he's on the firing line, the Mayor."

"There," mused the President, "is a potential problem." The Mayor was a volatile, outspoken man who might go off half cocked if he wasn't handled properly. "I think we better lay it on him face to face down here."

"And I think you'll also have to brief the Congressional leadership."

"Yes, but we'll hold it very, very tight. Find out exactly whom Kennedy brought into the early stages of the Missile Crisis." The President leaned back in his chair, clasped his chin in the cradle of his forefinger and gave his National Security Assistant an appraising glance. "Jack, what plan of action do you recommend?"

Eastman shuffled the papers in front of him for just a second. Then, with the low but commanding voice he had acquired in his years in the military, he began. "It seems to me, Mr. President, we've only got two practical approaches open to us to resolve this problem. The first is actually finding and disarming this device. You've given the brief on that to the FBI and the CIA. The second is getting to Qaddafi and convincing him that whatever his complaints against Israel are, threatening to destroy New York is a totally irrational and irresponsible way of resolving them.

"It occurs to me, Mr. President, that, as you said earlier, this is the ultimate terrorist situation. What we have here is a fanatic holding a gun to the heads of five million people. We've got to talk that gun out of his hand, get him into a negotiating position, which is probably what he wants anyway, just the way you'd maneuver a terrorist into a negotiating position in a hijacking situation. We've got a lot of people around with expertise on how to do it. I recommend we bring them together to give us their guidance."

"All right," the President agreed. "Get the best people we have into session at the White House immediately."

"Mr. President?"

This time it was the Army Chief of Staff. "I think we're overlooking one very vital point here. I agree that as long as there's a chance of that hydrogen device going off in New York we've got no military options open against Libya. That doesn't mean, however, that we shouldn't be preparing for the possibility of military action."

The President's chin thrust forward at his words.

"Not against Libya. Against Israel."

"Israel?"

"Israel, Mr. President. The bottom line of this crisis is that if that bomb or whatever it is is really in New York, you're going to have the lives of five million Americans at risk. Against those people in those settlements over there. Who shouldn't even be there in the first place. A bunch of far-out Zionists or New York City. It's no deal, Mr. President, no deal at all. I recommend we alert the Eighty-second Airborne and the divisions in Germany and hold the Sixth Fleet Marine transports in the eastern Mediterranean instead of sending them toward Libya with the carriers. If we're going to land the Marines, it'll be in Haifa, not in Tripoli. And I recommend State open very discreet communications with the Syrians." Just a suggestion of a smile turned the edges of the General's mouth. "I suspect they'll be ready to offer us landing facilities in Damascus if we need them."

"The General's right." It was Tap Bennington. "The fact of the matter is, those settlements over there are absolutely illegal. We've opposed them. You've opposed them. If it comes down to New York or them and the Israelis won't get those people out of there, then we damn well better be ready to go in and get them out ourselves."

"Whatever we think about those settlements," the President noted, "and you all know how I feel about them, forcing the Israelis out of them now would be yielding to Qaddafi's blackmail. It would be showing the world that this kind of act pays."

"Mr. President," Bennington answered, "that's a very fine moral point, but I don't think it's going to cut much ice with those good folk up there in New York."

Eastman had followed the exchange in discreet silence. "One thing is clear," he now interjected, "and that is, Israel is vitally concerned in this. The sooner we bring Mr. Begin into it, the better."

Just an intimation of distaste crossed the President's composed features at the mention of the Israeli Prime Minister's name. There was probably no political leader in the world he disliked quite so much. How many hours had he been forced to listen to his interminable lectures on the history of the Jewish people, the constant, self-important references to the Bible; to the Israeli's infuriating habit of arguing forever over the most trivial legal point. God, he thought, dealing with Begin had forced him to draw on reserves of patience which he had never imagined he possessed.

"You're right." He sighed. "Get Mr. Begin on the phone."

The early light burnished the Jerusalem limestone of the house at 3 Balfour Street to an amber glow. Just the suspicion of a breeze picked the tips of the Aleppo pines rising above the cement wall protecting the residence of the Prime Minister of Israel.

Inside, in the somber study that adjoined the sitting room, a slight figure stared moodily out the French windows to the flowered patio beyond. To his left, barely one hundred yards away, was the imposing roofline of the King David Hotel. His name would be forever associated with that building. It was there in 1946 that a commando of Menachem Begin's Irgun Zvai Leumi had killed ninety people, devastated a British headquarters and earned him a place in his unborn nation's history books.

Behind Begin, on one of the bookshelves stacked with encyclopedias, was a photograph taken of himself in the disguise which had allowed him time and time again to slip through the streets of Tel Aviv under the noses of Britain's soldiers: the flat black hat, black frock coat and straggly beard of a rabbi.

He turned and walked slowly back to the desk at which he had taken the President's phone call. He was dressed in a gray suit, a white shirt and a dark small-patterned tie, a reflection of a taste in clothes which, like so many other things, stamped him as a man apart in a nation in which ties were an anathema and baggy corduroys were preferred to well-pressed trousers.

Once again he reviewed the notes he had scribbled on a yellow legal pad during the President's phone call, punctuating his study with sips of the lukewarm tea flavored with Sucrasit, a sugar substitute, which had constituted his breakfast since his second heart attack five years ago. He uttered a silent prayer to the God of Israel. There was no question in Begin's mind about the significance of the information the President had passed him: it represented the most fundamental shift in power relationships in the Middle East in his lifetime. The American President would perceive it, as he would have to, in terms of the horrible threat being posed to the people of New York. Begin's duty was to perceive it in terms of the threat it posed to his people and their nation. It was mortal.

A crisis was at hand and Begin well knew that, in that crisis, he could not count on the friendship of the President. He had long ago sensed the rising tide of the animosity the American bore him. For his part, Begin did not dislike the President; rather, he mistrusted him, just as he mistrusted most non-Jews—and, indeed, a great many of his fellow Jews. He had, his political foes charged, a ghetto mentality, a narrow, ingrown attitude ill fitting a world leader, an inability to perceive a problem in anything other than its Jewish dimension.

That was the natural heritage of his formative years, his boyhood in the ghettos of Poland, his youth fighting as a Jewish partisan, his young manhood spent as an underground chieftain with a price on his head, struggling to drive the British from Palestine.

One vision had driven him during those years, the vision of his tutor, Vladimir Jabotinsky, whose writings lined his study. It was of Eretz Israel, the Land of Israel; not the truncated little Israel that his foe, David Ben-Gurion, had accepted like a crumb from the world's table in 1947, but the real land of Israel, the Biblical land God had promised his forebearers.

Consolidating Israel's claims to the land captured in 1967, which he referred to as Judea and Samaria, and bringing his people peace: those had been the two fundamentally irreconcilable aims of Begin's years as Israel's leader. Both seemed far away this December morning. The complex, painfully arrived-at Egyptian–Israeli peace settlement had proven to be a chimera. Its failure to come to grips with the Palestinian problem had left a raw and festering wound at the heart of the Middle East.

Instead of enjoying the benefits of the peace they so desperately wanted, his countrymen were living the most painful hours of their existence. Inflation and the heaviest tax burden any people on the globe were forced to carry stifled their economic life. Immigration had dwindled to a trickle of the infirm and the elderly. Many more Jews left Israel each year than arrived. There seemed little promise left in the Promised Land.

Most important, Israel's enemies, determined to destroy a peace settlement they believed to be a fraud, were gathering once again. Iraq and Syria were united, the Palestinians resurgent. Behind them, fanatical and militant, was the new Leftist Islamic Republic in Iran with its vast arsenal of sophisticated American weaponry seized in the overthrow of the Shah. Turkey, where once Israel had counted many a valuable friend, was openly hostile. The oil-producing states of the Persian Gulf, menaced by the Leftist tides to the north, no longer dared to counsel caution to their Arab brothers.

The focal point on which all their ambitions converged was Jerusalem and the Land of Judea and Samaria. Qaddafi's mad gesture seemed to Begin the inevitable culmination of the conflict that had opposed Arab and Jew for half a century.

Outside, he heard the rasp of approaching motorcycles. A few seconds later there was a knock on his door. His wife entered the study and placed on his desk a white envelope with a red slash across one corner. It was sealed and bore the words *"Sodi Beyoter —Ultra Confidential."* Prepared a few blocks away in an austere, barracklike building identified only by a number, 28, and the sign "Center for Research and Policy Planning," it contained the daily intelligence digest of the most important of Israel's three intelligence services, the Mossad.

The Prime Minister opened the envelope and smoothed the report out on his desk. At 7:01, it noted, Israel's seismograph laboratories had detected a shock of 5.7 on the Richter scale. Its source had been established as the area of the Awbari Sand Sea in southwestern Libya, an area not noted for earthquakes.

Reading the next paragraph, he started. At 7:31, the report continued, Mossad's Washington representative had spoken personally to the head of the CIA. The CIA director had given him his personal assurance that the shock was an earthquake.

Even in the most difficult hours of Israel's relations with the United States, the bonds between the CIA and her intelligence apparatus had been warm and intimate. There was almost nothing the Israelis learned that was not immediately passed to Washington. And now, in a matter critical to Israel's national existence, the Americans had deliberately, if perhaps only momentarily, lied to her. The implications of that were not lost on the Israeli Prime Minister.

He looked at his wife. She knew nothing of the crisis. But she saw he had suddenly gone pale, an almost grayish pallor seeping over his features.

"What's the matter?" she asked.

"This time, we are alone," he gasped, as much to his own stunned self as to her. "Completely alone."

The chimes of St. John's Monastery of the Cross were tolling nine, Jerusalem time, when Menachem Begin's black Dodge slipped below the Knesset, Israel's Parliament, and up to the unattractive, functional building that housed the center of the nation's government. A quartet of burly young men leaped out, each clutching in his left hand a black leather attaché case. Dressed in something other than their blue jeans and leather jackets, they might have been stockbrokers or a group of aggressive young salesmen rushing into company headquarters with their latest orders. Instead those cases contained the tools of their calling as the Prime Minister's bodyguards, an Uzi submachine gun, three extra magazines of 9mm. ammunition, a Colt .45 and a walkie-talkie.

A few minutes later, Begin took his place at the center of the oval table at which his Cabinet was gathered in emergency session. None of the men at the table had even the faintest intimation of the nature of the emergency that had brought them there. Begin had confided in no one. For a moment his regard swept the room, his dark eyes rendered outsized by the glasses he wore to correct his astigmatic vision. Carefully choosing his words, he began.

"Gentlemen, we are facing the gravest crisis in our history." With the phenomenal memory for which he was noted, he recollected every detail of his conversation with the President.

Nothing Begin could have told his ministers, no revelation he might have made, could have horrified them more than his words. For fifteen years their nation's survival had reposed on two strategic pillars, the support of the United States and the knowledge that in the ultimate crisis Israel alone in the Middle East possessed atomic weapons. Now the image of a mushroom cloud rising above the Libyan desert had destroyed the strategic basis of their state.

"We have no choice!"

The words thundered through the stricken silence left by Begin's speech, their impact underscored by the sound of a heavy fist smashing onto the ministerial table. They came from a barrel-chested man in an old sweater and open shirt, his suntanned face setting off a full head of pure white hair.

"We can't live with a madman pointing a thermonuclear gun at our heads."

Benny Ranan was one of the five authentic military heroes in the room, a former paratroop general who'd jumped at the head of his troops in the 1973 war in the spectacular transcanal operation which had paved the way for Arik Sharon's triumphant encirclement of Egypt's Third Army. As Minister of Construction, or "Minister of Bulldozers" as he was referred to, he was one of the most ardent supporters of the program to throw up new Israeli settlements on the land Begin called Judea and Samaria. He rose and strode around the table with the swaying gait his paratroopers loved to mimic.

His destination was the mural covering one wall of the room, a photograph of the Middle East taken by Walter Schirra from his Apollo 7 spaceship. Nothing could have illustrated more graphically the terrible vulnerability of their nation than that kaleidoscope of blues, whites and blacks, its vista sweeping from the Red to the Black Sea, from the Mediterranean to the Persian Gulf. Israel was just a sliver in its immensity, a strip of land clinging precariously to one edge of the photo.

Ranan gazed at it dramatically. "What this does is change totally the conditions of our existence. All Qaddafi has to do to destroy us is drop a bomb here—'' Ranan's thick forefinger thumped the map in the vicinity of Tel Aviv—''and here—and here. Three bombs and this nation will cease to exist.''

He turned back to his fellow ministers. The booming parade-ground voice dropped in register to a hoarse whisper. ''What would our life be worth here knowing that at any second, any minute, any hour, a fanatic who's been screaming for our blood for years can incinerate us instantly? I couldn't live like that. Could any of you? Could anybody?''

He paused, aware of the impact his words were having on the men in the room. ''Forty centuries of history has one lesson for us. We Jews must resist any threat to our existence with all our strength. We have to destroy him, gentlemen. Right now. Before the sun is high.''

Ranan placed his forearms on the table so that his heavy trunk leaned forward and the lingering smell of the garlic and cheese of his breakfast hung on the air. ''And we will tell the Americans what we intend to do once we've done it.''

Again, quiet muffled the room. The Deputy Prime Minister struck a match and thoughtfully lit his pipe. Yigal Yadin's bushy moustache and his bald head were as much a part of Israel's polit-ical scene as Ranan's bulky figure. He was an archaeologist, a humanistic warrior who was the architect of Israel's victory in the first war she had had to fight with her Arab neighbors, in 1948.

''For the moment, Benny,'' he noted, ''the people who are men-aced by Qaddafi's bomb are not here. They're in New York.''

''That doesn't matter. What matters is destroying Qaddafi before he can react. The Americans will thank us for doing it.''

''And suppose Qaddafi still manages to detonate that bomb and destroy New York? How much gratitude do you suppose that will inspire in the Americans?''

Ranan sighed. ''That would be a tragedy. An appalling, ghastly tragedy. But it's a risk we're forced to take. What would be a greater tragedy—the destruction of New York or the destruction of our nation?''

''For whom, Benny?'' Yadin asked. ''Us or the Americans?''

''There are three million Jews in New York,'' noted Rabbi Ye-huda Orent, leader of the religious party that was a part of Begin's ruling coalition, ''more than there are here.''

"This is where they belong." Ranan shook his head. "What's at stake here is more important than any number of Jews. We're the expression of the eternal vocation of the Jewish people. If we disappear, the Jewish people will cease to exist as a people. We'll condemn our seed to another two thousand years in the wilderness, in the ghettos, in dispersion and hate."

"Benny," the Prime Minister noted, "I must remind you the Americans have asked us to avoid taking any unilateral action against Qaddafi."

"The Americans?" Ranan gave a growling, scornful laugh. "Let me tell you something, the Americans are going to sell us out. That's what they're going to do." His hand waved toward a bank of black telephones in one corner of the room. "They're on the phone trying to talk to Qaddafi right now. Dealing away *our* land, *our* people, behind *our* backs."

"And suppose we do negotiate over those settlements."

Those words from the mouth of General Yusi Avidar, head of Shimbet, Israel's military intelligence agency, stunned the room. At the head of his tank battalion in 1967 he had defeated the Arab Legion in the crucial battle for the West Bank. "Giving them up won't mean the end of Israel. Most of the people in this country didn't want them there in the first place."

"What's at stake is not those settlements." Ranan's answering voice was deep and controlled. "Or New York. It's whether this nation can exist beside a Muammar Qaddafi armed with thermonuclear weapons. I say it cannot."

"And for that you're ready to run the risk of seeing five million innocent Americans slaughtered, of making enemies of the one people whose support and help we need?"

"I am."

"You're mad." Avidar sighed. "It's insane. It's this damnable, sick Massada complex driving us to destruction and suicide again."

Ranan was totally composed. "Every minute we waste talking brings us closer to our own destruction. We have to act right now, before the world can organize to stop us. If we wait, we'll have no West Bank, no Jerusalem, Yassir Arafat and his thugs on our doorstep, our hands tied behind our backs by the Americans, and Qaddafi posed to slaughter us. We will have no more will or reason to exist."

Menachem Begin had followed the argument without intervening, anxious to let every opinion enter into the debate. Now, softly, he spoke to his Defense Minister. "Does this nation have any military option to stop Qaddafi other than an all-out preemptive nuclear attack on Libya?"

The burly former fighter pilot who was the architect of Israel's Air Force slowly, despairingly almost, moved his head from side to side. "I can see none. We have no resources to mount and sustain an attack across hundreds of miles of open water."

Begin glanced at his hands, folded on the table before him. "I have lived through one holocaust. I cannot live under the threat of another. I believe we have no choice. I pray God the bomb in New York doesn't explode."

"Good God!" General Avidar gasped. "We won't have a friend left in the world."

Begin's face was set in a tragic, melancholy mask. "We have no friends now. We never have. From Pharaoh to Hitler we have been a people condemned by God and history to dwell alone."

He called for a vote. Scanning the raised hands, he remembered the May afternoon in 1948 when the leaders of the Jewish people had decided to proclaim their state—by just one vote. That was the margin before him—one vote. He turned to General Dorit. "Destroy Libya," he ordered.

No people in the world were better trained or better equipped to move fast in a crisis than the Israelis. Speed of reaction was a life-or-death reflex in a nation whose principal city could count on only two minutes' warning of an enemy attack from its northern borders, five minutes' from the south. As a result, the Israelis possessed probably the most highly perfected command communications network in the world, and on this December morning the speed with which it went into action was dazzling.

As soon as the Cabinet's decision was taken, General Dorit got up and went to a special telephone in the anteroom. That phone gave him a direct link to "The Hole," Israel's underground command post 160 feet below her Pentagon at Hakyria between Tel Aviv's Kaplan and Leonardo da Vinci Streets.

"The walls of Jericho," he said to the major sitting at the command console in "The Hole." His code phrase activated the command net which linked every one of Israel's twenty-seven senior military officers day and night. Whether they were jogging along the Tel Aviv waterfront, hoeing their garden, making love to a wife or a girl friend, or simply going to the toilet, each of those twenty-seven men was required to have a telephone or an ultrasophisticated portable short-wave, two-way radio transmitter within an arm's length of his person at all times. They were all assigned code names that were changed on the fourth day of the month by a computer at Hakyria, the new names being selected at random from an assigned category such as flowers or fruits.

Dorit ran out of the government headquarters, toward one of the two completely duplicated communications trucks which always traveled with his gray Plymouth. By the time he had settled into its seat, all twenty-six of his key subordinates were on line, standing by for his orders. Exactly three minutes had elapsed since Menachem Begin had given the order to destroy Libya.

In "The Hole," an Israeli female soldier, her khaki miniskirt clinging to her buttocks, unlocked the safe next to the command console. Inside were banks of envelopes, two for every potential enemy Israel possessed. The Israelis well knew there would be no time for planning once a crisis started, and those envelopes contained alternative sets of plans for a nuclear assault on any nation apt to menace her existence. Option A was designed to maximize the effect of the strike on the countries' population centers, Option B to maximize the effects on military targets. The clerk plucked out the envelopes for "Amber—Libya" and set them on the command console before the major who coordinated communications.

He quickly reviewed them by radio with Dorit. Everything the commander needed to know was contained in those envelopes: the radar frequencies; strike times calculated down to the last second; a complete description of Libya's radar and aircraft defenses; the best attack routes to each target; up-to-date aerial-reconnaissance photographs. In addition, duplicates of those envelopes were on file at the Israeli air bases where the pilots who would have to execute the plans they contained waited.

Dorit ordered Option B prepared. It would pose some spectacular problems: the commanding general wanted all targets struck simultaneously to heighten surprise. Because of the length of Libya's coastline, the planes hitting Tripoli would have to cover 1,250 miles; those striking the eastern borders, half that distance.

131

As Libya was beyond the range of Israel's Jericho B rockets designed to carry nuclear warheads six hundred miles, the strike would have to be delivered by her fleet of F-4 Phantom jets. Even more important was keeping the attack off unfriendly radar screens until the Phantoms were over their targets. Libya's radar was not a serious problem. But the radars of the U.S. Sixth Fleet steaming west from Crete were. Dorit ordered Ben-Gurion Airport to prepare Hassida for takeoff. "Hassida," Hebrew for "stork," was the code word for a Boeing 707. From the outside, it resembled a jet of Israel's national airline, El Al. The resemblance ended at the cabin door. Inside was a forest of electronic equipment.

Israel had pioneered the techniques of "masking" an aircraft's flight pattern from enemy radar with the material the plane contained. It was thanks to such Israeli skills that the planes bearing Egypt's commando assault team had been able to land at Nicosia airport undetected by Cypriot radar during their ill-fated effort to rescue a group of hostages held by Palestinian gunmen. In flight, that 707 would create a series of electronic "tunnels" through which the attacking Phantoms would streak, undetected, to their targets.

By the time Dorit's truck had reached the Monastery of Latrum, halfway to Tel Aviv, he had finished. In less than twenty minutes, enveloped by the olive groves, the ageless hills of Judea, he had planned the first preemptive nuclear attack in history.

One task remained: choosing a code name for the strike. The major manning the command console proposed one. Dorit accepted it immediately. It was "Operation Maspha," for the Biblical site where the thunder of Yahweh had routed the Philistines.

On every side the low and level sands stretched far away. Only the black stain of a herd of goats, the bleached white stone of a nomad's tomb or the bat-wing profile of a Bedouin's tent intruded on the endless ochre seas. Once the caravans of antiquity had passed by here; so, too, probably had the Children of Israel struggling homeward from their Egyptian exile. And here, under those Negev wastes, in three widely separated underground passageways, the children of modern Israel had stored for more than a decade the terrible weapons that were their nation's arms of last resort, a score of atomic bombs.

Instants after General Dorit's first alert had reached "The Hole," a series of red lights had erupted in a coded burst on the control panel of each tunnel, activating at the same time the wail of a klaxon siren.

At the sound, a score of technicians in each tunnel leaped from desks, bunks and backgammon boards and raced down the brightly lit corridors to the nuclear vaults. On one side of each tunnel, in airless containers, were shiny silver balls not much larger than the grapefruits grown in the orchards of the kibbutzim a few miles away. They were the plutonium cores of Israel's latest generation of nuclear weapons. As one team removed them from the containers, another was wheeling in the high-explosive cladding, the jacket into which each was designed to fit.

Their separation was a strategem. Since an atomic bomb existed only when these two halves were assembled, Israel had always been able to maintain publicly that she had not introduced nuclear weapons into the Middle East. It was a subterfuge similar to that employed by the aircraft carriers of the U.S. Seventh Fleet whenever they visited Japanese ports. Assembling them was a precise, delicate process, but those technicians spent hours every month rehearsing it until, like infantry soldiers breaking down and re-assembling a rifle, they could do it blindfolded.

Only once before had those bombs been assembled with the terrible knowledge that they might have to be used. It was in the predawn hours of October 9, 1973, barely seventy-two hours after the outbreak of the 1973 war. Earlier that night, the Syrians had pierced the last Israeli defenses standing in their path on the northern front. The heartland of Israel, the rich plains of Galilee, lay exposed and undefended before their columns. Moshe Dayan, in a state of extreme nervous agitation, had warned Golda Meir with an ancient Hebrew phrase that their nation faced a catastrophe comparable to the destruction of ancient Israel's Second Temple by Rome's rampaging legions.

Dismayed, dangerously close to suicide, she had responded with the order she had prayed she would never have to give, the order to prepare Israel's nuclear weapons for use against her enemies. The Syrians did not attack, however, and the crisis passed, but not before the Soviets had rushed a shipload of nuclear warheads from their Black Sea naval base of Nikolaev to Alexandria to be incorporated into their Scud missiles already in Egypt. CIA gamma-ray

133

detectors hidden along the Bosporus picked them up as they transited the waterway. That knowledge, in turn, led to Richard Nixon's global alert of U.S. forces.

Now, in their brilliantly illuminated tunnels, Israel's technicians prepared those bombs once again. In the control room of each tunnel, a high-speed Teleprinter gave the setting for each bomb's pressure detonator, fixing a few for ground-level burst, ordering the majority primed to explode at medium or high altitude to maximize their destructive radius.

As each was readied it was fitted into a special trolley designed to carry four fully armed bombs. The first trolleys were rolling down the corridors just eight minutes and forty-three seconds after the klaxon's first warning wail.

The atomic bombs speeding toward their elevators represented the final fruits of a program almost as old as the state of Israel itself. The man who had originally proposed it was Chaim Weizmann, Israel's first President and a brilliant scientist whose work in naval gunpowder for the British in 1914 had helped open Palestine for Jewish immigration with the Balfour Declaration. Over the objections of a number of his colleagues, David Ben-Gurion, the warrior-philosopher who presided over the state in its formative years, had committed Israel to the nuclear program in the early 1950s.

Israel's first allies in the search were the French, embarked in defiance of their Anglo-American allies on a nuclear-arms program of their own. Cut off from access to computer technology by the Americans, the French turned to the minds of the Weizmann Institute outside Tel Aviv for help in the interminable calculations the bomb project required. The Israelis also introduced the French to a technique they had developed to produce heavy water. In return, the French gave the Israelis access to their program and let them participate in the Sahara tests of their first bomb design, a gesture which relieved Israel of the need to test herself. Finally, in late 1957, the French agreed to sell her an experimental reactor fueled with natural uranium, a reactor that both nations' scientists knew could one day be used to produce weapons-grade plutonium.

Ben-Gurion himself chose the site for his atomic installation, a desolate strip of desert easily isolated and protected twenty miles south of his home kibbutz of Sde Boker. It was called Dimona, the name of a Biblical town that had existed there in the time of the Nabataeans. When Israeli engineers moved in to prepare the center, the government decided to conceal its real purpose by labeling it a textile plant. Thereafter, as the reactor's dome gradually began to rise above the desert floor, it was referred to by Israeli cognoscenti as "Ben-Gurion's pants factory."

A year later, the arrival of Charles de Gaulle in power in France in May 1958 put an abrupt halt to Franco-Israeli nuclear cooperation. For the nationalist de Gaulle, France's nuclear program was no one's business but France's. Israel found herself with the theoretical knowledge she needed to build a bomb and, until Dimona was ready, nothing to build it with. She found what she needed in the unlikeliest of locations, a shabby factory complex on the outskirts of Apollo, Pennsylvania, thirty-five miles northeast of Pittsburgh on Route 66. There the Nuclear Materials and Equipment Corporation (NUMEC)—founded in 1957 by Dr. Zalman Shapiro —made nuclear fuel and recovered highly enriched uranium from scraps of leftover fuel from the U.S. nuclear-submarine program. Between 1960 and 1967 an unbelievable 572 pounds of highly enriched, weapons-grade uranium disappeared from NUMEC. Well over half of it, the CIA later discovered, at least enough for a score of bombs. wound up in the Negev.

That NUMEC uranium fueled Israel's first generation of atomic bombs. The second generation was made from plutonium separated out of the burnt fuel of the Dimona reactor. Those efforts had left Israel, by the end of the seventies, far more than just the seventh nuclear power on the globe. The bombs rising out of their desert hiding places constituted part of a nuclear strike force which some intelligence agencies rated as good as England's and superior to China's.

"Stop here. I want to get some cigarettes." Yusi Avidar, the director of military intelligence, waved his driver to a halt on Jerusalem's Jaffa Road. He got out and walked to the tobacco shop just around the corner, where he bought a pack of Europa cigarettes.

When he came out, instead of returning to his car, he drifted up the street to the public telephone booth thirty yards away. No one recognized him there, fumbling through his address book for a telephone number. No one ever recognized Israeli intelligence directors; their faces and functions were carefully concealed from the public.

Avidar was not in fact looking for a number; he knew by heart the number he was thinking of calling. His hand trembled as he lit one of the cigarettes he had just bought. His face paled, and, standing there, pretending to study his address book, he felt his knees shake. His hand, a coin between his fingers, rose toward the phone. It stopped halfway. He turned to leave the booth, then stopped again. Swiftly, in one continuous movement designed almost to reach its culmination before any other impulse could stop him, he dropped the coin into the slot and dialed the number.

Forty miles away on the Tel Aviv sea front, the telephone rang in the office of the second political counselor of the U.S. Embassy.

Three blasts of a siren almost shook the half-dozen young men out of the leather easy chairs in which they sprawled watching closed-circuit television. Three blasts was the signal for an air-to-ground mission for those pilots of the Israeli Air Force; two would have signaled an air-to-air alert.

Grabbing their helmets and orange life jackets, they ran out of their ready room, across a graveled courtyard to the one-story bungalow from which their squadron was commanded. As they did, the first assembled nuclear bombs were already being fitted into their Phantom jets hidden in concrete abutments slotted into the desert floor so carefully they were practically invisible.

The pre-attack briefing was short. It concentrated on the radio frequencies they would employ in an emergency, the codes they would have to follow with total precision to be sure their assault was perfectly coordinated.

As one of the senior airmen in Israel, the squadron commander, Lieutenant Colonel Giora Lascov, was assigned to the huge Uba bin Nafi Air Base, formerly the U.S. Air Force's Wheelus Base outside Tripoli, as his target.

Like three quarters of Israel's pilots, the thirty-five-year-old Lascov was a kibbutznik. In his fifteen years as a member of the elite of Israel's armed forces, he had fought in two wars and accumulated over three thousand hours of flight time. So highly trained, so programmed, was he to respond to a crisis that the sudden revelation that this was not an exercise and that he would, in a very brief time, be dropping a twenty-kiloton nuclear bomb on an enemy target barely jarred his composure.

Because they had the greatest distance to cover, he and his wing man had the first launch. As he rose to head to the jeep outside waiting to speed him down the flight line to his Phantom, the full enormity of what he was about to do struck Lascov.

He turned to look back at the young pilots of his squadron. Their faces reflected the horror that had suddenly engulfed him. He stood there trying to find in his mind some words, some phrase, to leave his men. Then he understood that there were no words to fit so terrible a moment. Silently, Lascov turned to his jeep. Seconds later, he was racing toward his Phantom. It was 9:52. Exactly thirty-four minutes had elapsed since General Dorit had stepped out of the Cabinet Room and picked up the phone linking him to "The Hole."

Menachem Begin removed his steel-rimmed glasses. He lowered his head into the cradle of his left hand, slowly massaging his bushy eyebrows with his thumb and middle finger. There was a world of agony in that simple gesture, the reflection of a weariness so crushing that Israel's Prime Minister felt numb.

He looked at the terse communication on the paper before him. How had they found out? he wondered. Since 1973, every detail of Israel's nuclear strategy had been reviewed, pondered again and again, to be sure that no revealing detail of a coming attack could be picked up by a passing satellite, that no compromising communication could be intercepted by electronic surveillance. Yet, two minutes ago, he had received a phone call from the French ambassador. His voice hesitant with concern, the Frenchman had relayed the threat from the Chairman of the Central Committee of the Communist Party of the Soviet Union: if Israel went through with her nuclear strike against Libya, Soviet rockets would instantly annihilate their nation.

Were the Soviets bluffing? Were they just rattling their rockets the way Khrushchev had done at Suez? Did he have the right to risk the nation's existence on the possibility that they were?

Begin glanced at his watch. In twelve minutes the Phantoms would be arriving on target. No time to reconvene the Cabinet. The decision was his, and his alone.

He got up and walked to the window. Pale and trembling, the "Polish gentleman," as he was often described, studied the ageless sweep of the Judean hills, the monuments of modern Israel, the Knesset, the Hebrew University, the Israel Museum sparkling in the sunshine.

On a rise just beyond his line of vision was the one which meant more to Begin than any of the others, the white marble canopy of a "Tent of Remembrance" under which burned an eternal flame in memory of the six million victims of the holocaust—and most of his own family.

Begin had sworn on the altar of those six million dead that never again would his people live another holocaust. Would they if he went through with this? The Soviet threat was so devastatingly simple and direct. Yet Ranan was right. How could Israel exist constantly menaced with destruction at Qaddafi's hands?

Everything had depended on speed, on annihilating Libya and explaining why afterward. In the terrible chess game of global terror, there was only one move left that could check the Russians now, and it was the Americans who had to play it. Their counter-threat might stay the Russians' hand. But, Begin asked himself, were the Americans going to risk that when they discovered he had acted on his own, that he had not hesitated to imperil the city of New York to save his nation?

In a flash, Begin understood. The Russians hadn't found out. No one had. The Americans hadn't trusted them. They had realized that their own threat mightn't be enough to stay Israel's hand, to freeze her in position while they handled the crisis, so they had turned to the Soviets.

A phrase from Shakespeare's *Henry VIII,* "naked to mine ene-mies," flashed through his mind. That was Israel now, naked and vulnerable. He stared at his telephone. He had only to wait for it to ring now, for the start of the terrible pressures he knew would soon be on him, to abandon a dream, to break his nation's will, to dissemble its capital. Shrunken and suddenly aged, Menachem Begin turned back toward his telephone console.

Far below his streaking Phantom, Lieutenant Colonel Lascov could see the blue waters of the Mediterranean. His eyes swept incessantly over his instrument panel, looking for any flaw in the electronically controlled flight program hurling him toward the Libyan coast at almost twice the speed of sound. On his radar screen, he could already discern the outlines of the African shore. In nine minutes he would be climbing into the Tripolitan sky to prepare his bombing run.

Suddenly, a sharp buzz rose in his earphones. "Shadrock. Shadrock. Shadrock." Lascov tensed. Then, frantically, he began fingering his controls, swinging his plane in a 180-degree arc. The coastline of Africa faded from his radar screen. Operation Maspha had been stood down.

PART IV

MONDAY, DECEMBER 14:
3:30 A.M. TO 9:00 A.M.

"This is one crisis New York City can't live with."

I N THE CAPITAL OF THE UNITED STATES IT WAS JUST
after 3:30 A.M. Eastern Standard Time, Monday, December 14.
Three and a half hours had gone by since the explosion of Qaddafi's bomb, yet on the surface nothing in the sleeping capital indicated the crisis at hand. Beneath the surface, however, the best
technological resources of the U.S. government were already in
action in response to the orders that had been pouring out of the
Pentagon since midnight.

Eight miles off the I-87 linking Baltimore and Washington, in the
outskirts of Olney, Maryland, a red brick building vaguely resembling a submarine's conning tower peeped above the snow-covered
pastures. Buried five floors below those frozen fields was the National Warning Center. Its heart was a communications console on
which rested a round black dialing block slightly larger than the
dialing block of an old cradle phone. Its face bore only three digits
—0, 1 and 3. That phone was tied to 2,300 warning points across
the United States and through them to every air-raid siren in the
country. Twenty-four hours a day a man sat in front of it ready to
dial double three for Armageddon, the numbers that would warn
the United States that a nuclear attack was hurtling toward its
cities.

One floor below was an enormous computer programmed to
count the pieces which would be left over after Armageddon. The
havoc that would be wreaked on each metropolitan area in the
United States by any imaginable range of nuclear weapons was
stored on the computer. Now, in response to a query from its
technicians, it was spewing out an appallingly precise compilation
of the devastation a three-megaton blast would cause in New York.

A few miles away at Fort Meade, Maryland, some of the twenty
thousand employees of the National Security Agency skimmed
through the most complex and sophisticated computer facilities in

the world. Stored on them were the harvest of the NSA's worldwide eavesdropping systems, global electronic vacuum cleaners that scooped radio transmissions and telephone calls from the atmosphere, broke them down into key categories for rapid retrieval, then dumped them onto the NSA's computer. The information stored there had already allowed the NSA to foil a major terrorist operation on United States soil. Now the heirs to cryptologists who had broken Japan's naval code in World War II hunted for the word, the phrase, the message that would allow the FBI to foil this one.

At the FBI and across the Potomac River at CIA headquarters in Langley, Virginia, orders were flowing around the world instructing FBI agents and CIA station chiefs to undertake a relentless effort to find out who had delivered to Qaddafi the secret of the hydrogen bomb, how he had built it, and who might have been in charge of an effort to hide it in New York.

At the underground emergency command post in the Maryland countryside where the NEST nuclear-explosive search teams had been ordered into action, half a dozen tense officials prepared for the most complex and deadly search their organization had ever been asked to undertake.

Six times in its short history, NEST had rushed its teams into the streets of an American city. No one had found out about them. In a few hours, two hundred men and their detection equipment were scheduled to be prowling the streets of Manhattan in postal vans and rented Hertz, Ryder and Avis trucks and no one would know they were there or what they were looking for.

Two NEST aircraft, a Beechcraft King Air 100 twin jet and an H-500 helicopter, both bearing markings that could not be traced to the U.S. government, had already landed at McGuire Air Force Base in New Jersey, with an advance party of twenty men, a closed communications circuit for two hundred and a dozen boron trifluoride neutron detectors. From NEST's Western headquarters on Highland Street, Las Vegas, just two blocks from the Sahara Hotel and the neon glitter of the Strip, dozens of detection devices stored at the old Nevada nuclear testing ranges were being flown into McGuire by a unique facility at NEST's disposal—the largest fleet of rental jets in the United States, kept in Las Vegas for the city's high-rolling clients.

The man who would have the terrifying responsibility of leading the search was approaching New York on the New Jersey Turnpike in an unmarked government car. John Booth looked the quintessential Westerner: lean and muscled, well over six feet tall, with the coarse, grainy complexion of a man whose face was often exposed to the elements. As usual, he was wearing cowboy boots, a checkered shirt and, around his neck, a silver-and-turquoise Navajo charm suspended on a rawhide thong.

Booth's emergency call had caught him, as inevitably such a summons would, on a winter's weekend, skiing off the bowls of Copper Mountain, Colorado. Now, rushing toward the city ahead, Booth felt the nervous inroads of what he called his "but-for-the-grace-of-God feeling" knotting his intestines.

It was always there, that angry, half-nauseous sensation, whenever Booth's beeper called him to lead his NEST nuclear search teams into the streets of an American community. Those teams were Booth's brainchild. Long before the first novelist had written the first atomic-bomb-in-Manhattan thriller, Booth had seen the menace of nuclear terrorism coming. His first, apocalyptic vision of that possibility had come in the most unlikely of places, amidst the silvery-green olive groves and terraced fields of a little Spanish fishing village called Palomares.

He had been sent there with a team of fellow scientists and weapons designers in 1964 to try to find the nuclear weapons jettisoned by a crashing B-29. They had the best detection devices, the most sophisticated techniques available, at their disposal. And they couldn't find the missing bomb.

If they couldn't find a full-fledged bomb in the open countryside, it didn't require much imagination on John Booth's part to realize how terrifyingly difficult it would be to find a nuclear weapon hidden by a group of terrorists in an attic or a cellar of some city.

From the moment he had returned to Los Alamos, where he was a senior weapons designer, he had fought to prepare the United States for the crisis he knew would beset an American city one day. Yet, despite all his efforts, Booth was all too well aware of something few laymen would have even suspected looking at the sophisticated equipment his teams employed: how dreadfully inadequate they were, how tragically limited was their ability to perform the task for which they were intended. The problem was taking that equipment into the built-up downtown area of a big city. There the tightly packed blocks, the high-rise forests of glass and steel provided an abundance of natural screening to smother the telltale emissions that could lead his men to a hidden bomb as a scent takes a bloodhound to his quarry.

Outside, the sulfurous fumes, the roseate glow of the burn-off fires of the Jersey refineries flickered like the flames of a technological hell as they fell away behind his speeding car. He climbed up the Jersey Heights, then started the long loop down toward the Lincoln Tunnel. Suddenly, there it was before him across the black sweep of the Hudson: the awesome grandeur of Manhattan Island. Booth thought of something Scott Fitzgerald had once written, a phrase that had struck him years ago as an undergraduate at Cornell. To see Manhattan like that, from afar, was to catch it "in its first wild promise of all the mystery and the beauty in the world."

Booth shuddered. The skyline of Manhattan held no promise of beauty for him. What was waiting for him at the other end of the Lincoln Tunnel was the final refinement of the hell he most feared, the ultimate challenge to the techniques he and his men had so carefully assembled.

In Washington, D.C., half a dozen lights were burning in the West Wing of the White House. It was a little doll's house of a building sandwiched between the more familiar façade of the Executive Mansion and the gray Victorian hulk of the Executive Office Building. With its narrow corridors thick with wall-to-wall carpeting, its walls lined with Currier and Ives prints and oils of eighteenth-century Whig politicians, the West Wing looked more like the home of a Middleburg, Virginia, foxhunting squire than what it was, the real seat of power of the President of the United States.

Jack Eastman was upstairs in his second-floor office contemplating the unappetizing dish of Beefy Mac he had bought from the basement vending machine to replace the Sunday supper he had forgotten to eat. Like the walls of most Washington offices, his were covered with photos and citations, the milestones along the road that had taken him to the White House. There was Eastman as a young F-86 pilot in Korea, his graduation certificate from the Harvard Business School's Advanced Management Program; four sixteenth-century Delft porcelains he had purchased in Brussels during a tour at NATO headquarters. Before Eastman in a hinged silver frame were pictures of his wife and his nineteen-year-old daughter, Cathy, taken two years before on the June morning she graduated from Washington's Cathedral School.

The National Security Assistant picked listlessly at a twist of macaroni with his plastic fork. Inevitably, helplessly almost, his eyes turned back to the slender figure before him in her white graduation dress, her new diploma grasped defiantly in her hand. At first glance, the long, virtually angular face she had gotten from her mother seemed glazed with a solemnity appropriate to the moment. Yet Eastman could read there a hidden smile curling mischievously at the end of her lips. From the time she'd been a baby squirming in his arms that smile had been a secret bond between them, the special gauge of the love of father and daughter.

He stared at that smile now, unable to turn away, unable to think of anything except his proud girl in her white dress. The movements of his jaw slowed, then stopped. Nausea crept through his stomach. Slowly, despairingly, he lowered his head to the waiting cradle of his arms, struggling to stop the sobs, searching for the discipline he'd been so long trained to exercise. Jack Eastman's only child was a sophomore at Columbia University in New York City.

Laila Dajani hurried past the black limousines. They were always there, lined up like mourners' cars waiting outside the funeral of a politician or a Mafia chieftain. For an instant, she looked with pity and contempt at the knot of gawkers clustered by the door, waiting, despite the cold, the time, the fact that it was Sunday night, to savor whatever bizarre pleasure it was they got from watching someone famous walk into New York's Studio 54.

Inside, she was overwhelmed once again by the scene: the twelve landing lights of a Boeing 707, the multicolored strobes hurling a sparkling firestorm of light and color against the nylon drapes; the waiters slithering past in their satin shorts; the horde of liquid forms on the dance floor frozen, then released, in the incandescent glare of the strobes. Bianca Jagger was there, dancing frantically in satin jogging shorts; so, too, was Marisa Berenson, lolling on a banquette as though she were holding court. In front of Laila a frail black in leather pants, bare-chested except for a studded black leather vest, hands chained to a truss around his genitals, swayed in lascivious response to the ecstasy of some private dream.

Laila twisted through the crowd, waving, blowing an occasional kiss, indifferent to the hands caressing her black satin pants. When she finally found the group she was looking for, she glided up behind a boy whose long blond hair hung to the collar of a white silk shirt. She threw her arms around him, letting her fingernails scurry over the skin exposed by his unbuttoned shirt while her mouth nibbled his ear in quick, teasing bites.

"Michael, darling, can you forgive me for being so late?"

Michael Laylor turned to her. He had the face of an angel: blue eyes, features that were almost too perfect in their regularity, lips slightly parted; the whole framed in a halo of blond hair that gave him an open, innocent regard.

Innocence was not, as Laila had had the grateful occasion to discover, an attribute of his. He circled his hand under her hair so that the nape of her neck was caught in the soft vise of his thumb and other fingers. With a languorous movement he drew her face down to his and held it there, their lips barely touching. Finally, reluctantly, he released her.

"I'd forgive you anything."

Laila circled the banquette and slid down onto the cushion beside him. Across the way a joint was moving from hand to hand. Michael reached for it and passed it to her. Laila, still shaken by her experience in the garage, inhaled a full breath, holding the smoke in her lungs every second she could before letting it glide out her nostrils. Michael started to pass it on, but before he did she grabbed it back and gulped another lungful. Then she sat back, eyes closed, waiting, praying for the gentle numbness to seep through her. She opened her eyes to see Michael staring down at her, a crooked half-smile on his face.

"Dance?"

As soon as they reached the dance floor, she hurled herself into the music, eyes closed, racing off alone along the crashing tide of sound, away from everything, the grass finally enclosing her in its protective cocoon.

"Black bitch!"

The shrill scream shattered Laila's reverie. The young black she had noticed on the way in was slumping to the floor, blood spurting from his temple, his mouth open in a prayer of pain from the blow,

148

from the agonizing tear of his weird harness. His aggressor, a squat young white with a beer drinker's belly and a floppy leather hat, planted a vicious kick in his groin before two bouncers could shove him away.

Laila shuddered. "Oh God," she whispered. "How awful! Let's sit down." Her hand clutched Michael's tightly as they started back to their banquette. Dizzy from the grass, the scene on the dance floor, she leaned against him, raising her head toward his. Her eyes were glistening.

"What a hideous world we live in!"

Michael studied her. She seemed distant, distraught almost. Perhaps, he told himself, the new Mexican grass was too strong. He stroked her auburn hair as they sat down. He could see she was still far away, running down her own track.

"Why is it always the ones like him that get hurt?" she asked. "The weak, the helpless?" Michael didn't answer; he knew she didn't want an answer. "For people like that there's never any justice until they start to use the violence others use against them. And then there's more violence and more violence and more violence."

Hearing her own words, she trembled.

"You don't believe that, Linda."

"Oh yes I do. They"—she waved scornfully to the crowded dance floor—"never hear anything until it's too late. They're only interested in their bodies, their pleasures, their money. The poor, the homeless, the wronged—that doesn't interest them. Until there's violence, the world is deaf." Her voice fell until it was barely a whisper. "You know, there's a saying in our Koran. A terrible saying, really, but true: 'If God should punish men according to what they deserve, he would not leave on the back of the earth so much as a beast.' "

"Your Koran? I thought you were Christian, Linda."

Laila stiffened, suddenly wary of the grass. "You know what I mean. The Koran's Arabic, isn't it?"

From across the banquette someone waved another joint toward them. Michael pushed it away.

"Let's go back to the studio."

Laila cupped his face in her hands, her long fingers fondling the skin on his temples. She held him like that for a while, gazing at his beautiful face.

"Yes, Michael. Take me home."

As they walked toward the door, a chubby paw beckoned to them out of the darkness.

"Linda, darling! You're stunning, duh-voon!"

She turned to see the pudgy figure of Truman Capote, resembling a scaled-down Winston Churchill in a mauve velvet jumpsuit.

"Come meet all these lovely people."

With the pride of a jeweler pointing out his choice baubles, he introduced them to the gaggle of Italian pseudo-nobles fawning over him.

"The Principessa's giving a luncheon in my honor tomorrow," he gushed, indicating a gray-haired woman whose taut facial skin was evidence of more than one visit to the fashionable plastic surgeons of Rio. "You must come." The bright eyes swept over Michael. "And do bring this lovely creature along." Capote leaned over to her. "Everyone will be there tomorrow. Gianni is coming from Turino just for me." His voice fell to a conspiratorial whisper. "Even Teddy's coming. Isn't that marvelous?"

With a kiss and a promise, Laila managed to extricate them from Capote's grasp. Leaving, she heard his voice squealing through the shadows after them, its high timbre rising above the din of the club. "Don't forget Tuesday lunch, darlings! Everyone will be there!"

"They're here, sir."

The words had no sooner drifted from Jack Eastman's intercom than "they" were in his office, terrorist experts from State and the CIA: Dr. John Turner, head of the Agency's Psychiatric Affairs Division; Lisa Dyson, the thirty-five-year-old CIA officer who had what was referred to in the Agency as the "Libyan account"; Bernie Tamarkin, a Washington psychiatrist and a recognized world authority on the behavioral psychology of terrorists in stress situations.

Eastman scrutinized them all, noticing the faint flush on their faces, sensing the shortened rhythm of their breathing. Nervous, he thought. Everybody peaks when they come to the White House.

As soon as they had sat down, Lisa Dyson passed out copies of an eighteen-page document. It was enclosed in an embossed white folder bearing the pale-blue seal of the CIA, a "Top Secret" stamp and the words "Personality and Political Behavior Study: Muammar al-Qaddafi."

The study was part of a secret program run by the CIA since the late fifties, an effort to employ the techniques of psychiatry to study the personality and character development of a selected group of world leaders in intimate detail, to try to predict with some degree of certainty how they would respond in a crisis. Castro, Charles de Gaulle, Khrushchev, Brezhnev, Mao Tse-tung, the Shah, Nasser, all had been put under the dissecting glare of the CIA's analysts. Indeed, some of the perceptions turned up in the profiles of Castro and Khrushchev had been of vital help to John F. Kennedy in dealing with both men during the Cuban Missile Crisis.

Each involved prodigious expense and effort. Everything about a "target" was examined: what had influenced his life, what its major traumas were, how he had responded to them, whether he had developed certain characteristic defense mechanisms. Agents were sent all over the world to determine one precise fact, to explore just one facet of a man's character. Old military-school-mates were hunted down and probed to find out if a man masturbated, drank, was finicky about his food, went to church, how he responded to stress. Did he like boys? Or women? Or both? Had he had a mother fixation? Trace him where you could through his oral, anal, genital stages. Find out if he had a large or small penis. If he had sadistic tendencies. Once a CIA agent had been smuggled into Cuba for the sole purpose of talking to a whore with whom Castro had often gone to bed when he was a student.

Eastman turned back the folder of his study and looked at the portrait inside of the man who was threatening to massacre his daughter and five million other Americans.

He sighed and turned to Lisa Dyson. She had a mane of long blond hair that streamed below her shoulder blades. Her slender hips were forced into blue jeans so tight the men around her could not miss the welt made in them by the edge of her panties. "All right, miss, why don't you start by summing up just what that report of yours tells us about this son of a bitch and how he's going to act in a crisis," Eastman ordered.

Lisa reflected a moment, searching for the phrase, for the one all-embracing thought, that would capture the essence of those eighteen pages she knew so well.

"What this tells us," she answered, "is that he's as shrewd as a desert fox and twice as dangerous."

In New York, Times Square was empty. A chill wind sweeping up from the distant harbor twisted the cottony tufts of steam spurting from the Con Ed manhole covers and sent the night's harvest of litter scuttling along the sidewalks and curbs. The predominant sound was the clattering of the suspensions of the Checker cabs as they hurtled over the potholes of Broadway in their flight downtown.

At Forty-third and Broadway a pair of half-frozen whores huddled in the doorway of a Steak and Brew Burger, listlessly calling to the few late-night passersby. Three blocks away, in the warmth of a third-floor walkup, its walls and ceilings painted black, their pimp lolled on a mattress wrapped in a gold satin sheet. He was a lean black with a precisely trimmed goatee. He had on a white beaver hat with a three-inch brim, and, despite the almost total lack of illumination in the room, dark glasses screened his eyes. His hips, covered by the white silk folds of an Arab djellabah, twitched suggestively to the rhythms of Donna Summer's voice flooding out of his stereo system.

Enrico Diaz turned to the girl beside him. She was the third and newest member of his stable. He reached for the ornament dangling around his neck on a gold chain. It was a representation of the male sex organ and it was there that he kept his finest Colombian coke. He was about to offer the girl a jolt and a loving stroke, the assurance that she was his main woman, when the phone rang.

His irritation became evident displeasure when he heard a voice saying, "This is Eddie. How about a party?"

Fifteen minutes later Enrico's lime-green custom-built Lincoln paused at Forty-sixth and Broadway just long enough to allow a figure to emerge from the shadows and slip into the front seat.

As he guided the car into the traffic, Enrico glared disdainfully at the man beside him, the collar of his beige overcoat turned up to screen his face. Enrico was typical of dozens of men and women being contacted in these predawn hours in bars, on street corners, in restaurants and bedrooms around New York. He was an FBI informer.

He owed that distinction to the fact that he had been caught one night with a dozen dime bags of heroin in his car. It was not that Enrico scored horse. He was a gentleman. The bags were for one of his girls. But it had come down to doing eight to fifteen in Atlanta or walking—and talking, from time to time, with the Bureau. Besides pimping, Enrico, the son of a black mother and a Puerto Rican father, was a senior member of the FALN Puerto Rican underground, a group of considerable interest to the FBI.

"I got something heavy, Rico," his control agent said.

"Man," Rico sighed, maneuvering deftly through the late traffic, "you always got something heavy."

"We're looking for Arabs, Rico."

"No Arabs fucking my girls. They too rich for that."

"Not that kind of Arab, Rico. The kind that likes to blow people up, not screw them. Like your FALN friends." Rico eyed the agent warily. "I need anything you got on Arabs, Rico. Arabs looking for guns, papers, cards, a safe house, whatever."

"Ain't heard about none of that."

"Suppose you just ask around for us, Rico?"

Rico groaned softly, all the strains and tensions of his double life encapsulized in the sound. Still, life was a deal. You made, you took, you gave, you got. The man wanted something, the man give something.

"Hey, man," he said in that low gentle voice he reserved for special moments. "One of my ladies, she be in this thing with the Pussy Posse down at the Eighteenth Precinct."

"What *kind* of thing, Rico?"

"Hey, you know, this John, he don't want to pay and . . ."

"And she's looking at three to five for armed robbery?"

There was an almost reluctant, liquid roll to Rico's answer. "Yeahhh."

"Pull over here." The agent waved to the curb. "It's heavy, Rico. Real heavy. You get me what I need on Arabs, I'll get you your girl."

Watching him disappear down Broadway, Rico could only think of the girl waiting for him on the gold silk mattress, of her long muscular legs, the soft lips and the swiftly moving tongue he was training to perform the arts of her new calling. Sighing reluctantly, he drove off, not back toward his Forty-third Street flat but east toward the East River Drive.

For fifteen minutes, Lisa Dyson had kept the men in Jack Eastman's White House office captivated with her profoundly disturbing portrait of the man threatening to destroy New York City. Every facet of Qaddafi's life was covered in the CIA's report: his lonely, austere boyhood in the desert tending his father's herds; the brutal trauma of being cast from the family tent by his ambitious father and sent away to school; how he had been despised as an ignorant Bedouin by his schoolmates, humiliated because he was so poor that he had to sleep on the floor of a mosque and walk twelve miles each weekend to his parents' camp.

The CIA had indeed found his bunkmates at the military school where his political ambitions had begun to emerge. The portrait they gave of a youthful Qaddafi, however, was anything but that of a masturbating, eagerly lecherous young Arab male. He had been instead a zealous Puritan, sworn to a vow of chastity until he had overthrown Libya's King; abjuring alcohol and tobacco and urging his fellows to follow his example. Indeed, as Lisa Dyson pointed out, he still flew into wild temper tantrums when he heard that his Prime Minister was fooling around with the Lebanese hostesses on Libya's national airline or womanizing with bar girls in Rome.

The report described the carefully planned coup that had given him control on September 1, 1969, at the age of twenty-seven, of a nation with $2 billion a year in oil revenues, pointing out the code word he'd assigned the operations: "El Kuds"—Jerusalem.

It detailed the extreme, xenophobic version of Islam he had imposed on his nation: the return to the Sharia, the Koranic law, cutting off a thief's hand, stoning adultresses to death, putting drinkers under the lash; his conversion of Libya's churches to mosques, his decrees forbidding the teaching of English and ordering all signs and documents written in Arabic; how he had banned brothels and alcohol; how he had personally led, pistol in hand, the raids that had closed Tripoli's nightclubs, ordering strippers to dress, gleefully smashing up bottles like a Prohibition cop. There was his "cultural revolution" that had sent illiterate mobs into the street burning the works of Sartre, Baudelaire, Graham Greene, Henry James; smashing into private homes in search of whiskey; storming through the bunk rooms of the oilfield tool pushers, ripping *Playboy* centerfolds from their walls.

Most terrifying of all was the long history of terrorist actions for which he had been directly or indirectly responsible: his repeated attempts to assassinate Anwar Sadat, to organize a coup in the

154

Saudi Arabian Army; how he'd funneled millions into Lebanon to foment the bloody Lebanese civil war and other millions to aid the Ayatollah Khomeini's overthrow of the Shah.

" 'Muammar al-Qaddafi is essentially a lonely man, a man without friends or advisers,' " Lisa Dyson read with the singsong Scandinavian speech pattern of the tiny Minnesota village in which she'd been raised. " 'In every instance, his reaction to new situations has been to retreat back to the old and the secure. He has discovered all too often that rigidity works, and he will inevitably become rigid in difficult circumstances.' "

She cleared her throat and pushed a stray lock of hair from her forehead. " 'Most important, it is the Agency's conviction that in a moment of great crisis he would be perfectly prepared to play the role of a martyr, to bring the roof down over his head and destroy the house if he is not allowed to have his own way.

" 'He likes to be unpredictable, and,' " she concluded, " 'his favorite tactic in a crisis will be to lunge for his enemy's weakest spot.' "

"Jesus Christ!" Eastman groaned. "He certainly found it in New York City."

"That, gentlemen," Lisa Dyson noted, closing her report, "is Muammar al-Qaddafi."

Bernie Tamarkin had followed her, leaning tensely forward, elbows on his knees, his hands clasped so tightly together his knuckles glowed. He stood up and began to stride around Eastman's office, tugging nervously at his mat of curly hair. Without being asked, he started to offer his evaluation of the material Lisa Dyson had just read.

"We're looking at a very, very dangerous man here. First of all, he was humiliated as a kid and he's never gotten over it. He was the dirty little Bedouin boy despised by everybody else, and he's been out for revenge ever since. This business about keeping his family in a tent until everyone else in Libya has a house. Bullshit! He's still punishing his father for taking him out of his desert and throwing him into that school."

"I think there are some vital clues for us in the desert's impact on him," Dr. Turner, the CIA's Psychiatric Division head, noted. He was a big man, his bald head meticulously shaved, delicate gold-rim glasses on his nose. "Our key to getting to him may be religion—God and the Koran."

"Yeah, maybe." Tamarkin was still pacing. His own reputation as a terrorist negotiator had been considerably enhanced by his skillful use of an Arab ambassador familiar with the Koran during the Kannifi Black Muslim crisis in Washington a few years before. "But I doubt it. This guy thinks *he's* God. That stuff about raiding the nightclubs. The story about how he goes to the hospital disguised as a beggar asking for a doctor to come to help his dying father, then throws off his robes and orders the doctor out of the country when he tells him to give his father an aspirin. That's omnipotence. The man is playing God. And you don't negotiate with God.''

"Do we have to take this man at his word?" Eastman asked him. "Is he the kind of guy who really could go through with something like this? Could he be bluffing?"

"Not a chance." There was not, Eastman noted grimly, a hint of hesitation in Tamarkin's reply. "Don't doubt that son of a bitch even for a second. Don't ever, ever question his readiness to pull that trigger, because he'll pull it just to show you he can." Tamarkin moved to Eastman's desk. "The one vital, essential thing you've got to convey to the President or whoever's going to deal with Qaddafi is this: don't challenge him. We've got to forget our big nationalistic ego. We can't get into one of those macho, head-on collisions, have a couple of forty-five-caliber penises waving at each other. Do that and he'll feel threatened. And New York will go."

"All right," Eastman snapped, "I'll inform the President. But what are we supposed to do? That's what you're here to tell us."

"Well, right off I'd point out that the guy who wrote the book on how to handle situations like this is a Dutchman over in Amsterdam. I'd sure as hell like to have him here in our corner when push gets to shove."

"If he's a Dutchman and he's in Holland he's not going to do us much good tonight in Washington, D.C., is he?" barked Eastman.

"Look, that's not my problem. I'm just saying if there's some way to get him here it would be a big help. Now, as far as Qaddafi's concerned, the first thing I'd work on is the fact he's a loner. Has no friends. Whoever negotiates with him has to insinuate himself into his confidence. Become his friend."

Eastman made hurried notes on the yellow legal pad before him. "You know," he said to Tamarkin, "one thing that struck me in that report is the concern he's always shown for his people. Getting them better housing, things like that. Is there a reservoir of sympathy there we can play on to get him to respond to the people up in New York?''

The psychiatrist sat up with a sudden, almost spastic reflex. His dark eyes widened as he stared incredulously at the National Security Assistant.

"Never!'' he said. ''This man hates New York. It's New York he's after, not Israel, not those settlements of theirs. New York is everything this guy loathes. It's Sodom and Gomorrah. Money. Power. Wealth. Corruption. Materialism. It's everything that's threatening that austere, spartan desert civilization of his. It's the moneylenders in the Temple; it's the effete, degenerate society he despises.''

Tamarkin's eyes darted around the room to be sure that his message was registering on everyone there. ''The first thing you've got to understand is this: deep down inside, whether he knows it or not, what this guy really wants to do is destroy New York.''

The screaming jangle of an alarm bell galvanized the men manning the National Security Council communications center in the basement of the West Wing. The duty officer jabbed at three red buttons by his desk.

Thirty seconds later, Jack Eastman came running into the room.

"The *Allen* has found Qaddafi, sir!'' the duty officer shouted.

Eastman grabbed the secure phone that linked the room to the National Military Command Center in the Pentagon.

''Where is he?''

''In a villa, by the sea, just outside Tripoli,'' the admiral running the center announced. ''The *Allen* intercepted his voice on a call half an hour ago and traced it back there. The Agency confirms it's one of his terrorist headquarters.''

''Terrific!''

''I have just had Admiral Moore at Sixth Fleet on the blower. They can put a three-kiloton missile through the front door of that villa in thirty seconds.''

''Don't you fucking dare!''

Eastman had the reputation of being ''tight-assed,'' for never flapping no matter how severe the pressures on him were, but he screamed out his order to the Pentagon admiral. ''The President

157

has made it absolutely clear there's to be no military action in this situation without his express orders. You make damn sure everybody out there understands that.''

"Yes, sir.''

Eastman thought for a second. Should he wake the President? On his urging he had gone to sleep to husband his strength for the crisis. No, he told himself, let him get his sleep. He'll need it.

"Tell Andrews to start one of the Doomsday planes for Libya right away.'' The Doomsday planes were three converted 747s that bristled with electronic gadgetry and sensitive communications equipment. They could stay aloft for seventy-two hours and were designed to provide the President with an airborne command post in the event of a nuclear war. "I want them to set up a secure communications channel Qaddafi can use to talk from that villa to Washington.''

Eastman paused. He was sweating. "Get State,'' he ordered the duty officer beside him. "Tell them to have the chargé in Tripoli get out to that villa right away. Tell him . . .'' Eastman reflected carefully on his words. "Instruct him to inform Qaddafi that the President of the United States requests the privilege of a conversation with him.''

The thud of horse's hoofs echoed along the deserted bridle path of Paris's Bois de Boulogne. An early-morning ground fog wrapped the French capital's park, and the advancing rider emerged from the shadows enfolding the path like some phantom horseman of legend. It was appropriate that he did, for nothing could have better suited the character of the head of the SDECE, France's intelligence service, than that almost conspiratorial obscurity cloaking his morning ride.

In an age when the CIA pointed the way to its headquarters with highway signs and the names of British intelligence agents were bandied about in Parliamentary debates, the agency over which General Henri Bertrand presided remained obsessed with secrecy. No telephone book, no street directory, no Bottin contained its name or the address of its headquarters. No *Who's Who,* no *Baedeker* of French government officialdom listed Bertrand's name or that of any of his subordinates. In fact, Bertrand was not even the General's real name. It was a *nom de service* he'd adopted when, as a young captain in the Foreign Legion, he was recruited for the service in 1954 during the Indochinese War.

Expertly, Bertrand reigned his mount to a walk and started back to the stable of the Polo de Paris. He had belonged to that exclusive body for fifteen years, yet never once had his name appeared in the green members' directory the club published annually. Walking through its white gate, he started in surprise at the figure waiting in the shadows to greet him. Only a matter of gravest urgency could have brought Palmer Whitehead, the Paris station chief of the CIA, out here at this hour of the morning.

"*Alors, vieux?*" Bertrand said, swinging off his horse. Then, before Whitehead could reply, he suggested, "Come with me while I walk her down."

For five minutes the two men walked the horse around the huge greensward where Rothschild barons and Argentinian gauchos played polo. The CIA station chief did not reveal the existence of the bomb in New York to his French counterpart; he told him instead that the U.S. government had incontrovertible evidence that Qaddafi had made an atomic bomb, probably from plutonium diverted from the French reactor, and was planning to use it for terrorist purposes. They needed desperately the identity of anyone who might have been involved in the Libyan's project.

"You understand," Bertrand told the American when he'd finished, "that since this involves nuclear matters, I'll have to have the agreement of my principals before I begin. Although, in view of what you've told me, I'm sure there will be no problem."

The American nodded gravely. "I understand there's a personal message from the President on its way to the Élysée now." Leaving, he added one last phrase. "And please, Henri, be very, very discreet and very, very quick."

Sally Eastman awoke the instant she heard the metallic snap of the front door closing. The crunch of doors closing in the watches of the night had been the background music to her twenty-seven-year marriage: doors closing in bungalows adjoining Air Force bases in Colorado, France, Germany and Okinawa as her husband rushed off to alerts; in Brussels during their NATO tours, and here in Washington, first on Jack's assignments to the Pentagon, and now at the White House.

She lay awake listening to his footsteps follow their familiar course to the kitchen for a glass of milk, then their weary march up the stairs of their Colonial clapboard house.

She snapped on her night light as the bedroom door opened. The years had given Sally Eastman an unnerving ability to read in the lines of her husband's face the gravity of the crisis that had kept him from their bed. Seeing him, she sat up abruptly, hugging the blanket against her ten-year-old nightgown.

"What time is it?"

Her voice rang with those faintly imperious, metallic undertones so often found in women who had gone to Vassar or Smith in the early fifties, lived with roommates called Bootsie or Muffin and developed in the wasteland of their middle years an inordinate affection for alcohol.

Eastman sank onto the bed. "Just after four."

Three hours, he'd calculated; he had three hours to catch the sleep he so desperately needed while the Doomsday jet was streaking over the Atlantic.

"You look very worried. Is it something we can talk about?"

Eastman rubbed his weary eyes and shook his head as though somehow that gesture might ease the fatigue numbing his brain. On the maple chest of drawers opposite him was another picture in a silver frame. This one had been taken in Wiesbaden in 1961, and it showed Major Eastman and his wife proudly displaying their newborn daughter.

Eastman thought back to the President's injunction to secrecy in the Pentagon war room. The National Security Assistant was used to carrying the awful burden of secrecy. He had borne it many times, in many crises, although never one as personally painful as this.

"I'm afraid not, Sal." He looked at his wife, at her angular, decent face yielding sadly to age now, a mirror of the hurts and loneliness of their strained and empty marriage. Why the hell shouldn't I tell her? he suddenly thought. Doesn't she have at least as much right to know as I do? "If I tell you, neither you nor I have the right to tell anyone else, understand?"

His wife nodded her head dutifully.

"Anyone," stressed Eastman.

"Oh my God!" Sally Eastman shrieked after her husband had outlined Qaddafi's threat. "What a bastard!" Her body jerked upright almost violently. "Cathy! Jesus Christ, Jack, we've got to call Cathy right away and get her out of there." A perplexed, half-frightened, half-angry look swept Sally Eastman's features. "Haven't you called her already?"

Eastman shook his head.

"Why not, for God's sake?"

"Sally, we can't."

"Can't? What do you mean, can't? Of course we can. We have to."

"Sally, we don't have the right to."

"Jack, for God's sake, we don't have to tell her there's a bomb in New York! We'll tell her . . ." Sally Eastman's eyes flashed wildly. "I'll tell her Mother's going into the hospital for an operation."

"Sally, understand me. I've been crying my insides out all night for Cathy. But we just don't have the right to save our own family. Not when there are millions of families in New York who can't save themselves."

"Jack, we're not going to violate any secrecy."

"We're violating a trust."

"A trust? How about all the other people in that room? You don't think they're not on the phone right now, saving their daughters? Calling their girl friends? Or their goddamn stockbrokers? How about the President? Suppose one of his boys was up in New York. You don't think he'd call him back?"

"No, Sally, I don't. Not this President."

Joints creaking, Jack rose from the bed. He walked to the window. Nowhere in the neighborhood was there another light burning; all he could see was the regular pattern of street lights falling on the snow and the shadowy outlines of his neighbors' homes looming behind them. What decisions, he thought almost angrily, had they had to make tonight? Whether to have the vet put down the aging family dog? Whether they should have a child's teeth straightened? Was it time to trade in the station wagon?

He looked at his wife still clutching the blanket to her bare shoulders. "Sally, one person in that room, just one, breaks his trust." He was begging for her understanding. "He calls his mother. And she calls her brother. And he calls his partner. And he calls his daughter. And she calls her boy friend. And it's out. It's gone public. And Qaddafi blows the bomb, because that's what he's

161

threatening to do if this gets out. And five million people and our lovely Cathy die because someone in that room didn't live up to his trust, couldn't handle the moral obligation—"

"Moral obligation! My God, the only moral obligation we have is to our daughter. If she were a soldier on duty, all right. If we were betraying a secret, all right. But we're not. We're only saving her life."

"By using information I hold in trust."

"Oh dear God, Jack, it's not buying stocks with insider's knowledge! It's our daughter's life."

Sally Eastman looked at her husband through a film of angry tears. If there had been one constant in her feelings for him through twenty-seven years of marriage it was respect. Not understanding. Try though she had, she had never been able to understand his soldier's mind and, dear God, she could not understand it now. But respect him she did.

"All right, darling," she whispered, "come to bed."

Eastman undressed quickly and slipped under the covers beside her.

"What time do you have to get up?"

"The switchboard will call."

Sally leaned over him before switching off her night light, reading the deep hurt in his green eyes. Then she leaned down and kissed him.

On the other side of the Atlantic Ocean, it was just after 10 A.M. when a black Peugeot 204 maneuvered into its reserved parking place in front of one of the Flemish façades, all of them identical, of the red brick houses lining Amsterdam's Keerkstraat.

The man getting out of the car was a short, stocky sixty-year-old, his cheeks glowing with the healthy tone of a burgomeister in a Frans Hals oil. Tucked primly under one arm was a worn black leather briefcase. A few minutes later, in his austere office looking onto the Keerkstraat, Henrick Jagerman opened the case and took out the ingredients of the snack with which he inevitably began his working day: a steaming thermos of black coffee and an apple.

Jagerman was the son of a poor factory worker who had become a prison inspector in the slums of Amsterdam. Trailing along after his father, Jagerman had first felt the stirrings of the uncommon vocation which had brought him to his present office, a deep fascination with the criminal mind. He put himself through college and medical school guiding tourists along the canals and around the museums of Amsterdam, then became a psychiatrist specializing in criminology. When Holland's forward-looking government decided to set up a task force to study the best ways to deal with terrorist situations, Jagerman had been chosen to sit on it as its psychiatric counselor.

Four times since, when Palestinians seized the French ambassador to The Hague in 1974, when common convicts captured a choir visiting the capital's jail for a Christmas service, during the two train seizures staged by Holland's dissident Moluccan community, Jagerman had had the chance to put the theories he had developed in his long hours in prisoners' cells into practice. So successful were they that he had become known around the world as Dr. Terrorism, admired by policemen and feared by terrorists for the original and innovative methods with which he used manipulative psychology to resolve hostage situations.

He had, quite literally, written the bible on how to deal with terrorists. Compiled in a limited six-hundred-page edition, it was locked in the vaults of a score of national police services, the indispensable and rigorously secret tool they called on whenever terrorists struck on their soil.

Jagerman had barely turned his attention to the first item on his desk, when, unbidden, his secretary entered the office. He recognized immediately the flustered face of the American ambassador trailing behind her.

The ambassador indicated he had to talk to him alone, then told him what had happened. A jet of the Queen's Flight, he said, was waiting at Schiphol to fly him to Paris's Charles de Gaulle Airport, where Air France was holding the Washington-bound Concorde for his arrival.

"With luck," the ambassador remarked, giving his watch a nervous glance, "we can have you at the White House by nine Washington time."

Jack Eastman was snoring. His wife stared at his body, crumpled in the deep sleep he had long ago learned to force on himself in a crisis. Forgive me, Jack, she thought. Noiselessly,

Sally slipped from the bed and tiptoed out of the room. She walked carefully down the stairs to the telephone in the front hall. The first numbers she dialed were 212, the area code for New York City.

Laila lay on her back, gazing upward into the comforting nothingness of the high-ceilinged room, to the ill-defined point where all form and shape were obliterated by the darkness. The cloying odor of the incense Michael had burned mingled with the lingering fumes left by their grass and the pungent odor their love-making had wrung from their bodies.

It was dark except for one pale shaft of light falling across the room and onto the bed from a floor lamp burning in the studio next door. Here and there, along its advance, its soft glow highlighted bits and pieces of the clothing they'd flung about the room in their rush to the bed: Laila's black satin trousers crumpled in a heap by the door; Michael's silk shirt spilling from the bed; her flimsy panties wadded into a tight knot and hurled to the floor.

Michael was sprawled on his stomach. He was sound asleep, his head buried in the comforting arc of Laila's breast and shoulder. One arm lay across her body, its motionless fingers clutching her other breast. To her right, a traveler's alarm clock in a leather frame rested on Michael's night table. Its luminous dial read 6:15.

Tenderly, yet absentmindedly, Laila stroked the long hanks of hair spilling down Michael's back and tried to drive from her consciousness every thought except the recollected pleasure of her spent passion. The light cleaving the room caught the hairs along Michael's forearm, turning them into a gossamer's web of silver threads. Everything, it suddenly seemed to Laila, came down to that arm, to the hand encircling her breast. She had to perform one act, one deliberate reflex of the will to move it, to rouse her sleeping lover. All the rest would follow inevitably in the wake of that gesture, each inexorable step leading toward the act to which the luminous hands of the clock summoned her.

She thought of a line from Sartre: "Man can will nothing unless he has first understood that he must count on no one but himself."

There was no one there to make her move that hand, to put her feet onto the course she had chosen for them. The will to act—or not to act—was hers, and hers alone.

Her eyes stared into the darkness overhead. We have no destinies, Sartre had written, other than those we forge ourselves. Well,

164

she thought, I have forged mine. And for better or for worse, the time had come to accomplish it.

She took her free hand and lifted Michael's wrist from her breast. She drew it to her lips and tenderly kissed his fingertips. He stirred.

"You're not going?" His eyes blinked reluctantly open and peered up to her. Sleep had softened their hue from bright blue to a gentle gray.

"I have to, my love, the time has come."

"Stay," he whispered.

"Michael, my love, my darling. I can't. I have to go. I have to."

She lay there an instant, then she slid out from under his arms and slithered to the floor.

Michael watched dreamy-eyed as she wriggled into her tight black pants, pulled her blouse over her head, scooped her panties from the floor and stuffed them into her handbag.

"When will I see you again?"

"I don't know, Michael."

"Let's have lunch. My shooting will be finished at twelve."

"I can't today." There was an aching in her stomach now. "I'm having lunch with Calvin Klein's people."

"Then we'll go to Capote's lunch together tomorrow."

Laila felt as though someone had jammed a thick wad of wool into her mouth. She nodded, but it was seconds before her larynx formed the words she wanted.

"Yes, Michael. We'll go to Truman's together."

She came back to the bed and threw herself on top of him. Her mouth flayed at his, her twisting lips driving his back against his teeth until they hurt, her belt buckle, the heavy buttons of her blouse, driving into his bare flesh. Finally she slipped a hand around his neck, clasped the hair over his forehead, and slowly pulled his head back down onto the pillow. For a moment, she lay there on top of him, staring down at his face with such intensity it frightened him. Then, like an awakening dreamer, she shook her head. She got up.

"Don't move, darling. I'll let myself out."

He heard her voice calling to him through the shadows. "Goodbye, my love." Then he heard the door slamming behind her and she was gone.

A police ambulance on emergency call hurtled through the orange haze of Columbus Circle, the *hee-haw* bleat of its siren filling the empty square with a sound that was to many the background music of New York City. Laila Dajani watched it go, then continued her march toward the Hampshire House. Just ahead of her, Sanitation Department workers hurled black plastic sacks of garbage into the maw of their truck, its clanging metallic jaws piercing the slumber of the apartment dwellers in the buildings above them. In the darkened park to her left, the sneakers of the early-morning joggers were already crunching over the dry snow. From Brooklyn Heights to Forest Hills, in Harlem and the South Bronx, along Park Avenue and down to the Village, the lights were blinking on in the darkened façades as the seven million residents of the city she and her brothers meant to destroy prepared to face another day.

The proud, cantankerous, dangerous, dirty, awesome, difficult yet finally magnificent metropolis to which they all belonged was unique, the ultimate expression of man's eternal vocation to gather himself in communities. New York was emphatically not just another city; it was the very essence of cityhood, the example of the best and the worst the urban experience had produced. From the marshes beyond Jamaica to the tenements of Queens, the developments of Staten Island and the ghettos of Harlem, New York was a microcosm of mankind, a Tower of Babel in which all the races, peoples and religions of the world had their representation. The city contained such an assembly of peoples its population statistics were a cliché, yet, like most clichés, accurate. There were more blacks in New York than there were in Lagos, the capital of Nigeria; more Jews than there were in Tel Aviv, Jerusalem and Haifa combined; more Puerto Ricans than in San Juan, more Italians than in Palermo, more Irish than in Cork. Somewhere, in some corner of the five boroughs, there was a touch of almost everything the world had spawned: the smells of Shanghai, the clamor of Naples, the beer of Munich, the bossa-nova beat of Porto Allegro, the patois of Haiti. Tibetans, Khmers, Basques, Galicians, Circassians, Kurds, every oppressed and dissident population on earth chose to voice its miseries here. Its crowded, often decaying neighborhoods housed 3,600 places of worship, at least one for every cult, sect and religion invented by man in his ceaseless search for God.

It was a city of contrasts and contradictions, of promises made and promises unfulfilled. New York was the heart of the capitalist society, a symbol of unsurpassed wealth; yet it was also so broke it could barely meet the interest payments on its debts. New York contained the finest medical facilities in the world; yet, every day, people who couldn't afford them died from lack of care, and the infant mortality rate in the South Bronx was higher than it was in the bustees of Calcutta.

New York possessed a city university whose student body was larger than the population of many cities, yet one person in eight in New York couldn't speak English and her public-school system produced a regular flow of barely literate graduates.

As the pharaohs of Egypt, the Greeks of Antiquity, the Parisians of the Napoleonic era had set the architectural standards of their times, so the New Yorkers of the age of glass and steel had stamped the seal of their architectural genius on the urban skyline of the world. Yet a quarter of all the buildings in the city were substandard, and beyond the glittering magnificence of lower Manhattan, Park and Fifth Avenues loomed the wastelands of the South Bronx, Brownsville and Bedford-Stuyvesant.

No other metropolis in the world offered its inhabitants greater hope of material success or a wider variety of intellectual and cultural rewards. Its museums, the Metropolitan, the Modern, the Whitney, the Guggenheim, housed more Impressionists than the Louvre, more Botticellis than Florence, more Rembrandts than Amsterdam. New York was the United States's bank, its fashion model, designer and photographer; its publisher, advertiser, publicist, playwright and artist. The theaters, concert halls, ballets, jazz clubs of Broadway, off Broadway and off-off Broadway were the incubators in which a nation's taste and thought were nurtured.

The people awakening this Monday morning on the island purchased by Peter Minuit in 1626 for twenty-four dollars could, if they had the resources, buy virtually anything in their city: the ridiculous gold Mickey Mouse watches at Cartier's; the sublime, a Renoir at the Findlay Galleries; diamonds from black-frocked Hasidic Jews on Forty-seventh Street; stolen television sets in fence operations as elaborate as small department stores; chocolate-covered ants from Argentina, polar-bear steaks from Nepal, wildcat gizzards from Canton. Yet, in the midst of all that material affluence, an eighth of the population in New York lived on wel-

167

fare. Half the nation's drug addicts crowded her streets. Her police precincts recorded a theft every three minutes, a holdup every twelve, four rapes and two murders a day. More prostitutes circulated through her streets than in the avenues of Paris.

There were, in fact, three New Yorks: the oases of mid- and lower Manhattan, of corporate headquarters and high-rise splendor; a glittering world of discotheques, penthouses, Carey Cadillacs and rented limousines, candlelit sit-down dinners high in the glass sheaths of the Olympic Towers, 800 Fifth Avenue, the United Nations Plaza. There were the declining working-class suburbs of Queens, the Bronx, those parts of Brooklyn where trees still grew and a dwindling population clung to memories of the Brighton Beach Express, Ebbets Field and Coney Island's Steeplechase. There was the necropolis, the dying ghettos of Bronxville, Hispanic Harlem, Williamsburg, the South Bronx. And, in a sense, there was yet another New York, a transient city of 3.5 million people who daily crowded into the nine square miles south of Central Park. Space salesmen, television executives, lawyers, stockbrokers, doctors, odd-lot dealers, publishers, ad men, commodity brokers, bankers—they were the administrators of America's Rome, controlling an empire from their glass-and-steel towers.

Wall Street's name might be an epithet to the Marxists of the globe; it was still, seventy years after Lenin's voyage to the Finland Station, the unchallenged financial center of the world. On this December morning, men in its board rooms would discuss loans to France's railroads, Vienna's waterworks, Oslo's public transport, the governments of Ecuador, Malaysia and Kenya. Copper mines in Zaire, tin in Bolivia, phosphate in Jordan, sheep in New Zealand, rice in Thailand, hotels in Bali, shipping fleets in Ceylon would all be affected by the decisions made or postponed this Monday morning in two of the world's largest banks, the First National City and the Chase Manhattan.

At Rockefeller Center, CBS's "Black Rock" and the ABC Building, the United States's three television networks ordered programs that set values, influenced behavior, affected social change in the remotest areas of the earth.

Two blocks away were the citadels of the Prophets of Consumerism, the ad men of Madison Avenue. They had forced a revolution on the world, the revolution of rising expectations. Spread to every corner of the earth by the communications they had so effectively

168

mastered, its contagion had brought to millions the material benefits and spiritual dissatisfactions which were the malaise of the American Age.

Collectively, they were, those men and women, the most affluent, the most capable and the most influential people on earth.

They were also the ideal hostages for an austere zealot burning to reorder the world with the very technology and communications of which they were the proud inventors and masters.

The man who had the awesome and frustrating job of administering their city made an effort to scrunch down against the worn upholstery of his black Chrysler as it slipped through the early-Monday-morning rush-hour traffic already clogging the East River Drive. The gesture was understandable; no mayor of New York was anxious to be spotted by his constituents seventy-two hours after a major snowstorm had hit the city.

Abe Stern flailed at the pall of smoke filling his official limousine with a little pawlike hand. The Mayor was a diminutive fireplug of a man, barely five feet, two inches tall. He was completely bald and in three weeks he would be sixty-nine; yet vitality still snapped from his figure as static electricity sometimes snaps from light switches on a cold dry day. He turned to the source of the smoke, his three-hundred-pound detective bodyguard puffing an after-breakfast Dutch Master while he read the *Daily News* sports pages in the front seat.

"Richy," he growled. "I'm going to tell the Commissioner to give you a raise so you can buy yourself a decent cigar for a change."

"Sorry, Mr. Mayor. Smoke bother you?"

Stern grunted and turned his attention to his press aide in the seat beside him. "So how many trucks did we finally put on the streets?"

"Three thousand one hundred and sixty-two," Victor Ferrari replied.

"Son of a bitch!"

In barely two hours, Stern would have to face a snarling City Hall press corps, its members ready to savage him for his administration's failure to clean the city's streets quickly enough after Friday's snowstorm. It was an experience to which he looked for-

169

ward with a delight akin to that of a man going to his dentist for a root-canal treatment.

"Six thousand fucking trucks this city's got and the Sanitation Department can barely get half of them out on the streets!"

Ferrari squirmed. "Well, you know how it is, Mr. Mayor. Most of them trucks is twenty years old."

"Are, Victor, *are*. God," Stern groaned, "I've got a bodyguard who wants to choke me to death, a Sanitation Commissioner who can't get the snow off the streets and a press officer who can't speak English."

The press officer cleared his throat apprehensively. "There's another thing, Mr. Mayor."

"I don't want to know about it."

"Friedkin of the Sanitation Workers wants triple time for yesterday."

Stern stared angrily out at the black surface of the East River, trying to think how he could skewer the union leader at his press conference. For all his protesting to the contrary, he delighted in the rough give-and-take of a press conference. "Feisty" was the adjective most commonly employed to describe Abe Stern, and the word was well chosen. He'd been born in a tenement on the Lower East Side, the son of a Polish-Jewish immigrant father, a pants presser in a tailor shop, and a Russian-born mother who stitched up cheap frocks in a nonunion sweatshop in the Garment District.

It had been a tough neighborhood, predominantly Jewish with satellites of Irish and Italian immigrants along its fringes, a neighborhood where a kid's stature was measured by his skill with his fists. That had been fine with Abe Stern. He loved to fight. He dreamed of becoming a prizefighter like his idol, the light heavyweight champion Battling Levinsky. He could still recall drifting off to sleep in the tenement on the stifling summer nights, the murmur of conversation flowing through the open windows from the adults on the fire escape, while he dreamed of the triumphs his fists would win him one day.

A brutal physical reality had ended that dream of Abe Stern's. At sixteen, he stopped growing. If God had not given Abe the body to fulfill his boyhood dream, however, He had given him something much more precious: a good mind. Abe trained it first at CCNY, then studying the law by night at NYU. By the time he passed his bar exams, he had a new idol, a different kind of fighter from the boxer he had idolized as a boy. It was the cripple in the White House whose patrician accent offered hope to a nation mired in depression. Abe had become a politician.

He'd begun in the 1934 Congressional campaign as a Tammany district captain in Sheepshead Bay, working door to door, getting out the vote, cementing the first of the friendships that would ultimately carry him to City Hall and what was often regarded as the second elective office in the United States. There was no one who understood the complex chemistry of New York City and its governing structures better than the cocky little man in the back of his official limousine. Abe Stern had done it all in his long climb up the ladder. He'd worked the synagogues and the soda fountains, made the Wednesday-night smokers, the maudlin Irish wakes, the bingo games; sat attendant at saints'-day dinners honoring a procession of saints of a variety to bedazzle the most religious of minds. His stomach had been assaulted by enough blintzes, pizzas, chop suey, knishes, pretzels and foot-long red hots to ruin the digestive tracts of a battalion of Gaylord Hausers. His off-key tenor voice had sung the "Hatikvah" in Sheepshead Bay, "Wrap the Green Flag Round Me, Boys" in Queens, opera in Little Italy and Spanish love songs in Hispanic Harlem. Indeed, consciously or unconsciously, many of his electors had given him their vote because they saw in his tough little figure a mirror image of what they thought of as themselves. To them, Abe Stern was New York.

The car phone rang. Ferrari started to reach for it, but the Mayor's little hand shot past his.

"Gimme that. This is the Mayor," he barked. He grunted twice, said, "Thanks, darling," then hung up. As he did, a beatific smile lit up his face.

"What's up?" Ferrari asked.

"Would you believe it? The President wants to see me right away. White House just called the Mansion. They even got a plane waiting for me out at Marine Air Terminal." Abe Stern leaned close to his press aide and his voice fell to a conspiratorial whisper. "It's about the South Bronx redevelopment scheme. I got a hunch they're finally going to come up with our two billion bucks."

Laila Dajani, ravenous after her long night of lovemaking, blotted up the yellow remnants of her soft-boiled egg with a scrap of the slightly burned toast whose acrid aroma filled the kitchen of her Hampshire House suite. She took a final nervous swallow of the Chinese tea she had brewed herself as soon as she returned to the hotel, piled her dishes into the sink and looked around the suite. Everything was ready.

"WINS, ten-ten on your dial. It's seven-thirty and a chilly twenty-three degrees in mid-Manhattan," a voice announced from the transistor on her coffee table. "The weather man has promised us another clear, cold one. And don't forget, there are only twelve more shopping days left until Christmas . . ."

Laila snapped off the radio and picked up her Hermes address book. She ran a crimson fingernail down the entries under "C" until she found the one she was looking for—"Colombe." She stepped to the phone and dialed the number written beside it, methodically adding as she did the number 2 to each of its seven digits.

For a long time the phone rang unanswered. Finally Laila heard the click of a receiver being lifted from its cradle.

"*Seif* . . ." she said in Arabic.

". . . *Al Islam*," came the reply—the Sword of Islam, the code name Muammar al-Qaddafi had assigned to his nuclear program in 1973.

"Begin your operation," she ordered, still using her native tongue. Then she hung up.

The man who had answered Laila's call stepped into the storeroom of a Syrian bakery just off Atlantic Avenue in Brooklyn. Two men waited for him. All three were Palestinians. All three were volunteers. All three had been chosen by Kamal Dajani from among two dozen volunteers in a training camp of the Popular Front for the Liberation of Palestine, outside Aleppo in Syria, over a year before.

None of them had any idea who Laila was or from where she had been calling. They had only been told to wait by the telephone every morning at seven-thirty for the order she had just delivered.

They removed a lead chest from the storeroom's unused oven and methodically broke open the seals that held it shut. Its interior was divided into two halves. In one was a collection of metal rings the size of a nickel. In the other were several rows of greenish-gray pills about as big as Alka-Seltzer tablets. Carefully, they snapped a tablet into each of the rings in the chest.

When they had finished, they opened the first of three identical wooden crates stacked in one corner of the room and lifted out one of its inhabitants. It was a pigeon, not a homing pigeon but an ordinary gray pigeon of the kind raised by kids all over New York in rooftop lofts. They snapped a ring to the bird's leg, put him back in his crate and lifted out the next one.

As soon as the rings had been hooked to all the pigeons, the senior Palestinian embraced the other two warmly. *"Ma salaam,"* he murmured, "till we meet in Tripoli, *insh' Allah."* He picked up one of the three crates and left for a car parked in the street outside. The other two followed at fifteen-minute intervals.

Across the river, on the lower end of Manhattan Island, the Police Commissioner of the City of New York was enjoying a rare moment of silence and introspection. From the window of his office on the fourteenth floor of Police Plaza, Michael Bannion watched the first light steal over the rooftops of the city entrusted to his care. Ahead, looming behind the towers of the Alfred E. Smith housing project, was the familiar silhouette of the Brooklyn Bridge. To his left, far beyond the U.S. Courthouse in Foley Square, Bannion could just make out the tip of the eight-story tenement in which he had been born fifty-eight years before.

Bannion could spend the rest of his life in the filtered purity of offices like this; his nostrils would always be filled with the smells that had permeated that dark tenement's stairwells, the odors of his boyhood, the stench of the cabbage boiling in its kitchens, the reek of urine drifting from the toilets on each landing, the heavy aroma of the wax rubbed into its wooden banisters.

A telephone's ring summoned Bannion back to the massive mahogany table that was the unofficial symbol of his office, the desk used by Teddy Roosevelt in his years as Police Commissioner. It was his private phone. He recognized immediately the voice of Harvey Hudson, the assistant director of the FBI in charge of the Bureau's New York office.

"Michael," he said, "I've got something urgent which concerns us both. I hate to take you out of your office, but for a number of reasons I don't want to get into over the phone, I think we'd better discuss it over here. It will require,'' he added, ''the services of your Detective Division.''

Bannion looked at the crowded appointments list his detective secretary had laid out on his desk.

''You've got to be kidding, Harv?''

''No, Michael,'' Hudson answered. Bannion was struck by a curious catch in his voice. ''It's very, very urgent. It comes from the top, the very top.''

''Since when does your director tell the NYPD what to do?''

''It's not from the director, Michael. It's from the President.''

On the floor below the Commissioner's office, the Chief of Detectives, Al Feldman, was staring at a young man advancing toward his office door between the gray metal desks of the junior detectives' bullpen. He was a ''contract,'' a patrolman forced on his division because he'd had an uncle who'd been a deputy chief inspector in the Seventh Division. Just as Feldman had predicted he would, he'd fucked up.

Feldman waved a cold cigar at the youth, directing him toward the worn piece of carpet thrown over the linoleum flooring in front of his desk.

''You follow baseball, O'Malley?''

The question perplexed the red-faced young man. He was expecting a dressing-down, not a chat about sports. ''Yeah, sure, Chief. You know, I watch it on TV in the summer. Take the wife out to Shea once in a while, see the Mets.''

''So what happens, a guy's got two strikes on him, he swings and he misses?''

''Well, uh, he's out, Chief.''

''Right.'' Feldman snarled. He plucked a silver patrolman's shield from his desk drawer and flung it across the desk. ''And so are you. Tomorrow you're back in uniform.''

His gesture reflected the little-known fact that New York detectives served at the pleasure of their chief and could be instantly returned to the blue uniforms from which their gold detective's shield had freed them. Feldman had not even had time to savor the delight his action had given him when his phone rang.

"The PC wants you," the Commissioner's secretary announced, "forthwith."

There must have been half a million apartments in New York, more even, in which the almost identical scene was taking place this December morning. The TV was on, its volume, as always, turned up too high. Tommy Knowland, thirteen, moved an occasional spoonful of Rice Krispies and sliced bananas to his mouth with no apparent assistance from eyes that remained totally concentrated on *Good Morning America* blaring from the set before him.

Grace Knowland sipped her coffee on the chair beside his, studying her son with tender fascination. Even there at the breakfast table, without a trace of makeup, with thus far no effort at beauty beyond a dash of cold water on her face to rouse her and a few swift strokes of her hairbrush, she looked marvelous. Her eyes were clear, her face alive and engaging, the breasts that had excited more than a few admiring glances at Forlini's the evening before thrusting out against the lapels of the man's silk bathrobe she wore over her negligee.

"Aw, come off it!" Tommy's spoon fell to his plate with a clank. "Jeez, Mom, how can Howard Cosell say something like that?"

Grace laughed softly. "I'm sure I don't know. But what I do know is I can't send him a bill for a broken plate."

Her son grimaced and turned his attention back to the television set.

"Tommy, did you ever . . ." Grace sipped her coffee thoughtfully. "I mean after your father and I divorced, were you sad you didn't have any brothers or sisters?"

It seemed for an instant as though her question had made no impact on her son. Finally, when a female face appeared on the screen, he turned to his mother. "Naw, Mom, not really. Yeck," he squawked, "Rona Barrett's next. Turn it off, Mom."

"Gotta run." He sprang from the table, blotted his mouth with a napkin, grabbed for a pile of books and gave his mother's cheek a quick, wet stab with his lips. "Hey, don't forget I got my match at the armory tonight. You coming?"

"Of course, darling."

The door slammed. Grace sat pensively listening to the sound of her son's footsteps running down the hall. Running out of my life, too, she thought. How much time is left? Two, three years. Then he'll be gone. Off to his own world, his own life. Instinctively, her hand dropped to her negligee. Did she detect a first faint swelling there? Of course not. That was ridiculous, she knew. There couldn't possibly be a concrete manifestation yet of the life she carried inside her. She took a cigarette, struck a match, then stopped with the flame inches from its destination. If she was going to go through with it, she should stop smoking, shouldn't she? That's what all the doctors said. With a slow, uncertain movement, she shook out the match's flame.

Red-eyed from lack of sleep, Jack Eastman wrestled with the first assignment the President had given him for the day: how to keep the crisis enveloping the White House a secret. No head of state in the world lived as public an existence as the President of the United States. Brezhnev could spend two weeks in the hospital and not a word would appear anywhere. The President of France could drive to a regular appointment with a girl friend and get caught only because he was maladroit enough to bang into another car on the Champs-Élysées at four in the morning. Everywhere the American President went, however, he was dogged by his corps of journalists. When they were not being briefed, they lounged around the White House press room, their sensitive antennas always alert for the one off-key chord which would indicate that something unusual was going on.

"First thing," Eastman told the key aides he had assembled around his desk, "I don't want any reporters sniffing around the West Wing. If anyone in here's scheduled to see a reporter, tell them to take him down to the mess for coffee."

He picked up the President's schedule for the day from his desk. It was, as always, divided into two parts, the public program published every morning in *The Washington Post* and his private schedule circulated only to the White House staff. The public schedule for Monday, 14 December, listed four events.

9:00 A.M.   National Security Briefing
10:00 A.M.   Budget Meeting

11:00 A.M.   Remarks commemorating the anniversary of the adoption of the Universal Declaration of Human Rights
5:25 P.M.   Depart for lighting National Christmas Tree, Ellipse

The first item was no problem. Eastman thought for a moment about the second, the budget meeting.

"Let's get Charlie Schultz to sit in for the President," he suggested. Schultz was the chairman of the Council of Economic Advisers. "Tell him the President wants his opinion on the effect the budget cuts will have on the economy."

"Should we tell him what's going on?" someone asked.

"Hell, no. Why should he know about it?" Eastman turned to the press secretary. He had decided he would have to be informed of the crisis. "What about the Declaration and the Christmas-tree lighting?" Both were public events; both would have to be covered by the White House press corps. "Can we scrub them?"

"We'll have a hell of a lot of explaining to do if we do. Those guys out there will be all over us."

"Suppose we give him a cold?"

"Then they'll want to talk to Dr. McIntyre. 'Is he taking medication? What's his temperature?' Jack, you just can't fool around with the President's public appearances without an airtight cover story. And airtight cover stories aren't easily come by in this town."

"The Human Rights business I can see," Eastman answered. "If the shit hits the fan while he's in the Oval Office we can probably get him out of there in a hurry without anybody catching on. But, Jesus Christ, if something happens while he's down there lighting that Christmas tree, we'll never be able to rush him out of there without the whole world knowing something's going on."

"Still, if you want to keep this a secret you're going to have to take a chance and let him go." The press secretary stretched his long legs toward Eastman's desk. "The best way to keep this a secret is to keep up the front. That's how JFK's people played the Missile Crisis: people went out to dinners, stuff like that, to maintain a façade. We'll have to do the same thing."

"How are we going to get people in and out of here all day without the press finding out something's going on?" Eastman asked.

"Again," his colleague replied, "I'd say look at what the Ken-

177

nedy people did. They told people to use their own cars. Double up so that they didn't have a parade of limousines coming in. They even had Rusk and McNamara come in sitting on the floor of their cars.''

The Presidential Assistant started. Outside, on the snow-covered drive, he had just seen a familiar figure. Every President had his technique for keeping himself alert, for maintaining the flow of adrenalin in a crisis, and his employer was indulging in his. In a navy-blue track suit, his pale hair flopping about his head with each movement, the President of the United States was jogging around the grounds of the White House.

The headquarters of the SDECE, France's intelligence service, are on the Boulevard Mortier behind Père Lachaise Cemetery in Paris's Twentieth Arrondissement, a neighborhood so drab that even on the brightest of spring days it somehow seems as depressingly gray as a Utrillo winter scene. From the street, the building that houses the SDECE looks like an old army caserne, which it in fact is, its paint peeling away like dead skin flaking off a sunburned limb.

The decreptitude ends at the front door. Inside the headquarters, gleaming banks of computer consoles place all the wizardry of the electronic age at the disposition of a service traditionally known more for the Gallic panache of its operatives than for their technical skills. Years of Congressional probes and public outcries might have sanitized the SDECE's friendly rivals at the CIA; General Bertrand's service could still recruit the mercenary forces required to overthrow the odd African dictator, engage the services of Corsican gunmen whose normal pursuits involved the sale of a little white powder, or set up its Kuala Lumpur operative in a whorehouse. Such places were, after all, traditional venues for the exchange of information, and the French were far too appreciative of the foibles of the flesh to abandon them entirely in favor of devices as sterile as satellite photos.

The SDECE director, General Henri Bertrand, was seated at his desk deeply absorbed in a study of Vietnamese penetration into the Golden Triangle opium trade in Burma when his deputy came in with a thick computer printout. It contained everything the SDECE had on the sale to Libya of the reactor from which the Americans suspected Qaddafi had obtained plutonium.

178

Bertrand was familiar with much of the material. Security in nuclear matters had been a very delicate point in the French capital since the day in April 1979 when an Israeli hit team had blown apart the inner core of an experimental reactor destined for Iraq only weeks before it was due to be delivered to Baghdad. He glanced at it quickly and then told his deputy, "Ask Cornedeau to join me, would you?"

Cornedeau was the agency's nuclear scientist, a bald, intense young man who had graduated from the Polytechnique, France's great center of scientific learning, a decade before.

"Sit down, Patrick," Bertrand ordered. Swiftly, he reviewed for him what had happened.

Patrick Cornedeau smiled and took an unlit pipe from his pocket. He was trying to give up cigarettes and it was the security blanket he employed whenever he felt the urge for nicotine rising in him.

"Well, if Qaddafi is really after plutonium, he couldn't have picked a tougher way to get it."

"Perhaps, *cher ami,* it was the only one available to him."

Bertrand's scientist shrugged his shoulders. He had gamed dozens of ways by which a dictator like Qaddafi could get the bomb: hijack a plutonium shipment, do what the Indians did—buy a Canadian heavy-water reactor that runs on natural uranium and duplicate it right down to the thumbtacks. But this was different. Cheating with a standard light-water reactor was the toughest challenge of all.

Cornedeau got up and walked over to the blackboard hanging on one wall of Bertrand's office. For a minute he stood in front of it, idly tossing a piece of chalk in his hand, marshaling his thoughts like a schoolmaster about to begin a lecture.

"*Mon général,*" he said, "if you're going to cheat on a nuclear reactor, any reactor, you cheat with the fuel. When the fuel burns, or fissions, it gives off heat, boils water to make steam to run turbines to make electricity. It also sends a stream of stray neutrons flying around. Some of them"—he punched the blackboard —"go banging into the unburned fuel, lowly enriched uranium in this case, and start a reaction in there which converts a part of that into plutonium.

"In this reactor," he continued, making a sketch on the blackboard, "the fuel is in a pressurized core inside the shell that looks like this. You change it only once a year. It comes in enormous, heavy bundles of fuel rods. To get it out, you have to shut down your reactor. Then you need two weeks' time, a lot of heavy equipment and plenty of people. Don't forget we have twenty technicians assigned to it. There is absolutely no way the Libyans could have gotten the fuel out of there, spirited it away some dark night, without some of them noticing it.''

Bertrand drew on his Gauloise. "And what happens to that fuel when it comes out?''

"First of all, it's so hot, radioactively speaking, it would turn you into a walking cancer cell if you got close to it. The assemblies are packed in lead shells and taken to a storage pond where they're left to cool off.''

"And so the rods just sit there in the pond. What prevents Qaddafi from taking them out and getting the plutonium?''

"The International Atomic Energy Agency in Vienna has inspectors who are responsible for seeing that people don't cheat on these things. They run at least two inspections a year down there. And in between they have sealed cameras run on sealed lines which constantly monitor the pond. There are usually at least two of them there, timed to take wide-angle shots of the pond every fifteen minutes or so.''

"And that, presumably, doesn't leave him enough time to remove the rods?''

"Goodness, no. You've got to put them into huge, shielded lead containers if you don't want to be irradiated yourself. They have to be handled by heavy cranes. You need at least an hour for the operation. Two is more likely.''

"Could the inspectors alter the film?''

"No. They don't even develop them. That's done in Vienna. Besides, they also lower gamma-ray analyzers into the pond each time they make an inspection, to be sure the rods are radioactive. That way they can be sure a switch hasn't been made.''

Bertrand leaned back, his head pressed against the headrest of his chair, his half-closed eyes focused on one corner of the ceiling. "You make a very persuasive case against the Libyans being capable of obtaining plutonium from this thing.''

"I think it's very, very unlikely, Chief.''

"Unless they had complicity at some stage in their operations.''

"But where, how?''

"Personally, I have always managed to contain my enthusiasm for the workings of the United Nations.''

Cornedeau crossed the room and slumped into his chair, his legs sprawled uncomfortably before him. His superior was an old-school Gaullist and everyone in the house knew he shared the former President's distaste for a body de Gaulle had once referred to as "Le Machin"—the thingumajig.

"Sure, Chief," he sighed. "The agency has its limitations. But the real problem isn't them. It's that no one really wants effective controls. The companies that sell the reactors, like Westinghouse and our friends over at Framatome, give a lot of public lip service to the idea, but privately they oppose controls like poison. No Third World government wants those inspectors running around their country. And we haven't been very anxious to tighten controls ourselves, despite everything we say. There's too much at stake in our reactor sales."

"Well, my boy," the General murmured through the veil of cigarette smoke now cloaking him like a shroud, "a sound balance of payments is an imperative of state with which it's difficult to argue these days. I think you should get the inspection reports from Vienna immediately. Also ask our representative there whether he has any coffee-house gossip about inspectors being bought, bribed. Or too enamored of the bar girls or whatever it is they have over there now." There was a sudden brightening in the General's eyes as he recalled his last visit to the Austrian capital in 1971. "Handsome creatures, those Viennese. One could hardly blame the odd Japanese for going off the deep end for one of them." He leaned forward. "What about our own people down in Libya? What do we have on them?"

"We've got their security clearances over at the DST. And, of course, the DST has recorded all their telephone conversations coming into this country."

"Who was our senior representative down there?"

"A Monsieur de Serre," Cornedeau replied. "He's been back for a couple of months waiting for his next posting."

Bertrand looked at the Hermes clock in a black onyx frame on his desk. It was almost lunchtime. "Do we have his current whereabouts?"

"I believe so. He's here in Paris."

"Good. Get his address for me. While you're getting all that material from our friends at the DST, I'll see if I can't have a cup of coffee and a chat with Monsieur de Serre."

The sight of the three grave and unfamiliar men surrounding Harvey Hudson, the director of the New York office of the FBI, told Michael Bannion that something very, very serious was going on in his city. Just how serious dawned on the Police Commissioner when he heard the words "Los Alamos Scientific Laboratories" appended to his introduction to the suntanned man with an ornament around his neck sitting at Hudson's left.

Bannion looked at Hudson. The Commissioner had dark-blue eyes, "the color of Galway Bay on a June morning," his grandmother had once loved to tell him. They were clouded with fear and concern, with a question he did not have to articulate.

"Yes, Michael, it's happened."

Bannion sank into his place at the conference table.

"How long have you had it?"

"Since last night."

Normally, that answer would have provoked a burst of Celtic fury from Bannion. It was typical of the Bureau. Even in a matter that concerned the life and death of thousands of the people in his city, the FBI hadn't brought his force into their confidence immediately. This time, he reined in his fury and listened with growing horror as Hudson reviewed the threat and what had been done about it.

"We've got until three o'clock tomorrow afternoon to find that device," Hudson concluded. "And we've got to do it without anyone finding out that we're looking for something. We're under the strictest orders from the White House to keep this secret."

Bannion glanced at his watch. It was three minutes past eight. Just a month ago, he recalled, he and Hudson had discussed the possibility of nuclear terrorism together. "People have been shouting 'the nuclear terrorists are coming' for years," he had cynically remarked to his FBI colleague. "How, I want to know—galloping down the Hudson Valley like Lochinvar?" Now they had arrived and he felt totally, helplessly inadequate to deal with them.

"Don't your people out at Los Alamos have some technological resources we can employ to track it down?" Bannion asked Bill Booth. "These things have to give off some kind of radiation, don't they?"

It was indicative of the secrecy that shrouded NEST's operations that the Police Commissioner of New York didn't know that the NEST teams existed or anything about the way they operated.

Quickly, as succinctly as he could, Booth described to the Commissioner and the rest of the conference room how his teams would work.

"Aren't people going to spot your rented trucks?" the Commissioner asked.

"It's very unlikely. The only giveaway is a small device like a radar pod we attach to the undercarriage. You'd have to really look for it." Booth took a long drag on his cigarette. "The whole concept behind the operation is to be very discreet, unobtrusive. We don't want the terrorist sitting on his bomb up in the attic to know we're out there looking for him."

"How about helicopters?"

Booth glanced at his watch. "Our own choppers should be getting into the air now. We've borrowed three more from New York Airways and we're equipping them with detection devices. They'll be ready in an hour or so. I decided to start them on the waterfront. The choppers are very effective down there. They can run over the wharves very quickly and they can read through those thin warehouse roofs without much trouble." He grimaced. "Although if it's in a ship, we'd have to do a foot search to pick it up. The deck layers would shield out the rays we're looking for."

Those words brought all the frustrations, the hopelessness of his task welling up in Booth. He stubbed out his cigarette with an angry, impatient gesture. "Look, Commissioner, don't expect any miracles from us, because there aren't going to be any. We've got the best technology there is and it's completely inadequate."

The scientist saw the startled bulge of the Commissioner's blue eyes, the nervous tic of his Adam's apple. "All the tactical advantages are with our adversaries. My trucks can only read up to four stories. The choppers can only read down two at best. Everything in between's a blank. If whoever put this bomb there wanted to shield it, all they would have to do is throw a water bed over it and we couldn't pick it up three feet away." Booth's nervous hands went up to the Navajo medallion Bannion had noted on his neck.

The scientist made no effort to conceal his anguish, his deep sense of implicit guilt at being forced to admit to the men around him that he was incapable of finding in the streets of their city one of the terrible weapons he had spent a lifetime designing.

"Without intelligence, gentlemen, to narrow down the search

area there's no way in the world we can find that bomb in the time we've been given.''

Two stories below the director's conference room, a telephone rang in one of the offices assigned to the FBI's intelligence unit. The agent picked it up.

"Hey, man, this is Rico."

The agent sat up, suddenly alert. He activated the device that would record his incoming call.

"Watcha got for me, Rico?"

"Not much, man. I spent the whole night looking, but the only thing I got is this brother, he be asked to get some medicine for an Arab lady."

"Drugs or medicine, Rico?"

"No, man, this is straight. Something for her stomach. She didn't want to get no prescription, didn't want to have to mess with no fuckin' doctor."

"What'd she look like?"

"The brother, he don't know. He just take it to her hotel."

"Where was that, Rico?"

"The Hampshire House."

Upstairs, Al Feldman, the Chief of Detectives, rolled his cold cigar in his mouth and pondered Bill Booth's despairing words. Figures, he thought. Just like those scientific bastards. They always expect someone else to clean up their shit after them.

"So what exactly are we looking for?" he asked.

Booth circulated a sketch and description of the device prepared at Los Alamos from Qaddafi's blueprint.

"Do we know approximately when this came into the country?" Bannion inquired.

"No, we don't," Hudson, the New York FBI chief, replied. "But the assumption is it was recently. The CIA figures it would have been shipped from one of six places: Libya, Lebanon, Iraq, Syria, Iran or Aden. They may have smuggled it across the border from Canada. That doesn't take much doing. Or they may have run it through a normal port of entry disguised as something else."

Down the table, Hudson's superior, Quentin Dewing, the assis-

184

tant director for investigation for the Bureau, flown up from Washington during the night to take overall command of the search, cleared his throat. He had old-fashioned clear-plastic-rimmed glasses, gray hair slicked to his head with lashes of Brylcreem, a dark-blue suit, and a white handkerchief squared to a precise half an inch rising from its pocket. An insurance executive, Feldman had thought contemptuously when he had been introduced.

"What this means is we're going to have to go through every waybill and manifest for every piece of cargo that's come in from one of those countries in the last few months. We'll start with the latest shipments and work our way back."

"By three o'clock tomorrow?" asked the stunned Police Commissioner.

"By three o'clock today!"

Feldman ignored their exchange, scrutinizing instead the material Booth had circulated around the room. "Tell me something," he asked the scientist, "could this be broken into pieces, smuggled in and reassembled here?"

"Technologically, I'd say that's almost impossible."

"Well, it's nice we got some good news today." Feldman pointed his cigar at the drawing. "That fifteen-hundred-pound weight is going to eliminate a lot of shipments. It's also going to rule out high floors in buildings without elevators." He laid the material back on the table. "How about the people who put it there? Do we have any leads on them at all?"

"For the moment we have nothing precise." Hudson pointed to a flaxen-haired agent in his midthirties seated across from Feldman. "Farrell here is the Bureau's Palestinian expert. He came up from D.C. last night. Frank, give us a quick rundown on what we do have."

Ranged neatly on the table before the agent were computer summaries of all the Bureau's ongoing Middle East investigations. They included items as diverse as a suspected traffic in prostitutes between Miami and the Persian Gulf, an illegal shipment of four thousand M-16 automatic rifles to the Christian Lebanese Phalange, the efforts of the Iranian revolutionary regime to infiltrate assassination squads into the United States to carry out their revolutionary justice on United States soil, and the document Farrell picked up in response to Hudson's order.

"We have files on twenty-one Americans who went through

185

Qaddafi's terrorist training camps. All of them were Arab born. Nineteen Palestinians. Seventeen males, four females.''

''Have you jumped them? What did you turn up?''

The young agent coughed nervously in answer to Feldman's query. ''Most of them went over there between 1975 and 1977. We put them under surveillance when they came back, but they never did a damn thing wrong. We couldn't even catch them lifting a candy bar from the five-and-ten-cent store. So we ran out of court orders for the surveillance because of lack of probable cause.''

''So you stopped watching them?''

The FBI man nodded.

''My God!'' Feldman's already dumpy figure slumped deeper into his chair. ''You mean to tell me Qaddafi has the perfect terrorist sleeper operation set up in this country and the FBI hasn't got a single one of those people under surveillance?''

''That's the law, Mr. Feldman. We've been after them since last night and managed to locate four of them thus far.''

''That isn't a law! It's a fucking covenant for a suicide pact.''

Michael Bannion turned to his angry Chief of Detectives, anxious to calm him and at the same time intrigued by what had just been said. ''You know, Al, you'd have to be interested by the fact that the Arab community in New York is within walking distance of the Brooklyn docks. Do we have anything on PLO activity over there?''

''Not a helluva lot,'' Feldman replied. ''There are a couple of bodegas, little family grocery stores, we suspect are fronting a gun traffic that may have PLO ties. When Arafat came to the UN, his bodyguards gave our people the slip a few times and wound up over there. Now, you might think they went over for a cup of coffee. Or you might choose to think they went to set up some sleepers.'' Feldman shrugged. ''Take your choice.''

''Do your people have any penetration into the PLO?''

Bannion turned to the speaker, Clifford Salisbury, an assistant director of the CIA, specializing in Palestinian affairs. ''The only penetration activity we're allowed these days is against organized crime. Besides,'' Bannion added acidly, ''I can't afford two patrolmen in my police cars. I'm certainly not going to waste money trying to penetrate the PLO.''

What the Police Commissioner did not bother to add was that there were only four Arabic-speaking officers among the 24,000 men and women on his force, and none of them was assigned to cover Palestinian activities. The fact was, Brooklyn's Arabic community had always been notably law-abiding. There had been, since the early sixties, a sharp rise in immigration, many of the newcomers Palestinian; still, there had been only one recorded incident of attempted PLO terrorism in the New York area.

Dewing, the deputy director of the FBI, rapped his knuckles on the conference table. "Gentlemen, we've got to get this search organized and under way as fast as we can. Can we agree, in view of the words 'New York Island' in Qaddafi's threat message, to concentrate NEST's efforts on Manhattan?"

There was a mumble of agreement.

"Booth will run his operation independently for secrecy's sake. We'll support him with drivers to protect his men."

The scientists had chosen to work with the tight-lipped agents of the Bureau rather than local police officers since they had begun operations.

"Where do I start?" Booth wanted to know. "The Battery or the Bronx?"

"I'd suggest the Battery," Bannion said. "You're closer to the waterfront down there. They would have had less distance to carry that thing. Besides, everybody hates Wall Street."

"Right," the deputy director rejoined. "Second: manpower. We're running an 'All Hands' on this, bringing in five thousand agents. I've ordered Treasury, Customs, Narcotics and the Task Force on West Fifty-seventh to make their personnel available. Commissioner, can we have the services of your Detective Division?"

"You've got them."

"If Washington wants us to be discreet with this, what are we going to use for communications?" Feldman asked. "Too much traffic on our frequencies will make the guys in the press room at headquarters sit up. The family fights, the horseshit jobs'll pass right over their heads. But something like this they'll pick up right away. The volume would be a tipoff."

"We'll use our gold band," Dewing said. The FBI employed ten frequencies, five locally in their blue band, five nationally in what was referred to as their gold band. "And whenever possible the telephone."

"Al," Hudson turned to the Chief of Detectives, "what's the best way to set this up?"

"I'd recommend a one on one," the Chief replied. "One fed

with one of my men. That way you can pair up your feds who don't know the city with my guys who do.

"We'll break them down into task forces," he continued. "Assign one the docks, a second the airports. We'll have a third task force to systematically comb all the usual places, hotels, car-rental agencies." Feldman bit down on his cold cigar. "Arabs coming into this town, they go to Queens and it'll be 'Oh-oh, there goes the neighborhood,' right? But like the PC says, over there in Arab town Brooklyn they'd blend in. We ought to start our third task force there. Search the place inside out. See if we can find anything out of synch."

"Yeah, I agree," Hudson said.

Feldman was leaning back, thinking. "We've got to narrow this thing down if we're ever going to get anywhere. Get a tighter focus on the kind of people we're looking for. What the hell kind of people are they, anyway?"

Hudson turned a commanding eye to the Bureau's Palestinian expert.

"Well, as a general rule," Farrell noted, "they tend to live pretty well on assignments. They have plenty of money. They go middle class, which most of them are anyway. I mean, they usually don't go hiding out in slums or rabbit warrens. They learned a long time ago the best way to blend into the stream is to posit yourself just above the middle-class level. The other thing, they tend to stay pretty close to their own kind. Don't seem to trust the other ethnics very much."

The Chief of Detectives digested his words. "Something else too, I'd say. If you wanted to pull off a caper like this, you'd put it in the hands of someone who knew his way around, been here before. Otherwise, your people'd leave a string of clues behind them. Blow the operation right away."

"Mr. Feldman has a very good point." It was Salisbury, the CIA representative. "We can also assume, I think, that the kind of people who would do this would be sophisticated, cold-blooded and smart enough to realize that their chances of success lay in holding it very, very tight. I'm convinced we're looking for a small, coherent group of intelligent, highly motivated people.

"And," he continued, "I'm also convinced the kind of person Qaddafi would assign an operation like this to would have already left his—or her—traces somewhere in one of the world's intelligence services. We're in touch with every intelligence agency in the world that has files on Palestinian terrorists. They're sending us descriptions and photographs of everyone in their files. I suggest that we separate out those who have spent time in this country and are intelligent, sophisticated and educated, and concentrate on them."

"How many do you figure that would be?" Feldman demanded.

Salisbury made a few silent calculations. "There are about four hundred known and identified Palestinian terrorists at large. My guess is we'll find fifty to seventy-five of them who meet our specs."

The detective shook his head in dismay. "That's too many. Too fucking many. Job like this, you gotta get it down to two or three to have a chance. If we're going to save this city, my friend, we've got to have one or two faces, not a portrait gallery."

The first of the two agents flashed his gold shield at the desk clerk so discreetly that the young man didn't realize who his visitors were until he heard the words "FBI." Then, like most people confronted with a federal law-enforcement officer, he came quickly to attention.

"May we see your register, please?"

The clerk dutifully submitted the black bound guest register of the Hampshire House to the agents' scrutiny. The index finger of the senior man ran down the pages, then stopped at the address Hamra Street, Beirut, Lebanon, after the name Linda Nahar. Suite 3202, he noted, and glanced up at the key bank. The key was missing.

"Is Miss Nahar in 3202 in?"

"Oh," replied the clerk, "you just missed her. She checked out forty minutes ago. She said she'd be back, though. In a week."

"I see. Did she tell you where she was going?"

"The airport. She was flying out to LA on the earlybird flight."

"Did she leave you a forwarding address?"

"No."

"Do you suppose you could tell us something about Miss Nahar?"

Ten minutes later, the two agents were back in their car, smoking. The clerk had been singularly unhelpful.

"What do you think, Frank?"

"I think it's probably a waste of time. Some woman who's afraid of doctors."

"So do I. Except she did decide to leave this morning, didn't she?"

"Why don't we get your informer and work over his contact?"

"That might be a little heavy. Rico deals with some bad people." The agent looked at his watch. "Let's check the flight lists and find out what plane she took. We'll have somebody do a check on her when she gets out there."

"There's one major point we've all overlooked." Authority flowed from Michael Bannion's voice like sound waves from a pitching fork, and everyone in the room turned to him. "Are you going to apply the White House's injunction to secrecy to the men running the investigation, Harv?"

"No, certainly not. How are we going to get them to pull out all the stops if we don't tell them the truth?"

"Good God!" Bannion shook his head in dismay. "Tell my men there's a hydrogen bomb hidden on this island, that it's going to go off in a few hours and wipe the city off the face of the earth? They're human. They'll panic. The first thing they'll say to themselves is, 'I gotta get the kids out of here. I gotta call the old lady. Tell her to get the kids outa school and head for her mother's up in Troy.' "

"You seem to have singularly little confidence in your men, Commissioner."

Bannion's blue eyes flashed as he looked down the table to the austere presence of Quentin Dewing, the assistant director of the FBI.

"My men, in whom I have the greatest confidence, Mr. Dewing, don't come from Montana, South Dakota and Oregon like yours do. They come from Brooklyn, the Bronx, Queens. They've got their wives, their kids, their mothers, their uncles, their aunts, their pals, their girl friends, their dogs, their cats, their canaries trapped in this goddamned city. They're men, not supermen. You'd better find a cover story to give them. And let me tell you something else, Mr. Dewing, it had better be a goddamn good cover story, because if it isn't, there's going to be a panic on this island the likes of which neither you nor I nor anybody else has ever seen."

Grace Knowland turned up her coat collar to deflect the wind that hit her as soon as she emerged from the BMT's Chambers Street subway station. It was almost 8:45. Hurrying through City Hall Park, Grace almost fell on the ill-cleaned, half-sanded path. The Mayor, she thought tartly, can't even keep his own sidewalk shoveled.

She smiled at the policeman manning the gate leading to the Mayor's offices and stepped into the noisy bustle of the press room. Still clutching her coat about her, she pulled her mail from her pigeonhole, tossed a quarter into the paper cup by the coffee machine and poured herself a steaming cup of black coffee.

A stir at the doorway interrupted her. Vic Ferrari, a blue cornflower twisted into the lapel of his gray flannel suit, stepped into the room. "Ladies and gentlemen, I have a brief announcement. His Honor is very sorry, but he won't be able to keep his appointment with you this morning."

Ferrari, unfazed, let the storm of jeers and catcalls which followed his words abate. Tolerating the ill-humor of the New York press was only one of the minor trials involved in being the press secretary of the Mayor of New York.

"The Mayor was invited to Washington earlier this morning by the President to discuss certain budgetary questions of concern to them both."

The room erupted. New York's chronic financial problems had been a running story for years, and the questions flew at Ferrari.

"Victor," Grace asked, "when do you expect the Mayor back?"

"Later on in the day. I'll keep you posted."

"By shuttle, as usual?"

"I suppose so."

"Hey, Vic," a television reporter yelled from the rear of the circle of newsmen around Ferrari, "would this have anything to do with the South Bronx?"

Just the faintest glimmer of acknowledgment crossed Ferrari's face, a swift illumination akin to the look on a mediocre poker player's face when he's filled an inside straight. One journalist in the room caught it—and Grace Knowland was probably the only

191

person there who didn't play poker. "I said I didn't want to speculate on the subject of their meeting," Ferrari insisted.

As unobtrusively as she could, Grace slipped to her phone and dialed the *Times* city desk. "Bill," she whispered to her editor, "something's up on the South Bronx. Stern's gone to Washington. I want to shuttle down and try to ride back with him." Her editor agreed immediately. Before leaving, she decided to make a second call, this one to Angelo. His phone seemed to ring interminably.

Finally an unfamiliar voice replied. "He's not here," he said. "They're all off at a meeting someplace."

Funny, Grace thought, hanging up the phone, he told her he was going to catch up on his paperwork this morning.

As she edged, almost surreptitiously, toward the door, she heard a snarl rising from the circle in which the others still clustered around the press secretary. "All this is lovely, Vic," a voice asked, "but we happen to have a real problem on our hands here. Just when does this city plan to finish getting the fucking snow out of Queens?"

The man the City Hall press corps was so anxious to question was at that moment entering the private office of the President of the United States.

"Mr. President, you're looking terrific. Wonderful. Marvelous." Abe Stern's adjectives succeeded each other in little barks, like a string of exploding Chinese firecrackers. He seemed to bounce across the room to the man at the desk as though he was being propelled by springs concealed in the soles of his shoes. "Job must agree with you. You've never looked so good."

The President, who was wan and haggard from lack of sleep, waved Abe Stern to an apricot sofa and waited while a steward poured coffee for them both. In the background, barely audible, were the strains of Vivaldi's *Four Seasons*. The President preferred the intimacy of this room to the imposing formality of the Oval Office next door with all its symbols and majestic trappings, constant reminders of the authority and burdens of the Presidency of the United States. He'd furnished it with the comfortable memorabilia of his past: an old musket, his Navy commission, an oil portrait of his wife and children. Before his inkstand he had set the famous sign that had once graced Harry Truman's desk. Its words seemed grimly appropriate this morning: "The Buck stops here."

"So," the beaming Stern declared as the steward left the room, "we're finally going to get together on the funding of the South Bronx, are we?"

The President set his coffee cup onto its saucer with a rattle. "I'm sorry, Abe, I had to practice a little deception to get you down here this morning. That's not why I asked you here."

The Mayor's eyebrows twitched into peaks of incomprehension.

"We have a terrible crisis on our hands, Abe, and it involves New York City."

Stern emitted a sound that was half a sigh, half a growl. "Well, it can't be the end of the world, Mr. President. Crises come, crises go, New York City's lived with them all."

There was a sudden watery glimmer in the President's eyes as he looked at the little man before him. "You're wrong, Abe. This is one crisis New York City can't live with."

Harvey Hudson, the director of the FBI's New York office, clambered up the steps of the auditorium, followed by the Police Commissioner and his Chief of Detectives. While the New Yorkers settled into chairs between the American flag and the blue-and-gold banner of the Bureau, Hudson moved to the speaker's lectern. It was not yet nine o'clock in the morning of Monday, December 14. Hudson looked at the gathering for a second, took a slow breath and leaned toward the microphone.

"Gentlemen, we have a crisis on our hands."

His words produced a nervous rustle, then dead silence. "A group of Palestinian terrorists have hidden a barrel of chlorine gas somewhere in New York, almost certainly here on Manhattan Island." Behind Hudson, Bannion studied the faces of his detectives, watching for their reaction to the FBI director's words.

"I'm sure I don't have to remind you of the toxic qualities of chlorine gas. You probably all remember what happened up in Canada not so long ago when they had that chlorine gas spill after a train accident and had to move a quarter of a million people. It's deadly, dangerous stuff.

"The fact that it's here and we're looking for it must be kept a total secret. We're explaining it to you because you're all intelligent, responsible police officers, but if it ever got out to the public, the panic the news might cause could be devastating."

Bannion's experienced eyes read the worry and concern on his detectives' faces. Christ, he thought, what would have happened if we'd told them the truth?

Hudson moved through the remaining details of the cover story: a Palestinian commando was somewhere in the area with orders to detonate the barrel of gas if the Israelis didn't release ten of their fellow terrorists being held in Israeli jails. "The lives of an awful lot of people are going to depend on our getting to that barrel before they can blow it up. This is what it looks like."

A blowup of Los Alamos' sketch of Qaddafi's bomb, its nuclear details carefully masked, appeared on the screen behind Hudson. "Some of you will be assigned to try to run down the perpetrators, others will do an area-by-area combing operation; the rest of you will scour the piers and docks to see if we can pick up some trace of how it came in. We'll do a one on one, NYPD with fed, Bomb Squad with Bomb Squad, major case with major case, kidnap with kidnap, and so on down the line."

"Oh, for Christ's sake," a voice called out from the rear of the auditorium, "why doesn't someone just tell the Israelis to give the Arabs their goddamn prisoners back and get off our backs?"

Bannion stirred at the sound of the New York accent ringing through the anonymous speaker's voice. He had expected that reaction. He gestured to Hudson, then strode to the lectern and took the microphone from the FBI director's hands. "That's the Israelis' problem, not yours." The dead air in the auditorium seemed to quiver under the impact of his angry words. "Your job is to find that goddamn barrel." The Police Commissioner paused, trying to infuse his voice with just the right blend of urgency and anger. "And find it in one God-awful hurry."

The Secret Service agent waiting outside the main entrance of the Treasury Building in Washington, D.C., moved up to the two men as soon as they got out of their black government Ford. He verified with a discreet glance their papers identifying them as senior officials of the Department of Defense, then gestured to them to follow him into the busy Treasury lobby. He led them along its marble hall to a heavy door marked "Exit," down two flights of stairs to the building's cellar, then along a dimly lit corridor to a second door, this one locked.

That door gave onto an almost unknown aspect of the American

White House, a tunnel running underneath East Executive Avenue into the basement of the East Wing. The passage had been employed for years to keep the identity of participants in affairs of state—and occasionally that of individuals involved in affairs other than those of state—a secret. Already it had been used a dozen times in this crisis to bring people into the White House without anyone in the press or the public becoming aware that they were there.

Preceded by their Secret Service escort, the two men entered the tunnel. From overhead, the rumble of traffic rang through the shadowy passage like a clap of distant thunder.

David Hannon was a senior civil servant in the Civil Preparedness Agency; Jim Dixon was his assistant for research into the effects of nuclear weapons. Each had devoted the major part of his adult life to the study of one horrifying subject: the devastation that nuclear and thermonuclear weapons could wreak on the plains, the cities and the people of the United States. The unthinkable was as familiar to them as a balance sheet to a CPA. They had been to Hiroshima and Nagasaki, followed the test shots in the Nevada deserts, helped plan and construct the tidy Colonial homes, the cute bungalows, the lifelike John and Jane dolls on which the military planners of the fifties had measured the effects of each successive generation of nuclear warheads.

Their escort took them through the East Wing basement under the White House itself and into the West Wing offices of the National Security Council, where he turned them over to a Marine Corps major.

"The meeting's just started," the major informed them, indicating a couple of folding chairs near the NSC conference-room door. "They'll be getting to you in a few minutes."

Inside the conference room, the President had just waved Abe Stern into the chair beside his, while the regular members of the NSC Crisis Committee took their places at the table. The black bar of white numerals on the wall recorded the time, 9:03.

"We're keeping the Governor of New York informed by phone of the crisis," the President began. "I personally gave the Mayor a very brief review of what's happened a few moments ago and asked him to join us here. Because it's his city and his people who are at risk, we'll waive our normal classification procedures for him.''

He nodded to Tap Bennington. By tradition, the NSC Crisis meetings began with a briefing by the director of the CIA.

"First of all, our request to the Soviets to intervene with the Israelis following the call to our people in Tel Aviv worked. Sixth Fleet Intelligence reports the Israelis stood down an assault on Libya at three-twenty-seven A.M. I think we can now consider them contained.''

A tilt of the CIA director's head acknowledged the approving mumble his words had produced. "The thrust of the Agency's efforts right now is to uncover some precise indication of who physically could have put this in New York for Qaddafi, to aid the Bureau's search for the device.'' He paused. "Unfortunately, thus far we have nothing concrete.''

"Has there been any answer from the chargé in Tripoli to Eastman's message?'' the President asked.

"Not yet, sir. The plane is now on station, though. We're ready to set up a communications channel as soon as we have Qaddafi's reply.''

"Good.'' The swiftness with which the President articulated the word was revealing of his deeply held conviction that once he had contacted Qaddafi he would be able to reason with him, to lead him, through the power of the faith and logic in which he himself so firmly believed, to some acceptable resolution of the crisis.

"Tap, how much lateral movement has Qaddafi got? Does he run his own ship? Are there any constraints on his options?''

"No, sir. He's under no constraints at all. Not from his military. Nor from his public. He runs it all himself.''

The President frowned, but said nothing. He turned to the director of the FBI. "Mr. Webster?''

As, one after another, the men at the table reviewed their agencies' actions in the past few hours, Abe Stern listened in silence. He was still stunned, still dazed by the mind-numbing words the President had uttered to him a few minutes earlier. When Admiral Fuller concluded, however, with the news that the Sixth Fleet's carriers and nuclear submarines were nearing their positions off the Libyan seacoast, he leaned forward, his chubby little hands clasped on the table before him. It was as though he were waking from a nightmare.

"Gentlemen, the Israelis were right."

The sober faces around the NSC conference table turned to the stranger in their midst.

"You shouldn't have stopped them. The man is an irresponsible international criminal and the Israelis had the right answer: destroy him!"

"Our first concern, Mr. Mayor," Jack Eastman quietly noted, "has been the lives of the people in your city."

There was no stopping the Mayor, however. "The man is another Hitler. He's violated every single precept of international behavior there is. He's killed, murdered and terrorized every corner of the globe to get his way. He destroyed Lebanon with his money, which he poured into Beirut right through our good American banks, by the way. He was behind Khomeini. He's out to kill every friend we have in the Middle East from Sadat to the Saudis and then destroy us by shutting off our oil. And we've sat on our asses for five years and let him get away with it like we were a bunch of Chamberlains cringing before another Hitler." Stern's face was red with anger, with his fury at what his city faced. He looked at the President. "Even your own damn fool of a brother made an ass out of himself and you—running around this country licking his boots. Like those idiots in the German-American Bund barking 'Heil Hitler' at their rallies in 1940."

The Mayor paused just an instant to catch his breath, then was off again. "Now he's gone and put a bomb in my town, in the midst of my people, and you propose to get down on your hands and knees and give him what he wants? To a Hitler? To a madman? Instead of clobbering the bastard?"

"The fact of the matter is, Mr. Mayor," Admiral Fuller replied, "clobbering Libya isn't going to save New York."

"I don't believe that."

"It happens to be the case."

"Why?"

"Because destroying Libya isn't going to give us any guarantee that the bomb in New York won't go off."

The Mayor slapped both his hands on the table. He half rose out of his seat, his eyebrows twitching in anger, as he looked down the table to the beribboned Chairman of the Joint Chiefs of Staff.

"You mean to sit here and tell me that after all the billions and billions and billions of dollars we've poured into your goddamn military machine for the last thirty years, all that money my city needed so badly and never got—after all that, you're telling me your navies and your armies can't save my people, can't save my city from a crackpot, half-mad tinhorn dictator running a country that's nothing but a lot of sand and camel crap?''

"And oil," someone remarked.

The Admiral's bony face took on the mournful look of an aging bloodhound. "There's only one thing that can save your city for sure, Mr. Mayor, and that's finding the bomb and defusing it."

"Who'd they give you?"

Detective First Grade Angelo Rocchia wiped his hands on the towel rack of the FBI's washroom as he addressed the question to his detective partner, Henry Ludwig. Ludwig gestured with his heavy hand toward a slim, curly-haired black smoking at the far end of the room. "Joe Token down there. Who'd you get?"

Angelo gave a disdainful glance toward a young agent running a comb through his wavy blond hair a few washbasins away. He exhaled a weary breath, then leaned forward to ponder his own face in the mirror over Ludwig's basin. He could see a few glistening traces still remaining of the antiwrinkle cream he rubbed under his eyes and around his mouth every morning. It was something he'd been doing since August, since just after he'd begun his affair with *The New York Times*'s Grace Knowland.

His appearance was something that had always concerned Angelo. He had learned as a young detective on Manhattan's East Side that dress and respect went hand in hand. First you had to impress the doormen to get up to see your "clients"; then, once you got there, a little respect was just the attitude you wanted to inspire in them.

Angelo's money, his pals joked, went two places, into his stomach and onto his back. He never gambled. Never played the ponies. Never pissed it away on the broads. This morning he was wearing a navy-blue suit, $350 marked down at F. R. Tripler, a heavy cotton shirt with the French cuffs and the initials on the pocket, a brocaded white silk tie, one of half a dozen ties he bought each year at the Customs Shop's January clearance sale.

Angelo touched his tie and brushed his hair with his hand. "Know something, Dutchman?" he mumbled to his NYPD partner. "Something's wrong with this one. Too heavy. FBI's focusing in. Task Force is focusing in. I seen four Narcs. All for one shitty barrel.''

Without waiting for an answer he strolled along the row of white washbasins to the FBI agent with whom he had been assigned to work. "Terrific-looking tie you've got there, son," he said, casting a pitying glance at the narrow, stringy piece of cloth dangling around the young man's neck. "Where'd you get it?''

"Oh.'' Jack Rand smiled. "Do you like it? I got it at Denver Dry Goods.''

The mention of his base station reminded the twenty-eight-year-old agent of just how tired he was after his all-night flight into the city. Despite himself, he yawned sleepily. Angelo gave his partner a sour glance, then clapped a heavy hand on the agent's shoulder. "Come on, kid. Let's see where they want us to go.''

In a large room nearby, a dozen gray government-issue desks had been pushed into a square. At one, an agent and a senior detective handed out pier assignments. At others, men drew up duty rosters, set radio code signals, issued radios. Everyone was shouting at the same time: "We don't have enough radios. Call the Plaza, we need more radios.'' "Get us some unmarked cars. Kind that don't look like police cars.'' "We getting overtime for this?'' "Who's covering at nine tomorrow?''

A hand brushed Angelo's elbow as he moved to the assignment desk. He turned to find himself looking into the sparkling black eyes of the Chief of Detectives. Feldman put his face close to his. "Pull out all the stops on this one, Angelo. Don't worry about anything. Civilian complaints. Nothing. We'll cover you.''

Without waiting for a reply, Feldman moved across the room in search of the next ear to which he could whisper his injunction.

Rand returned from the assignment desk and passed Angelo a slip of paper with their destination on it. The New Yorker looked at it, then at the knot of men crowding the desk where each team was being given an FBI radio set for their New York police car. That operation, Angelo concluded, was going to take all day. Casually, he eased his way over to the desk, stooped down, tucked a radio under his arm and began to slide away.

"Hey!'' the FBI desk clerk screamed. "Where the hell do you think you're going with that?''

"Where am I going?'' Angelo growled. "To the Brooklyn Army

Base piers, where I'm supposed to go. Where else would I be going? To Roosevelt Raceway?"

"You can't do that!" The bespectacled clerk was almost beside himself with rage. "You haven't signed the form. You gotta sign the paper. It has to be dated and signed."

Angelo gave Rand a disgusted glance. "Would you believe that? A barrel of gas out there ready to kill a bunch of people and we have to sign a paper before we can go out and look for it?"

He grabbed the paper the frantic clerk was waving at him. "I tell you, kid, if the world was about to blow up there'd still be a fucking clerk out there somewhere, saying, 'Hey, wait. First you gotta sign the fucking paper.' "

For the first time in his life David Hannon was face to face with an American President. He removed a circular blue-and-white plastic wheel not much thicker than a dime from his breast pocket and set it on the table before him. It was a nuclear-bomb-effects computer designed by the Lovelace Foundation, the revised 1962 edition computed for sea-level conditions. Hannon was never without it. There was almost nothing he couldn't tell you about nuclear explosions with that wheel: how many pounds pressure per square inch would break a glass window, snap a steel arch or hemorrhage your lungs; the degree of burns you'd get twenty-three miles away from a five-megaton burst; how much fallout it would take to kill you 219 miles away from an eighty-kiloton explosion; the time the fallout would need to reach you—and how long you'd go on living once you'd been exposed to it. He glanced at the wheel. New York, he thought reassuringly, was at sea level. There would be no need to make any adjustments in his calculations.

"Let's get going."

Hannon recognized the familiar face of the President's National Security Assistant. He self-consciously touched his wavy white hair to make sure it was in place and gave a nervous tug to his striped tie.

"Sir, in New York with a three-megaton thermonuclear explosion we've got a situation that is unique in the world. All those tall buildings. The thrust of our studies has always been what we can do to the Soviets, not what they can do to us. And since they don't have any tall buildings, this is a circumstance where the data runs out, so to speak." Little dew balls of sweat began to gleam on Hannon's head. "The fact of the matter is, we just can't say with total precision what this weapon is going to do to Manhattan. The damage would be so great, it's almost inconceivable."

Hannon rose and walked to the map of the New York area his deputy had just pinned to the display board of the conference room. A series of concentric circles, blue, red, green and black, moved out from the narrow pencil of Manhattan Island at its center. "What we've done is work out here our best estimate of the destruction it would cause, based on our computer calculations. Since we don't know exactly where this device is, we've assumed for the purpose of our study that it's here." His finger indicated Times Square. "In that case, the blue circle represents Zone A from ground zero out to three miles."

He moved his finger along its circumference, down Chambers Street in lower Manhattan in the south, over the East River by the Williamsburg Bridge, through Greenpoint in Brooklyn, Long Island City in Queens, across upper Manhattan at Ninety-sixth Street, and, west of the Hudson, around Union City, Hoboken and parts of Jersey City. "Nothing inside this circle is going to survive in any recognizable form."

"Nothing?" the President asked, incredulous. "Nothing at all?"

"Nothing, sir. The devastation will be total."

"I just can't believe that." Tap Bennington thought of the view he had so often had of Manhattan Island driving down to the Jersey entrance of the Lincoln Tunnel: of those glittering ramparts of glass and steel stretching from the World Trade Center up through Wall Street to midtown and beyond. That all that could be flattened by one thermonuclear device was inconceivable, the CIA director thought. This had to be an overstatement of some bureaucrat too long lost in his charts.

"Sir," Hannon replied, "the blast wave a device like this will produce is going to generate winds unlike anything that has ever existed on earth."

"Not even at Hiroshima and Nagasaki?"

"Remember we employed atomic, not hydrogen, bombs in those cities. And with comparatively low yields. The winds they created were just summer breezes compared to what this one's going to produce."

The bureaucrat turned back to the slender blue ribbon twisting around the heart of Manhattan Island: Wall Street, Greenwich Village, Fifth and Park Avenues, Central Park, the East and West Sides. "We know from our studies in both of those cities that modern steel and concrete buildings just disappeared. Poof!" Hannon snapped his fingers. "Like that. With the winds this is going to produce, you're going to have skyscrapers literally flying all over the landscape. Disintegrating in seconds. They'll blow away like Long Island beach huts in a hurricane."

Hannon turned to his audience again. He was so controlled and composed he might have been addressing a class at the War College. "If this really goes off, gentlemen, all that will be left of Manhattan Island as we know it today is a smoldering pile of debris."

For seconds, the men at the table struggled to digest the enormity of Hannon's words.

"How about survivors in the area?" Abe Stern asked, nodding toward the blue circle inside which were trapped, at that very moment, perhaps five million people.

"Survivors? In there?" Hannon gave the Mayor a look of total incredulity. "There won't be any."

"Good God!" Stern gasped. For an instant he looked as though he was going to suffer a stroke.

"And fire?" asked Harold Brown, the Secretary of Defense.

"The fire this will create," Hannon replied, "will be unlike anything in human experience. If this device explodes, it's going to release a heat burst that'll set houses on fire all over Westchester County, New Jersey and Long Island. You'll have tens, hundreds of thousands of wooden houses bursting into flames like matches exploding."

Hannon glanced at his map. "Inside the first circle, what will happen first is that the thermal pulse, the heat of the fireball, will be passed little diminished through the glass sheaths of all those modern buildings in the center of Manhattan. Now, when you look inside those glass skyscrapers, what do you see? Curtains. Rugs. Desks covered with papers. In other words, fuel. What will happen is, you'll have a million fires lit instantly on Park Avenue. Then, of course, the blast will hit and turn the place into piles of smoking rubbish."

"Christ!" One of the deputies along the conference room wall said. "Imagine those poor people in those glass buildings!"

"Actually," Hannon replied, "according to our calculations, glass buildings may turn out to be less dangerous than you'd imagine, provided, of course, they're well away from the shot. At the enormous pressure those things generate, those glass structures are going to fragment into millions of tiny pieces which are not going to have a high degree of penetration. I mean, they'll make you look like a pincushion, but they won't kill you."

Is this guy for real? Eastman asked himself. He stared at Hannon, the square pink fingernails of his thumbs pressed tensely together, his heavy shoulders and upper body untidily enclosed in a gabardine suit. Doesn't he realize he's talking about people, Eastman thought, living flesh-and-blood people, not a chain of numbers spat out by a computer?

"What are the possibilities of survivors outside your first circle?" the President asked.

"We'll begin having survivors," Hannon answered, "inside the second circle, three to six miles from ground zero." He mechanically ran his finger along the circle's red circumference encompassing the rest of lower Manhattan, South Brooklyn, Jackson Heights, La Guardia Airport, Rikers Island, Secaucus and Jersey City, the guts of the most important metropolitan area in the world. "Fifty percent of the population in this area will be killed. Forty percent will be injured. Ten percent will survive."

"Only ten percent?" Abe Stern's voice was a whisper. He looked at Hannon's map, but he didn't see those colored circles, the rigid crisscrossing pattern of streets and highways. He saw his city, the city he had walked and studied, loved and cursed through half a century of politics and campaigns. He saw the Jewish neighborhoods out around Sheepshead Bay where he had hiked through stairways redolent with the smell of gefilte fish in the thirties getting out the vote; the frightening vistas of the South Bronx he had come here to save; the boardwalk at Coney with the guys in the stands hawking frozen custard, Nathan's Famous and foot-long franks; the barrios of Spanish Harlem and the crowded alleys of Chinatown smelling of salted fish, smoked duck and preserved egg; of Little Italy festooned in red and green for the saint whose gaudy statue was paraded through an exultant throng; of those endless neighborhoods of two-family row houses and tenements in Bensonhurst, Astoria and the Bronx; the homes of his people: the cabdrivers, waiters, barbers, clerks, electricians, firemen and cops who had spent a lifetime of struggle to get where they were, all of them now trapped because they lived inside a thin red line on a map.

"Do you mean to tell me only one New Yorker in ten in there is going to come out unscathed?" he asked. "Half of them are going to die?"

"Yes, sir."

"What about the impact of this on your other areas?" the President queried.

"Most of Jersey City, upper Manhattan and Flatbush are just going to fall over. Low-rise buildings will collapse. Anything under ten stories will come down."

"What are the chances of survivors inside the green circle?" Eastman asked, the sharp upward flaring of his voice revealing the depth of his personal concern. The campus of Columbia University lay inside its boundary.

"Out there," Hannon answered, "glass is going to be flying. Interior partitions are going to go. Anybody who's not in a cellar is going to risk being badly bruised or cut up by flying glass and debris. We reckon ten percent in that belt dead and forty to fifty percent injured.

"The black outer circle," he continued, "defines the blast-damage limit." It went as far as JFK Airport and the southern border of Westchester County and enclosed a great swath of New Jersey's wealthiest bedroom communities. "Glass, light walls will go down there. Anybody outside will risk severe body burns."

"How about the fallout?" the President queried.

"God forbid, sir, if there is an onshore wind blowing when this thing explodes to drive the fallout up into New York State and New England, it'll contaminate a swath of land thousands of miles square. Right up into Vermont. Nobody will be able to live there for generations to come."

"Look, Mr. Whatever-your-name-is." Abe Stern had begun to recover his composure. "I'd like to know one thing from you. God forgive me for using the expression for something like this, but I want the bottom line. How many of my people are going to be killed if this things goes off?"

"Yes, sir." Hannon opened the pages of a stack of papers enclosed in a stiff black cover ostentatiously stamped "Top Secret." That pile of paper was the indispensable crutch of the modern bureaucrat, a computer printout. This one had been spewed out during the watches of the night by the computer in the National Warning Center. Everything that would happen to the Mayor's city should Qaddafi's bomb explode was on those pages. It was as if some computerized Cassandra had uttered an infallible prophecy recording in minute, macabre detail the instant future which awaited New York in that awful eventuality; what percentage of the buildings along Clinton Avenue in Brooklyn would remain standing (zero); the number of dead on Eighth Avenue, Manhattan, between Thirty-fourth and Thirty-sixth Streets (100 percent); the percentage of the population of Glen Cove, Long Island, that would die from exposure to radioactive fallout (10 percent); how many private dwellings in East Orange, New Jersey, would suffer severe damage (7.2 percent); the destiny of the people of Queens (57.2 percent would die from blast and fire, 5 percent from the fallout, 32.7 percent would be injured).

It was a multimillion dollar *Baedeker* to the unthinkable, right down to how many nurses, pediatricians, osteopaths, plumbers, hospital beds, airport runways, and, naturally, government tax records, would survive in each corner of the affected area. Hannon methodically toted up the horror encapsulated in those dark chains of numbers.

"The total dead, sir, for the conditions we've been given in the five boroughs and New Jersey would be 6.74 million."

PART V

MONDAY, DECEMBER 14:
9:15 A.M. TO NOON

"Fox Base has cut the circuit."

An INTERMINABLE CLUTTER OF NEW YORK traffic loomed up before Angelo Rocchia's four-year-old Corvette, blocking its route to the exit ramp. Beside Rocchia, Jack Rand gave his watch an anxious glance. "Maybe we ought to check in."

"Check in? What for, for Christ's sake? To tell them we're stuck on the Brooklyn Bridge?" This kid's really got a bug up his ass, Angelo thought. He plucked a peanut from the bag tucked into the pocket of his suit jacket. "Here," he said, "relax. Enjoy the sights. The good part's coming up. The asshole of Brooklyn."

Slowly, painfully, he funneled the car off the bridge ramp, sped along the Brooklyn-Queens Expressway and then the Gowanus Expressway, until he turned toward Second Avenue, Brooklyn, and his destination. The young agent gawked at the sight spreading along their route: a line of three- and four-story tenements, every other one of them, almost, a gutted shell. The walls, those that were still standing, were covered with obscene graffiti. Windows were broken everywhere. Those on the ground floor were barred. Doors were padlocked. Rubbish littered the sidewalks. The place stank of urine, of feces, of ashes.

On the street corners, men and kids warmed their hands over flickering fires of rubbish set in old trashcans or lit on a patch of the sidewalk. Rand stared at them, blacks and Hispanics, an occasional flash of hatred for their passing car illuminating the otherwise expressionless faces of those for whom the American dream was a nightmare, a distant, unobtainable mirage quivering mockingly from across the narrow neck of water over which their car had just passed.

"Got anything like this in South Dakota?" Angelo asked. "You know what they get for murder one down here? Ten bucks. Ten bucks to kill a man." He shook his head sadly. "Used to be a nice neighborhood, too. Italian. Few Irish. Some of these people they got here now, they live worse than animals in the Bronx Zoo. Arabs be doing us a favor, they gas the place."

The FBI radio on the seat between them crackled. There was no mistaking the speaker's flat Midwestern accent. Angelo burst into laughter.

"You remember when they snatched Calvin Klein's kid a couple of years ago?"

Rand didn't.

"We had a bunch of you guys from South Dakota in on that one too. I'm riding in this thing monitoring your frequency plus the pigeon with a wire. We've already sprung the kid, got the perp, but the FBI, they wanted to stay out. Thought there might be more people. And suddenly I hear"—Angelo mimicked the accent—" 'Foxtrot Four to Base. There are two suspicious-looking Negro males loitering on the corner of One Hundred Thirty-fifth and St. Nicholas Avenue.' " Angelo laughed again, a short, harsh burst of noise. "Shit! That's all they got up there, for Christ's sake, is suspicious-looking spades. Hanging around. Scoring dope. You could rupture every nose in South Dakota with the coke they sell up there."

Rand looked at him. There was a taut, teeth-baring smile on Angelo's face, but there was no smile in his eyes. Something, the young agent thought, is disturbing this man.

"Angelo, I live in Denver."

"What's the difference?"

"Considerable, in fact. Have you ever been out West?"

"Out West? Sure, I been out West." Angelo gave the agent a regard that mixed pity with contempt. "I was up in Albany once." He produced another mirthless laugh. "You know what they say, kid? Once you get past Yonkers, everything out there's Bridgeport."

He waved a hand past the sagging façade of a Catholic church. "Over there," he noted, with a certain pride in his voice, "is Joey Gallo's old turf. His docks are down there."

Rand followed his gesture toward the low-lying piers pushing into the gray sludge of the harbor. "Do the rackets still control the piers?"

What's with this guy? Angelo thought. Next thing he'll want to know is, is the Pope Catholic? "Of course. Profacci family. Anthony Scotto."

"And you guys can't break them?"

"Break them, you kidding? They own all the stevedore companies that lease the piers. And the union local on every pier is owned by the mob that owns the stevedore company. If a guy hasn't got an uncle, a brother, a cousin inside the union to recommend him, forget it, he don't work. What happens his first day down there, guy comes up to him, says, 'Hey, we're taking a collection for Tony Nazziato. Broke his leg over to Pier Six.' He says, 'Tony who?' and he never works again. Because old Tony, he's up there in the union hall, and he could run the hundred on that broken leg of his. It's an understanding. Like everything on the piers."

Enough of this, Angelo thought. He gave the agent a quizzical regard. "They sent you all the way from Denver just for a crummy barrel of chlorine gas."

Rand swallowed hastily. "I'd hardly call chlorine gas crummy. You heard what they said about how toxic it was."

"Yeah, well, you know what I figure? At least two thousand of you guys been pulled in here, all for that little barrel."

The New Yorker's face, Rand noted, seemed relaxed, but the cold set of his gray eyes had not changed.

"I wouldn't know about that," the agent replied. He hesitated a moment. "You must be getting close to retirement age, Angelo."

Okay, Angelo said to himself, the kid wants to change the subject, we'll change the subject. "Sure. I could retire. I got the years. But I like the job. Like the excitement. Nobody's breaking my balls. What would I do, I retire? Sit out there on Long Island somewhere and listen to the grass grow?"

Just the thought of retirement reminded him that it was here, in this precinct, that he had walked his first beat. In 1947. He'd been so close to home he could drop in for coffee in the house where he'd been born, kiss Ma, talk with the old man in the tailor shop he had set up when he came over from Sicily after the first war, lounge in the back room where Angelo had pushed the needle himself on Saturday afternoons, listening to the Metropolitan Opera, to his old man belting out *Rigoletto, Trovatore, Traviata.* Knew them all, his old man. Where did they go, all those years, Angelo thought, where did they go?

"You been with the Bureau long?" he asked Rand.

"Three years. Since I got out of Tulane Law School."

Figures, Angelo thought. I always get the veterans.

Angelo fell silent for a moment, looking again at the once familiar neighborhood, resembling now the blasted-out villages he'd fought over north of Naples in the winter of '43. Those years in the service, the force. He'd done all right. For an Italian. The Police and Fire Departments in the city belonged to the Irish. The Italians had the Sanitation. Jews owned the teachers. They said New York was a melting pot, but its heat could thaw things out only so much.

"You married, kid?"

"Yes," Rand replied. "We have two children. How about you?"

For the first time he noted a softening in the detective's gray eyes. "I lost my wife to cancer some years ago. We had one child, a daughter." The words were issued like pronunciamento, a definitive statement that permitted no further questions.

Angelo turned off the avenue and drew up to a gate. He flashed his detective's shield at the guard inside, who waved them ahead. They rolled down a slight incline to a huge three-story façade of yellowing cement opening before a dark cavern that looked a little like a covered railroad stand. Overhead, a walkway linked the building to a pair of massive warehouses. They were quintessential U.S. government functional: squat and tasteless, without any redeeming frill or folly. Four railroad tracks ran into the pier's dim recesses. Painted overhead in black block letters were the words "PASSENGER TERMINAL."

"The end of the line for the kid in Upper Seventeen," Angelo mused.

"What?" the startled Rand asked.

"Shit. Forget it. It was an ad during the war. You weren't even born then." He flicked a peanut into his mouth and shook his head as though in disbelief. "I shipped out of here in 'forty-two."

A bitter gust of wind tore off the bay, flinging up to their nostrils the putrid odor of the dirty sea water lapping the docks. Angelo headed toward a shacklike booth at the end of the pier, its windows coated with fly specks, grime and dust.

"Would you believe that?" he asked. "U.S. Customs Office. You could walk a circus elephant past those windows and the guy inside wouldn't notice."

Angelo led the way into the dimly lit office. Decals of the Knicks, the Jets, old postcards, a yellowing *Playboy* centerfold were stuck to the walls. In one corner sat a hot plate in a little puddle of cold coffee. It was surrounded by an open can of Nescafé, a pair of mugs, their handles chipped, a jar of Creem, a few cubes of sugar, each capped with its matching crown of flies. The Customs officer had his feet up on the desk, a copy of the *Daily News* open to the sports page on his lap.

"Oh yeah, they told me you were coming," he said at the flash of Angelo's gold shield. Without getting up, he added, "They're waiting for you next door in the stevedores' office."

That office was little different from Customs. Stacked by month on a table were six piles of paper, almost a foot high, the manifests of the ships that had called at the pier in the last six months.

Angelo took off his overcoat and folded it neatly over a filthy cabinet. He plucked a few peanuts from his pocket and offered them to Rand. "Have a peanut, kid, and let's get to work. Remember, *che va piano, va sano.*"

"What the hell does that mean?"

"It means, my friend, a good cop is a guy who takes his time."

The Mayor's chubby hands, the hands Abe Stern had once imagined jabbing and punching their way through the glare of a prize ring, were pressed flat against the White House window-pane. Despair etched every line that seventy years of toil and struggle had left upon his face. Six million seven hundred thousand people, he thought over and over again, six million seven hundred thousand! A holocaust even worse than the tragedy that had swept the remnants of his father's family into the gas chambers of Auschwitz; and all of it accomplished in the glare and incandescence of a few terrible seconds.

"Mr. President." His voice was a harsh plea. "We gotta do something for those people up there. We got to."

The President was perched on the corner of his desk, his weight supported by one foot. He had brought the Mayor back here to his private office after the NSC meeting to try to both brace and prepare him for the ordeal they were going to share.

"We are, Abe," he answered. "We're going to negotiate our way out of it. No man can be as unreasonable, as irrational as this. In the meantime, what's important is to keep calm, not to let ourselves give in to panic."

"Mr. President, that's not enough for me. You have to perceive your responsibilities in this mess to the people of this country as a whole. Me, I have to perceive mine in terms of those six million people up there that that fanatic is threatening to kill. What are we going to do to save them, Mr. President?"

The President rose and walked to the window. His countrymen had elected him to this high office despite the fact that many among them still questioned his strength, his capacity to lead the nation in a crisis. Now his abilities as a leader were being tested as no American President's had been since the war. In the last great national crisis President Kennedy had been able to stand eyeball to eyeball with Khrushchev, he knew, because he had behind him the awesome power of the United States. That was denied him here. How could he even threaten Qaddafi with the U.S.'s military power when the Libyan well knew its use would mean three or four Americans dead for every Libyan killed?

"Abe, for God's sake," he said, his voice cracking slightly as he spoke, "don't you think if I knew something more we could do for those people we'd be doing it?"

"How about evacuating the city?"

"You read his letter, Abe. If we start doing that, he says he's going to explode the bomb. Do you want to risk that? Before we've even talked to him?"

"What I don't want to do is let that son of a bitch dictate his terms to us, Mr. President. Can't we find some way to clear the city without his finding out about it? Do it at night? Cut the radios, the television, the phone systems? There's got to be a way."

The President turned from his window. He could not bear the beauty of that sight this morning, the clean sweep of snow, the Washington Monument soaring into the blue sky, the spartan rigidity of its design bespeaking another, simple time.

"Abe." His voice was quiet and reflective. "He's thought this through very carefully. The whole key to his strategic equation is the fact that in New York he's got that uniquely vulnerable dense concentration of people. All his calculations depend on that. He knows if we clear the city he's dead. He's got to have someone hidden up there with a powerful shortwave radio transmitter ready to flash him the word the moment someone says 'evacuation.' "

"Mr. President, there's only one thing I can think about and that's the six million seven hundred thousand people in New York City this thing may kill. The least I can do for them is to warn them. Get on radio and television and tell them to run for the bridges.''

"Abe." There was no reproach in the President's voice. "Do that and maybe you'll save a million people. But they'll be the rich with cars. How about the blacks, the Hispanics in Bedford-Stuyvesant and East Harlem? They'll barely be out of the front door when the bomb goes off.''

"At least they'll write on my tombstone, 'He saved one million of his people.' ''

The President shook his head, agonizing with the little man in his dilemma. "And the history books may also say, Abe, that you helped cause the death of five million others by acting precipitously.''

For a minute, neither man said anything. Then the President went on. "Besides, Abe, can you imagine the pandemonium you'd cause trying to evacuate New York?''

"Of course I can." Petulance flared from the Mayor like a flame spurting from a sharply struck match. "I know my people. But I've got to do something. I'm not going back up there and sit around Gracie Mansion for the next thirty hours, Mr. President, waiting for your charm and persuasive talents to save six million New Yorkers from a madman.''

The Mayor thrust an outstretched index finger toward the vista beyond the window. "How about all those guys over there in Civil Defense at the Pentagon, been spending millions of dollars of our money for the last thirty years? What are we waiting for? Let them start earning their money. Give me the best people you got. I'll take them back with me and sit them down with my people. We'll see if they can't come up with something.''

"All right, Abe," the President replied, "you got them. I'll have Harold Brown get them out to Andrews right away." He placed one of his outsized hands on the Mayor's shoulder. "And if they come up with something, anything, that looks like it might work, we'll do it, Abe. I promise you." He squeezed the older man's shoulder. "But it won't come to that. Once we get through to him, we'll find a way to talk him out of this. Believe me. In the meantime," he sighed, "we've got to put up a good front." He took a slip of paper from his desk and stood up. "I guess the time to start is right now.''

A score of White House journalists were waiting outside. The

President smiled, bantered with a couple of them, then read the innocuous three-line statement on his paper. They had discussed the question of federal aid for New York in the new budget, it read, and had agreed to close, continuing discussions on the matter over the next few days.

"Mr. Mayor," a voice called from the circle of reporters, "what the hell's going to happen to New York if you don't get the money?"

The President could see that the question had caught Abe Stern by surprise, his thoughts far closer probably to the East River than to the Potomac.

"Don't you worry about New York City, young man," he snapped, when his mind had returned to the White House. "New York City can take care of itself."

Jeremy Painter Oglethorpe spooned the egg from the double boiler at the first tinkle of his three-minute timer, flicked a slice of Pepperidge Farm stonemill oatmeal bread toast from the toaster, and poured a cup of coffee from his Mr. Coffee machine. With meticulousness born from twenty years of habit, he set the ingredients of his breakfast down in the breakfast nook of his Arlington, Virginia, split-level. Breakfast, like the rest of Oglethorpe's life, was a series of well-worn rituals. He would close the working day now opening before him as precisely as he had begun it, a rigid eight and a half hours hence, with the rattle of the ice in a pitcher of martinis on the sideboy in the dining room.

Oglethorpe was fifty-eight, stout, myopic and given to wearing floppy bow ties because a secretary had once told him they gave him a debonair look. Professionally, he was an academic bureaucrat, a product of that curious union between the groves of academe and the capital's corridors of power spawned by the nation's universities in their insatiable thirst for federal funds. "Think tanks," research institutes, government consultancies—the organizations which employed men like Oglethorpe had sprung up like mushrooms after a warm rain along the Potomac in the years since the war. A projection of the impact of zero-base population on housing starts in 2005; the future cadmium-stockpile requirements of the computer industry; the impact accuracy of the MX missile over a spectrum of reentry speeds—no subject was too arcane for their scrutiny. Even, as Senator William Proxmire had learned to his fury, a study of the social pecking order in South American whorehouses.

Oglethorpe belonged to one of the most prestigious among them, the Stanford Research Institute attached to Stanford University in Palo Alto, California. His specialty was figuring out how to evacuate American cities in the event of a Soviet thermonuclear attack. Except, of course, that the word "evacuation" was never used in his work to refer to the operation. The government bureaucracy had decided it was a negative-association word like "cancer" and had replaced it with a more palatable term, "crisis relocation."

For thirty years, Oglethorpe had devoted himself to the subject with a zealousness no less total than the devotion offered by one of Sister Theresa's nursing nuns to the poor of Calcutta. The crowning achievement of his career had been the recent publication of his monumental 425-page work *The Feasibility of Crisis Relocation in the Northeastern United States*. It had required the services of twenty people for three years and had cost the U.S. government more money than even Oglethorpe cared to admit. Since then, he had devoted most of his working hours to the most difficult challenge that report had posed, evacuating New York City—and that despite the fact that he had never lived there and personally couldn't stand the place. His lack of firsthand knowledge of the city whose evacuation concerned him, however, had never troubled the federal bureaucracy; such things seldom do.

What had troubled Oglethorpe during those long years was the massive indifference of his countrymen to his efforts to provide for their well-being on the day of the Ultimate Disaster. Approaching retirement, it sometimes seemed to Oglethorpe that he was a kind of ultimate disaster himself, a man of undisputed talent and ability whose hour had never seemed to come.

Yet, on this morning of Monday, December 14, it had. Oglethorpe had just given two sharp raps of his spoon to his egg when the phone rang. He almost choked hearing a Pentagon colonel introduce his caller as the Secretary of Defense. No one higher than a GS10 had ever called him at his home. Two minutes later, his breakfast in the nook uneaten, he was getting into a gray U.S. Navy sedan, preparing to speed first to his office to pick up the documents he would need in the hours to come, then to Andrews AFB.

Across the Potomac from Oglethorpe's Arlington home, the haggard advisers who were gathered around Jack Eastman's conference table in the West Wing of the White House each reacted in a different way to the Dutch psychiatrist joining their group. To Lisa Dyson, the CIA's blond Libyan Desk officer, he brought a promise of fresh air to a gathering going stale from a night of intense and occasionally acrimonious discussion. Bernie Tamarkin, the Washington psychiatrist who specialized in dealing with terrorists, looked on Henrick Jagerman with the awe of a young cellist about to meet Pablo Casals for the first time. Jack Eastman saw in his stocky figure the incarnation of the one hope he had for a nonviolent resolution to this ghastly crisis.

The introductions completed, Jagerman took the seat Eastman indicated at the head of the table. Barely an hour ago, he had been hurtling across the Atlantic at twice the speed of sound, sipping ice-cold Dom Perignon champagne and studying the psychological portrait of Qaddafi a CIA operative had given him at Charles de Gaulle Airport. Now here he was in the councils of the most powerful nation on earth, expected to offer a strategy that could prevent a catastrophe of unthinkable dimension.

"Have you established contact with Qaddafi yet?" he inquired when Eastman concluded his review of the situation.

"Unfortunately, we haven't," the American admitted, "although we do have a secure communications channel set up which we can use when we do."

Jagerman looked at the ceiling. There was a large black mole in the middle of his forehead. It resembled, he was fond of pointing out, the *tikka,* the stain Hindus often painted there to represent the Third Eye that perceives the truth beyond appearances.

"In any event, it's not urgent."

"Not urgent?" Eastman was aghast. "We have barely thirty hours left to talk him out of this mess and you say getting hold of him isn't urgent?"

"After the success of his test in the desert the man is in a state of psychic erection—clinically speaking, a state of paranoic hypertension." Jagerman's tone had the authoritative ring of a distinguished surgeon offering his diagnosis to a circle of interns. "That explosion has confirmed to him that he now possesses what he's been looking for for years, absolute, total power. He sees at last that all the possibilities he sought are open to him: destroying

Israel, becoming the undisputed leader of the Arabs, master of the world's oil supplies. Speaking to him right now could be a fatal error. Better let that stewpot cool down a bit before we take off the cover to see what's inside."

He pinched his nostrils with his fingers and tried to clear his aural passages, blocked by the Concorde's abnormally rapid descent in response to the White House's orders for speed.

"You see," he continued, "the most dangerous moments in a terrorist situation are the first ones. Then the terrorist's anxiety quotient is very, very high. He's frequently in a state of hysteria that can drive him to the irrational in a second. You must ventilate him. Let him express his views, his grievances." The Dutchman started. "By the way, these communications facilities, I presume, will allow us to hear his voice?"

"Well, there's a possible security problem, but . . ."

"We *must* hear his voice," Jagerman insisted. A man's voice was for him an indispensable window onto his psyche, the element with which he could evaluate his character, the shifts in his sentiments, eventually predict his behavior patterns. In a hostage crisis, he recorded every word exchanged with the terrorists, then listened over and over again to their voices, hunting for shifts in speech patterns, in tone, in usage, looking for hidden clues that could guide his own search for mastery of the situation.

"Who should talk to him?" Eastman asked. "The President, I suppose."

"Absolutely not." Jagerman sounded almost shocked that Eastman had even suggested it. "The President is the person who can give him what he wants—or at least he thinks he is. He's the last person who should talk to him." The psychiatrist took a sip of the cup of coffee someone had placed at his elbow. "Our aim," he went on, "must be to gain time to allow the police to find that bomb. If we let the President speak to him, how are we going to stall for time if we have to? Qaddafi can force him into a corner, a yes-or-no situation. He can demand an immediate answer he knows the President can give him."

Jagerman noted with satisfaction that the people around the table were following his logic. "That's why you insert the negotiator between the terrorist and authority. If the terrorist asks for something immediately, a negotiator can always stall by telling him that he has to go to speak to those in authority to get it for him. Time," he smiled, "is always on the side of authority. As time goes by, terrorists become less and less sure of themselves. Vulnerable. As one must hope Qaddafi will."

"What kind of person should this negotiator be?" Eastman asked.

"An older man. It's possible he might perceive a younger man as a threat. Someone placid, a man who will listen, who can draw him on if he lapses into silence. A father figure the way Nasser was to him when he was young. Above all, someone who'll inspire a sense of confidence. His attitude must be: 'I sympathize with your aims. I want to help you achieve them.' "

The Dutchman knew that task well. Five times he had had to fill it, talking terrorists through their first irrational, dangerous stage, coaxing them slowly back to reality, imposing the rhythms of normality on them, finally bringing them to accept the role he had in mind for them: becoming conquered heroes by sparing their hostages' lives. Four times those tactics had worked brilliantly. Better in this situation, he thought, not to think about the fifth.

"The first contact will be decisive," he continued. "Qaddafi must realize immediately that we're taking him seriously." His quick bright eyes surveyed the room. "In view of what he's done, what I'm about to say may sound grotesque, but it's a vital part of the strategy. We must begin by telling him he's right. That not only is his complaint against Israel perfectly justified, but we're prepared to help him find a reasonable solution to it."

"All this presumes, of course," Lisa Dyson observed, "that he'll talk to us. It would be very much in character for him to say," she gave Jagerman an angelic smile, "please forgive my French, Doctor, 'Screw you. Don't talk to me. Just do what I say.' "

These American girls, Jagerman thought. Their language is worse than a Dutch prison warden's. "Don't worry, young lady," he replied. "He'll talk. Your excellent study makes that clear. That dirty little Arab boy from the desert the kids all ridiculed once is now going to become the hero of all the Arabs by imposing his will on the most important man in the world. Believe me, he'll talk."

"I hope to Christ you're right." Eastman had been following Jagerman with feelings that were a mixture of his skepticism of the psychiatrist's trade and his desperate hope that this man could provide them with the answers they needed. "But don't forget, Doctor, we're not dealing here with some wild-eyed terrorists holding a gun against a little old lady's head. This man has the power to kill six million people in his hands. And he knows it.''

Jagerman nodded. "Quite right," he agreed. "But what we are dealing with are certain immutable psychological patterns and principles. They apply to a chief of state just as well as they do to a terrorist gunman. Most terrorists see themselves as oppressed luminaries striving to avenge some wrong. Clearly, the man we have in front of us here is a luminary, a true religious fanatic, which complicates matters, because religion can always radicalize a man, as we all saw in Iran with Khomeini.''

Jagerman glanced toward Lisa Dyson, an approving, paternal air in his regard. "Once again, your portrait is most instructive. He knows that you Americans, like the English, the French, even the Russians, think he's crazy. Well, he's going to prove you're wrong. He, that miserable, despised Arab, is going to force you to make his impossible dream come true. And to prove to you he's not as crazy as you think he is, he's ready to pay the final price: to destroy you and himself and his own people if he has to to get his way.''

Angelo Rocchia glanced at the group of men warming their hands by the old coal stove in one corner of the office of the pier boss of the Hellenic Stevedore Company. Dock bosses. Italians mostly, with a token black in their circle, the Mob's reluctant concession to the pressures of the times. In their leather caps, their faded lumberjackets and dungarees, they were a casting man's dream for a remake of *On the Waterfront*. Their conversation was a series of guttural grunts, a mixture of English and Sicilian, touching on sex and the cold, money and the Knicks, punctuated by regular hostile glances at Angelo and the FBI man beside him.

No one, the detective knew, was as unwelcome on the docks as a cop. Those guys, he thought cheerfully, have got to be going crazy trying to figure out what the hell we're doing here. Beyond the office, from the huge pier of the Brooklyn Ocean Terminal, Angelo could hear the snarl of forklift trucks, the clang of metal, the grinding of the cranes hoisting pallets of cargo out of the holds of the four ships tied up to the terminal's wharves. It was a soup-to-nuts pier, one of the few piers left in the Port of New York that still handled the old loose cargo slung onto the pallets, an anachronism in the days of containerized cargo.

Angelo remembered the old days when everything had come in on pallets and the longshoremen went at them like a rat pack, eating away at their loads at every stage of their progress along the docks. Pilferage then had been a fringe benefit of being a longshoreman.

Not anymore. Everything was containers now. Three, four days it would take to unload by crane and hand the ships tied up at the terminal. Across the bay, in the modern container ports at Elizabeth and Newark, they took off thirty tons in half an hour, snapped a hustler, a tow cab, onto each container and drove it away. The savings to the shippers were enormous and the conversion had probably saved the Port of New York.

It had done something else too, and Angelo was well aware of what it was. It had turned the port into a smugglers' paradise. Customs had to pay the cost of busting open a container, unloading it and repacking it while the shippers stood by screaming bloody murder because their shipment was being harassed. As a result, the random sampling of goods for Customs' purposes had been practically abandoned. Customs just didn't touch a container unless they had hard intelligence on it. You could run a hundred barrels of whatever this stuff was they were looking for across those docks over there in Jersey, Angelo reflected, and there was no way in the world anyone would find out what you were doing.

He rubbed his eyes and turned his attention back to his methodical progress through the manifest of the *Lash Turkiye,* fifty-two cargoes, each one different, it seemed, each loaded in a different port. Already he had picked up two shipments that had fitted into the frame they were looking for. There was nothing in the last dozen cargoes. Wearily, Angelo tossed the manifest on top of the others he had already finished and reached for the next one in the pile before him.

As he spread it out on the table, he felt a familiar rumble in his stomach. "Hey," he called to the pier boss. Tony Piccardi was seated at a long counter in front of a row of bank-teller-like windows. "That restaurant, Salvatore's, over there on Fifth Avenue. It still open?"

Piccardi looked up from the documents he was checking for one of the truckers standing in front of his window. "No. The old guy died a couple of years back."

"Too bad. He made a manicotti you wouldn't believe."

Jack Rand glanced impatiently at his detective partner. Bullshitting. Since he arrived he had spent half of his time bullshitting with these guys, mostly in Italian. Impatiently, the young agent flicked over a page of his manifest. He started at the sight of the first entry on his new page.

"I've got one," he called, his voice sliding sharply upward with excitement.

Angelo leaned over and followed Rand's finger across the manifest.

Shippers: Libyan Oil Service, Tripoli, Libya.
Consignees: Kansas Drill International, Kansas City, Kansas.
Marks and Numbers: LOS 8477/8484.
Quantity: Five pallets.
Description: Oil Drilling Equipment.
Gross Weight: 17,000 lbs.

"Yeah," he agreed, "that's a live one all right. Better call it in."

Rand moved off toward the phone, and Angelo went back to his own manifest. It was the shortest one he'd studied, listing barely a dozen items. Guy owns this ship, Angelo mused, can't be making much money. He went quickly through the usual run of Mediterranean products: Greek olive oil in tins, Syrian copperware. He stopped short at the word "Benghazi."

That had a familiar ring. Uncle Giacomo. That's where the British captured Uncle Giacomo in 1941. In Benghazi, Libya. He studied the entry.

Shipper: Am Al Fasi Export, Benghazi.
Consignee: Durkee Filters, 194 Jewel Avenue, Queens.
Marks and Numbers: 18/378.
Quantity: One pallet.
Description: 10 barrels of Diatome.
Gross Weight: 5,000 lbs.

Angelo thought for a second. Ten barrels, so each one weighed five hundred pounds, well below the size they were looking for.

"Hey, Tony," he said to the pier boss. "Take a look at this." He thrust the manifest at Piccardi. "What's this stuff?"

"Kind of white powder. Busted-up seashells."

"What the hell do they use that for?"

"I don't know. Filtering water, I think. Swimming pools, you know?"

"Sure. I use mine all the time." Angelo noted the word "Filters" by the name of the consignee. "You know this ship?"

Piccardi looked at the head of the manifest. "Yeah. An old rust bucket. Been coming in here with that shit about once a month for the last three, four months."

Angelo pondered the paper a moment. You'd look an awful fool downtown sending them after five-hundred-pound barrels when the one they're looking for weighs fifteen hundred. This was a heavy case. No time and no manpower to waste. Besides, there was a regular pattern to the shipping. He laid the manifest on his stack of completed papers. As he did, the name of the ship that had delivered the cargo caught his eye. It was "S.S. *Dionysos.*"

Huge sunglasses, their lenses as dark as eye patches, shielded the pimp's eyes from the harsh light of day. Morning was not Rico Diaz's best time. From his tape deck the echoes of Bobby Womack's "Road of Life" vibrated through his customized Lincoln; soul had seemed more appropriate for this meeting than disco. He hurried the car down Seventh Avenue, putting as much space between him and his turf as he could. No reason to be spotted by the brothers with these two in the car—although, he thought with a contemptuous sideways glance at his FBI control agent, they could easily pass for a pair of Johns off to party time with his ladies.

"Rico, we got a little problem."

Rico did not answer his control. His eyes, invisible behind the shades, were studying the man in the back seat in the rearview mirror. He had not seen him before, and he did not like what he saw. The man had a mean and sterile face, the face of someone who enjoyed squashing little bugs between his fingertips.

"That Arab girl you told us about. She left the Hampshire House this morning. To fly out to LA."

Rico gestured indifferently at the filthy gray ridges of snow along the avenue. "She be a lucky lady."

"Except she didn't get on the plane, Rico."

The pimp felt a chill quiver of apprehension flick through his stomach. He regretted now that he hadn't taken a wake-up jolt of coke before leaving his pad. "So?"

"So we'd like to talk to your friend who dealt with her."

The quiver of apprehension became a knot squeezing Rico's bowels. "No way, man. He a mean motherfucker."

"I didn't expect he'd be studying for the priesthood, Rico. What's he do?"

The pimp emitted a low, soft groan. "You know, man. He make a little dope here and there."

"Good. That's good, Rico. We'll bring him in to have a talk about dope. No way in the world he'll trace it back to you."

"Come on, man." Rico could feel a trickle of sweat sliding along his spine, and it wasn't because he was warm in his five-thousand-dollar knee-length mink-lined coat. "You say to him, 'Arab lady, Hampshire House' and they be only one nigger in New York he gonna be thinking about."

"Mr. Diaz."

It was the man in the back seat. Rico studied the flat, emotionless face. "What we have here is a matter of greatest importance. And urgency. We need your help."

"You got it already."

"I know that and we're very appreciative of what you've already done. But we're very, very anxious to find that girl. We've got to talk to your friend." The agent took a pack of cigarettes from his pocket, leaned forward and offered one to Rico. The black pushed it away.

"You're very important to us, Mr. Diaz. We're not going to do anything that would compromise you in any way, believe me. There will be no way your friend can trace our visit to you from the nature of our questions. I promise you." The agent lit his own cigarette, took a deep breath and exhaled slowly. "Frank," he said to Rico's control in the front seat, "I understand one of Mr. Diaz's girl friends is in some difficulty with the New York police."

"Yeah," Frank replied, "if you consider five years in the slammer difficult, she is."

"Can you arrange to get the charges dropped? In view of the importance of Mr. Diaz's cooperation?"

"I suppose so."

"Today?"

"If I really had to."

225

"You will."

Through the rearview mirror, Rico noticed the man turn his eyes back to him. "The girl is yours, Mr. Díaz, but we need your help. Believe me, there'll be no way in the world your friend'll trace this back to you. No way."

Why, Rico thought angrily, why did I ever put a bag of shit in this machine? Anita was the only hundred-dollar tricker he had. There was a gold mine in her pussy. Two, three thousand dollars a week she brought in, twice the earnings of his other girls. She was the principal mainstay of a very expensive lifestyle and no one had to explain to Rico what was going to happen to that if he didn't come through for these two. They'd clean her slate all right if he talked; but keep his mouth shut and it would be bye-bye, baby, five years upstate for Anita and some mean times for Rico until he found a girl to replace her.

"You sure they no way this get back?"

"Trust us."

Rico slammed the heel of a hand onto the steering wheel. Dumb bitch, he thought. I told her never to stiff a John. He swallowed nervously, running the fine calculations through his street-smart brain, reckoning up the dangerous balance, pitting the risks against the spiraling cost of good coke, against the cash required for the out-front display a man had to have to keep his standing on the street.

His control agent had to lean forward to catch the whispered reply when bitterly, reluctantly, it came. "Franco. Apartment Five A, 213 West Fifty-fifth."

The girl the FBI agents were looking for was thirty-five miles north of Manhattan driving a Budget Rent-a-Car up the New York State Thruway toward Albany. Laila Dajani had picked the car up in Buffalo two weeks earlier. As an additional precaution, she had removed the car's license plates and replaced them with a pair of New Jersey number plates stolen by Palestinian agents six months earlier from a U.S. tourist's car parked in Baden-Baden, Germany.

Whalid was in the seat beside her. It was 10 A.M. and he was fiddling with the dials of the radio, trying to catch a news bulletin. "Maybe"—he smiled at his sister—"they'll have something on the Israelis starting their pullback."

Laila gave him a hurried glance. There's been quite a change in my brother in the past few hours, she thought. Perhaps it was the medicine she'd gotten him. He hadn't complained about his ulcer since she'd picked him up.

Laila eased the car into the outside lane to pass a huge refrigerated truck, being careful as she did to stay well within the fifty-five-miles-per-hour speed limit. This was no time to be arrested for speeding. If he's so relaxed, she told herself, maybe it's because it's over for him now. All he had to do was sit in the safe house she'd found in the upstate countryside and wait while she and Kamal spent another twenty-four hours in the city, Kamal standing vigil over the bomb with his rats and his air gun, she in the hotel to which she'd moved waiting to bring him to the safe house two hours before the bomb was due to explode.

Once Qaddafi's plans had been implemented—and Laila had no doubt that the Americans would accept his ultimatum—he would tell Washington where the bomb was and radio the code that would break the firing circuits. They, in the meantime, would have worked their way west to Canada, using false Canadian passports and papers. Their destination would be Vancouver, where a second safe house awaited them. A Panamanian freighter, Greek-run but Libyan-owned, was due there to pick them up December 25. The Canadians, they calculated, wouldn't be watching their piers too closely on Christmas Day.

Laila turned off the Thruway at Spring Valley and a few minutes later pulled into a huge shopping mall, being sure to drive well to the back of its half-empty parking lot.

"Whalid," she told her brother, "you've probably got a less memorable face than I have. Why don't you do the shopping? There's no sense in taking any chances we don't need to."

Whalid smiled and slipped out of the car. As he did, Laila flicked on the radio. She felt herself growing more nervous, more desperate, with each passing moment. She played with the dial until she settled on the loud wail of a Dolly Parton lament. She turned it up as loud as she dared, hoping that somehow the din would overwhelm the black thoughts assailing her. Almost desperately, she clutched at the steering wheel. Don't, she told herself, don't, don't, don't think.

But Michael's image would not leave her: Michael calcinated to black ash; Michael at the instant the incandescent heat seared the life from his body in a flash of pain. It's not going to go off, she

227

kept telling herself. It's not. But in the depths of her soul there was the whisper—what if it does?

She started, her painful reverie broken by the sound of Whalid opening the car door. He got in and Laila reached for the ignition key. As she did, she caught a glimpse of the shopping bag he had set on the seat between them. Aghast, she half pulled a fifth of Johnnie Walker from the bag. "What about your ulcer?"

"Don't worry about my ulcer." Her brother smiled. "It's fine now."

In Paris, the lunch hour was already over. General Henri Bertrand's eyes were half closed and the vacant expression on his face as he advanced along the corridor of an apartment in the city's elegant Sixteenth Arrondissement gave the impression his mind was miles away. It was, in fact, concentrated with a connoisseur's delight on the twitching buttocks of the Spanish maid leading him toward her employer's study.

"Monsieur will be with you in a moment," she intoned, opening the door.

The director of France's intelligence agency nodded gravely and entered the room. It was a miniature museum. One wall was a large window overlooking the Bois. The other three were lined with display cases, each subtly illuminated and backed with velvet fabrics that set off the priceless collection of Oriental and Greco-Roman antiquities they contained. Bertrand himself had been born in Indochina and he had more than a layman's appreciation of Oriental art. Some of the Hindu pieces, notably a finely chiseled stone representation of Shiva which Bertrand judged to date back to the seventh or eighth century, were priceless.

The centerpiece of the collection was an enormous Roman head three or four times life size locked in a display cabinet in the center of the room. Wrapped in the diffused glow cast by a spotlight overhead, that ancient marble radiated a beauty such as Bertrand had rarely contemplated.

Behind him, the SDECE director heard a door opening. He turned to find himself facing a portly bald man in a scarlet silk dressing gown buttoned tightly around his neck, its flaring skirt falling to his ankles. A mandarin, Bertrand thought, or a cardinal on his way into the Sistine Chapel for a conclave.

Paul-Henri de Serre was a senior member of France's nuclear

establishment. He had begun his career working on Zoé, France's first atomic reactor, a device so primitive its control rods had been manipulated with an engine taken from a Singer sewing machine. Most recently, he had supervised the Libyan project, overseeing the reactor's construction, then presiding over its functioning during the critical first six months of its operation.

"How like our American friends to wave an accusing finger at us," he sighed when Bertrand, after apologizing for disturbing his host's siesta, explained the reason for his visit. "They've been jealous of our program for years. The very idea the Libyans could have somehow extracted plutonium from our reactor is ridiculous."

Bertrand took out a Gauloise and politely asked de Serre if he minded if he smoked. Seconds later, the cigarette was in its usual resting place in the right-hand corner of his mouth, fixed there so firmly it appeared to be an appendage to his lips. He sat back in the high leather wing chair de Serre had offered, his hand folded over the slight paunch forming on his midriff.

"Our scientific people confirm what you say," he noted. "Damned embarrassing for us if it did happen, however. Tell me, *cher monsieur,* did anything take place down there that gave you any grounds for suspicion? Anything that seemed unusual, out of the ordinary?"

"Nothing at all." De Serre sipped thoughtfully on the coffee that Paquita, the Spanish maid, had brought them. "Now, this is not to say I don't believe that Qaddafi wouldn't like to get his hands on some plutonium. Every time the word 'nuclear' comes up, there's a gleam in his people's eyes. I'm merely saying he didn't get it from us."

"Would you have any idea where he might have gotten it?"

"Quite frankly, no."

"How about your personnel? Were there any among them with pronounced sympathies for the Arab cause? Sympathies that might have made them amenable to a plea for help from the Libyans?"

"As you know, all of our people were given security checks by the DST before being assigned to the project. To weed out just the sort of individual you're talking about. They all came down more or less sympathetic to the Arab cause. Although, I might add, working with the Libyans tended to disabuse most of them of those notions rather swiftly."

"Difficult people, are they?"

"Impossible."

The General noted with interest the vehemence with which de Serre seemed to spit out the word. Here is one man, he thought, who bears the Libyans no affection.

Their conversation continued for another half hour. Nothing in it, it seemed to the head of the SDECE, opened up an avenue his agency might want to explore. The source of Qaddafi's plutonium was probably elsewhere; an outright theft, perhaps.

"Well, *cher monsieur,* I think I've taken up quite enough of your time," he declared, rising from his armchair.

"If there's anything else I can do, please don't hesitate to call on me," his host murmured.

Turning to leave, Bertrand was once again struck by the breathtaking beauty of the head locked in its display case in the center of the room, by the perfect serenity of that marble mask casting its stone gaze across the centuries.

"A remarkable piece," he said admiringly. "Where did you get it?"

"It came originally from Leptis Magna on the Libyan seacoast." De Serre's eyes caressed his treasure with an expression so adoring that it struck his visitor. "It is beautiful, isn't it?"

"Indeed." Bertrand waved at the glowing display cabinets lining the study. "Your entire collection is extraordinary." He stepped to the head of Shiva he had noted earlier. "This is quite unusual. At least a thousand years old, I should have thought. Did you get it in India?"

"Yes. I was assigned out there as a technical adviser in the early seventies."

The General stared appreciatively at the delicately wrought stone sculpture. "You're a fortunate man," he sighed, "a fortunate man indeed."

Jack Rand finished the last manifest of the Hellenic Stevedore Company's Brooklyn pier and laid it carefully on the stack of papers on the desk. He buttoned his shirt collar and started to tighten his tie, noting irritably as he did that his partner had already finished. Angelo Rocchia's feet were propped up on the desk and he was gnawing a Hostess cupcake to which he had helped himself from the clutter of half-eaten jelly doughnuts and pastries scattered around the office's hot plate. Once again Angelo and Tony Piccardi were bullshitting.

"I think everything's fine here," Rand announced. "Let's get on to the next pier."

Angelo concealed his annoyance with a cold smile. Slowly, very deliberately, he licked the chocolate-cupcake crumbs from his fingertips. This guy, he thought, is an unmitigated pain in the ass. I've never seen anybody in such a fucking hurry. Unless, it suddenly occurred to him, someone's told him something they haven't bothered to tell me.

The detective lowered his feet to the ground and contemplated for a moment his own stack of completed manifests. Then he reached over, flicked through it and pulled one out. Ignoring Rand, he turned to the pier boss. "Hey, Tony, you got any other paper on this shipment?"

Piccardi glanced at the manifest of the *Dionysos,* then reached for a black looseleaf notebook. He kept one on every ship that left cargo on the pier. It contained a copy of the bill of lading for each piece of cargo unloaded, the arrival notice sent to the broker handling the cargo, his delivery order cleared by Customs, and a pier sheet. Piccardi turned to the pier sheet for the ten barrels of diatome consigned to Durkee Filters in Queens. It gave the name of the trucker who had made the pickup, the license number of his truck, the time he left the docks and the details of his load.

"Oh yeah," he said. "I remember this. Murphy usually picks this guy's stuff up. Their guy didn't come in that day. Guy in a Hertz truck made the pickup."

Rand peered down at the manifest. "Angelo," he said, "these barrels weigh five hundred pounds apiece."

"No kidding?" Angelo gave Piccardi a look of ill-feigned wonder. "Kid here, he's got a mind like a computer."

"So, in view of that, why are we wasting time on this when we've got two more piers to cover?"

Angelo twisted around on his stool until he faced the young agent. The smile, the wide toothy smile, was there, but his eyes had lost none of their chill. "Kid, you know something? You are right. Send this thing downtown, it'll be 'What'samatter? Can't those guys divide?' But just for us, let's check it out. That way tonight, over there in that Howard Johnson Motor Lodge they got you in, you put your head on the pillow, you're going to sleep.

You'll know you've covered. Haven't left anything hanging. Tony,'' the detective interrogated the pier boss, ''anybody here deal with this likely to remember anything about it?''

Piccardi pointed to two names at the bottom of the pier sheet. ''Maybe the checker and the loader that handled the stuff.''

Angelo got up, his knee joints creaking. *''Paisan,* how about you taking us up there and introducing us to them?'' He gave a wave of his index finger to Rand. ''Come on, kid. Here's your chance to see what a Brooklyn pier looks like.''

The Brooklyn Ocean Terminal was an endless dark cavern as wide as a football field and twice as long. The odor of burlap mingled in the dust-clogged air with the scent of spices, nuts and coffee, giving it a strange resemblance to an Oriental bazaar. At intervals along its length, shafts of light penetrated the dimness from the doors opening onto the ships tied up at the pier. Forklift trucks darted and circled through the pools of light they formed like water bugs skimming the surface of a pond.

Marching down the pier, Angelo Rocchia and Jack Rand passed pyramiding stacks of Greek olive oil, silver cans of cornseed oil from Turkey, dried raisins from the Sudan, sacks of Indian cashew nuts, bales of cotton from Pakistan, stinking cowhides from Afghanistan, burlap bags of coffee beans from Kenya.

The New Yorker waved at the row of goods disappearing into the shadows. ''You poke around in the corners, you wouldn't believe the shit these longshoremen got stashed away.''

''Hey, Tony,'' Angelo called after Piccardi, ''tell me something. You get many rental trucks making pickups down here?''

''Naw,'' Piccardi replied. ''Two, three a week. Depends.''

He led them up to a cluster of longshoremen unloading pallets of copper tubing and beckoned to a short swarthy man, a cargo hook dangling from his right hand. Angelo noted the whites of the man's eyes. They were spiderwebbed with little pink tracings. Likes the *vino,* he thought.

Piccardi showed the man the sheet. ''Guy here wants to know you remember anything about this pickup.''

Behind the man, work had stopped. The circle of longshoremen looked at Rand and Angelo in sullen, hostile silence. The docker didn't even bother to look at Piccardi's sheet. ''Naw,'' he said, his voice a hoarse rasp. ''I wouldn't remember nothing about it.''

Booze has got his voice too, Angelo mused. He reached into his pocket for a pack of Marlboros. It had been years since he'd given up smoking, but he always carried a pack, right beside his peanuts.

"Here, *gumba*," he said to the docker in Italian, "have a smoke."

As the man lit up, Angelo continued. "Look, what I got here got nothing to do with putting anybody locally in the can, you know what I mean?"

The docker gave Piccardi a wary glance. At that instant, all Angelo's seemingly meaningless chatter in Piccardi's office had its reward. With a barely discernible movement of his eyebrows, the pier boss indicated he was all right.

"What do them barrels look like?" Angelo prodded gently.

"Hey, you know, they're big cans. Big fucking cans. Like garbage cans."

"You remember the guy made the pickup?"

"No."

"I mean, you know, was he a regular? A guy who knows his way around down here? Do the right thing and all?"

It was the tradition of the piers to "smear" the longshoremen who handled your load, to slip them five or ten dollars for their help. Angelo's mention of the custom brought to the docker's face the first intimation of a feeling, other than that of ill-will, that the detective had seen on it.

"Yeah." The reply was a long growl. "Now I remember that jerk. He forgot. We had to let him know something was dragging. You know—" he half whistled, half blew a spurt of air through his teeth—"put a little kabootz on him. When he got the message, he come half a yard. Sure." There was even a smile on the docker's saturnine features. "I remember him."

Angelo's thick eyebrows rose. Who comes up with fifty bucks? he wondered. No Italian. No Irishman. In fact, no one who's been around the docks. Has to be a stranger, a guy who isn't onto it.

"You remember what he looked like?"

"Hey, you know, he was a guy. What could I tell you? A guy."

"Angelo." Rand's voice was sharp. "We're wasting our time here. Let's get on to the next dock."

"Sure, kid, we're on our way." Angelo indicated Piccardi's pier sheet. "How about the other guy that handled the load? The checker?"

"He's on a break over at the Longshoremen's Club."

"Okay, kid, let's stop in there on our way out." Before Rand could articulate the protest Angelo knew was coming, the detective threw an arm around his shoulder. "Let me tell you what happens in an Italian club like this longshoremen's place, kid," he said, his voice a friendly growl. "They play Italian card games. You know how an Italian card game is? Everybody sits at the same side of the table."

He gave a jovial laugh and slapped Rand on the back. "You interview guys at an Italian card game, it goes like this. 'Who shot the guy?' 'Hey, I don't know, I didn't see nothin'. I was playing cards. Had my back to the door.' So you ask the next guy, 'What'd you see?' 'Nothing, what could I tell you? I was sitting my back to the door. Playing cards.'

"It's always like that. Everybody sits on the same side. With their backs to the door. Nobody's ever on the other three sides." Angelo laughed, then stopped his march back down the pier. This guy, he told himself, is going to be no help to me in that club. I won't get the time of day out of anybody with him standing beside me.

"Look, kid," he cajoled. "You're in a hurry. I'm in a hurry." He took the pier sheet from Piccardi and pointed to the license number of the truck that had made the pickup. "While I'm in there, why don't you go to Tony's office, call Hertz, find out where this truck comes from and get what they have off the rental agreement?"

Less than five minutes later, Angelo was back. His visit to the club had been totally unproductive. Rand handed him a slip of paper with the details of the Hertz truck's rental agreement on it. The truck had been rented at a Hertz truck agency on Fourth Avenue, just behind the docks, at ten Friday morning, a few minutes before the pier sheet showed it had reached the pier. It had been returned at the end of the day. The man who had rented it had used his American Express card to pay. His New York State driver's license gave his name and address: Gerald Putman, Interocean Imports, 123 Cadman Plaza West, Brooklyn.

Angelo gave the address an appraising glance. "Looks legitimate to me. Let's just check it out. One telephone call and we know we're clean." He picked up the telephone directory, found Interocean's number and dialed it.

Rand heard Angelo identifying himself to a switchboard opera-

234

tor, then asking for Putman. In the silence that followed, the New Yorker gave the agent a bemused smile. "Ever heard of a truck driver who's got a secretary?"

"Mr. Putman," he announced. "Detective Angelo Rocchia, New York Police Department. We've been informed by the Hertz Rent-A-Truck office over on Fourth Avenue, Brooklyn, that you rented one of their vehicles last Friday morning around ten and we'd just like to—"

Three feet away, Rand could hear Putman's surprised and angry voice interrupting the detective. "I what? Listen, officer, last Friday was the day I lost my wallet. I spent the whole morning right here in this office."

The headquarters of the pier search of which Angelo Rocchia and Jack Rand were a small part was in New York's emergency command center. It had become operational a few minutes after nine. Buried three floors below the State Supreme Court Building on Foley Square, it was an ideal place to manage a crisis in secret. So infrequently had the center been used in the years since it had been installed by the Lindsay administration that nearly everyone involved with it, including the City Hall press corps, had forgotten it was there.

It was entered through an obscure side door to the courthouse. Basically, it was just a huge underground cavern divided into areas by salmon-pink wood panels eight feet high. Everything else in it was administrative gray: gray walls, gray floors, gray filing cabinets, gray redundant furniture thrown out of City Hall, gray faces on the policemen assigned to watch over it twenty-four hours a day. The last time the place had been used was during the great blackout in July 1977, when, to the Police Department's embarrassment, its lights had gone out along with everyone else's. Someone had forgotten to keep its generators serviced.

Quentin Dewing, the FBI assistant director for investigation, had taken on the job of organizing the center. He did it in the methodical, careful manner for which the Bureau was famous. By the time the Police Commissioner and Al Feldman, his Chief of Detectives, had finished dispatching their manpower, he was ready to give them a guided tour of the place. The first room, designed to be the center's switchboard in an emergency, he had assigned to the effort to run down the Arabs who, according to their I94 forms, had come into the New York area in the last six months. The room had fifty telephone lines. Each was manned by an agent, some holding open phones to JFK or the Immigration and Naturalization Service in Washington. On one desk was a minicomputer serving as a central locator file. Every incoming name and address was punched into it. If the person belonging to the name hadn't been found and cleared in two hours, the computer dumped the name into a higher-priority file.

The operation next door was even more impressive. It had been designated by Dewing as the headquarters for the pier search. Maps of New York and New Jersey's 578 miles of waterfront hung on the walls. All of the waterfront's two hundred piers were listed on charts under the maps.

Every time one of the teams working the piers came across a suspicious piece of cargo, the name and address of the consignee was telephoned to the center. If the cargo had been delivered in the New York area, the center dispatched a team of Customs inspectors or drug enforcement agents to track it down. If it had been shipped outside New York, an agent from the nearest FBI office was sent after it.

The tour completed, Dewing took Bannion and Feldman to his own command post set up in what was meant to be the Mayor's suite in an emergency. Next door, the CIA and the FBI had installed multiflex printout receivers to deliver to the New York operation the harvest of their files and their overseas contacts.

While the Chief listened, resting against an old desk, his arms folded across his chest, Dewing explained how Clifford Salisbury of the CIA was combing through the terrorist files, sorting out those individuals who had spent time in the United States and appeared to have a high level of sophistication. On a morning like this, Al Feldman looked every one of his sixty-two years. His hair, what was left of it, was grayish white and greasy, popping out from his skull in disorderly little spirals that invariably sprinkled a glaze of dandruff on the shoulders of his dark suit. He picked his nose and looked at the CIA man, at the pile of dossiers on his desk.

Terrific, he thought, he'll have a hundred of those things before he's through. And they would be perfectly useless. What would you do with them? Take them out to some bartender in Arab town and say, "Hey, have you ever seen this guy? This guy? This guy?"

After three or four photos, the guy would have switched off. Be so confused, he wouldn't be able to recognize a picture of his sister.

Feldman pulled a Camel from a pack that looked as if he'd slept on it and lit it. He had a lot of respect for the methodical, almost ponderous approach the Bureau used. Most investigations were, after all, like this one, shaped like a pyramid. They started across a broad base and worked, hopefully, to one very precise point. It was a proven system. Given a week, ten days, it got results.

The trouble is, Feldman thought, this guy has forgotten he's only got thirty hours. Qaddafi will have fried this place and he'll still be in Phase Three of his investigation. If all this is going to get anywhere, Feldman mused, we've got to have that big break, the Son of Sam parking ticket, the one face in the crowd to look for. And we've got to have it awfully fast.

"Excuse me, Mr. Dewing," he said, looking at his watch. "I told my intelligence officer who covers the Arab neighborhoods over in Brooklyn there to bring in the material he's got on the PLO. I'd better go find him."

"Of course, Chief. It would be helpful if we could have a look at anything worthwhile you might have." The tone of the FBI man's voice made it clear how unlikely he thought that possibility was.

The intelligence officer was a genial, freckle-faced Irishman to whom the Department, with a fine sense of balance, had also assigned the responsibility of following the activities of the Jewish Defense League. His files contained almost nothing worthwhile and hadn't since the passage of the Freedom of Information Act. Police intelligence represented educated gossip, a tip picked up by a cop on the beat from a friendly bartender or grocer, an item squeezed from an informer: "The Arab Red Crescent Society, 135 Atlantic Avenue, which has filed for a tax exemption as a charity, is suspected of raising funds for the PLO." "The Damascus Coffee House, 204 Atlantic Avenue, is frequently patronized by supporters of George Habbash."

With the FOI that material could eventually come under public scrutiny, and since no one wanted it out, nothing worthwhile ever went into the files. The good stuff was held "on the hip," in an intelligence officer's personal notebook that no one but he had the right to open, and the Irishman's listed this December morning thirty-eight PLO suspects, most of them among the younger, poorer Palestinian immigrants living in the neighborhoods crowding up toward the fringes of the black slums of Bedford-Stuyvesant.

"At least we know where they are," Feldman commented. "Not like the ones they've got in there. Bring them all in. Grill them. Establish everything they've been doing in the last seventy-two hours."

"On what grounds, Chief?"

"Find some. Immigration papers. Half of 'em probably are illegals anyway."

"Christ! We do that, we'll have every civil-rights lawyer in the city on our backs."

And so what, Feldman was about to add, there may not be any civil-rights lawyers around in a couple of days anyway, when a plainclothesman interrupted. "Telephone, Chief."

It was Angelo Rocchia. The Chief was neither surprised nor irritated by the fact that Rocchia had called him directly, short-circuiting the formal chain of command that Dewing had just finished showing him. He knew who the good guys in his division were, the solid diggers whose work could make him look good upstairs, and those guys he had always encouraged to act independently, to come directly to him with a problem. He listened to Angelo's story, then uttered the three words used more often than any others in the Detective Division of the New York Police Department: "Repeat that again."

This time, Feldman scrawled a series of hasty notes on a pad on the desk. When Angelo had finished, it took him five seconds to reach a decision.

"You get over to that guy's office in Brooklyn and see if you can get a line on who grabbed his wallet," he ordered. "I'll have someone else cover your piers."

As he talked, he was already dialing the head of the Pickpocket Squad on a second phone. "Get the photos of all the dips who work Brooklyn," he ordered, "and get your ass over to 123 Cadman Plaza West."

"Got something, Chief?" the intelligence officer asked.

"I doubt it," Feldman growled. "I'm going to get a cup of coffee, though."

The Chief headed toward the custodian's office, where he had spotted a Silex and a hot plate. It was the first moment he'd had to himself since he left his office two hours earlier, and, meditating almost, he blew at the hot black coffee, then glanced at the wall over the hot plate. Stuck to it was what appeared to be an old Civil Defense poster bearing the once familiar "CD" in its black circle and white triangle. He noted its government printing number and the headline "PROCEDURE TO FOLLOW IN THE EVENT OF A THER-MONUCLEAR ATTACK."

Seven points were listed there, beginning with "1. Stay clear of all windows."

Feldman scanned the list.

5. Loosen necktie, unbutton shirt sleeves, and any other restrictive clothing.
6. Immediately upon seeing the brilliant flash of a nuclear explosion, bend over and place your head firmly between your legs.

At the last line, the detective burst out laughing. No words could have summed up better than the ones he saw there the insane, desperate mess they were in:

7. Kiss your ass goodbye.

"We got a situation in this town . . ." Angelo Rocchia, Jack Rand noted with exasperation, was embarked on yet another of his monologues.

The FBI agent was still burning at the freewheeling manner with which the New Yorker had bypassed the chain of command and gotten them taken off their pier assignment to go chasing pickpockets. Like the Marines, the FBI taught its recruits that discipline was the key to success: spiritual discipline to build character, intellectual discipline in an investigation, collective discipline when working as a team so that every team member knew he could count on every other team member to do exactly what he was supposed to do. That kind of discipline, Rand reflected sourly, was a quality conspicuously lacking in his New York partner.

If Angelo was aware of the young man's anger, however, he gave no indication of it. He went on as though he were lecturing a group of recruits at the Police Academy. "Dips in this town'll pick your pocket by appointment. No big deal. Custom work, they call

239

it. Fence comes to the dip, says, 'Hey, Charlie, I need some fresh cards noon tomorrow. No more than two, three hours old. Wanta buy a color TV for the old lady, it's her birthday.' So the dip takes the job on consignment. He gets to keep the cash in the guy's wallet and gets a couple of yards for his ID and two, three cards. Guy's got a whole lot of plastic, the dip'll hold a few cards back. Sell 'em to somebody else for a dime apiece. He'll make two, three hundred bucks on the deal. That ain't bad.''

Yards, Rand thought, dimes. They can't even speak English in this city. "So, Angelo, if I understand you, what you're suggesting is that something like this might have happened here.''

"I think it might have, yeah.''

"Angelo, how many pickpockets would you reckon work the New York area?''

Angelo whistled softly, maneuvering his Corvette as he did into the inside lane to get a jump on the traffic at the stop light ahead. "Three, four, five hundred.''

Rand tapped the crystal of his Rolex. "It's after eleven, Angelo. And that damn barrel's supposed to go off at three o'clock tomorrow afternoon. Do you really think we're going to find and interrogate five hundred pickpockets? Pick out of that mess the one who may—or may not—have stolen the guy's wallet, find out whom he gave it to, locate that guy, all by three o'clock tomorrow?''

"Kid, how the fuck would I know?'' Angelo was moving along Fulton Street now, and he could see the outlines of Cadman Plaza rising by the exit loops of the Brooklyn Bridge. "But for now, it's the best thing we've got. In fact, for now it's the only thing we've got.''

He was already searching for an illegal parking place close to their destination. "Besides, you and I aren't going to bust this thing. None of us are here. We're just window-dressing. It's the people in Washington who gotta handle this one, not us.''

The people in Washington had been in semipermanent session since their first Crisis Committee meeting with Abe Stern. The President came and went, depending on his schedule and his efforts to maintain a façade of normality for the benefit of the press. He had just rejoined the meeting after turning over the session of his Council of Economic Advisers to Charlie Schultz.

"Have we heard from Tripoli? Is Qaddafi ready to talk?" he asked the Deputy Secretary of State as he lowered himself into his chair.

"Sir, we've just had the consulate on the blower," Warren Christopher replied. "The chargé's still out at the villa where Qaddafi's supposed to be staying."

A few seats away, Harold Brown spoke. It was almost as though he was thinking out loud. "You know, since the beginning of this thing no one has actually seen Qaddafi or heard his threat articulated from his own lips. This is, after all, such a fantastic escalation of the threat level. Are we sure he's behind it? Could he have been kidnapped? The victim of some kind of Palestinian coup?"

Almost automatically, the attention in the room shifted to the CIA's Bennington. The stack of papers in front of his chair was conspicuously higher than anyone else's. That reflected the fact that since the Cuban Missile Crisis it had been government policy to make the raw input of intelligence sources available to the President in an emergency even if they differed, rather than having an agency analyst synthesize the material for him.

"We've looked at that one," Bennington replied, "and our decision is no. The nuclear program has always been strictly Qaddafi's work. He keeps his own Palestinians on a tight leash and under close guard. His relations with Arafat and the PLO have been more than strained since he broke with them because he accused them of being too ready to compromise. And our voice analysts have now confirmed that that's his voice on the original tape."

"Better late than never," the President tartly observed. "Do we have anything new from New York?"

Before William Webster of the FBI could answer, the red warning light on Warren Christopher's telephone flashed. "Sir," he said, after listening a second, "the operations center is pulling in a Cherokee NODIS from Tripoli." A Cherokee NODIS was the State Department's highest cable priority, a term assigned it by Dean Rusk in honor of his native Cherokee County, Georgia. "We'll have it in a second."

In the Department's seventh-floor operations center the incoming coded text was automatically fed into a computer which decoded it instantaneously and printed a clear text on the duty officer's cable console. He, in turn, relayed it immediately to the White House communications center, where a warrant officer pushed a button on another console that spewed out a printed text as fast as the cable's words rose on the screen. Christopher had barely hung up his phone when the warrant officer handed the message to Eastman.

"Sir," he said, glancing at it, "the chargé has just spoken personally with Qaddafi."

"And?"

"And he says everything he has to say is in his original message. He refuses to talk to you."

The New York Police Department, Gerald Putman thought, is a much maligned body. He had not even bothered to report his wallet to the police as lost or stolen, assuming, as he supposed any citizen in a similar situation would, that his report would be lost in a morass of bureaucratic indifference and ineptitude. Yet here in his office were an obviously senior detective, the head of the Pickpocket Squad and a federal officer, all trying to help him establish what had happened to his wallet.

"All right, Mr. Putman," Angelo Rocchia said, "let's just go through that one more time. You spent all Friday morning here in this office. Then, at about . . ."

"Twelve-thirty."

The detective checked his notebook. "Right. You went over to the Fulton Fish Market to Luigi's for lunch. At approximately two P.M. you reached for your wallet to get your American Express card to pay the check and found your wallet was missing, right?"

"Right."

"You returned here, where you keep a record of all your credit card numbers, and had your secretary call them to report the loss."

"That's correct, Officer."

"And you didn't bother to notify the local precinct?"

Putman gave Angelo an awkward smile. "I'm sorry, Officer, I just thought that with everything you people have to do these days, something like this would, you know . . ." His voice dwindled to an embarrassed mumble.

The detective returned the smile, but his gray eyes were cold and appraising. Angelo liked to give people like Putman the impression he was a little slow, a bit of a plodder. It never hurt to disarm a client, to get him to relax a bit. Putman was in his midthirties, medium height, a trifle stocky, with a dark tan and a swarthy complexion. Maybe an Italian had wandered into the bed of one of Putman's WASP ancestors, Angelo mused.

"Now, Mr. Putman, let's go over everything that happened to you that day very slowly, very carefully. First of all, where do you keep your wallet?"

"Right here." Putman tapped the right hip pocket of his pants. He was wearing gray slacks, a blue button-down shirt and a striped tie. Everything in his office, the thick wall-to-wall carpeting, the understated mahogany furniture, the huge window looking over to the tip of Manhattan, indicated upper-middle-class affluence.

"You were wearing an overcoat, I suppose?" This time the question came from the head of the Pickpocket Squad whom Feldman had ordered to meet Angelo here.

"Oh yes," Putman replied. "I've got it right there."

He walked to a closet and took out a Cheviot tweed coat he had bought at Burberry's in London. The head of the Pickpocket Squad examined it, then slipped his fingers up its high-cut center vent.

"Convenient." He smiled.

Methodically, prompted by Angelo, Putman recreated his activities of Friday, December 11. He'd gotten up at 7 A.M. in his home in Oyster Bay. His wife had driven him, as she did regularly, to the station, where he'd bought *The Wall Street Journal* and waited only two minutes on the platform for the 8:07 Long Island Rail Road train. On the way in, he had sat next to his friend and squash partner Grant Esterling, an IBM executive. He'd gotten off, as always, at the Flatbush Avenue Terminal and walked the rest of the way to his office. He remembered absolutely nothing unusual, out of the way, on the train, at the terminal or on his ten-minute walk to the office: no one bumping into him, no one shoving him, no jarring movement, nothing.

When he had finished, the room was so quiet that all four men could hear the tick-tock of the old-fashioned grandfather's clock in one corner of Putman's office. Rand impatiently crossed, then uncrossed his legs.

"It sounds like we got a very artistic bit of work here," the head of the Pickpocket Squad noted with respect.

"It sure does." Angelo made a swift doodle in his notepad, a stick figure of a doll. My good idea, he mused, doesn't look so good anymore. He rose. "Mr. Putman," he said, "we're going to show you some pictures. Take all the time you want to look at them. Study them very carefully and tell us if you think you've ever seen any of these people anywhere before.''

If travel broadened, the young men and women in the procession of photographs Angelo laid one by one on Putman's desk should have constituted a unique cultural elite. Only a handful of experienced travelers could claim the knowledge of the capitals of the world they possessed. No great international gathering from the Olympic Games in Montreal or Lake Placid, the election of a Pope in the Vatican, the Queen's Jubilee in London, the World Cup in Buenos Aires could be celebrated without their presence. They were the best of the world's pickpockets, and, almost without exception, the dark-haired, dark-complexioned youths in the mug shots passing through Gerald Putman's hands were Colombian.

As the Basque country exports shepherds, Antwerp diamond cutters, so that Latin American nation exported coffee, emeralds, cocaine—and pickpockets. There were in the miserable *calles* of Bogotá, the Colombian capital, a whole series of Faginesque pickpocketing schools. Poor farm children were literally sold into servitude to the schools' masters to learn the trade. In the Plaza Bolivia, along the Avenue Santander, they were taught every trick of the art, how to slit a pocket with a razor, open unnoticed a handbag, pluck a Rolex watch from an unsuspecting wrist. As a graduation exercise they had to demonstrate fingers so skilled they could slip a wallet from a pocket to which was sewn a line of jingle bells without causing a single bell to ring.

Once trained, they assembled into teams of twos and threes, because a good dip never worked alone, and fanned out all over the world in search of the crowds, conventions, tourists and unsuspecting pockets from which they extracted well over a million dollars a year.

Putman had gone through almost fifty photos when suddenly he stopped and stared at the photo of a girl, dark rolls of hair falling to her shoulders, her breasts thrusting challengingly against a tightly drawn white silk blouse.

"Oh yes," he said with a nervous half-chuckle, "I think I recognize this one. I think that's the girl I nearly knocked down the other day at the foot of the stairway coming down the train platform." The memory of the incident came flooding back. "Of course. It's her all right. It was quite embarrassing. I ran right into her and she had to grab onto me to keep from falling."

244

"Mr. Putman," Angelo asked very quietly, "could the other day have been Friday?"

The importer hesitated, trying to reconstruct the moment in his mind. "My goodness," he said, "you know, I think it was."

The detective took the photograph back and studied the girl's pretty face, her provocative breasts so defiantly exposed to the policeman's camera. "You didn't bump into her, Mr. Putman, she bumped into you. They love to work with girls with big tits. She jams those knockers into you while the dip boosts your wallet."

He noticed a flush on the importer's cheeks. "Don't worry, Mr. Putman. Everybody gets turned on by girls with big tits. Even guys like you from Oyster Bay."

Abe Stern glanced angrily at Jeremy Oglethorpe. The evacuation expert was bustling around the Police Commissioner's office, hanging flow charts, diagrams, maps with those damnable colored circles all over them onto walls and easels, displaying an energy so frenetic he might have been a Madison Avenue account executive about to make a presentation for a new toothpaste account.

The Mayor had elected to bring him here rather than to City Hall because the Police Commissioner's office was more secure than his. They had come by helicopter right from the Marine Air Terminal to the pad on the roof.

"Well," Oglethorpe announced, surveying his display with quiet pride, "I think I'm ready if your people are."

The Police Commissioner turned to one of the two inspectors he had summoned to the meeting. "Where the hell is Walsh?" he growled.

"He's on his way, sir."

Walsh was Timothy Walsh, thirty-seven, a six-foot-three-inch Brooklyn-born lieutenant who presided over the NYPD's Office of Civil Preparedness. He was a shrewd, ambitious empire-building Irishman who had been moved to Civil Preparedness from the Intelligence Bureau with orders to make it snap, and snap it did. Any kind of catastrophe that might strike the city was supposed to be in his bailiwick. Walsh, however, had a solid preference for those that were the high-media-exposure areas, the areas that could get you applause from the Commissioner's office, beef up your budget, swell your staff; things like power failures, hurricanes, flooding, blizzards. Evacuation and civil defense were at the bottom of the pile. The problem with civil defense, Timothy Walsh was fond of remarking, was, "People don't want to know. It's 'Hey, look, don't bother me with those fucking Russian bombs. I got a foot of snow in my driveway.' "

His own thoughts on the subject were succinctly summed up in a phrase he often repeated to his deputy: "Every so often I go down to Washington and genuflect on the altar of the thermonuclear holocaust so I can keep the federal money coming in for the things that really count in this city, like getting some more portable generators for our next power failure."

Now, whistling cheerfully, Walsh nodded at the detective manning the electric gate leading to the Police Commissioner's suite and found himself quickly ushered into his office. At the sight of all the heavies in the room, Walsh's cheerfulness disappeared.

"Walsh, have we got a plan to evacuate this city in a crisis?" the Police Commissioner demanded.

Oh-oh, Walsh thought, why is he asking that? Better use a little soft-shoe routine here. Toss a few balls in the air and see which way the wind is blowing. Such a plan did, in fact, exist. It was called "The New York Target Support Area Operational Survival Plan, Volume I, Basic Plan." Drawn up in 1972, it contained 202 pages and was generally acknowledged to be worthless. So worthless, Walsh had never bothered to read it; nor, as far as he knew, had anyone else in his department.

"Sir, the last time we looked at evacuation was a report we did in December 1977 for Commissioner Codd. Con Ed wanted to start running liquefied natural gas up the East River to their storage farm at Berrian's Island and we were asked if we could clear the East Side in a helluva hurry if there was a spill."

"And?"

"And the conclusion was it was an absolutely hopeless job. Better not to let the LNG up the river in the first place."

The Police Commissioner grunted. "Well, sit down and listen to this man here. Between now and four o'clock this afternoon, you and he have got to come up with a plan to clear this city in the shortest possible time."

Walsh folded his large frame onto the Police Commissioner's blue sofa, a whole series of alarm bells ringing in his psyche as he did. He watched Oglethorpe moving to his charts. There was some-

246

thing vaguely familiar, it occurred to him, about the face of the man above the blue polka-dot tie.

Oglethorpe took up a rubber-tipped pointer and began, a professor lecturing a class. "Fortunately, the problem of evacuating New York City is one that we have spent a great deal of time in studying. I don't need to tell you it's a staggering challenge. The shortest time we've been able to come up with for clearing the city in our crisis-relocation studies is three days."

"Three days!" Abe Stern snapped. "That son of a bitch over in Tripoli is barely giving us three hours!"

Oglethorpe grimaced his acknowledgment. Unfortunately, as he explained, all Civil Defense evacuation plans were built around what he called "a wartime scenario." In it, the United States would have five to six days warning of a Soviet thermonuclear attack because of certain preparations the Russians would have to make which would be observed by U.S. satellites. This prospect was one they hadn't thought a great deal about.

"To be safe," Oglethorpe went on, "we've got to plan on evacuating Manhattan, the southern Bronx, most of Queens and Brooklyn and a strip of New Jersey river shore four miles deep."

"How many people will that involve?" Abe Stern asked.

"Eleven million."

The Mayor groaned softly. Walsh looked at him. Jesus, Mary and Joseph, he thought, what do you evacuate eleven million people for? Only one thing.

Oglethorpe turned back to his map. "One thing we do know, it's going to be a ground burst. That means fallout, bad fallout. Looking at New York's prevailing winds tells you that Queens and Long Island have the highest probability of getting heavy fallout. We've got the Weather Service monitoring the winds for us now and it looks like they're going to get drenched if this goes. The best natural fallout shelter for those people is the cellar. In New York State you've got one of the highest cellar percentages in the country—seventy-three percent." Oglethorpe was on familiar ground now, dealing with statistics, numbers, figures. "Unfortunately, that figure drops down to twenty-two percent out on Long Island because the island's got a high water table. Those people are going to be in a lot of trouble out there if this thing explodes."

"Shouldn't we evacuate them too?" the Mayor queried.

"How?" Oglethorpe replied. "They can't swim off that island,

and if we pull them back toward the bridges we'll be exposing them to more fallout and the possibility of burns." Normally the mild-mannered Oglethorpe wouldn't have replied in so brutal a fashion, but New Yorkers, he firmly believed, liked tough, pragmatic speakers.

"The one thing we've got to avoid at all costs is moving people into fallout. So that means unless there's a shift in the weather patterns our evacuation is going to have to go north up into Westchester and west into Jersey.

"The first thing I'd do is shut off all access to the city when we get our 'go.' Make all access one way—outbound. Now, here in Manhattan only twenty-one percent of your people have first cars. Very low figure compared to the national average. That means eighty percent of the people have got to get out by other means. We'll want to mobilize all the buses we can lay our hands on. Any large truck fleets we can get, too. Luckily, we've got the use of the subways, which were more or less denied to us in our wartime scenario. We'll want to make large use of them. Load them up, switch them into the express lanes and tell them to go like hell. Send as many as we can into the upper Bronx. Take people as far up there as you can, and tell them to get out and walk."

"Jesus Christ!" It was the Police Commissioner contemplating the chaos Oglethorpe's ideas were going to produce. "Can you imagine the field day the looters are going to have?"

Oglethorpe smiled. "Sure, there are going to be plenty of scavengers combing your luxury high-rises," he admitted. "But if they're ready to run the risk of being incinerated for a color TV, well, so be it. You can hardly expect your police, whom you're going to need for more important matters anyway, to run around booking them as though Manhattan was going to be here on Wednesday morning."

"Where are you going to put all those people?" the Mayor asked. "You can't just take them out and dump them in a street in the Bronx or over in the Jersey Flats in the middle of winter."

"Well, sir." Oglethorpe straightened up. "Crisis relocation is based on the concept of risk areas and host areas. We move population from overpopulated risk areas to underpopulated host areas. In our New York 'wartime scenario' "—he was looking at a map of New York State—"we contemplated moving people as far out as Syracuse and Rochester. Here we'll want to work much closer in. Ask the authorities in Westchester to prepare to welcome these people in what we in Civil Defense call 'congregate care facilities' —schools and hospitals.''

Terrific, Walsh thought, listening to him. This is beautiful. Can you imagine the look on the Police Chief's face up there in Scarsdale when we call up and say, Hey, Chief, look, we're sending you up half a million of our best Bedford-Stuyvesant blacks for the weekend? The guy'll go fucking bananas.

Suddenly it occurred to Walsh where he'd seen Oglethorpe before. It was in Washington at a briefing in the Pentagon on crisis relocation. He'd come away from it convinced the idea of even trying to evacuate New York was bullshit. The New York temperament, the unruliness of the population, the sheer staggering size of it, it was all too overwhelming; better not to even think about it.

"How about the old, the infirm, the people who just can't get up and move like that?'' the Mayor was asking.

Oglethorpe gave a hopeless shrug. "You'll just have to tell them to go underground and pray.''

He turned back to his chart. It had all been so clear in their studies. Why, they had gamed the evacuation of New York three times in Washington in March 1977 on the computer, gradually working the time down from three days eighteen hours to three days flat. Everything was beautifully laid out, indexed and tabulated. You knew you had 3.8 million housing units in your risk area, with an average occupancy of 3.0 persons, ranging from 3.8 in Suffolk County to 2.2 in Manhattan. You knew you had 75,000 persons, 21,400 occupied units and 19,600 first autos per zip code in Nassau County, 40,000 persons, 19,400 units and 4,300 first autos in Manhattan.

They were going to use, for example, 310 commercial aircraft flying out of eight risk-area airports, seventy-one flights an hour over three days to move 1.24 million people. They had said it couldn't be done, but they had found out how, turnaround times, everything. The trains. They knew how they'd use the six rail routes in and out of the city, how they'd maximize traffic flow. They had even figured out how they'd use the freight cars in the Jersey yards, thirty box cars and three locomotives a train; 2,500 people, which gave you an average space allowance of six square feet per person.

They had counted in the Staten Island ferries, reckoning that taking over the automobile space they could get five thousand people onto a ferry. Even New York's 125 tugboats and 250 open barges were included in their plans.

They had spent weeks identifying nine special highway routes suitable for getting people out of the city. It was all so well thought out—right down to the fact that there were a quarter of a million people on Manhattan Island with pets who'd drive you crazy if they couldn't take them along and half a million people with no luggage. But it was all based on three days—three days of careful, organized effort, not one spastic surge for the bridges like they were being asked to look at here.

Oglethorpe shook his head, trying to root out the dismay this disorderly problem caused his orderly mind, and plowed ahead. "The highways and the subways will have to be our principal modes. Everybody inside the five-PSI circle"—that was the five-pounds-per-square-inch-over-pressure circle, the second ring the Mayor had seen in Washington—"has got to come out. Personally, I'm happy if we can evacuate down to two PSI. Do that and we'll be in great shape.

"We've got to maintain an orderly flow of cars out of the city. There are lots of ways. We can do it alphabetically. Broadcast the instructions on radio and TV: 'Vehicles registered in the names of people beginning with A through D leave now!' Or odd-even license plates. Do it by zip codes. Start with the high-risk zip codes at the Manhattan core and roll our risk out."

"Look," the Police Commissioner pointed out, "this place is an island. Cars are going to break down, overheat, run out of gas and jam the tunnels and bridges up. People are going to overload them with their families and their belongings. Remember those pictures of the people on the roads in France in 1940? Pushing baby carriages full of pots and pans?"

"Yes," Oglethorpe agreed, "but our psychologists assure us that if a family has a car, they'll use it. It gives them mobility and provides them with a sense of security."

Timothy Walsh stirred uncomfortably. I think I'm dreaming here, he told himself. All these beautiful charts, these maps, these nice ideas. He looked at the Mayor and the Police Commissioner, so desperately attentive it was almost as though they were silently wishing that somehow all this could really be done.

"Look, mister," Walsh said, "I don't want to throw sour grapes around here, but I'm not sure you understand some of the facts of life in this town. You want to evacuate alphabetically? Tell Mr. Abbott to get in his car and go first? And you think Mr. Rodriguez up there in Spanish Harlem is going to sit around and watch him go tooling off? Sure he is. What Mr. Rodriguez is going to do is to be down there on the street corner with his Saturday-night special and he's going to tell Mr. Abbott to get the fuck out of his car and walk. He's riding.''

"That's what the police are for. To maintain order and prevent that sort of thing.''

"The police?'' Walsh couldn't help laughing. "What makes you think the cops are going to obey? I tell you half of them are going to be out there on the street corner with their thirty-eights. Right beside Mr. Rodriguez. They are going to take over the first car they see and head for the hills, too.'' Walsh shrugged at the impracticality of it all. "All this stuff is great if you've got a bunch of trained soldiers. But you haven't got any soldiers here. Just a bunch of scared people.''

"All right, Walsh,'' the Police Commissioner barked angrily, "that's enough of that.'' Yet, despite his irate words, a sickening voice inside him told him that the lieutenant was probably right. He looked at Abe Stern. There was no expression on the Mayor's face, no hint of what he really thought of all this.

"We will rely on TV and radio as an instant channel to communicate with the population,'' Oglethorpe continued, grateful for the Police Commissioner's support. "I'd close the banks immediately and announce you've done it. Otherwise, everyone will rush to draw out their savings.''

A sudden burst of inspiration registered on Oglethorpe's face like a tide of sunlight flooding out from behind a storm cloud. "For radio and TV, I recommend we employ an old scheme of ours called CHAT.'' He smiled, almost condescendingly. "That's an acronym for Crisis Home Alert Technique. Unfortunately, the FCC would never let us use it.

"What you do is have all the radio and TV stations announce an important message from the President—in this case, the Mayor. As soon as he goes on, all the radio and television stations reduce their modulation to sixty percent of normal. That way, everybody has to turn the volume way, way up to hear him. As part of his speech, he tells everybody to leave their radios and televisions on all the time to receive instructions. "Now, when you have something important to announce, you tell the stations to move their modulation back to normal. I can tell you the noise that will come out of these TV sets will shake the house down. Of course," Oglethorpe added apologetically, "it's not very much help if you're deaf."

Oh boy, Walsh thought. Still, there was one reassuring thing in what Oglethorpe had said—use radio and television. Because one thing you sure as hell weren't going to use if you wanted to alert anybody was the old Civil Defense siren system. Once in the fifties there had been 750 sirens in the city, tested once a week, audible to ninety-five percent of the population. Now, Walsh knew, there were barely three hundred that worked, and most of those were crumbling in disrepair. The siren system's most recent contribution to the city's welfare had come in Herald Square when one had toppled into the street, almost killing a lady shopper heading for Macy's.

"It's very important," Oglethorpe was saying, "that all the messages we give the public over TV are very supportive. The public must be assured that we have a plan, that everything's been worked out and they'll be taken care of when they get to where they're going. Our plans must be precise enough and credible enough to reassure the people and prevent panic."

He turned next to a chart on one of his stands. Its heading was one word, "TAKE." "We can show this chart on the television at intervals so that people will take the right things with them."

Walsh looked at the list. Extra socks, a thermos of water, a can opener, candles, matches, transistor, toothbrush and toothpaste, Kotex, toilet paper, special medicine, Social Security card, credit cards.

Oglethorpe turned the page. The one beneath was headed "DO NOT TAKE." It listed firearms, narcotics, alcohol.

The man is a genius, Walsh thought. He's managed to find the three items nobody in this town is going to go anywhere without in an emergency.

"What we've got to do is get on top of it and stay on top of it," Oglethorpe declared. "I'd like to devote the next three hours to a helicopter survey of your access routes to confirm our SRI information. Then I'd like to get over to the Metropolitan Transportation Authority headquarters on Jay Street in the Bronx with your people to set up a subway plan."

Oh my God, thought Walsh. Jay Street's in Brooklyn! This guy's going to save New York and he doesn't even know the difference between Brooklyn and the Bronx!

"Just a minute." It was Abe Stern's authoritative voice. "It seems to me we're overlooking one of the most important elements in the whole damn picture here. This city has, or at least it used to have when Rockefeller was governor, one of the best systems of air-raid shelters in the world. Why the hell aren't we using them?"

Oglethorpe beamed. No one needed to remind an old Civil Defense warhorse like him of Rockefeller's program. In the late fifties and early sixties, thanks to Rockefeller's zealousness, New York's shelter program had been the pride of the whole Civil Defense establishment. The U.S. Army Corps of Engineers and the city's Public Works Department had selected and licensed sixteen thousand shelters designed to accommodate 6.5 million people in cellars and at the core of the city's buildings. The yellow-and-black fallout-shelter sign had become as familiar a part of the city's landscape as the white and red "WALK" and "DON'T WALK" signs introduced at about the same time. Millions of city and matching federal dollars had been employed to stock the shelters with the basic ingredients that would allow their occupants to survive underground for fourteen days: carbohydrate candy, protein crackers wrapped in individual packs in wax paper, twelve crackers per individual three times a day providing the minimum survival ration of 750 calories; medical kits, penicillin, drinking water, the containers convertible into chemical toilets, chemical toilet paper, Kotex and miniature Geiger counters so that survivors could periodically crawl outside and check the level of radioactivity in the rubble above their heads.

"Of course, Your Honor," Oglethorpe replied. "Those shelters should be a vital part of our program."

"Walsh," the Police Commissioner growled, "just what sort of condition are they in?"

That was not a question Walsh was anxious to answer. The people the shelters were accommodating most frequently these days were teenage junkies. They had discovered the phenobarb pills in the medical kits and it was now a race to see who could get them out first, the junkies or Walsh's men. The junkies were winning.

"The Department of General Services' Division of Public Struc-

253

tures is responsible for them, sir. I believe they look at them periodically." Like about once every ten years, Walsh thought.

"And those crackers and all that stuff, are they still good?"

"Uh, there may be a little problem with them, sir."

"What kind of problem, Walsh?"

"Well, you see, when they had that big hurricane and flood in Managua, Nicaragua, in 1975, we pulled a bunch of them out and sent them down to the people down there."

"So what's the problem?"

"Everybody who ate them got sick."

It was a few minutes before half past four, Paris time, when General Henri Bertrand, the director of France's intelligence service, returned to his office from his interview with Paul-Henri de Serre, the man who had installed Libya's French reactor. The initiatives he had ordered earlier in the day after his first contact with the CIA's Paris station chief had borne fruit. On his desk were four attaché cases belonging to the DST, France's internal-security agency. They contained the dossiers of all the Frenchmen assigned to work on the Libyan reactor and transcripts of all the telephone calls they had made to France.

The transcripts represented only a miniscule part of the material swept from the atmosphere each day by the DST in its communications laboratory on the top floor of its Rue de Saussaies headquarters, just behind the Ministry of the Interior. There white-smocked technicians functioning in a controlled, dust-free environment employed oscilloscopes, high-speed computers, ultrasensitive direction finders and listening devices to record every transmission and international telephone call originating on French soil, then stored them up on the computers from which they had been patiently culled. It was the ultimate transposition of the old concierge-as-watchdog system to the technology of the twentieth century.

Bertrand was still signing for the DST's documents when his phone rang. It was his scientific adviser, Patrick Cornedeau. "Chief," he said, "the inspection reports came in from Vienna an hour ago. I've just finished going through them and there's something I should see you about right away."

Cornedeau brought a file of papers three inches thick enclosed in a blue-and-white folder stamped with the seal of the United Nations into the General's office. Bertrand gasped looking at it.

"Dear Lord! Did you have to wade through all that?"

"I did," replied Cornedeau, scratching his bald pate, "and I'm confused."

"Good," his superior replied. "I prefer confusion to certitude in my operatives."

Cornedeau placed the reports on Bertrand's desk and began to thumb through them.

"On May seventh, the Libyans informed the IAEA in Vienna they had found radioactivity in their reactor's cooling system. They said they had concluded they had a faulty fuel charge and they were shutting down the reactor to take out the fuel."

Cornedeau pointed to his report. "The IAEA immediately sent a team of three inspectors to Libya. A Jap, a Swede and a Nigerian. Good people. They were present while the fuel was taken out and put into the storage pond. They installed their sealed cameras I told you about this morning around the pond. They've run two inspections since."

"To what result?"

"Everything is perfect. The cameras' records are complete. They saw no sign whatsoever of any attempt to take out the fuel. And at each inspection they checked the level of radioactivity coming out of the fuel in the pond with their gamma-ray analyzers. It was perfect."

"In that case," the General remarked, "I don't see the reason for your confusion."

"It's this." Cornedeau got up and returned to his blackboard. "To make a bomb, you want very, very pure plutonium 239. Normally, the plutonium you'd get out of the fuel burned up in a reactor like this one contains a very high percentage of another isotope, plutonium 240. You can make bombs with it, but it's a tricky business."

"Interesting," Bertrand commented, "but what's the relevance here?"

"Time," Cornedeau continued. "The shorter the time the fuel is in the reactor, the more plutonium 239 it's going to contain."

Bertrand squirmed apprehensively in his chair. "And how much would there be in the fuel they took out?"

"That's what concerns me." Cornedeau turned to the black-

255

board to reconfirm the calculations he had already made in his head. "If you wanted to get ideal, ninety-seven-percent weapons-grade plutonium out of this reactor's fuel, you'd leave it in the reactor exactly twenty-seven days."

He turned back to Bertrand. "Chief, that happens to be just how long they kept the fuel in that reactor down there."

The idea for the meeting was Quentin Dewing's. Every ninety minutes, the FBI's assistant director for investigation had decreed that the principals running the New York search effort would gather around his desk at the underground command post to review their progress. He looked at them now, coughed nervously and pointed to the FBI assistant director in charge of the effort to locate every Arab who had come into the area in the past six months.

"All the names we're after have come in from Washington or JFK and are on the computer next door," the man announced. "There are 18,372 of them."

The dimension of his figure sent a shock wave through the room. "I've got two thousand people out there running them down. They've already cleared 2,102 names. Those they can't locate on first effort but which seem okay we're putting into Category Blue on the computer. Those who were unavailable but who looked doubtful are going into Category Green. Clear cases of infiltration we're putting into Category Red."

"How many of those have you got?" Dewing asked.

"Right now, two."

"What are you doing about them?"

"I've stripped fifty agents out of my pool and put them to work on the Red and Green names. As we clear more people, I'll be shifting additional agents to the effort."

Dewing nodded, satisfied. "Henry?"

The question was addressed to the director of the Washington Bureau, who'd been sent up to run the pier operation.

"Things are moving a little faster than we'd hoped, Mr. Dewing. Lloyd's Shipping Intelligence in London and the Maritime Association down at 80 Broad Street have furnished us the list of all the ships we're looking for, the dates they came in and the piers they used. There were 3,816, about half the ships that called on the port

256

in the last six months. Our dock teams have gotten through the manifests of eight hundred of them. We've been able to clear the cargoes on about half of them in the last hour. Washington's really got the bureaus around the country fired up.''

"Good. Mr. Booth?" Dewing said to the director of NEST. "What have you got for us?"

Booth heaved himself wearily from his chair and walked to a map of Manhattan he had pinned on the wall. "We've had our organization fully operational since ten up in the Seventh Regiment Armory at 643 Park. Right now, I've got all two hundred of my vans and our choppers working lower Manhattan." His finger ran along the tip of the island. "From Canal Street down to the Battery."

"Anything suspicious yet?" Dewing queried.

The scientist turned glumly to the FBI man. "Sure. The problem with those detectors of ours is they don't just pick up nuclear bombs. So far we've gotten an old lady who collects Big Ben alarm clocks with radium dials, the dump that supplies half the gardens in the city with fertilizer and two people coming out of a hospital who'd had barium milkshakes for a stomach X ray. But no bomb." He looked once again at his map. "We're covering the streets and the rooftops very thoroughly. But, as I told you gentlemen this morning, if it's above the third story of one of those buildings, we're not going to find it. We just haven't got the equipment or the manpower to walk through them."

When Salisbury of the CIA had made his report, Dewing turned to Harvey Hudson, the Bureau's New York director. He had control of coordinating the rest of the investigation.

"I've got two things, Quent. One just came in from Boston and it looks very, very promising. It's one of those guys who was trained in Qaddafi's camps. Here's his ticket and picture." He passed a sheet of mimeographed paper around the room.

"This guy disappeared from his home Sunday morning about ten A.M. and hasn't been seen since. New England Bell just finished a run-through of his phone records. He got a collect call from a pay phone at Atlantic Avenue, Brooklyn, two hours before he took off.''

"Terrific!"

"He drives a green Chevelle, Massachusetts number plates 792–K83. I'm going to send the flying squad"—the flying squad was a team of fifty FBI agents and New York detectives being held in strategic reserve—"into Brooklyn right now to see if they can pick up some trace of him."

"That's the best lead we've had all morning," Dewing said enthusiastically. "What was the other thing you've got?"

"One of our informers, a black pimp with FALN ties, gave us a second-rate drug dealer who got some medicine Saturday for an Arab woman up at the Hampshire House. She checked out this morning and apparently gave the hotel a false lead on where she was going."

Hudson picked up the sheaf of paper on which he'd made a few notes on his way to the meeting. "We had to come down on the drug dealer pretty hard to get him to open up. It turned out she called him. A PLO/FALN link. Knew the right words. Asked him to get her the medicine because she didn't want to go to a doctor herself. The problem is, the guy swears he never got a look at her. Just left the medicine at the desk, which the hotel confirms, by the way. She was a pretty good tipper, so we had some trouble getting the hotel staff to talk. Seems to be involved in fashion. A jet-set type."

"What was the medicine?"

"Tagamet. It's for ulcers."

"So that's our clue. We're looking for an Arab with ulcers." Dewing scowled in disgust. "Chief," he said to Feldman, "what have you got?"

Feldman reacted as though he had been caught daydreaming. He had in fact been trying to assess the importance of these two leads the FBI had turned up and decide what, if anything, his division could do to expand them. "Not much. The detective in charge of one of the pier teams," he gave a deferential inclination of his gray head to the FBI agent running the pier search, "called me to say he'd found some barrels from Libya that were well under our weight specs but which had been picked up by someone using stolen ID. I've got a car out checking the barrels' consignee right now."

Dewing mulled over his words. Working out of channels, he thought, but probably better not to make waves. "Good, Chief, keep us informed."

He had just picked up his papers, closing the meeting, when a shirtsleeved agent from the radio room burst in. "Mr. Booth," he cried, "your headquarters is on the line. One of your choppers got radiation!"

Booth shot from his seat and ran after the agent to the radio room. "Patch me onto my chopper," he shouted at the duty operator.

"What are you reading?" he called to the technician as soon as he was through.

Booth could hardly hear the man's voice over the thump of the helicopter's rotors. "I got a real positive indication." NEST never employed figures or the word "rads" over an open line in case anyone was eavesdropping. "It's a few tenths."

Booth whistled softly. A few tenths was a very, very hot reading, particularly since it almost certainly had to have filtered up from one or two stories below roof level.

"Where's it coming from?"

Using maps in the radio room, Booth and a pair of New York detectives narrowed down the area from which the radiation seemed to be emanating to four high-rises in the southeastern corner of the Baruch Housing Project just inside the East River Drive, a few dozen yards from the Williamsburg Bridge.

"Tell the chopper to get the hell out of there so we don't tip our hand," Booth ordered, "and call in the manual search teams."

Before the radio operator could deliver his instructions, Booth was running out of the underground command post, heading up the stairs two at a time toward the unmarked FBI car waiting for him in Foley Square.

In Paris, Henri Bertrand had been pacing his office in silence for several minutes digesting what his scientific adviser had told him about the IAEA inspection reports on Libya's French-made reactor. Finally, Bertrand lit a new Gauloise from the stub of the one he was smoking and sank into his leather armchair.

"Is there no way of verifying that there really was something wrong with that fuel they took out of there so early?"

"Not for another six months or so. Until the rods have cooled down enough so you can work with them."

"How very convenient." Bertrand grimaced ever so slightly.

259

"What puzzles me is why Monsieur de Serre didn't mention the incident when I talked to him."

"Perhaps," Cornedeau volunteered, "he felt it was too technical to be of interest to you."

"Perhaps."

The General bestowed what he hoped was an ironic smile on his young adviser. "You nuclear physicists are all alike. You really are a little Mafia trying to keep the rest of us away from the treasury of your knowledge. Because, one supposes, you're persuaded that in our ignorance we'll stop you from bestowing on the world the fruits of your great wisdom."

Bertrand reached for the attaché cases the representative of his sister service, the DSI, had left on the desk. "We'll have to bring in some people and start going through this material very, very carefully."

His fingers picked their way through the thick stack of manila envelopes, each bearing a red "Ultra Secret" stamp, until he had found the name he was looking for.

"Personally," he said, "I think I shall start at the top with the dossier of Monsieur de Serre."

Angelo Rocchia was still chuckling over Gerald Putman's last words when he, Rand and the head of the Pickpocket Squad got back to his Corvette. "It certainly is gratifying," the importer had said to them, "to see the lengths to which the Police Department is prepared to go to help just one citizen recover a stolen wallet."

"Okay," Angelo said, settling back in his car, "what have you got on her, Tommy?"

While his colleague searched for the girl's identity file in his briefcase, Angelo gave an almost surreptitious glance at Rand in the back seat. Our impatient young stud, he reflected with satisfaction, has calmed down a bit. Angelo took the girl's card from the pickpocket expert's hands.

Yolande Belindez, AKA Anita Sanchez, Maria Fernandez
Born: Neiva, Colombia, July 17, 1959
Hair: Dark
Eyes: Green

Complexion: Medium
Identifying Marks or Scars: None
Arrest Record: London, Queen's Jubilee, June 1977. Sentenced two years, one suspended.
Munich, Oktoborfest, October 3, 1979. Sentenced two years, one suspended.
Known Associates: Pedro "Pepe" Torres, AKA Miguel Costanza, NYPD Ref 3742/51.

Tom Malone, the pickpocket expert, drew Torres's photo and identity card from the file. Torres's arrest record paralleled the girl's.

"It isn't much," Angelo sighed, "but it's something. Where do we go looking for them, Tommy?"

"There's an area over here where they hang out," Malone replied. "The South End. Off Atlantic Avenue. Let's go down there and see if I can find somebody who owes me a favor."

Before Angelo could start the car, the FBI radio on the seat beside him cackled. "Romeo Fourteen, respond to Base."

Angelo got out of the car and walked to the pay telephone booth on the corner. Its walls were covered with obscene graffiti, its receiver dangled from the phone on a half-torn cord, and its coin box had been ripped open by vandals. "Bastards," the detective growled. "I hope that goddamn barrel's in their back yard." He waved to Malone to bring the car and started up the avenue looking for another phone booth.

He found one, occupied by an elderly, gray-haired woman chatting feverishly about the Pentecostal service she had attended Sunday night. Angelo waited impatiently a moment, then flashed her his shield. The woman half shrieked in fright and yielded up the phone.

The men in the car couldn't miss the change that had come over Angelo when he stepped out of the booth. He was whistling "Caro Nome" loudly and expertly; his stride was full of energy and purpose; and a grin, a real one this time, was spread all over his face. He slipped into the driver's seat, turned and whacked Rand's knee with a heavy hand. His craggy features glowed with pride and satisfaction as he looked at the younger man. "That was Feldman on the phone. They sent a team out to that address in Queens where the barrels went. The place is a locked-up house with a big

261

garage out back. Every barrel that company ever got is in there, kid. Every fucking barrel except one."

An idea struck John Booth as his FBI driver threaded their car through the narrow and crowded streets of lower Manhattan. Information about the buildings they were searching—the thickness of the walls, the ceilings, the roof, the materials employed in their construction—was vital to his NEST teams. "This housing development," he asked, "the city must have built it, right?"

Before his agent driver had even answered, Booth had picked up the radio and called his headquarters in the Seventh Regiment Armory. "Get someone down to the Municipal Building," he ordered, "and pick up the plans for the Baruch Houses. I'll be waiting for them in our control van at Columbia and Houston."

As their car reached Houston Street, Booth spotted a yellow Hertz van parked at the corner. Four black metal discs, not much larger than silver dollars, and the slim pod slung from its undercarriage were the only indications the truck wasn't being used to deliver packages or move someone's furniture.

It was, in fact, a rolling scientific laboratory, one of the two hundred that Booth's NEST teams were using throughout the city. The little black discs were hooked to a boron trifluoride neutron detector that could pick up neutrons flowing from the tiniest speck of plutonium. The pod was connected to a germanium gamma-ray scanner tied, in turn, to a minicomputer in the van of the truck with its own televisionlike screen for an oscilloscope. Not only could that detector pick up gamma rays over the maximum distance possible, a distance that was a closely guarded secret, but it could "read" them, determine what isotope of what element was throwing them off.

Booth walked over to the suntanned man beside the driver. Jack Delaney was a weapons designer at Livermore, a Ph.D. from Berkeley, who got his suntan scaling the Sierras on his weekends.

"Nothing," Delaney said.

Booth looked down the street toward the housing project, its thirteen-story towers thrusting into the skyline with a brutish inelegance born of municipal economy. "Not surprising. It's got to be on the top floors."

He continued to study the project. Over two hundred people,

most of them on welfare, in thirty-five apartments. Moving around in there without being noticed wasn't going to be easy. A second, unmarked FBI car glided up behind them. An agent got out and handed Booth a thick roll of blueprints.

Booth climbed into the crowded rear of the van. At the back, an FBI agent was already undressing Delaney. "You wiring him?" Booth asked.

The agent nodded. He was taping to Delaney's chest a Kel, a radio microphone that would allow Booth to follow his progress through the project from the truck. An ivory plastic button like a hearing aid was stuck to his ear, the receiver on which he'd get Booth's instructions.

The NEST director spread out the blueprint on a small camp table and studied it. A matchbox, he thought. The emanations they were looking for weren't going to have any difficulty penetrating the walls and the ceilings of the Baruch Houses.

"Okay," Booth announced after a few calculations. "We'll do the top six floors. Although there's almost no chance it's below the top four. You two guys take Building A. Why don't you be insurance salesmen?"

The New York FBI agent who was going to accompany Booth's scientist waved a warning finger. "Down here a debt collection agency's better."

"If you say so," Booth agreed. Getting in close to pin down a bomb site with precision after a first reading was the trickiest, most dangerous part of the business, and he wasn't going to go against a local agent's advice. His scientists, for the most part, knew nothing about firearms, so they had to work with an FBI agent to protect them. They needed an infinite variety of disguises that would allow them to glide unnoticed through those areas where a bomb might be hidden and armed terrorists might be alert for their presence: telephone repairmen, gas meter readers, delivery men. For Building B he had already decided to use a black chemist and a black female FBI agent.

Delaney picked up his portable detector. It was a box the size of an attaché case or a traveling salesman's sample case.

As soon as the two had gone, Booth supervised by radio the dispatch of teams to the remaining buildings. Then, with the blueprint before him, he followed the progress of his teams, apartment by apartment, floor by floor, through the buildings.

Delaney came on, his final floor completed.

"Listen," Booth ordered, "go up and have a look at the roof."

Delaney groaned. "The elevator's broken down."

"So what?" his boss answered. "You're a mountain climber, aren't you?"

Several minutes later, the panting Californian emerged on the roof. There was nothing before him except the distant skyline of Brooklyn. His detector was silent. He looked, disgusted, at the grayish stains speckling the roof. "John," he reported, "there's absolutely nothing up here. Nothing but a lot of old pigeon shit."

As he watched the members of the White House press corps drift into the Oval Office, it occurred to the President that they represented the only element in this crisis that was under control. How much longer, he wondered, are we going to be able to go on saying that?

While they formed into a crescent around his desk, jockeying for position, some striving to make those self-conscious jokes with which they deceived themselves and their colleagues into thinking they were on intimate terms with the President of the United States, he scanned their faces, searching for any indication that one of them might be privy to his government's frightful secret. To his relief, he sensed most of them had nothing more important on their minds at the moment than deciding where to have lunch.

In any event, nothing in his own manner could have betrayed the strain he was under unless it was the quick tap dance of his fingertips on his massive oak Presidential desk framed from the timbers of H.M.S. *Resolute* and offered by Queen Victoria to Rutherford B. Hayes.

The little ceremony his press secretary opened with a few ritual words was part of the charade they were acting out to convince the press that nothing unusual was going on. It was the Presidential proclamation of the thirty-third anniversary of the adoption of the Universal Declaration of Human Rights, and the Chief Executive was halfway through it when he saw Jack Eastman glide unobtrusively into the room and lean against the office wall. With his index and forefinger, his national-security adviser made a scissors movement across his tie—cut it short.

The President rushed through the remaining text, then, as quickly as he could while still appearing to be unhurried, moved for the door. The instant he had settled into his private office, Eastman joined him.

"Mr. President," he announced. "He's ready to talk!"

       Timmy Walsh and Jeremy Oglethorpe walked slowly up Broadway, then turned toward the big plate-glass doors of the New York State Office Building. For a moment they let the outflow sweep past them; the pretty black secretaries flaunting their style and elegance, their makeup all in place, flaring glasses frequently setting off the high arch of their cheekbones; the pasty-faced, over-weight state office workers huddling together in conversations so intense they might have been discussing a multi-million-dollar high-way extension when in fact, Walsh knew, they were probably ar-guing the point spread on tonight's Knicks' game.

He'd selected the building as the first of their "random" sample of New York's air-raid shelters deliberately. Given Rockefeller's and Albany's interest in the shelter program, the building should have the Rolls Royce of New York City's shelters.

They pushed through the lobby, past the elevator banks to the familiar yellow-and-black sign over a door leading to the cellar. At least, Walsh noted, the sign was clean.

He gave his shield to the janitor at the desk in the building superintendent's office. "New York Police, Office of Civil Pre-paredness," he announced. "Doing a survey of the air-raid shel-ters, want to see how the biscuits, the portable toilets and all are being maintained."

"Oh sure," the janitor said. "Air-raid shelter. Got the keys right here." He got up and walked to a huge box on the wall spilling over with keys of every imaginable size and shape. "One of these in here . . ." The voice faltered a bit. "Right here someplace." He began to scratch his head. For over three minutes, he stood there studying the board, fondling, then rejecting one key after another. "I know they're here. Gotta be here someplace. Harry!" he shouted in exasperation. "Where the hell's the key to the fucking air-raid shelter?"

A black assistant custodian came over and gazed with equal consternation but, apparently, no greater sense of enlightenment at the cluttered key box. "Yeah," he said, his head moving back and forth as though in prayer, "it's gotta be here somewhere."

Oglethorpe's eyes were on the clock on the wall. By now, five minutes had gone by and no key. Five minutes during which, in a crisis, his planner's mind told him pandemonium, sheer pandemonium, would be building up in the corridors outside.

"Here it is!" the janitor announced triumphantly.

"Man, you sure that's the key?" his aide asked, squinting at a heavy key hung on a red plastic ring. "It don't look like the key to me."

"Gotta be," his superior rejoined.

It wasn't.

By the time they got back, over ten minutes, Oglethorpe noted, had elapsed. Finally the janitor found the missing key skillfully concealed under three others dangling from the same bank.

It unlocked a huge, cavernous area, the ceiling interlaced by heating ducts so low Walsh had to bend in half to pass under them. Hung on the wall was a clipboard with a yellowed piece of paper flapping from it. It was a Civil Defense inventory dated January 3, 1959, listing the materials stored in the room: 6,000 water drums, 275 medical kits, 500 miniature Geiger counters, 2.5 million protein crackers.

Walsh's flashlight swept the huge chamber's horizons, its gloom unmolested by the few light bulbs hanging from the ceiling. "There they are!"

Along one wall, under his flashlight's beam, were thousands of khaki barrels and cases and cases of protein crackers. He tapped a barrel with his knuckles. It gave out a hollow echo.

"Funny," he said, "they're supposed to be full." He tapped another. It gave up the same unpromising sound. The men began to tap cans at random along the darkened walls until it seemed to shimmer with the hollow echoes they produced. Not a single barrel was full. Some Civil Defense expert on that January day two decades before had carefully lined up all those barrels—and then gone away leaving them empty.

Walsh and Oglethorpe exchanged dismayed glances. "We better take a look at another one," Walsh said, consolingly handing Oglethorpe the list of shelters in the neighborhood. "Pick one. Any one."

The one Oglethorpe chose was in the cellar of the MacKenzie Explosives Company at 105 Read Street. Their arrival was greeted with a certain undertone of consternation, the natural reaction, perhaps, to a visit from the police in an establishment of that sort. Its office manager, a young man in his middle thirties in shirtsleeves and a striped tie, smiled in evident relief when Walsh told him why they were there.

"Oh sure, that Civil Defense stuff. My father told me about that once. It's down in the cellar."

He guided the trio down two flights of wooden steps into a subbasement. They spotted what they were looking for immediately, neatly stacked against the wall in the midst of a bunch of old filing cabinets and broken desks. Walsh stepped over and thumped a water barrel. It gave out a resounding *bonk*.

"Full up," he reported.

Walsh studied the wall. Three quarters of the way to the ceiling, just above the level of the cases of protein crackers, was a wiggly yellowish line. The surface of the wall below the line was notably darker than that above it.

"What's that?" he asked.

"Oh, that," the office manager replied. "That's the high-water mark of the flood we had a few years back."

"Flood?"

"Had water that deep down here for three weeks almost."

Oglethorpe looked at Walsh. Then the bureaucrat ripped open the top case of protein crackers and thrust his hand inside. He drew out a sodden mass of yellow-brown sludge.

Any last illusions Jeremy Oglethorpe had about the current viability of New York City's shelter system faded as they entered the next shelter on their sample, the Hotel James at 127 Chambers Street. The room clerk's alcove was the clue to the kind of place it was. It was screened off behind bars and a partition of bulletproof wire-meshed glass. The half-dozen young men lounging in the lobby were out the front door before Walsh had completed his introductory remarks, which he had begun with the word "Police." The desk clerk had never heard of an air-raid shelter in the Hotel James—or, for that matter, any place else.

Walsh suggested that what they were looking for might be in the cellar. The clerk paled at the notion that anyone would be crazy enough even to think of going into the cellar of the Hotel James. Walsh persisted. With a shrug of incomprehension, the clerk pointed to a door across the hallway.

The two started down a flight of creaking wooden steps, ducking under heating pipes from which torn cobwebs and shreds of asbestos stroked their faces. Out of the darkness ahead came a series of quick, rustling sounds.

"Rats," commented Walsh. "Nice place to spend a few nights."

The lights switched on and a skinny little guy emerged from the shadows. He was wearing a baseball cap and a warmup jacket. All of the athletic insignia that had once decorated it had been removed. Now the jacket was covered with buttons, medallions, decals, sew-on badges carring messages like "Jesus Is Your Savior," "The Redeemer Is Coming," "Let Christ's Way Be Your Way."

Walsh spoke to him. He replied in Spanish, a tongue made no easier for Oglethorpe to comprehend by the fact that the man had a cleft palate.

For several minutes he and Walsh exchanged words in Spanish. "He says he's never heard of the Civil Defense stuff," Walsh reported. "But he remembers seeing some stuff he doesn't know anything about out in a back room somewhere."

The little Puerto Rican led them through several back rooms stacked high with old hotel furniture until he came to the one he was looking for. Like a Swiss mountain guide trying to dig out a skier buried under an avalanche, he attacked the mound of junk before him, heaving his way through mattresses littered with rat droppings, old bedsteads, box springs, bits and pieces of chairs and tables. Finally, with a guttural shout of victory, he flung away a last shattered chest of drawers and stood back. There, buried at the bottom of his pile of rubble, were the familiar khaki barrels and cracker cases of the old Civil Defense program.

Oglethorpe gasped in dismay. Walsh moved over to him and draped his heavy arm around his shoulders. "Jerry, listen," he whispered. "Up there, in the Police Commissioner's office, I didn't want to say anything, you know? In this town, you got to let the big guys down easy. These shelters, ten, fifteen years ago, maybe they might have saved somebody. Today? Forget it, Jerry. They ain't going to save anybody today."

The Puerto Rican spoke up. "He says it's his lunch hour," Walsh reported. "He's got to go over to Brooklyn to hand out pamphlets for his church."

"Certainly," Oglethorpe said. "We're finished."

The little Puerto Rican smiled and started off. Then, as though

268

he'd forgotten something, he stopped and pulled from his pocket two of the pamphlets he'd be giving away in a few moments. He gave Walsh and Oglethorpe each one.

Walsh looked at his. "Jesus Saves," it read. "Bring your problems to Him."

He turned to the shattered bureaucrat. "You know, Jerry," he remarked, "I think maybe the guy's got something here."

In the White House the members of the Crisis Committee were waiting in the National Security Council conference room when the President came downstairs from his press briefing. With the exception of the military, they were in shirtsleeves, ties askew, their disheveled hair and haggard faces indicative of the terrible strain under which they had been laboring for hours. They started to rise as the President entered, but he waved them to their places. He was in no mood for protocol formalities. While Eastman reviewed what had happened, he too removed the jacket of his gray suit, undid his tie and rolled up his shirtsleeves.

"The chargé received a call from Qaddafi's Prime Minister, Salam Jalloud, a few minutes ago," Eastman said. "He would like to speak to you at sixteen hundred GMT." The National Security Assistant glanced up at the clocks on the wall. "That's in twenty-seven minutes, over the Doomsday aircraft facilities we proposed to him early this morning. Qaddafi speaks English, but we are reasonably certain he'll insist, initially at least, on speaking Arabic. These two gentlemen"—he gestured to a pair of middle-aged men sitting tensely halfway down the conference table—"are State's senior Arabic translators.

"The way we propose to proceed if you agree is this: One of these two men will give us a simultaneous, confidential translation of Qaddafi's Arabic so that we can know immediately what he has to say. Each time Qaddafi pauses to let us translate, the second interpreter will take over. While he's interpreting, we'll have a few moments to consider our answers. If we need more time, the second translator can interrogate Qaddafi on the precise meaning of one of his words or phrases."

The President nodded his approval.

"We're also, of course, taping both his words and the translation and taking him down in shorthand. The girls outside will type up

269

the material for us in relays. And we have down there"—Eastman pointed to a black plastic console with a televisionlike screen attached to it—"a CIA voice stress analyzer, which will reveal any sign of nervous strain or tension in his voice."

"Better not use it on me." The President smiled grimly. "You may be disappointed with the results you get."

Eastman coughed. "That brings us to another point, Mr. President." He turned to Henrick Jagerman, Bernie Tamarkin and the CIA's Dr. Turner, seated halfway along the table next to the edgy State Department Arabists.

Their presence came as no surprise to the President. Although the fact was little known to the public, the counsel and observations of psychiatrists, particularly those attached to the CIA, had been employed in crises at the highest echelons of the U.S. government for years.

"It is their very strong recommendation, based on their own experience in terrorist negotiations, that you do not speak to Qaddafi yourself."

The suddenness with which the President swiveled his head toward the psychiatrists revealed his irritation, but his voice remained calm and studiously courteous. "I want to thank you gentlemen for coming here to help us. Particularly you, Dr. Jagerman."

The Dutchman gave a ritualistic bob of his head.

"Now, why is it you don't want me to talk to him?"

Jagerman quickly repeated the arguments he had made earlier to Eastman.

"There is a second reason," Tamarkin added. "To keep him tied up in a dialogue with a negotiator while we're working out our strategy quietly and calmly. We force him to respond under pressure while we create the situations to which he has to respond in an orderly environment."

"It seems to me that we're the ones who are responding under pressure at the moment," the President noted tartly. "Who do you suggest should do the negotiating?"

"We hope he'll agree to work with Mr. Eastman," Jagerman replied. "He's known around the world for his closeness to you personally. His office gives him the necessary authority. And we think he has the proper personality for the job."

The President's fingertips stroked the tabletop. "Very well, gentlemen," he agreed. "I'll accept your recommendation. We'll see if he will. Your understanding of the psychology of power may not be as complete as your understanding of the psychiatry of terrorists. Now I want you to explain to me what would drive a man to do something like this. Is he crazy?"

Jagerman clasped his hands before him and leaned forward, wishing he were in his office in Amsterdam, anywhere but here in this room with these terrible pressures weighing down on him. "It really doesn't matter whether he's crazy or not, Mr. President. What matters is how and why he behaves as he does; what motivates him."

"Then why in hell has he done such a mad thing?"

"Ah!" The black arcs of Jagerman's eyebrows spurted upward, setting the mole in the middle of his forehead dancing on a ridge of flesh. "The most striking aspect of this man's character is that he is a loner. He was a loner as a boy at school, at the military academy in England. He's a loner as a ruler. And isolation is dangerous. The lonelier a man is, the more dangerous he is apt to become. Fundamentally, terrorists are lonely, isolated people, outcasts of society banded into small groups by an ideal or a cause. The more isolated they are, the more they feel compelled to act. Violence becomes the terrorist's way of proving to society that he exists.

"As Qaddafi has found himself more and more isolated internationally, more and more cut off from the world community, the need to act, to prove to the world he's there, has become greater and greater. Loneliness gives terrorists a superiority complex. They become gods, a law unto themselves, absolutely convinced of the rectitude of their position. Clearly, Qaddafi is absolutely persuaded of the righteousness of his point of view. And now with this H-bomb of his, he has become God, beyond reason, ready to administer justice himself."

"If the man is beyond reason," the President interjected, "then why are we wasting our time talking to him?"

"Mr. President, we're not trying to reason with him. We are going to try to convince him of the necessity of giving us time just as we try to convince a terrorist of the necessity of giving us his hostages. Often, with time, the isolated, unreal world the terrorist lives in crumbles around him. Reality submerges him, and his defense mechanisms collapse. This could very well happen in Qaddafi's case. All the unforeseen consequences of his action may suddenly overwhelm him.''

The psychiatrist's index finger shot up as it did whenever he wanted to issue a warning or stress a point. ''That instant, if it comes, will be terribly dangerous. At that moment, a terrorist is ready to die, to commit suicide in a spectacular way. The risk that he may then destroy his hostages along with himself is immense. In this case . . .''

Jagerman did not need to finish the sentence. Everyone had understood. ''But there is also, at that moment, the golden chance to take the terrorist by the hand, so to speak, and lead him away from danger. To convince him he is a hero, a conquered hero yielding honorably to superior forces.''

''And you hope that, somehow, we'll be able to manipulate Qaddafi like that?''

''It is a hope. No more. But the situation offers very little else.''

''All right. But how? How will we do it?''

''That's the ultimate goal, Mr. President. The tactics we will have to work out as we talk to him. That's why opening a dialogue is so crucial. We will adapt our tactics from what we learn listening to him. One must always continue saying, 'We accept the situation because we know we'll win in the end.' ''

Except, the Dutchman thought as he heard his words drift through the crowded room, in the end one doesn't always win.

A bell over the door jingled. It was as though an alarm had gone off. Everyone in the bar's dark interior, the half-dozen young men on its worn moleskin barstools, the squat, unshaven bartender, the trio in black leather jackets playing pinball, turned to stare at the three policemen invading their sanctuary. There was not a sound in the place except for the *click-clack* of the lead ball still bouncing from bumper to bumper in the pinball machine and the *ting* of the lights flashing on its back panel.

''You would have to say,'' Angelo muttered to Rand, ''that these guys know the heat when they see it.''

Malone, head of the NYPD Pickpocket Squad, walked slowly down the bar, his eyes scrutinizing each face along his way. They belonged to the dips who were the regulars at the Flatbush Avenue Terminal of the Long Island Rail Road, resting up with coffee and tequila between rush hours. He stopped a few feet from the pinball machine, pointed at one of the three young men, then beckoned to him with his forefinger.

"Hey, Mr. Malone." The young man gave a nervous wriggle that would have passed as a clever move on a disco dance floor. "Why for you jostling me? Is nothing I've done. Nothing."

"We want to have a little talk with you. Out in the car."

The car was around the corner. Malone put the pickpocket into the front seat and got in beside him. Angelo circled the car to get in on the other side. Rand headed for the rear. "No," Angelo ordered, "you go back and keep your eyes on the bar. Just in case."

Squeezed between the two detectives, the Colombian seemed to shrink under the impact of his nervous concern. His head swiveled from man to man like a weathervane buffeted by a swirling wind. "Why you busting me, Mr. Malone? Is nothing I do, I swear." The voice was now almost a whimper.

"I'm not busting you," Malone replied. "Just giving you a chance to get on the plus side for the next time we take you in."

He took out the photos of Yolande Belindez and Torres and placed them before the pickpocket. As he did, Angelo's attention was totally concentrated on the young man's face. For a fleeting instant he saw there what he was looking for, the sudden apprehensive flicker of recognition.

"Know these guys?" Malone asked.

The pickpocket paused. "No. I no know. Never seen." Before he knew what had happened, Angelo had slipped the young man's right forearm between his own arms, grasped his fingertips and was slowly, steadily pushing them backward.

"My friend here asked you a question."

Sweat broke out on the pickpocket's forehead. Again his head swiveled wildly from one detective to the other. "Hey, man, I no see. No see."

Angelo squeezed harder. The pickpocket squealed in pain.

"You ever tried boosting somebody's wallet with your hand in a cast? You don't talk to my friend there, I'll snap these tendons like crackers."

"Hey," the pickpocket screamed in pain. "I talk. I talk." Angelo eased the pressure. "They new in town. I only seen them once. Maybe twice."

"Where they live?"

"Hicks Street. Over by the Expressway. I no know house. Only one time I see, I swear."

Angelo released his fingers. *"Gracias, amigo,"* he said, opening the door to let the dip out. "Appreciate your help."

Henri Bertrand loathed reading the transcripts of wire-taps. The director of French intelligence had no scruples about their morality. It was rather that he inevitably found the exercise depressing. Nothing, he had discovered long ago, revealed quite as completely the emptiness, the banality, the squalor of most lives as did that harvest of the electronic scanning of an unguarded soul.

When he had started to comb his way through the transcripts of Paui-Henri de Serre's conversations, it was with the expectation that he would find in them the imprint of an exalted spirit, of a man with the love of beauty needed to assemble the collection of ancient objects Bertrand had admired in his apartment.

He had found instead a petty, scheming bureaucrat; a dull, banal man with no trace of the weaknesses someone might exploit to get his cooperation. He had no mistresses; or, if he did, he didn't talk to them. Indeed, the man's rigorous marital fidelity, Bertrand had thought with a chuckle, might be seen as the only aberration in his character.

The interminable transcript through which he was laboring dated to November a year ago. It was with the administrative director of the Fusion Research Center at Fontenay-aux-Roses, and, Bertrand noted with relief, it was finally concluding with a personal exchange. He skimmed it rapidly.

ADMINISTRATOR:	By the way, *cher ami,* we're going to have a Nobel here.
DE SERRE:	Don't be fatuous, Jean. The Swedes will never give a Nobel to anyone even remotely connected with our program.
ADMINISTRATOR:	Well, you're wrong. Do you remember Alain Prévost?
DE SERRE:	That rather ploddy type who worked on the submarine reactor at Pierrelatte years ago?

ADMINISTRATOR:	That's he. In strictest confidence, he and his people at the laser-beam complex have just made the fusion breakthrough we've all been hoping for.
DE SERRE:	They blew up the bubble?
ADMINISTRATOR:	Shattered it. Prévost has been invited to the Élysée at four next Tuesday to tell Giscard and a select Cabinet what it all means.
DE SERRE:	My God! Perhaps you're right. Give Prévost my congratulations. Although I never would have dreamed he had the intellectual resources for such a thing. Au revoir.

Alain Prévost. Bertrand took a slow, meditative drag on his Gauloise, trying to remember where it was he had heard that name before. Then he had it: the murder in the Bois de Boulogne.

A strange voice filtered into the National Security Council conference room over the same white plastic squawk box through which Harold Agnew had revealed barely eighteen hours before the existence of Qaddafi's hydrogen bomb. It belonged to an Air Force brigadier general sitting at the communications console of the Doomsday 747, thirty-five thousand feet above the Mediterranean.

"Eagle One to Eagle Base," he said. "Secure communications circuit to Fox Base is now operational." "Fox Base" was the code designation for Tripoli. "All contacts verified and functioning. Fox Base advises Fox One will be on line in sixty seconds."

The mutter of conversation in the room stopped at the words "Fox One." For a moment, there was no noise except for the whir of the ventilation equipment and the occasional scraping of a chair. Each of the men and women present reacted in his or her own way to the fact that in a few seconds they would be listening to the voice of the man threatening six million of their countrymen.

A cackle of static broke from the squawk box, and suddenly Qaddafi's voice filled the conference room. Since he was speaking over a secure, scrambled line, his voice had a peculiar resonance as though it was percolating slowly upward through a vat of water

275

or had been taken from the sound track of a late-night movie about an extraterrestial invasion of planet Earth.

"This is Muammar al-Qaddafi, Secretary General of the Libyan People's Congress," the voice said in Arabic.

Jack Eastman leaned forward as soon as the translators had finished. "Mr. Qaddafi, this is Jack Eastman, the President's National Security Assistant. I wish first to give you the personal assurances of the President of the United States that the communications channel over which we are speaking is a secure voice channel audible only to the people around you and the people here with me in the White House. For the purposes of our conversation I have with me Mr. E. R. Sheehan of the Department of State, who will translate our remarks into Arabic for you, and yours into English for us."

Eastman gestured with his head to the translator.

"Your arrangements are satisfactory," Qaddafi replied when he had finished. "I am now ready to address the President."

"Thank you, sir," Eastman answered politely. "The President has asked me to tell you first that he takes the contents of your letter with the utmost seriousness. He is conferring now with our senior people to discuss how we can best take action on your proposals, and has asked me to serve as his personal liaison with you as we try to reach together some resolution of the issues you have raised. There are a number of points in your letter on which we would like to ask you for clarification. Have you considered what interim security arrangements are to be made on the West Bank as the Israelis withdraw?"

The three psychiatrists exchanged satisfied smiles. Eastman was slipping brilliantly into his role of negotiator, ending with a question that would force Qaddafi to go on talking and at the same time lead him to believe he was going to get what he wanted.

There was a long silence before Qaddafi came back on the line. Even in Arabic, everyone in the room could detect the change in his tone.

"Mr. Eastman. The only person in your country to whom I am prepared to speak is the President."

The men at the table waited for Qaddafi to continue, but only the faint drone of the sound amplifier emerged from the squawk box.

"Stall," Tamarkin said to Eastman. "Tell him you've summoned the President. He's on the way. Tell him anything you want, just as long as you keep him talking."

Eastman had resumed speaking for only a few seconds when Qaddafi's voice came back on the line. This time the Libyan spoke directly in English.

"Mr. Eastman, I am not going to tumble into your traps as easily as that. If what I have to discuss with the President is not important enough for him to receive my communication himself, I have nothing further to say to you. Do not contact me again if the President is not prepared to talk personally with me."

Again the drone of the amplifier came over the open line. "Mr. Qaddafi?" Eastman said.

"Eagle one to Eagle Base." It was the Air Force Brigadier in the Doomsday jet. "Fox Base has cut the circuit."

Angelo Rocchia and Jack Rand cruised slowly southeast down Hicks Street, the street indicated by the pickpocket Angelo had grilled a few minutes earlier. The street, it seemed to the Denver-based agent, was almost as miserable, as depressing as the one they had driven through earlier on their way to the docks: the same obscene graffiti on the walls, the same shattered windows, padlocked doors, the same cannibalized hulks of the cars abandoned by the curb. In a third-floor window just above their car, Rand spotted an old derelict, a woman, peering down at them. Yellow-gray hair was strewn around her head in a disordered jumble. One hand clutched a faded housecoat around her shoulders, the other the neck of a pint of Four Roses. Pasted to the window, just beneath her gaunt face, was a string of paper cut-out dolls. Rand shuddered. There was more despair, more hopelessness writ upon that face than the young agent was prepared to handle. He turned to Angelo beside him.

"What do we do?" Rand asked. "A door-to-door?"

Angelo was silent a moment, thinking. "No," he answered. "We do that, the word'll get around the heat's on the street. They'll figure we're from Immigration. Half of these people are illegals. Hit some of these places here, what you have to be concerned about is you don't get trampled by the mob running out of the front door. We got to figure out something else."

They passed a tiny grocery store, a hole in the wall with a couple of half-empty crates of wilted vegetables piled against its window. Angelo noted the proprietor's name painted in white on the door panel.

"I got an idea," he said, looking for a parking place.

The two picked their way along the rubble- and garbage-littered sidewalk, back to the grocery store.

"Let me do the talking in here," Angelo warned.

Once again there was the familiar tinkle of a bell over the door. The odor of garlic, of cheap salami and of cold cuts assaulted their nostrils as they stepped inside. It was, Rand observed, a cramped cubbyhole of a place, not even half the size of the Holiday Inn bedrooms he had so often slept in. Cans, bottles of oil, packages of pasta, dried soup, noodles were strewn about in a disordered jumble. Along one wall were gallon jugs of cheap wines: muscatels, sauternes; reds, whites, each glowing with its gold or ruby promise of a few hours' release from the miseries of Hicks Street.

The face of a plump elderly woman in black, gray hair gathered in a tight bun at the nape of her neck, rose up above a refrigerating cabinet crammed with milk, butter and an array of frozen junk foods. She eyed warily the two unfamiliar faces intruding into her store.

"Signora Marcello?" Angelo asked, coming down hard with the accent.

The woman grunted.

Angelo moved a step closer to her, consciously stressing the space separating him from Rand. His voice dropped to a husky half-whisper. "I got a problem. I need a little help." There was no question of telling her he was a cop, he knew that. Older women like her, born in the old country, didn't talk to cops, period. "Niece of mine, nice Italian girl, got mugged last Sunday coming home from the ten-o'clock Mass over there to Saint Anthony's on Fourth Avenue."

He leaned toward the woman, as though he was a priest about to hear her confession. "That's the *fidanzato*," he whispered, jerking a thumb at Rand. An intimation of dislike crossed his face. "He's not an Italian, but what are you going to do, kids the way they are these days? Good Catholic boy, though. German."

He drew back slightly, sensing the bond of understanding that was growing between him and the woman. His heavy head moved back and forth in apparent sadness and disbelief. "Would you believe that people could do a thing like that to a nice girl, one of ours, just received Our Lord, right there almost on the church steps? Beat her up, grab her bag?"

278

He stepped closer until his face was only inches from Signora Marcello's, his voice a whisper, each of his words designed to arouse her prejudices. "South Americanos, they were. Spics." He spat out the last word. "They come from around here."

Angelo reached into his pocket and drew out the photos of Torres and Yolande Belindez. "Friend of mine, Italian detective downtown, got me these pictures." Angelo grimaced. "But cops, you know, what could they do?" He tapped the pictures. "Me, I'm the oldest. I'm going to get them. For the honor of the *famiglia, capito?* You ever seen these two?"

"Ai, ai," the old woman groaned. "Jesus, Mary, Joseph! Whatsa become this place?" She reached for a pair of broken glasses. "This one I know." A gnarled finger thumped the picture of the girl with the big tits. "She come in here every day, buy a bottle of milk."

"You know her name?"

"Sure. Itsa Carmen. Carmen something."

"You know where she lives?"

"Down the street, next to the bar. Three buildings, all alike. She lives there."

The only person in the National Security Council conference room not shocked by Qaddafi's brutal interruption of his communication with Eastman was the President. He had expected it. Heads of state, no matter how irrationally they may behave, do not respond to the same psychological imperatives as desperate and isolated terrorists.

"Wait a decent interval," he ordered, "then tell the Doomsday I'm on the line ready to talk to him." He glanced along the table to the three psychiatrists. "Gentlemen, while we're waiting I want you to give me the best advice you can on how to deal with this man. Dr. Jagerman?"

Jagerman sighed, regretting again the web of circumstances that had brought him into this room. "First of all, Mr. President, you must neither threaten him nor give in. But plant in his mind the idea that what he wants is not totally impossible."

"Even though it in fact is?"

"*Ja, ja.*" The Dutchman underlined his words with two abrupt inclinations of his head. "We must deceive him into thinking that he can succeed." Jagerman caressed the skin of his mole with his fingertips, almost as if he were touching a talisman. "Try to avoid direct confrontation, because that will only reinforce his negative attitudes. From his first few words, he seems quite composed and in command of his emotions. Contrary to what you might think, that's good. It's weak, insecure people who frighten easily that are dangerous. They're apt to lash out at you at the slightest provocation."

There was a slight pause while the psychiatrist marshaled the last of his thoughts. "Tactically, sir, I would try to persuade him to accept the dialogue with Mr. Eastman. Tell him that that way you yourself will be free to concentrate all your time and energy on resolving the problems he has raised in his letter. It's really very, very important that we lure him into that ongoing dialogue."

The President folded his hands on the desk, composing his thoughts, preparing himself for the ordeal ahead. He took a breath that swelled the frame of his thoracic cage until his blue shirt went taut, then let it out in one long, weary burst. "All right, Jack," he said. "I'm ready."

As the President leaned to the white squawk box, a flush of pink seeped above the ridge line of his collar like water spreading over a blotter. It was a manifestation of his hidden anger; his anger at the humiliation he felt having to act out this comedy; his anger as the proud leader of the most powerful nation on earth at being forced to humble himself before a man who would kill six million of his fellows.

"Colonel Qaddafi," he began as soon as the Libyan leader was back on the line, "this is the President of the United States. The message which you addressed to my government yesterday has been the object of a close and detailed study by my principal advisers and myself. We are still in the midst of that process. However, you must have no doubt, sir, that both I and my government condemn the action you have taken. No matter how strongly you feel about the issues that divide us in the Middle East or the injustices that have been inflicted on the Arab people of Palestine, your attempt to resolve the problem by threatening the lives of six million innocent Americans in New York City is a totally irresponsible and deplorable action."

The President's blunt words sent concern sluicing over the faces of the psychiatrists. Tamarkin grabbed a silk foulard from the breast pocket of his jacket and dabbed at the sweat glistening on his temples. Jagerman sat stiffly upright, his head cocked slightly backward as though he was already waiting to hear the distant rumble of the Apocalypse. The Chief Executive ignored them. He jabbed his finger at the State Department's Arabist.

"Translate that. And don't you damn well modify my tone by so much as one iota."

The President leaned forward as the translator's last phrase ended, determined to resume speaking before Qaddafi could break in with a reply.

"You are a soldier, Mr. Qaddafi, and as a soldier you know that I have, at my fingertips, the power to destroy, instantly, every living creature in your nation. I want you to understand that I shall not hesitate to use that power, whatever the consequences may be, if you force me to do so."

Eastman smiled in silent approval. He hasn't listened to a damned thing the psychiatrists had to say, he thought.

"Most men in my position, sir, would have used that power to destroy you the minute they read your letter. I did not because it is my ardent desire to find a peaceful solution to this problem. To find it together with you and your help. As you are perhaps aware, I have never, during my Presidential campaign and since my inauguration, ceased to proclaim my conviction that there can be no durable resolution to the problem of the Middle East which does not take into account the legitimate aspirations of the Palestinian people. But you must not forget, sir, that the attainment of the objectives you set forth in your letter does not depend on my government alone. That is why I would like to suggest to you that my close counselor, Mr. Eastman, remain in permanent contact with you as a link between us while I negotiate with Jerusalem."

Drained, emotionally, by his effort, the President slumped back in his chair. "How'd we do?" he asked Eastman, tugging at his sweat-dampened shirt collar as the translator started to work.

"Terrific!" his adviser replied. "A-okay."

A few minutes later, the Libyan's answering voice poured forth from the squawk box. Its tone seemed slight, almost as though the dictator was subconsciously trying to apologize for intruding on the White House gathering. There was nothing apologetic, however, about the words Qaddafi employed.

"Mr. President, I have not called you to discuss my letter. Its terms are very clear. They require no discussion or amplification on my part—only action on your part. I have no intention of entering into a discussion with you now or in the future."

Qaddafi paused to allow the State Department expert to interpret his words. Jagerman and Tamarkin gave each other quick glances of professional concern.

"Mr. President," The Libyan continued. "The sole reason for my communication is to warn you that we have discovered on our radar screens and radio channels the presence of your Sixth Fleet menacing our shores. I will not be intimidated by your martial posturing, Mr. President. I will not be threatened."

"That arrogant son of a bitch!" The voice, skirting *sotto voice* under the interpreter's words, belonged to Delbert Crandell, the Secretary of Energy. "*He* thinks *he's* being threatened?"

"Those ships are now twenty kilometers off my coastline. I want them withdrawn immediately to a distance of at least one hundred kilometers from my shores, Mr. President. If they are not, I shall reduce the time in the ultimatum I gave you by five hours, from twenty-one hundred GMT tomorrow to sixteen hundred GMT."

The President shook his head, stupefied by the boldness of the man. Handing out ultimatums seemed to come easily to him.

"Mr. Qaddafi, in view of the threat you yourself have already posed to the citizens of New York City, I find your request not only extravagant but wholly unexpected. However, because of my very real desire to find, with you, a peaceful solution to this crisis, I am prepared to discuss it immediately with my advisers and convey to you our decision in a few minutes' time."

The Chief Executive gave an angry, accusatory regard to the men around him. "None of your well-thought-out game plans predicted this, gentlemen," he noted acidly. "How the hell do we handle it?" He turned to the Chairman of the Joint Chiefs. "Harry, what do you recommend?"

"I'm very much opposed to pulling those ships back, Mr. President," Admiral Fuller replied. "The whole purpose of this exercise was to provide him with a highly visible reminder of what the consequences of setting that bomb off are going to be. Very clearly we've succeeded. Take those ships away and their absence just might make it easier for him to set the bomb off if it comes to it."

"Harold?"

"I concur," the Secretary of Defense answered.

"Mr. Peabody?"

The Secretary of State, recalled from Latin America, twisted a ballpoint pen in his fingers, subconsciously playing for a few seconds to run the alternatives past the screen of his brain one more time. "Military considerations aside, I think that with a man of his reputation it would be a fatal mistake to open a negotiation with a concession like this. I'm convinced it'll tend to make him wholly untractable farther down the line. I say refuse."

"Tap?"

"The man seems bent on a showdown, Mr. President. If that's what he's looking for, then shouldn't we let him know right now we're ready for it?"

The President's blue eyes focused on Bennington's blandly self-assured patrician face. My CIA director, he thought, always ready to answer one question with another so that on the record you can never nail him to a position. He must have studied under Henry Kissinger when he was at Harvard.

"Jack?"

Eastman leaned back in his chair, uncomfortably aware of the attention on him. "I'm afraid that I'm going to go against the consensus, Mr. President. The problem we face is how do we keep those six million people in New York alive, and I say it's with the one thing Qaddafi's trying to take away from us, time. We need those five hours in New York to find that bomb a lot more than we need the Sixth Fleet off Libya's seacoast."

"You're recommending we pull those ships back?"

"Yes, sir." Eastman tried to force the image of the slender girl in her white graduation dress from his mind, to be sure he was responding to the President's question on nothing other than a cold analysis of the situation. "The reality of those extra hours is far more important to us than Qaddafi's perceptions of our strength or weaknesses. And if it comes to that, we certainly don't need the Sixth Fleet to destroy Libya."

"I find one thing strange in all this," the President remarked. "Why five hours? Why not fifteen? Why not right away? If he's really so upset, why such a minimal demand?" He was silent a second, trying, unsuccessfuly, to provide himself with an answer to his question. He shifted his attention to the psychiatrists. "How do you people analyze this?"

Once again, Henrick Jagerman felt his skin prickle with nervous apprehension. What he was about to recommend would be bitterly resented, he was sure, by half the men in the room.

"First, to answer your question, sir, I think his request betrays a fundamental insecurity on his part. He is subconsciously testing the water, hoping for your acquiscence as a reassurance that this awful gamble of his is going to pay off. We see this attitude all the time in terrorists on our first contact. They're aggressive, demanding, 'Do this right away or I'll kill a hostage.' My advice then is do what the terrorist asks, and my advice to you is do what Qaddafi asks. You will be showing him he can get things done by working through you. You will implant very subtly in his mind the notion that, ultimately, he may succeed if he goes on working with you. But I would attach a price to it. Use your agreement as a lure to get him into the discussion he's resisting."

The President nodded and lapsed into silence, trapped now in that hard and lonely place referred to in Harry Truman's plaque on his desk, the end of the line where the buck stops and one man has to make the decisions in the solitude of his soul.

"All right," he sighed. "Harry, tell the fleet to get ready to pull back."

"Jesus Christ! You can't cave in to that bastard like that, Mr. President. You'll go down in history as America's Neville Chamberlain if you do!"

The President turned his heavy head with exquisite slowness toward the Secretary of Energy. "Mr. Crandell, I am not about to cave in to Qaddafi or anyone else." He doled out the words with the slow, measured cadence of a funeral drum. "I am playing for what Mr. Eastman has properly pointed out is the most valuable asset in this crisis—" the blue eyes glanced up at the clocks on the wall—"time."

He used the same measured tone with the Libyan leader. "Mr. Qaddafi," he said, explaining his decision, "I want you to know that I am doing this for one reason only: to show you how serious and sincere I am in my desire to find with you a way out of this crisis that will be satisfactory to us both. My order is conditional on your agreement to begin intensive discussions on how we can do it."

An abnormally long delay, filled only by the menacing buzzing on the empty voice channel, followed his words. Something strange is going on in Tripoli, Eastman thought.

When Qaddafi's voice returned at last, he spoke once again in English. "As long as your ships are there, no discussion. When they have gone, we will talk. *Insh' Allah*."

The squawk box went dead.

PART VI

MONDAY, DECEMBER 14:
NOON TO MIDNIGHT

"The President is lying!"

ANGELO ROCCHIA STUDIED THE THREE BUILD-ings the Italian shopkeeper, Signora Marcello, had indicated to him. They enjoyed a similarity of decay: shabby four-story tenements, broken fire escapes dangling down their façades like limbs splintered off a tree, the same faded paint peeling from their barred windows and doors. "Rooms to Let—Inquire Superintendent 305 Hicks," read a sign on one.

"Railroad flats," Angelo observed. "Probably belong to some slumlord waiting for a fire. Stuffs illegals in here and charges them by the head."

The pair stepped into the hallway of 305 Hicks. Garbage was piled to the level of the stairs in a stinking mound of rotting food, bottles, beer cans, cartons. Even worse was the stench, the acrid, all-enveloping odor of urine that seemed to hang on the stairwell like a moist, invisible film.

"Watch this, kid." Angelo picked up a bottle and lobbed it at a pile of garbage. Before the agent's horrified eyes, a gray battalion of rats came scurrying out of the heap of refuse.

Angelo chortled at the young man's sudden loss of poise, then walked over to the door marked "Superintendent" and gave a gentle rap. There was a clatter of chains. The door, firmly secured on the inside, opened just a crack. An elderly black in denim overalls peered out. Angelo flashed his badge so fast the man could only catch a glittering of gold. Rand almost choked in disbelief at what he heard next.

"Working with the Board of Health," Angelo told the black. He jerked his head toward the mound of garbage. "Got a lot of garbage over there. Fire hazard. Gonna have to do something here.'

While Rand and Angelo watched, the apprehensive superintendent undid one by one the locks and chains sealing him into the security of his little room. "Look, mister, what can I do? These people here, they animals. They just open the door, throw the stuff down here." He shook his head in helpless dismay, seeking Angelo's sympathy for the impossibility of his job.

"Yeah, well, we got a lot of violations here. Gonna have to write some of them up." Angelo reached into his pocket for the photograph of the girl pickpocket. "Hey, by the way, you know this girl here? Colombian. Big tits. You could spot 'em a mile away. Carmen, they call her."

The superintendent looked at the photo. A nervous roll of his Adam's apple, the quick dart of his tongue on his lips betrayed to both men the recognition he wanted to conceal. "No, no, I don't know her."

"Too bad." Angelo looked straight into the black's eyes. "I thought we could help each other out, you know what I mean?" The detective sighed and drew out his notepad. "At least a dozen violations you got here." He started by waving at the garbage, at the ill-lit stairwell.

"Hey, mister, wait a minute," the super pleaded. "Don't get excited. Landlord, he makes *me* pay the summonses."

"Yeah? Well, it looks to me like you got about five hundred bucks' worth."

Angelo could see the nervous, frightened glimmer the mention of that sum brought to the super's eyes. He was probably, Angelo calculated, a decent hard-working guy trying to raise a family in that jungle. And Angelo also knew that the poor man was well aware his tenants would gladly put a knife in his back if they thought he'd given any of them up to the police. He threw his arm around the black's shoulders.

"Look, friend, I don't want to stiff you with all this paper. Just tell me what flat she's in. We know she's here."

For an instant, the super's eyes seemed to roll as wildly as an epileptic's in a seizure, looking for any half-open crack in the doors along the hallway.

"She's in 207, second floor. Second door on the right."

"She up there now?"

The super shrugged. "They all the time in and out. Fifteen people up there sometimes."

Angelo and Rand loitered just a second on the sidewalk outside. "Angelo," Rand urged, "we should call in help. This could be big, very big."

288

"Yeah," the detective mumbled. "Fifteen guys. You might want to think about that. Only two of us." Angelo picked at the stubble on his chin. "But, generally, pickpockets aren't armed. They don't want to go in for armed robbery. On the other hand . . ." He shook his head, "Sneaking a bunch of cops into a neighborhood like this is going to be like trying to sneak the sun past a rooster. Come on." He had made up his mind. "We'll take them ourselves."

As he started up the stairs, Angelo reached not for his gun but for his wallet. He took out a Chase Manhattan calendar printed on a supple but firm slip of plastic. He flicked the card at Rand. "I'll open the door with this. You step in and freeze them."

"Jesus Christ, Angelo," the agent almost gasped. "We can't do that. We haven't got a warrant."

"Don't worry about it, kid," Angelo said, drawing up to the second door on the right on the second floor. "It ain't a perfect world."

"Gorgeous!"

Michael Naylor pirouetted around the model frozen in artificial grace under the arc lights of his studio, then dropped to one knee at just the point where he knew he would catch the mauve lights reverberating off the satin of her Saint-Laurent evening gown. "Fantastic!" He clicked his Haselblad. "Unbelievable!"

He continued through a dozen shots and a dozen adjectives, each word more extravagant than the one that had preceded it, then straightened up, sweating from the strain and the lights. "Thanks, darling," he told the model, "that'll be all for now."

He saw Laila as he stepped out of the circle of the spots. She had slipped in so quietly he hadn't even noticed her arrival.

"Linda!" he gasped. "I thought you had a—"

She stifled his words with a kiss. "I got out of my lunch," she said. "Take me to lunch."

"Police—don't move!"

The angry words ricocheted around the flat with the force of a caroming pelote ball. Angelo and Jack Rand stood just inside the door the detective had opened with his plastic bank calendar. They were in the classic policeman's half-crouch, each clasping his revolver before him with outstretched hands. The suddenness of their entry, the intimidating sight of their arms froze the room's half-dozen occupants.

The place was, just as Angelo had expected it would be, wall-to-wall mattresses, a squalid, ill-lit room reeking of sweat and cheap cologne. A clothesline filled with dripping undershorts, bras, tee shirts and blue jeans bisected it like a limp set of signal flags dressing an aging vessel's masthead. There was only one piece of furniture in the room, a dilapidated sofa, its springs popping through its torn upholstery. Sitting on one end of it, stirring a casserole set on a hot plate on the floor, was the girl with the big tits.

Angelo recognized her immediately. He stood up, put his pistol back into his holster, stepped over one Colombian sprawling terrified on a mattress and drew up beside her. He sniffed at the stew bubbling in the casserole.

"Smells good," he remarked. "Too bad you're not going to get to eat it. Get your coat, *muchacha*. You're coming in."

Angelo was about to articulate the first question he wanted to ask her when the answer came springing like a fury from a mattress along the wall and bounded toward him, shouting, "Why you take my *mujer?*"

"Freeze!"

It was Rand, still in the doorway, his weapon drawn. Torres, the man in the second photo, stopped instantly. He was a gaunt-faced youth with drawn, tubercular cheeks, a sallow complexion and a mass of uncombed black curls spilling over his forehead.

"Take that thing off," Rand ordered, waving his combat Magnum at the geometric patterns of the red poncho enveloping the Colombian. Despite Angelo's comments on the street, the agent was going to take no chances on an arm being hidden under its folds.

"Thanks, kid." There was both gratitude and new respect in Angelo's tone.

Torres pulled the poncho over his head. He was naked except for unmatching socks and filthy yellow-gray jockey shorts. Angelo stepped over to him, took the pickpocket's photograph from his pocket, studied it, then looked up, smiling, at Torres.

"Well, now," he said, "you, my friend, are just the guy we're looking for. You're coming in, too."

Torres began to babble a protest of his innocence in a blend of

Spanish and English. Angelo cut him short. "The guy whose wallet you boosted down at the terminal Friday picked your picture out of a pile. You're going in. But first you and I are going to have a little talk."

One of the three men sprawled on the mattresses stirred at Angelo's words. He was a sour-looking older man. "Officer, he new in town. He no much score yet." His hand was groping under his mattress for his roll of cash. "I help straighten out." He looked at the detective with a leering smile.

"Fuck you!" Angelo growled. "This isn't a shakedown." He pointed to the man, the two others in the room and a second girl crouched in one corner. "All of you get out of here. Right now! Or I'll call in Immigration to check your papers."

The four South Americans vanished at the mention of Immigration with an alacrity that was astonishing. As the door closed on the last of them, Angelo returned his attention to Torres. "I want to know one thing from you. Where'd that card go? Who'd you make the dip for?"

From behind him, Angelo heard a quick burst of idiomatic Spanish. He understood only one phrase, *derechos civiles*—civil rights. He gave the girl with the big tits an annoyed stare. She was still perched over her bubbling casserole, her pretty face suffused with sullen hostility. This one, Angelo mused, has got to go. He looked at Rand, still standing in the doorway. Goody-goody two shoes over there, too.

"Take her down to the car," he ordered. "I'll bring him down as soon as he gets his clothes on."

Rand hesitated a moment. He's going to work him over, he thought. He wanted to say something, but not in front of these two. Too much was at stake to let them glimpse at any difference between them. "Let's go," he said to the girl with the big tits.

Torres had picked up a pair of jeans and was starting to put them on when Rand and the girl left.

"Drop those things," Angelo commanded. "You're not going anywhere yet. I said I wanted to talk to you. Where'd the cards from the wallet you boosted last Friday go? Who buys your fresh cards?"

"Hey, what you mean?" Torres was trembling, but he tried to force an air of defiance into his voice.

"You heard me. You did that dip in the terminal Friday on

consignment. You were told to set up a guy just like the guy you hit. I want to know where that fucking card went.''

Torres stepped warily back a couple of paces, almost tumbling over a mattress as he did, until he was only inches from the wall. On the hot plate, the girl's stew was still bubbling noisily. Angelo followed him.

"Meester," the Colombian was pleading, "I got civil rights."

"Civil rights? You got no civil rights, you little cocksucker. Your civil rights are down there where you left 'em, in Bogotá.''

The detective moved closer to Torres. He was at least a head taller than the Colombian. Torres was shivering from the cold, from fear, from the terrible sense of impotence nakedness always imposes in a prisoner before his captors. His hands were spread over his genitals, drawing together his shoulders and making him look even more emaciated than he was. He had just taken another half-step toward the wall when Angelo moved. The detective's gesture was so swift Torres didn't even see it coming. Angelo's right hand shot up, caught him by the neck under the chin and literally threw him against the wall. The Colombian's head banged twice against the plaster. He went limp. His hands fell to his sides. As they did, Angelo's left hand ripped into his crotch, grabbing and squeezing his testicles with all his strength.

The Colombian shrieked in agony.

"Okay, motherfucker," Angelo growled. "Now you either tell me where that card went or I'll rip these things out of here and stuff them down your goddamn throat."

"Talk! I talk!" Torres shrieked.

Angelo relaxed his grip slightly.

"Union Street. Benny. The fence there."

Angelo squeezed again. "Where on Union Street?"

Torres shrieked, tears of pain rolling down his face. "By Sixth Avenue. Across from supermarket. Second floor."

Angelo released the pickpocket. He tumbled to the floor, writhing in pain.

"Get your pants on," Angelo ordered. "You and I are going to see Benny."

Laila Dajani had been silent through most of her lunch at Orsini's, picking indifferently at her *tagliatelle verdi* and salad, barely touching her Bardolino wine, destroying, apparently, what

292

little appetite she had with half a dozen cigarettes. Yet, on the way to the restaurant, she'd told Michael at least three times she had something very serious to talk about.

Her silence had not disturbed her lover. Michael had devoured a plate of *fettucine,* followed by *fegato alla Veneziana,* calf's liver and onions, all to still the ravenous appetite for which she was largely responsible. The waiter cleared away their dishes and gave the table a desultory flick of his napkin.

"Dessert?"

"No," Michael replied. "Two espressos."

As he left, Michael leaned toward Laila. She had changed her clothes and was wearing an eggshell-white Givenchy blouse that clung hungrily to every indentation of her braless breasts. "You said you had something you wanted to talk to me about."

Laila reached for another cigarette, lit it, exhaled slowly, thoughtfully. "I want to think about us a moment."

Michael grinned lasciviously. "Okay, I'm thinking."

"Michael, we need more fantasy in our lives."

Michael had just taken a sip of his espresso, and he almost spilled it with the laughter that followed her words. "Darling, what did you have in mind? Do you want me to whip you or something?"

"Michael, we've got to do crazy, wonderful things together. Like that." She snapped her fingers. "On a whim. Just because we want to. Because it's for us."

Michael gave a gentle laugh and reached for her hand. "Like what?"

Laila swallowed nervously, trying to feign thought. "Crazy things. I don't know. Like going off somewhere on the spur of the moment together. The two of us, alone. No baggage even, just ourselves." A smile suddenly brightened her face. "Look, I've got to go to Montreal one day this week to see a collection. I'll go tomorrow on the first plane. You come up tomorrow, too. There's a direct flight to Quebec at noon. We'll meet at the Château Frontenac. Do you know it?" She was rushing on, now trying to sweep him up in the torrent of her words, painfully aware of the undertow of hysteria in her voice. "It's the most marvelous place! Lovely, quaint streets just like Paris. We'll ride on sleighs and eat warm croissants in bed for breakfast and walk along the Saint Lawrence and go shopping in the wonderful little shops they have. Oh, Michael darling, do it. For me. Please."

Her hands took his, stroking them tenderly.

Michael kissed her fingertips. "Angel, I can't. Impossible. I've got two *Vogue* shootings tomorrow I can't possibly cancel. Besides, I thought we were going to Truman Capote's lunch."

"Oh, Michael! Who gives a damn about that little creep and all those fawning toads swarming around him? I want us to do something for ourselves, for ourselves alone."

Michael sipped his espresso. "Now, if you want to do something really crazy, I have an idea. I've got a friend at one of the agencies who has a flat down in Acapulco. He's always offering to lend it to me. We'll take the Friday-night plane and spend a mad, crazy weekend in the sun together." He shivered. "I mean, Quebec, it's cold up there."

Laila extended a hand and lovingly caressed his cheeks, playfully skimming the skin of his ears with her long fingernails. "That's a wonderful idea, darling." She paused. "But I just have this feeling about tomorrow. You know how superstitious we Arabs are. Come on, let's do it. Please."

Michael picked up the check the waiter had just set on the table. "Angel, I can't. Really. If I break these shootings I've got tomorrow, I might as well go down and sign up for my unemployment checks."

Laila watched him counting out the money for the check. How far do I dare go, she asked herself, how far?

Outside, the air was chill with the moist, gray promise of snow. "Do you have another shooting?" she asked.

"No, I'm through for the day."

Laila slipped an arm around Michael's waist. "Then let's go back to the studio," she said.

"To what," the Baron Claude de Fraguier, Secretary General of the French Foreign Office, asked Henri Bertrand, "do I owe the pleasure of this unexpected visit?"

The director of France's intelligence service was looking for an ashtray. With a gesture of his head, the Baron indicated one on an Empire gueridon halfway across the room.

"On April fifteenth, 1973," Bertrand replied, returning to his armchair, the outsized ashtray clutched awkwardly in his hand, "you people signed a Monsieur Paul-Henri de Serre of the Atomic

Energy Commission to a three-year contract to serve as a technical adviser to India's nuclear program. He returned to this country in November 1975, some six months before his contract was due to expire. The dossier which my colleagues at the DST have given me on Monsieur de Serre fails to indicate why he came home early. Perhaps your people could enlighten me?"

The Baron stared at Bertrand. He disliked both the man and his service. "May I ask why you wish to know?"

"No," Bertrand replied, concealing with his inscrutable features the pleasure he took in pronouncing the word. "You may not. Although I might add that my inquiry has the sanction of the highest authority."

These people, the Baron reflected distastefully. Constantly invoking the office of the Presidency to cover their intrusions into the domains of others. "You will probably find, *cher ami*," he said, ordering up the dossier, "a reason as commonplace as a poor widowed mother dying of cancer in the Dordogne."

When an aide laid de Serre's dossier on his desk, the Baron opened it himself, careful to keep its contents well out of reach of Bertrand's eyes. A reference tab was affixed to the document terminating de Serre's Indian service. It referred to a sealed envelope in the dossier containing a letter from the French ambassador in New Delhi to the Baron's predecessor. The Baron opened it and read it, studiously ignoring as he did the manifest impatience of the SDECE director. When he had finished, he folded the letter, placed it back in its envelope, returned the envelope to its place and passed the dossier back to his assistant.

"Just as one might have expected," he said, his voice as cutting as long years of practice could make it, "a sordid little affair. Just the sort of thing to interest your services. Your friend Monsieur de Serre was caught employing the diplomatic valise to smuggle Indian antiquities out of the country. Quite valuable objects, as it turned out. Rather than risking any embarrassment with our Indian friends, he was recalled and returned to his post at the Atomic Energy Commission."

"Interesting." Bertrand methodically twisted his cigarette stub into the ashtray in his hand. So there is our fissure, he thought. The search for these little flaws, for the barely perceptible cracks in the smooth façade of a man's character that could be widened and exploited, was the very essence of Bertrand's calling. The

295

heavy hands of the brass Empire clock on the Baron's desk showed that it was already half past six. The velvet mantle of evening, the magic hour of legend and lovers, was settling over Paris. If he was going to pursue this tonight, he would have to hurry. He hesitated. Really, he should leave it to the morning. Still, his CIA colleague had seemed very concerned. And the Arabs, he knew, worked late.

"I'm sorry, *mon cher,*" he informed the Baron. "I'm going to have to use your facilities to get off an urgent message to our man at the embassy in Tripoli. In view of what you've just told me, it can't wait until I get back to my headquarters."

Jeremy Oglethorpe, Washington's evacuation expert, gawked at the sight before him like a little boy on Christmas morning discovering on his living-room floor an electric-train set that went beyond his wildest fantasies. Spread over an entire wall of the command center at the Metropolitan Transit Authority Building in Brooklyn was an action map of New York's subway system, each of the 450 stations of its three divisions identified by name and a light, every one of the 207 trains moving at that moment on its 237 miles of track marked by a flashing red light.

"Wonderful!" he gasped. "Even more impressive than I imagined it would be."

He was sitting in the superintendent's glassed-in central booth in the center of the room with the chief of operations, a genial, slightly overweight black. Spread on the desk before him was a map of the system and beside it a thick sheaf of notes in a gray-and-white Stanford Research Institute binder. "I've done a lot of work studying your system, Chief. You've got six thousand cars available?"

"We had 5,062 today. You've always got some in for repairs, inspections."

"And you can put two hundred and fifty people in a car?"

"Only if you want to start a riot. Two hundred's our limit."

Oglethorpe grunted. My figure is good for my scenario, he thought. "Chief, I want you to think about a problem with me. Suppose we've got to evacuate Manhattan in an emergency. Fast, real fast. And we don't want to take people out to Brooklyn or Queens. We want to move them up here." Oglethorpe's pudgy fingers skirted the terminals of the upper Bronx, 242nd Street, Woodlawn Road, 205th Street, 241st Street, Dyre Avenue, and Pelham Bay Park.

The chief twisted a Styrofoam cup of black coffee in his hand and studied Oglethorpe with a skeptical eye. "Why would you want to do all this?"

"Well, say we're afraid there's a nuclear bomb in Manhattan. Or the Russians are coming."

The chief thought awhile, then stood and peered down at the system's map. "Okay. The first thing you'd want to think about are the trains already moving in the system when you sound your alert. I guess you keep 'em going all the way through. Take an IRT number five going into Fulton Street in lower Manhattan. Give the motorman an announcement, 'We have to evacuate Manhattan because of an emergency threat.' Then tell him to run straight up to Dyre Avenue nonstop and dump his load."

Oglethorpe was frantically noting down his words.

"Now," the trainman continued, "that might be a little difficult. New Yorkers don't like being told what to do very much." He gave a little laugh. "You'll want some help there in the Bronx. Some of those people aren't going to want to get off the train. They'll insist on going back to get their wives or their kids, or their mothers-in-law. Or their pet canaries. We'd have to devise a loop. Up to the Bronx. Drop them. Out to Brooklyn," he continued.

"Why all the way to Brooklyn?" Oglethorpe queried.

"Because we can't turn trains around in the middle of the system. You'd use the local track to load and go onto the express track once they're loaded. Run 'em nonstop right up to the Bronx and start all over again."

"Terrific!" Oglethorpe was almost trembling with excitement. Obviously, this was the answer. With a little order, a little control. "Now tell me," he said, "on the basis you've outlined here, allowing for the minor problems that always crop up, how much time do you think it would take under this plan to clear Manhattan?"

"Probably four to six hours. Maybe a bit more."

"And if we asked you to take people out of Queens and Brooklyn too?"

"Then we've got a much bigger problem."

Oglethorpe sat down, studying his notes, going through the papers of his SRI study. He was beaming. He looked at Walsh, the smile on his face almost triumphant. "I told you this was the answer. Now look, Chief, if you started right now, with any help you wanted, could you get this plan down on paper for me, everything, logistics, signaling systems, timing, everything, in two hours?"

"I think so."

"Terrific." Oglethorpe looked again at Walsh. "We're going to have a terrific plan."

"Sure, you'll have a terrific plan, mister," the chief agreed. His voice was low and cool, so fully controlled he might have been an anchor man reading out the evening news. "And there'll only be one thing wrong with it."

"What's that?"

"It won't work."

"Won't work?" Oglethorpe looked as though he'd just received a blow in the stomach. "What do you mean it won't work?"

"Who do you think are going to drive those trains for you?"

"Why," Oglethorpe replied, "your motormen. Who else?"

"Not if they know there's an atomic bomb on Manhattan Island, my friend. They'll take their first train up to Dyre Avenue all right. And then they'll be out of the station door with everyone else. The switchmen, the yardsmen you need to turn the trains around—they'll be gone, too."

"Well," Oglethorpe muttered, "we won't tell them. We'll say it's a practice."

The chief laughed, a rich, warm laugh from deep in his overextended stomach. "You're going to clear three and a half million people off Manhattan Island and try to make them believe you're doing it for fun? For some kind of exercise?" The pitch of his laughter skirted upward at the thought of how ludicrous it all was. "Mister, there's not a New Yorker alive who'd believe horseshit like that. I tell you, half an hour after you start this, every car in the system'll be laid down on the tracks up there in the Bronx and every motorman in town'll be running for the hills."

Oglethorpe listened in dismayed silence, one hand clutching his carefully written notes and the papers of his SRI study.

"You can't evacuate this city with the subways," the chief said, "or any other way, for that matter." He looked sadly at the papers in Oglethorpe's fingers. "All you got there, mister, is a handful of dreams."

Puzzled and angry, John Booth followed the steady cackle of NEST's ultra-high-tranmission network. The normally phlegmatic NEST director was as distraught as a man who has just been told his wife is expecting triplets. Three times since he had gotten back to his Seventh Regiment Armory headquarters, his helicopters overflying lower Manhattan had reported high radiation readings only to see them mysteriously disappear when his foot search teams moved in.

Like everything else in NEST, the radio facility set up in the locker rooms used by the tennis players who usually employed the armory's main floor was designed to be independent and self-contained. Everything from batteries, spare parts and screwdrivers to hand-carried transreceivers and portable sender-receivers for the trucks and helicopters had been flown in from Las Vegas. That way Booth could feel reasonably certain that local CB fans, newspapers or TV stations wouldn't pick up any indication of what was going on by eavesdropping on his transmissions.

On the wall of the locker room were huge color aerial-survey maps of New York's five boroughs, maps whose resolution was so fine you could identify with a loop the color of a hat on a woman walking down Fifth Avenue. They were part of a file of maps of 170 U.S. cities held available twenty-four hours a day at NEST's Washington offices.

Suddenly Booth heard an excited call rise over the chatter on the network.

"Feather Three to base. I have a positive." Feather Three was one of the trio of New York Airways helicopters Booth had pressed into service.

Jesus Christ, Booth prayed, please don't let this be another false alarm, I'll go crazy.

The technician and the pilot were back on the air, pinning their reading down to a hotel two doors from Twenty-third Street and Sixth Avenue, when one of them shouted, "Son of a bitch, it's fading!" A few seconds passed and his voice was back.."No, it's not, John. It's moving! It's moving up Sixth Avenue!"

Booth hit his forehead with the heel of his hand. Of course, that was it! The clever bastards had hidden the bomb in the back of a truck and were circulating through the city.

Trembling with nervous excitement, Booth and the men in the command post followed the steady progress of the target up Sixth Avenue, across Thirty-fourth Street. Suddenly the chopper, whose pilot had been trying to get some idea of which truck in the maze of traffic below was giving off radiation, came back on the air. "Target no longer moving."

"Where is he?"

"Seems to be at Bryant Park, Sixth and Forty-second!"

Booth ordered half a dozen NEST vans and FBI cars to converge on the intersection.

"I've got it!" shouted the technician in the first van to reach the scene.

"Where are you?" Booth demanded.

"Just down Fifth from the corner," came the answer, "right in front of the New York Public Library."

The numerals on the bar clock hung on the wood-paneled wall of the National Security Council conference room read 1428. A sense of helplessness infused the room. Coffee cups, half-eaten sandwiches, ashtrays overflowing with cigarette stubs littered the table along with piles of top-secret cables from CIA, State and Pentagon. Nothing in those cables or the messages delivered to the room over its sophisticated communications network had brought its occupants any solace, any promise of a satisfactory resolution to the crisis. Barely twenty-four hours before the expiration of the ultimatum of the zealot of Tripoli they were, as Harold Brown had so bitterly observed, the "pitiful giant" once mockingly described by Mao Tse-tung, all the vast panoply of U.S. resources useless. Little by little as they had followed the progress of the search for the bomb in New York in regular hourly reports from the city, one thing had become appallingly clear: so frightening were the dimensions of the task, so painfully slow the manner in which it had to be carried out, there was no hope of finding the device in the time Qaddafi had allocated them. As for the secret messages that had reached the White House from every major world capital and leader, they all, without exception, urged the President to remain firm in the face of Qaddafi's menace. None of them, however, had offered the slightest specific suggestion on how to do that without imperiling New York and its people. It was the Iranian crisis all over again. America's allies were free with their advice but notably timorous when it came to help or action.

Just after half past two, a Navy chief petty officer interrupted a

CIA report from Paris with the announcement that the last of the Sixth Fleet's ships had reached the one-hundred-kilometer limit set down earlier by Qaddafi. The President greeted the news with a mixture of relief and concern. Fundamentally, he was certain all their hopes came down to the enterprise he could now begin: trying to reason with a man four thousand miles away, a man who, only a generation ago, would have been just the inconsequential ruler of a lot of sand, but who, thanks to oil, the technological genius of twentieth-century man and his own countrymen's madness in hurling their most precious knowledge into the public domain, now had the power to force his zealot's vision on the world. Mankind could afford tyrants in the day of the sword, the President reflected. Not anymore.

While the white squawk box buzzed with the space-age jargon of the Doomsday jet reestablishing the communications link to Tripoli, he gave a last glance at the yellow legal pad before him. On it were the notes he had made listening to the psychiatrists' advice:

> Flatter him; play up to his vanity as a world leader.
> He's a loner. Must become his friend. Show him I'm the person who can help him out of the corner into which he's painted himself.
> Voice always soft, nonthreatening.
> *Never* give him the impression I don't take him seriously.
> Keep him in a position of fundamental uncertainty; he must never know exactly where he's at.

Good maxims for a police negotiator. But were they really going to be any help to him? He swallowed, feeling the tension constrict his throat. Then he turned to Eastman and indicated he was ready.

"Mr. Qaddafi," he began, once he had confirmed that the Libyan had followed the fleet's withdrawal. "I want to address the very grave problem posed by your letter. I understand how ardently you want to see justice done for your fellow Arabs in Palestine. I want you to know that I share those sentiments, Mr. Qaddafi, I—"

The Libyan cut into his speech. His voice was as gentle as it had been two hours before, but his words were no more encouraging than they had been then.

"Please, Mr. President, do not waste my time or yours with

speeches. Have the Israelis begun to evacuate the occupied territories or have they not?''

"No stress reading at all." the CIA technician monitoring the voice stress analyzer reported. "He's perfectly relaxed."

"Mr. Qaddafi," the President pressed on, striving to control his own emotions, "I understand your impatience to reach a settlement. I share it. But we must lay together the basis for a durable peace, one that will satisfy all parties concerned, not one forced on the world by a threat such as the one you have made to New York."

"Words, Mr. President." The Libyan, to the Chief Executive's irritation, had interrupted him again. "The same kind of hollow, hypocritical words you have been feeding my Palestinian brothers for thirty years."

"I assure you I speak with the utmost sincerity," the President rejoined—to no avail. Qaddafi, ignoring him, was continuing. "Your Israeli allies bomb and shell Palestinian refugee camps in Lebanon with American planes and guns, kill Arab women and children with American bullets, and what do you offer in return? Words—while you go right on selling the Israelis more arms so that they can go on killing more of our people. Every time the Israelis seize my brothers' lands with their illegal settlements, what do you do? You give us more of your pious words, your spokesmen wringing their hands in public in Washington. But have you ever done anything to stop the Israelis? No! Never!

"Well, Mr. President, from now on you and the other leaders of your country can save your words. The time for them has passed. At last the Arab people of Palestine have the means of obtaining the justice that should have been theirs long ago, and they are going to get it, Mr. President, because if they do not, millions of your people are going to die to pay for the injustices that have been committed against them."

The impact of Qaddafi's words was heightened by the flat, monotonous voice in which he uttered them, a voice so devoid of passion it seemed to Eastman that the Libyan leader could have been a broker reading off stock quotations to a client, or a pilot going through his preflight checklist. For Tamarkin and Jagerman, the precise, well-controlled voice was the final confirmation of something each had suspected: this man would not hesitate to carry out his threat.

"I cannot really believe, Mr. Qaddafi," the President continued, "that a man like you, a man so proud of having carried out his revolution without bloodshed, a man of compassion and charity, can really be serious about employing this satanic device, this instrument of hell, to kill and maim millions and millions of innocent men and women."

"Mr. President." For the first time, there was a slight undercurrent of stridency in Qaddafi's tone. "Why can't you believe it?"

The President was staggered that the man could even ask the question. "It's totally irrational, a wholly irresponsible act, sir. It's—"

"Such as your act when you Americans dropped a similar weapon on the Japanese? Where was the compassion and charity in that? It's all right to kill, burn, maim thousands of yellow Asiatics or Arabs or Africans, but not clean, white Americans. Is that it? Who created this satanic device, as you call it, in the first place? German Jews. Who are the only people who have ever used it? White Christian Americans. Who are the nations that stockpile these engines that can destroy the world? Your civilized, advanced, industrial societies. They are products of your world, Mr. President, not mine. And now it is we of the other world who are going to use them to right the injustices you have committed against us."

The President was frantically scrutinizing his yellow legal pad. How inappropriate the words he had written there seemed to him now that he was actually confronted by this man. "Mr. Qaddafi." The usually stern and confident baritone wavered. "No matter how strongly you may feel about the injustices done to the Palestinians, surely you will acknowledge that it's not my innocent countrymen in New York who are responsible—the blacks in Bedford-Stuyvesant, the Puerto Ricans, the millions of ordinary, hard-working men and women struggling there to make a living?"

"Oh yes, they are responsible, Mr. President," came the reply. "All of them. Who is responsible for creating Israel in the first place? You Americans are. Who provided them with the arms they used in four wars against us? You Americans did. Whose money keeps them alive? Yours."

"Do you suppose that, even if the Israelis should agree, temporarily, to withdraw, they would let you get away with this?" the President asked. "What guarantees can you hope to have that this solution of yours can last?"

Clearly, the President's question was one for which the Libyan

303

was prepared. "Order your satellites that are observing my country now to study our desert along our eastern border from the seacoast to Al-Kufra. Perhaps you will find some new constructions there. My SCUD missiles are not like yours, Mr. President, they cannot travel around the world and strike a pin as yours can, but they can fly a thousand kilometers and find the coast of Israel. That is all they have to do. They are all the guarantee I will need when this is done."

My God, the President thought, it's even worse than I had imagined. He doodled frantically on his legal pad, hoping for some magic thought that would strike the responsive chord he had thus far been unable to find.

"Mr. Qaddafi, I have followed the progress of your revolution with genuine admiration. I know how well you've used your great oil wealth to bring your people material progress and prosperity." He was groping and he knew it. "Whatever your feelings are about New York, surely you don't want to see your nation and your people destroyed in a thermonuclear holocaust?"

"My people are prepared to die for the cause if necessary, Mr. President, just as I am." Again the Libyan had lapsed into English to shorten the exchange.

"Mao Tse-tung accomplished the greatest revolution in history with a minimum of bloodshed," the President rejoined. That was a lie, but it reflected the psychiatrists' advice. Invoke Mao, they had said, he sees himself as an Arabic Mao. "You have the same opportunity if you will be reasonable, remove your threat to New York and work with me toward a just and lasting Middle East peace."

"Be reasonable, Mr. President?" came the answer. "Being reasonable to you means that Palestinian Arabs can be driven from their homes, can be forced to live in refugee camps for thirty years. Being reasonable means that Palestinian Arabs should stand by and watch the creeping annexation of their homeland by these Israeli settlements. Being reasonable means that we Arabs should let you Americans and your Israeli allies go on preventing the Palestinians from enjoying their God-given right to a homeland, a nation, while we continue selling you the oil to run your factories and your cars, to heat your homes. All that is reasonable. But when my brothers and I tell you, who are responsible for their misery, 'Give us the justice you have denied us so long, or we will strike,' suddenly that is unreasonable. Suddenly, because we ask for justice, we are fanatics. You cannot understand just as you couldn't understand when the Iranian people turned their wrath on you.''

As Qaddafi was speaking, Jagerman slipped a piece of paper up the table to the President. On it he had written the words "The greater-goal tactic?" The phrase summarized a maneuver the Dutchman had suggested earlier: trying to persuade Qaddafi to drop his threat to New York by getting him to associate with the President on some specific plan to achieve an even greater goal than the one he was seeking. Escalate his ambitions into something beyond those he had defined. Unfortunately, no one in the National Security Council conference room had been able to suggest a practical way of applying the theory. Suddenly, as he looked at the note, an idea struck the President. It was so bold, so dramatic, it might capture Qaddafi's imagination.

"Mr. Qaddafi," he said, unable to conceal the excitement in his voice. "I have a proposal to make to you. Release the millions of my fellow Americans in New York from your dire menace and I will fly to Libya immediately, unescorted, in *Air Force One*. I, the President of the United States, will allow you to hold me as your hostage while together we work, hand in hand, to find a plan to give the world and your Palestinian brothers something even greater than what you have proposed—a real, durable peace, acceptable to all. We will do it together, and yours will be a glory greater than Saladdin's, because it will have been won without bloodshed.''

The President's wholly unexpected proposal stunned his advisers. Eastman was aghast. It was absolutely unthinkable: the President of the United States becoming the hostage of an Arab oil despot, locked up in some desert oasis like a commercial traveler kidnapped for ransom by the Barbary Coast pirates two hundred years ago.

Finally, Qaddafi's voice once again filled the room. "Mr. President, I admire you for your offer. I respect you for it. But it is not necessary. My letter is clear. Its terms are clear. That is all that we ask. There is no need for any further discussion between you and me either here or anywhere else.''

"Mr. Qaddafi." The President almost interrupted the Libyan. "I cannot urge you strongly enough to accept my proposal. We have been in contact in the last two hours with every major leader in the world. And all your fellow Arab leaders: President Sadat, Mr. Assad, King Hussein, King Khalid, even Yassir Arafat. All of them, without exception, condemn your initiative. You are alone, isolated as you will not be if you agree to my proposal."

"I do not speak in their names, Mr. President." The Libyan's Arabic continued to flow into the room in the slow, unmodulated cadence he had employed almost from the beginning. "I speak for the people, the Arab people. It is their brothers who have been dispossessed, not those of our leaders and kings rotting in their palaces." Suddenly there was a shift in Qaddafi's tone, a stirring of impatience and irritation. "All this talk is useless, Mr. President. What must be done must be done."

"We're getting some strain," the technician manning the voice analyzer announced.

"You had thirty years to do justice to my people and you did nothing. Now you have twenty-four hours."

Anger seized the President in a swift, uncontrollable tide. "Mr. Qaddafi!" To the psychiatrists' dismay he was virtually shouting. "We will not be blackmailed. We will not be coerced by your unreasonable, impossible demands, by your outrageous action!"

A long, ominous silence followed his outburst. Then Qaddafi's voice returned as calm and as unhurried as it had been earlier. "Mr. President, there is nothing impossible about my demands. I am not asking for Israel's destruction. I only ask for what is just —that my Palestinian brothers have the home God meant for all people to have on the land He gave them. We Arabs were in the right for thirty years, but neither war nor political methods allowed us to achieve our objective, because we did not have the strength. Now we do, Mr. President, and either you will force the Israelis to give us the justice that is ours or, like Samson in your Bible, we will pull down the roof of the temple on ourselves and all the others that are in it."

While Muammar al-Qaddafi was delivering his threat to the President, one of the terrorists he counted on to help carry it out if necessary was getting ready to make love in a bedroom in New York City. Why am I here? Laila Dajani asked herself. She knew the answer. Because I'm weak. Because I lack the steel in

306

my soul the others have, that steel Carlos always said was the one indispensable ingredient of a revolutionary. I'm fatally prone to the terrorist's mortal sin, she admitted. I think too much.

The door opened and Michael walked in, a bath towel knotted around his slender waist, a glass of white wine in each hand. He bent down, kissed her gently, handed her her glass, then lay down on the bed beside her. For a moment they lay there in silence, Michael's hand slowly, distractedly almost, running over the surface of her breasts.

"Michael?"

"Yes, darling."

"Come to Quebec tomorrow."

Michael propped himself up on his elbow and stared down at Laila. Even in the half-light of his bedroom, he could see the sorrow on her face, the nascent sparkle of tears rising in her eyes.

"Linda, for Christ's sake, what is it with this Quebec thing? You're obsessed with it."

Laila rolled over, squashed out her cigarette, pulled a new one from her pack and lit it. "Michael, I told you I was superstitious, didn't I?"

Michael let his head sink back onto his pillow. So that's it, he thought.

"There's an old Egyptian fortuneteller I go to over in Brooklyn. An incredible place. Once you get inside you'd think you were on the banks of the Nile. His wife is all done up in black like a Bedouin woman. Her face is tattooed. She brings you a cup of *masbout*, Arabic coffee." She paused.

"He takes your cup and holds it. He asks your name, your mother's name, your date of birth. Then he goes into a kind of trance, praying. You're not allowed to smoke or cross your legs or your arms—that cuts the current between you. Every so often, he stops praying and talks to you."

Laila sat up, leaning against the backrest of the bed, smoking intently. "Michael, you wouldn't believe me if I told you some of the things this man has predicted for me."

"Like a secret rendezvous in Quebec?"

She ignored him.

"I went to him this morning. At the end, just before I left, he tensed up as though something terrible was happening. He said, 'There is someone very close to you. A man. A young blond man.'

307

He said in Arabic, 'He's a *messawarati*.' Michael, do you know what a *messawarati* is?''

Michael rolled his head on his pillow. ''A lecherous infidel?''

''Please, darling. Be serious. A photographer. How could he possibly have known that, Michael? He said, 'He's in very great danger here. Very soon. Tomorrow. He must leave New York before tomorrow.' ''

Laila clasped his hand, awed by the chance she was taking. ''Michael, please. Go to Quebec tomorrow.''

Michael rose up again on one elbow, looking at her sorrowful face, at the two tears glistening on her cheekbones. What ridiculous, superstitious creatures women can be, he thought.

Tenderly, he kissed away each teardrop. ''You're sweet, my darling,'' he said, ''to think of me like that.'' Then he laughed softly. ''But really I haven't got room in my life for the prophecies of old Arab fortunetellers.''

Laila rolled over on top of him, her back and shoulders raised so that the long swirls of her hair hung down around his face, enclosing it in an auburn canopy. I tried, she thought, gazing solemnly at her lover, God knows I tried.

''Too bad, Michael,'' she whispered. ''Oh, too bad!''

In Washington, the President was trembling. Qaddafi's reference to Samson's destruction of the Temple had shaken him as nothing had since he'd watched the Libyan's fireball exploding on the Pentagon's screens at midnight.

''Jack,'' he ordered, his words coming in a hoarse whisper. ''Tell the Doomsday to arrange for some communications problems over the next few minutes. I want some time to think about this.''

When the squawk box fell silent the Chief Executive studied the faces around the table. They too were aghast. It was as if the full measure of the drama they faced had only just become apparent in the obduracy and fanaticism of the man in Libya.

''Gentleman,'' the President asked, ''what do you think?''

At the end of the table, Admiral Fuller seemed to pull his head down into his shirt collar like a wizened old sea turtle withdrawing into his shell. ''Sir, I think he's only going to leave us one option —military action.''

''I don't agree.'' Andrew Peabody, the Secretary of State, had intervened almost before the Admiral had finished. ''There is another option, and I think we should make a decision to act on it very quickly. Instead of going on trying to reason with a very unreasonable man, we must use the precious time we have left to force some kind of an accommodation out of the Israelis that will satisfy him and save New York."

"That, at least, has the advantage of being an initiative that requires very little time," Bennington noted sarcastically. "Only the thirty seconds it's going to take Begin to say no. The Agency has been pointing out for the last five years that those damn settlements were a menace to peace and were going to land us in serious trouble one day. Unfortunately, no other agency in the government wanted to do anything about them."

For just a second, listening to his advisers, the President yearned to unleash a primal scream. Was there no crisis so terrible it couldn't shake the agencies of the U.S. government out of their stereotyped pattern of response: the Pentagon urging us to blow the bastard to bits; State recommending we back down; the CIA trying to cover its ass the way it has been ever since Iran?

"Jack?" he said wearily to his National Security Assistant.

"I come back to what I said half an hour ago, Mr. President. The essence of this crisis is time. If we can get the Israelis to come up with some kind of concession, then maybe we can use it to get Qaddafi to lift his threat. Or at least extend his deadline so we'll have a better chance of finding this damn thing in New York before our time runs out."

The President's eyes passed over Delbert Crandell. He had no desire to read the intimation of a prophecy fulfilled that he knew he'd find on the Energy Secretary's face. "What do you people read into this?" he asked the psychiatrists.

Tamarkin looked at the notes he had hastily jotted down while listening to Qaddafi. He was horrified by how inadequate they appeared, by how little, finally, he had to offer the President. "I think we're dealing with an omnipotent personality here. One with a slight but by no means disabling streak of paranoia. People like that tend to have trouble handling open-ended situations. Multiple possibilities. The thing is not to give him a fulcrum on which to crystallize his actions. He's probably counting on you to either capitulate or threaten him with destruction. In other words, to make his decision for him. If, instead, you throw a whole series of specific, peripheral problems at him he might be at a loss."

"I'm inclined to agree with my young colleague," Jagerman

noted approvingly. "If I may, sir, I would suggest there is little to be gained by pressing him further on the *why* of his action. He's quite convinced he's right, and you're only going to make him more intractable by arguing the point. I think you should get instead onto the *how* and try to distract him with a lot of low-level, semitechnical questions about how to implement his plan. You recall my reference to the 'hamburger or chicken option'?"

The President nodded. Jagerman's phrase sounded grotesque in the present situation, but it described a technique for handling terrorist-hostage crises that was in every secret-police manual in the world. Jagerman himself had helped formulate it. Distract the terrorists, it maintained, keep them busy dealing with an unending stream of questions and problems not related to the central point at issue. The example invariably given to demonstrate how the principle worked was the recommended response to a terrorist's request for food: What did he want, hamburger or chicken? The leg or the wing? Rare or well done? Mustard or ketchup? On a bun? Toasted? How about relish? Sweet or sour? Pickles? Did he take it with onions? Distracting a terrorist with such an unceasing barrage of questions frequently helped to calm him down, to expose him to reality and, ultimately, to make him more malleable. The Dutchman added a number of refinements to the technique. For example, he always had food sent in on normal china, glasses and silverware. This, he maintained, subtly introduced an element of civility into the police–terrorist relationship. Furthermore, he had the terrorist, where possible, wash the plates before returning them, to force him to begin responding to authority.

"If you can succeed in getting a variant of that working," Jagerman counseled, "then you can perhaps suggest he continue with Mr. Eastman while you are talking with the Israelis."

"We can always try," the President replied grimly. "Get him back, Jack."

"Mr. Qaddafi," he began again, "there are now, as you know, forty-eight Israeli settlements in what you refer to as the occupied territories. Over ten thousand people are settled there. The logistical problems involved in moving them in the very limited time you've given us are staggering."

"Mr. President." The Libyan's quiet, courteous tone was unchanged. "Those people set up their settlements in a few hours. You know that. They sneak in under the cover of night, and at dawn they present the world with a *fait accompli*. If they can go in a few hours, they can leave in twenty-four."

"But, Mr. Qaddafi," the President persisted, "now they have their homes, their possessions, their factories, their farms, their schools, their synagogues. You can't expect them to walk away and leave all that in twenty-four hours."

"I can and I do. Their property will be guarded. Once the Palestinian Arab nation is established they will be allowed to return and collect what is theirs."

"How can we be sure that we won't have chaos and disorder as the Israelis withdraw?"

"The people in their joy at rediscovering their homeland will preserve order."

"Joyous they may well be, but I'm not sure that's going to be enough to preserve order, sir. Shouldn't we ask King Hussein to furnish Jordanian troops?"

"Certainly not. Why should that imperialistic stooge reap the glory of this?"

"How about the PLO?"

"No. They are compromising traitors. We must use the men of the Refusal Front."

"We will need to work out arrangements very, very carefully. Know what units would be involved. Who their commanders are. Where they will come from. How they would identify themselves. How will we coordinate their movements with the Israelis? All this requires close planning and discussion."

There was another of Tripoli's long and unexplained silences before Qaddafi replied. "You shall have it."

"And the bomb in New York? I presume when these arrangements are made you will tell us where it is and radio instructions to your people who are guarding it to deactivate it?"

Again there was a long silence. "The bomb is set to detonate automatically at the expiration of my ultimatum. The only signal its radio is programmed to receive is a negative signal known only to me to deactivate it."

Eastman let out a low whistle as the interpreter finished his work. "What a clever bastard! That's his guarantee we don't dump the missiles on him at the last moment. We have to keep him alive to save New York."

"Either that," Bennington answered, "or it's a very shrewd . . ."

He pursed his lips, thinking. "He could be lying, you know. And lying about the SCUD missiles too." He turned abruptly to the President. "Mr. President, it would make all the difference to our planning to know if he's lying or not. We have a device here that we've developed at the Agency which could be invaluable to us if we can get him to agree to speak to you over a television linkup."

"What is it, Tap?"

"It's a machine that employs laser beams to scan the musculature of a man's eyeballs at ultra-high speeds while he's talking. It picks up certain characteristic changes in the muscle patterns that occur if a man is lying."

The President gave Bennington an admiring smile. "You're right. Let's try it."

"Mr. Qaddafi," he said as he resumed his dialogue, "in the very complex discussions we're going to have to have here on movements on the West Bank, it would be helpful if we could see as well as hear each other. That way we can work out our arrangements on maps and aerial photographs so that there's no chance of error. Would you be agreeable to setting up a television link between us? We can fly in immediately the necessary equipment."

Again there was a long pause from Tripoli. Bennington distractedly twisted a pipe cleaner in the stem of his Dunhill, silently praying that Qaddafi would agree. To his astonishment the Libyan did, with no reluctance at all. Further, he had his own equipment immediately available in his headquarters.

Poor bastard, Bennington thought, detecting a note of pride in his reply. Probably so caught up with technology as a plaything that he keeps forgetting how far we're ahead of him.

While the technician on the Doomsday jet prepared to set up a television link that would relay Tripoli's signal to the Atlantic COMSAT satellite, then back to the antennas and communication discs in the space-age garden adjoining the CIA's headquarters, a pair of Agency scientists wheeled their eye scanner into the National Security Council conference room.

The conferees looked on, fascinated, as they set up this latest gadget in an arsenal of weapons designed by the CIA to break down the most resistant barriers of the human conscience and force men to divulge emotions so hidden they were sometimes unaware they had them. It looked vaguely like a portable X-ray machine. Two small black metal tubes like the eyepieces of a pair

312

of fieldglasses protruded from the top. From these, two beams of light were already dancing over the television screen on which Qaddafi's face was expected to appear. High-intensity laser beams, they would be trained on his eyeballs and would read for the mini-computer at the heart of the scanner the slightest variations in the size or shape of their surface. The results would be instantly compared to the control data already stored in the computer bank, and be printed out on the mini-television screen attached to the scanner.

For a few seconds, Tripoli's television signal expanded and contracted on the screen as haphazardly as a multiplying amoeba caught under a microscope's glare. Then, suddenly, it coalesced into a sharp image of the Libyan leader. Curiously, the sight was almost reassuring. Qaddafi appeared so boyish, so timidly serious, that it seemed inconceivable that he could carry out his threat. In his simple khaki blouse with no decoration other than his colonel's epaulets, he looked more like a professor of tactics at the infantry school than a man who would be the avenging sword of God.

Eastman could detect no hint of strain or tension on his face. Indeed, there was only one register of feeling there, the intimation of an ironic smile trying, with minimal success, to intrude on the precise set of his mouth.

The little pinpoints of light from the scanner skated over the screen, then came to rest astride each eyeball like a pair of contact lenses.

"We're registering," one of the technicians stated.

This time, you son of a bitch, we've got you, Bennington thought, taking as he did a long, satisfied puff of his pipe.

Opposite the President, a red light glowed on the television camera relaying his image back to Tripoli.

"They're set," Eastman whispered.

The images of the two leaders were now projected side by side on the screens of the conference-room wall, the President trying, despite the strain, to force some indication of personal warmth onto his face, Qaddafi's regard as devoid of emotion as a Roman bust.

"Mr. Qaddafi," the President said, resuming the dialogue, "I think we will both find this visual link we've established very helpful in dealing with the difficult problems we face. When we were speaking a few moments ago, I believe you had just told me that the bomb in New York is controlled by an automatic timing device which only you can alter by a radio signal from Tripoli. Is that correct?''

Every face in the room was turned to the image of Qaddafi on the screen, the two bright lights of the scanner riveted to his eyeballs. Before he replied to the President, his right hand reached up to the pocket of his battle blouse. He unbuttoned it with almost tantalizing slowness. Then he drew a pair of dark sunglasses from its folds and, while the audience in the White House looked on in dismay, placed them defiantly over his eyes.

''Son of a bitch!'' gasped one of the CIA technicians.

The smile that had been struggling for ascendancy on the Libyan's face burst forth. ''Yes, Mr. President,'' he answered, ''you are correct.''

Compared to the National Security Council conference room the underground command post from which Muammar al-Qaddafi was addressing the President was almost spartan in its simplicity. Not much larger than a pair of double bedrooms, it was divided in half by a chest-high cement partition topped by a thick panel of glass. Qaddafi sat in one half at a simple wooden desk on which was trained the television camera transmitting his image to Washington. Just off camera was a twenty-eight-year-old Libyan graduate student from the University of Texas who was serving as his interpreter in much the same way as the State Department Arabists were serving the President.

In the second room, five men sat at a gray metallic desk. There were no maps on the wall, no blinking telephones at their elbows, no piles of secret cables offering advice stacked before them. There wasn't even a rug on the floor. They included Qaddafi's Prime Minister, Salam Jalloud; his chief of intelligence; Vladimir Illitch Sánchez "Carlos," the elegant Venezuelan terrorist; and a short man with thick eyeglasses and long, unkempt blond hair. He was a German, born in a little village in the Bavarian foothills, who had found his true vocation at West Berlin's Free University in the early sixties as a professional student radical. Among his several degrees was a doctorate in psychology, and it was that which accounted for his presence in the Villa Pietri. In return for $50,000 in a Swiss bank, he had agreed to become Qaddafi's psychiatric adviser. The fact that Qaddafi was even speaking to the President went against his primary recommendation. It was he who had persuaded the Libyan to reject the chargé's first initiative. Qaddafi's reluctance to agree and his instant and irrational rage at sighting the Sixth Fleet on his radar had confirmed the German's conviction that, as his Washington counterparts had suspected, Qaddafi really did want to talk to the President.

"My time, Mr. President," Qaddafi was saying, "is as valuable as yours. I have no intention whatsoever of becoming involved in a long and revealing dialogue with your adviser Eastman while leaving you free to concentrate your energies on other things."

"But," the President protested, "I've got to talk with Mr. Begin about your note."

The German smiled. That was exactly the reply he had told Qaddafi the American would make.

The Libyan stared at the television camera from behind his dark glasses. A faint smile twisted away at one side of his mouth. "Surely, Mr. President," he said, his voice suddenly chill, "you don't mean to tell me that fifteen hours have gone by since my explosion and you have not yet started discussing the implementation of my demands with the Israelis?"

The image of the President was being screened on an ordinary commercial television set, a twenty-four-inch Philips color receiver. The Americans were delivering a tight closeup of his head and shoulders. That was the shot the psychiatrists had recommended. A close visual contact with a figure of authority often aided a terrorist negotiation.

It aided, in any case, the task of the two young men manipulating the machine which fixed a pair of light beams to the eyes of the President on the screen before them. Manufactured by the Standarten Optika of Stuttgart, the machine had come to Carlos's attention when the West German police had used it to interrogate the suspected killers of German financier Dietrich Vallmar. With the German psychiatrist's help, he had brought it to Tripoli.

"Of course I have," he answered. "At great length and in great detail. And I can assure you Mr. Begin's initial reaction is very favorable. That's why it's so important that I resume my discussions with him."

One of the two technicians training the eye scanner on the President's face started. The green line darting across the oscilloscope

315

of the screen of his machine had taken a jagged, sawtooth pattern as it ran over the high-speed computerized printout of the President's words. He hit a red button that allowed him to speak to Qaddafi, isolated in the other room.

"*Ya sidi,*" he said, "the President is lying!"

The Libyan didn't move a facial muscle. He took off his dark glasses and leaned to the camera. "Mr. President," he said, "I thought you were an honest, decent man. I find out you are not. Not only are you despising of our abilities to cope with the technology of your world, but you have lied to me. Further conversation between us is useless. You now have twenty-four hours left in which to put the terms of my letter into effect or the bomb will explode."

From inside his red Avis Econoline van, the technician of the first NEST team to reach Forty-second Street and Fifth Avenue surveyed the broad steps of the New York Public Library. The oscilloscope of his detector registered a steady gross gamma count of .14 millirads an hour. Yet, to his utter astonishment, there were no other trucks, no cars immobilized in front of the library. Nothing stood between the pods of his detector and its monumental staircase.

"What in hell is going on?" the uncomprehending scientist asked rhetorically.

He did not have time to answer his question before John Booth had climbed into the front of the van. He studied the oscilloscope, then the view from the van, as wholly mystified as his scientist. From the radio net, he got the helicopter confirmation: the telltale emission was coming from somewhere across the street. By now, the area was full of unmarked FBI and police cars. Two more NEST vans had driven up behind his. Each confirmed the first van's reading.

Booth studied the scene, completely baffled. Was it possible that someone had carried a ton-and-a-half device into that building before the first van had reached the spot? He looked at the building. No, he told himself, the radiation would never get through its thick floors and ceilings to the choppers.

"Shit!" he growled. "Maybe we've been following some guy who had a barium milkshake who's just got off the bus here."

He ordered four scientists with portable detectors across the

316

street, then followed himself in the footsteps of their FBI escort. The four men drifted through the kids on roller skates gliding along the sidewalk, earphones glued to their ears so that not a note of the disco rhythm to which they moved eluded them, past a pair of handsome blacks in Afros and a sidewalk vendor selling kitchenware.

They worked in a kind of triangular pattern, approaching the steps from different angles so that they could converge on the direction from which their readings were coming.

"It's over there," said the technician beside whom Booth was walking. He tilted his head toward Prudence, one of the two stone lions guarding the steps. Half a dozen people reading the morning paper or a paperback book or just staring into space sat along the granite wall behind the lion.

"It's got to be one of them," Booth said.

As they approached, the emanation shifted. Sure enough, one of the people on the wall, an elderly, stooped woman in a frayed black coat, had begun to shuffle down the steps. Indicating to the others to move back, Booth, the scientist and an FBI agent followed her, then as discreetly as possible drew around her. She had a gaunt, waxen face, colored only by two russet circles of rouge on her sunken cheeks; sad, jaded reminders of what might have been her vanished beauty. At the sight of the agent's shield, she clutched to her shrunken bosom the black plastic shopping bag she was carrying. A hurt and bewildered air seized her features.

"I'm very sorry, Officer," she stammered. "I didn't know it was wrong to do it. I'm on welfare."

With one of her bony hands she brushed at the wisp of gray hair dangling from under a cloth stocking cap and smiled imploringly at the bulky agent. "Times are fearfully bad and I, I . . ." she stammered again, "I just didn't see no harm in pickin' it up to take home. I didn't know they were government property. Honest, I didn't."

Booth leaned forward. "Pardon me, ma'am, what did you pick up?"

Timidly she opened her plastic shopping bag and offered it to Booth for his inspection. He looked in and saw a gray mass. He plunged in his hand and drew out the still-warm body of a dead pigeon, recognizing as he did the deadly substance dangling in the ring on its leg.

317

"Oh, my God!" he exclaimed. "How long ago did you pick this up?"

"Only about five minutes ago. Just before you folks come up the steps."

Dear Christ, Booth thought, staring down at the tablet in its metallic ring. So that's it. That's why all those readings kept disappearing on us.

He looked pityingly at the old woman. "Ma'am, we'd like to ask you, for your own good, to come with us to the hospital. You see, some of these pigeons have bad diseases"—he patted her arm reassuringly—"but they'll give you a fine dinner there tonight, you'll see."

For the third time in barely five hours, the men responsible for the search for the bomb in New York City were gathered around the desk of Quentin Dewing in the underground emergency command post.

"Harvey," Dewing asked the director of the FBI's New York office, "have you picked up any trace of that guy from Boston that trained in Qaddafi's camps?"

Hudson shook his head. "Negative. And we've had fifty guys pounding the pavements over there in Brooklyn for the last two hours. The dockers who handled those barrels at the Brooklyn Army Terminal didn't recognize him, either."

"Well, widen the search. I want every belly-dancing joint and Arab restaurant from New Haven to Philadelphia checked out. I still think that's the best thing we've got going."

There was a sharp cough from the far end of the conference table. "What's the matter, Chief?" Dewing asked Al Feldman.

The Chief of Detectives plucked at one of his nostrils with a forefinger. "If these guys are half as smart as you people tell us they are, the last place they're going to be eating lunch is in some Arab restaurant. They're probably going to a pizza joint or a Hamburger Heaven."

"Well, we've got to cover everything. How about our forensic operations? What do we have on the house where the barrels went, Chief?"

Dewing had assigned the job of sifting through the Queens house for clues to the NYPD's forensic unit. The Hertz van that had picked up the barrel he'd turned over to an FBI forensic team flown up from the National Crime Laboratory in Washington. Both groups were responsible for picking through their targets in painstaking detail, searching for anything, a fingerprint, a hairpin, a matchbox, soil on the doormat or grease caught between the treads of the van's tires, that could reveal something about the people who had used them.

Feldman took a black notebook from his inside pocket and laid it on the desk. "The place belongs to a retired stockbroker out in Bay Shore. Inherited it from his sister. Woman rented it from him last August. She gave him a year's rent in cash, so he wasn't inclined to ask her too many questions. We had an Identikit drawing on that Arab lady who checked out of the Hampshire House this morning done up from the clerks and the maid who knew her and ran it past him. He thinks it was her."

"The embassy in Beirut finally came up with her visa application," Salisbury of the CIA interrupted. "The name she registered under at the Hampshire House, the whole thing's a fake. They've sent us her picture, but none of our intelligence sources have anything on her. The only thing we know is she came into the country at JFK on TWA Flight 701 November twenty-sixth."

Dewing grunted. "Keep after her. How about the house itself, Chief?"

"From what the neighbors say, whoever was using it wasn't around very much. My forensic chief says there aren't a lot of signs of life inside either. But we do have a numbers guy on the corner who thinks he saw a Hertz truck around there last week."

"What sort of sewage system do they have out there?"

Feldman, barely able to suppress a laugh, turned to his questioner, Bill Booth. What the hell kind of a question is that? he asked himself. "City sewers."

"I'm going to send some of my people out to have a look at them. People who are in close physical contact with the material used in this will leave radioactive traces in their urine and feces. It's not much, but if we find something it will at least give us confirmation that this is the shipment we're after."

Dewing acknowledged his words with a crisp authoritative gesture and went back to Feldman. "When can we expect your report?"

"In an hour or so. They've dusted a couple of fingerprints. We're scouring the neighborhood, the stores and all for people who might have known them. And the phone company's getting a call report together for us."

"How about our people with the truck, Harv?"

Hudson had checked on their activities before coming to the meeting. "They're just setting up, Mr. Dewing. All we know at the moment is the truck had two hundred and fifty-two miles on the clock when it came back in that night. Which tells us that the bomb can be anywhere within a circle with a 125-mile radius."

That, Dewing thought, is really helpful.

"And our efforts to follow up on the stolen ID?" he asked Feldman.

"We've got the dip and we're moving in on the fence he did it for."

"Isn't there some way we can speed that line of investigation up?" the FBI assistant director demanded impatiently.

"Mr. Dewing, you want to be a bit gentle here. Some of these guys, you come down too hard, too fast and they'll shut up on you. Then you're nowhere, my friend, nowhere at all."

"Up there."

Pedro Torres, the Colombian pickpocket, gestured with his head to the second story of the brick tenement across the street. He was in the back of Angelo Rocchia's Corvette, wrists handcuffed in his lap, his hands resting protectively over his throbbing groin. Carmen, his girl, was already at the Seventy-eighth Precinct being booked.

Angelo and Rand scrutinized the building from the car's front seat. The windows were filthy and a fire escape obstructed what little view inside the grime allowed.

"What's it look like in there?" Angelo asked.

Torres shrugged. "Big room. One girl. Benny in there."

The detective grunted. "Typical. They try to set up so they look like some kind of wholesale house. Secretary in a glass cage and all. Buy anything. Cameras, TVs, power tools, rugs, auto parts, whatever. Lot of 'em rent guns. Have sixty to seventy Saturday-night specials stashed in there. Rent 'em out for twenty bucks a night and a cut of the take."

He turned down Sixth Avenue and began to look for a parking space well out of the line of vision from the fence's window.

"We've set 'em up ourselves. Open a shop. Send a couple of streetwise guys into the bars. Tell the bartender, 'We're doing a job, fixing up this new place there. We need some tools, you know? Couple tools. Cost so fucking much money for drills and all. Hell, I seen one up the street there, guy wants a hundred and forty dollars for it.' Next thing you know, a guy comes in, says, 'Hey, you want to buy a drill?' 'Yeah, what kind of drill?' 'Brand new,' the guy replies. 'I'm a plumber by trade. Normally I wouldn't do this, but I gotta have money, get some bus tickets. Got a sick aunt up there in the Catskills.' " Angelo gave a gleeful laugh, one of the first Rand had heard from the New Yorker. "Operation like that you can bring in guys like our friend there in the back seat by the carload."

As he was talking, Angelo had deftly slipped the car into a tight parking space half a block up Sixth. "Okay," he said, yanking on the hand brake, "bring him in." He jerked his thumb at Torres. "A minute after I get in there. Throw a coat over his bracelets so you don't draw a crowd."

He took a cigar from his coat pocket and lit it, then picked an old racing form out from under the dashboard and strolled off up Sixth, his face buried in the form sheet.

He paused at the light on the corner. Up Union, just fifty yards from the fence's building, a blue-and-white Con Ed truck was stopped. Its crewmen were setting up sawhorses and unloading a jackhammer. Must be ours, Angelo figured. At the rear corner of the building, three spades in denims, goatees, black sunglasses and floppy berets lounged against the wall, laughing loudly. They too, Angelo realized, were probably fellow detectives.

The fence operation was marked only by a sign on the door, "Long Island Trading," and the proprietor's name, B. Moscowitz, in the lower right-hand corner. As Angelo had predicted, a mousy secretary, listlessly polishing her fingernails, sat by the door.

She looked at Angelo. Clearly, she wasn't expecting visitors. "What can I do for you, mister?"

Benny was in the next room, behind a glass partition. He was a wizened little man in his late fifties, wearing a vest and shirt-sleeves, his shirt undone, his tie askew. Horn-rimmed glasses perched on his bald head. His lower lip, the detective noted, pushed forward like that of a pouting child fighting to hold back tears.

"It's him I want to see," Angelo replied. Before the girl could protest, he had stepped across the room into Benny's office.

"Who the fuck are you?" Benny snarled.

Angelo gave him the shield.

The fence's face didn't betray even a flicker of emotion. "Whatta you want with me? I run a legitimate business here. Legitimate trading company. I got nothing to do with cops."

Angelo stood above his desk looking down at the agitated fence. He slowly rolled his cigar between his thumb and forefinger, striving to fix Benny with his gray eyes, giving the little man the full force of what he called his Godfather look. Finally he lifted his cigar from his mouth. "Got a friend of yours here, wants to say hello to you."

He turned to the door, and, as he had hoped, Rand and Torres were standing there. Angelo waved them into the office.

"Who is this fucking creep?" Benny roared. "I never seen him before in my life."

From the Godfather, Angelo became the Prosecuting Attorney. "Pedro Torres," he intoned, "do you recognize and identify Mr. Benjamin Moscowitz here present as the individual who requested you to pick the pocket of a commuter in the Long Island Rail Road Terminal for his identity papers Friday morning and to whom you delivered same?" The legal jargon was utterly meaningless, but it occasionally shook up guys like Benny.

Torres shifted on his feet. "Yeah," he replied, "it's heem."

"The fucking spic don't know what he's talking about," Benny shrieked. "What is this anyway, some kind of setup?" He leaped to his feet, his arms flailing in the air.

Angelo turned to Rand. "Get him out of here," he said. He pointed his cigar at the fence. "Sit down, Benny, I want to talk to you."

The fence, still babbling a protest, settled in his chair. Angelo perched on one corner of his desk so that he towered over him. He rested there, his face set, building the edge, letting the flow of Benny's angry words trickle away to nothingness like the last sparks spurting from a dying Roman candle. The room, he noted, was a pigsty of papers, files, overflowing trashcans.

"Look, Benny, I know from the Colombian there you're doing fifty cards a week." Angelo's voice vibrated with the husky, sincere tone of a salesman trying to close an order. "But I'm not interested in fifty. I only want to know about the one you did for order last Friday."

"Hey, what do you mean? I don't do nothing like that."

Angelo bestowed a cold smile on Benny that was meant to tell him that they both knew how meaningless that protest was. "Torres out there hits the guy at the terminal after the nine A.M. train. Brings the papers here. Ten o'clock some guy is renting a Hertz truck with them over on Fourth Avenue."

"Listen, you guys got some fucking nerve." Benny's snarls were as defiant as ever, but under their surface Angelo detected the first tremulous quiver of concern. "This is a legitimate shop here. I got records. All kinds of records. Tax records. You want to see my records?"

"Benny, I don't want to see nothing. I just want to know where that card went. It's very important to me, Benny." An understated sense of menace seeped into the friendly salesman's tone on the last words, but if it frightened the fence, he gave no indication of it.

"I didn't do nothing wrong. I'm a secondhand dealer. I got all that stuff there, legitimate." He waved at the vast jumble of goods he was fencing.

"Benny." There was no friendly intimacy left in Angelo's voice now. "I don't give a fuck what you've got here. Talk to me about this day, this one day, last Friday. Torres there comes in with some ID he found, right? We all know he found it. And it went right back out. Where, Benny? Where did it go?"

Behind Angelo the office door opened and closed softly. It was Rand. He had turned Torres over to a backup team downstairs. The mousy secretary, Angelo noted, was still doing her nails as though nothing unusual was happening. She must be used to seeing cops in here, he thought. Her boss probably gets busted all the time and gets off with a good lawyer.

"I don't know nothing about that."

"Benny." Angelo waved his cigar at an "Out to Lunch" sign behind the office door. "You don't cooperate with us, we're going to close you down. You're going to be flying that thing for a month."

Benny sat, despondent but defiant, in his chair.

"We'll close you down, Benny. And if we do, I hope you got a lot of fire insurance." Very slowly, very deliberately, Angelo scattered the ashes from his cigar over some of the rubbish strewn on the floor. "Real firetrap you got here. Owner's away, fires happen, you know what I mean?"

Benny paled. "You son of a bitch. You wouldn't . . ."

"Who said anything?" Angelo asked, flicking some more ashes on the papers on the fence's desk. "Hell of a fire this place'd make, though."

"I'll get you on a civilian complaint. Tell 'em you threatened to burn me out."

Angelo remembered Feldman's whispered injunction a few hours earlier. "You know what you can do with your civilian complaint, Benny? You can shove it up your ass."

The fence blinked, perplexed. He had been arrested six times and walked each time. This time there was an element of menace, of coercion, he hadn't experienced before. "Okay," he said, resignation creeping into his voice. "I don't keep much cash around here, but we'll make a deal."

"Benny." Angelo's voice was low but firm. "That's not the kind of deal I'm talking about. I don't give a shit what you're doing in here. I don't give a shit how many welfare checks you're making, whatever. I only want to know one thing, Benny: where did that card go?"

"Hey," Benny said, mustering what defiance remained. "You gotta let me call my lawyer. I got a right to call my lawyer."

"Sure thing, Benny." The mirthless smile spread over Angelo's teeth. "Call your lawyer." The cigar came out of the detective's mouth. With a low chuckle, he tapped the ashes on the fence's desk. "What is he, anyway, your lawyer—some kind of fucking fireman?"

The dark-brown eyes that had been so full of fury a few minutes before were soft and liquid now, brimming with tears. Angelo studied his quarry. There came in every interrogation a critical moment like this when a man hovered on the brink, when one deft thrust could nudge him over. Or when, afraid of the consequences of giving somebody up, he'd step back, go in and take the collar. The detective leaned close to Benny, real warmth on his features this time. His voice was a hoarse seductive whisper. "All I need to know is where that card went, Benny. Then you and I got no problems."

The lip, the lower lip, thrust out in its permanent pout, quivered slightly. The fence's chin sank into his chest. It remained there awhile before he looked up at the detective. "Fuck it," he said, "bust me."

"Angelo." It was Rand, his voice as soft and well modulated as that of a bank vice-president extending a new client a line of credit. "Perhaps you could let Mr. Moscowitz and me have a word together before we take him in?"

The detective looked irritably at the younger man, then at the fence. A sense of impotent rage, of humiliation, caused by his failure in front of Rand overwhelmed him. "Sure, kid," he replied, making no effort to conceal his bitterness. "Talk to the motherfucker if you want." He got up from Benny's desk, his joints creaking, and walked wearily to the door to the anteroom. "Try to sell him a little fire insurance while you're at it."

"Mr. Moscowitz," Rand said as the door closed behind his partner, "you are, I presume, of the Jewish faith?" He let his eyes rest on the gold Star of David peeking through the fence's open shirt.

Benny looked at him, stunned. What the fuck have we got here, he thought scornfully, some kind of professor or something, talking like that, "of the Jewish faith"? His chin thrust defiantly forward. "Yeah. I'm Jewish. So what?"

"And you are, I presume, concerned about the security and well-being of the State of Israel?"

"Hey," Benny's poise was returning. "What are you cops doing? Selling bonds for Israel?"

"Mr. Moscowitz." Rand leaned forward, his arms resting on the fence's desk. "What I'm about to tell you, I'm telling you in the strictest confidence, because I think you of all people should know it. It is of far greater concern to the State of Israel than the sale of a few bonds."

Angelo was watching them through the glass panels. Benny seemed first skeptical, then concerned, then intensely interested. Finally his puckered little face exploded with emotion. He leaped up from his desk, barged through the door into the anteroom, headed past Angelo toward the window without even glancing at the detective. He thrust an angry outstretched arm at the window.

"It was a fucking Arab son of a bitch who wanted it." He pronounced the word A-rab. "Hangs out there in that bar down the street!"

Tiens, General Henri Bertrand thought. Our cardinal has metamorphosed into Sacha Guitry going to Maxim's. Once again he was in the elegant study of Paul-Henri de Serre, the nuclear physicist who had supervised the construction and initial operations of Libya's French-built nuclear reactor. This time de Serre was dressed in a burgundy velvet dinner jacket and black tie. On his feet, the director of the SDECE noted, were black velvet pumps, their toes embroidered with gold brocade.

"So sorry to keep you waiting." De Serre's greeting was effusive, particularly so in view of the fact that Bertrand's visit had interrupted a small sit-down dinner he was offering a group of friends. "We were just finishing dessert." He went to his desk and picked up a mahogany humidor. "Do have a cigar," he said, opening its heavy lid. "Try one of the Davidoff Château-Lafites. They're excellent."

While Bertrand carefully prepared the cigar, the scientist stepped to the bar and poured two balloons of cognac from a crystal decanter. He offered one to Bertrand, then sank into a leather armchair opposite him, savoring as he did his first taste of his own cigar. "Tell me, any progress on the matter we spoke of this morning?"

Bertrand sniffed his cognac. It was superb. His eyes were half closed, a weary, melancholy gaze on his face. "Virtually none at all, I'm afraid. There was one point I thought I should review with you, however." The fatigue of his long and difficult day had weakened the General's voice. "That early breakdown that forced you to remove the fuel rods."

"Ah, yes." De Serre waved his cigar expansively. "Rather embarrassing that, since the fuel in question was French-made. Most of our uranium fuel, as you are perhaps aware, is American-made."

Bertrand nodded. "I was somewhat surprised you hadn't mentioned the incident in our chat this morning."

"Well, *cher ami*"—there was no indication of concern or discomfiture in de Serre's reply—"it's such a technical, complex business I really didn't think it was the sort of thing you were interested in."

"I see."

The conversation between the two men drifted on inconclusively for fifteen more minutes. Finally, with a weary sigh, Bertrand drained his cognac glass and got to his feet.

"Well, *cher monsieur,* you must excuse me once again for imposing on your time, but these matters . . ." Bertrand's voice dwindled away. He started for the door, then paused to stare in rapt wonder at the bust glowing in its cabinet in the center of the room.

"Such a magnificent piece," he remarked. "I'm sure the Louvre has few like it."

"Quite true." De Serre made no attempt to conceal his pride. "I've never seen anything there to match it."

"You must have had an awful time persuading the Libyans to give you an export permit to take it out of the country."

"Oh!" The scientist's voice seemed to ring with the memory of recollected frustrations. "You can't imagine how difficult it was."

"But you finally managed to persuade them, did you not?" Bertrand said, chuckling softly.

"Yes. After weeks, literally weeks of arguing."

"Well, you are a lucky man, Monsieur de Serre. A lucky man. I really must be on my way."

The General strolled to the door. His hand was on the knob when he stopped. For a moment he hesitated. Then he spun around. There was no hint of fatigue on his face now. The eyes that were usually half closed were wide open, glimmering with malice.

"You're a liar!"

The scientist paled and tottered half a step backward.

"The Libyans didn't give you an export permit to take that bust out of the country. They haven't given anybody a permit to take anything out of there for the past five years!"

De Serre staggered backward across the room and collapsed in his leather armchair. His usually florid features glistened with the clammy pallor of the physically ill; the hand that clutched his cognac glass quivered slightly.

"This is preposterous!" he gasped. "Outrageous!"

Bertrand towered above him like Torquemada contemplating a heretic stretched out on his rack. "We spoke to the Libyans. And incidentally had a chance to learn about your misadventures in India. You've been lying to me," he intoned, "since I walked in that door this morning. You've been lying about that reactor and how the Libyans cheated on it, and I know damn well you have." The General was following his instincts, stabbing in the dark for the target the inquisitor in him told him was there. He leaned down and placed his powerful thumbs in the ridges of the scientist's collarbones. "But you're not going to lie anymore, my friend. You're going to tell me everything that happened down there. Not in an hour. Not tomorrow morning. Right now."

The General squeezed de Serre's collarbones so hard he squirmed in pain. "Because if you don't, I shall personally see to it that you spend the rest of your life in Fresnes Prison. Do you know what prison is like?"

The word "prison" brought a wild, almost hallucinated flicker to de Serre's eyes. "They don't serve Davidoffs and Remy Martins after dinner at Fresnes, *cher ami*. What they do after dinner at Fresnes is sit around and bugger helpless old bastards like you silly."

Bertrand felt the panic beginning to overwhelm the man. It was now, in these first instants of fear and hysteria, that all the advantages were with the inquisitor. Break him, the General's instincts told him, break him quickly before he can start to reassemble his shattered psyche. Those long-honed instincts also suggested where the trembling man in the armchair would be most vulnerable.

"You think you're going to retire in a few months, don't you?" He almost hissed the words. "And you're going to need every sou of your pension to go on living like this, aren't you? I know because I spent the afternoon studying your bank accounts. Including the secret one you've been building up illegally in the Cosmos Bank in Geneva."

De Serre gasped.

"You're going to cooperate with me, Monsieur de Serre. Because if you don't, I'm going to ruin you. By the time I'm finished with you, your wife won't have enough money to bring you oranges out at Fresnes."

Bertrand relaxed the pressures on de Serre's collarbones and allowed his voice to take on a more gentle tone. "But if you do cooperate, I'll promise you this. What brings me here is very important. So important that I shall go personally to the President of the Republic and intercede with him on your behalf. I'll see that this is written off as completely as your little episode in India was."

De Serre's face was gray now. His chest heaved twice and his jaw fell open. My God, Bertrand thought, the bastard is going to have a heart attack on me. A gagging sound rumbled up from the depths of de Serre's bowels. The scientist let his cognac glass tumble to the floor and clapped his hand to his mouth to staunch the flow of vomit that spurted through his fingers and cascaded in a vile-smelling yellow-green stream down his burgundy dinner jacket's lapels and onto the lap of his black trousers. Desperately, he pawed at his pocket for a handkerchief.

Bertrand grabbed his own handkerchief to clean him up, but the scientist had already half collapsed, holding his head in his hands, his chest shaking with sobs.

"Oh God, oh God!" The voice was shrill. "I didn't want to do it. They made me!"

Bertrand picked up the cognac glass, went to the bar and filled it with Fernet Branca, the dark-brown liqueur the French use to settle queasy stomachs. He had his man. There was no need to continue playing the Spanish Inquisitor. He brought the glass back to the shaking scientist. As de Serre gratefully sipped it, Bertrand dabbed at the worst of the mess on his dinner jacket.

"If you were coerced," he said, his tone as reassuring as that of an aging family physician at the bedside of a familiar patient, "it will make everything easier. Begin at the beginning and tell me exactly what happened."

De Serre sobbed, "I didn't want to," three more times before he was able to continue.

"Every weekend I used to go down to Leptis Magna. One could find things occasionally in the sands there, particularly after a storm." He took out a handkerchief and blew his nose, fighting to regain his composure. "There was a Libyan guard I met there. Sometimes, for a few dinars, he'd indicate where I could find things. Then one day he asked me into his hut for tea. He had that bust." He pointed to the stone head glowing in its cabinet with what seemed now a mocking beauty. For a pathetic instant, de Serre stared at it as an older man might look at a younger woman with whom he is desperately in love at the moment of parting. "He offered it to me for ten thousand dinars."

"An insignificant sum, I suppose, for such a piece?"

"God, yes." De Serre sniffled. "It's worth millions. Two weeks later, I was going to Paris for the Pentecost weekend. The Libyans had never, never looked at my bags, so I decided to take it with me."

"And at the airport, Customs went right for your bags?"

"Yes." De Serre seemed puzzled by the swiftness of Bertrand's observation.

"Why wouldn't they, since they had set you up? And then what happened?"

The wild, terrified look that had swept de Serre's face earlier at the mention of the word "prison" illuminated his features with a fear akin to that of a trapped animal. He gagged and gulped at the Fernet Branca.

"They put me in prison." The man, Bertrand saw, was becoming hysterical. "Their prison was a black hole. A black hole with no light and no windows. I couldn't even stand up. There was nothing in it, no bed, no toilet bowl, nothing. I had to live in my own excrement." De Serre shook. A touch of madness glowed on his face now, a glimpse of how close he must have come to insanity in that hole. Poor son of a bitch, Bertrand thought. He knew something about holes like that. No wonder he almost went over the edge when I mentioned the word "prison." The scientist's fingers clutched the flesh of Bertrand's arms. "There were rats in there. In the dark I could hear them. I could feel them brushing against me. Biting me." He shrieked involuntarily at his recollection of the rats' nibbling bites, their jabbing little paws. "They gave me rice once a day. I had to eat it with my fingers before the rats could get it." De Serre was crying uncontrollably now. "I got dysentery. For three days I sat in a corner in my own shit screaming at the rats.

"Then they came for me. They said I had violated their antiquities law. They refused to let me call the consul. They said I would either have to spend a year in a jail like that or . . ."

"Or help them divert plutonium from the reactor?"

"Yes."

The word was a quick, despairing gasp. Bertrand rose, took de Serre's empty glass and refilled it with Fernet Branca.

"After what they had put you through, who can blame you?" he said, passing the glass to the trembling scientist. "How did you do it?"

De Serre took a gulp of the drink, then sat still a moment, panting, trying to regain his composure.

"It was relatively simple. The most frequent problem in any light-water reactor is faulty fuel rods. Some failure in the cladding that surrounds them. The fission products that build up in there as the fuel burns leak out through the fault into the reactor's cooling water and contaminate it. We pretended that had happened in our case.''

''But,'' Bertrand said, thinking back to his talk with his scientific adviser, ''those reactors are such complex machines. They have such an array of safety devices built into them. How did you manage such a thing?''

De Serre shook his head, still trying to force the ugly images of the last few minutes from his mind. ''*Cher monsieur,* the reactors themselves are perfect. They are equipped with so many marvelous safety systems they are, indeed, inviolable. It's the little things around them that are always vulnerable. It's like . . .'' de Serre paused. ''Years ago, I had a dear friend who raced Grand Prix cars. I was with him once at the Grand Prix in Monte Carlo. He was racing with Ferrari then, and they had given him a superb new twelve-cylinder prototype. Worth millions, it was. The car broke down the first time he went past the Hotel de Paris. Not because anything was wrong with Monsieur Ferrari's beautiful engine. But because a two-franc rubber gasket failed to hold.

''In this case, we started with the instruments that measure the radioactivity in each of the reactor's three fuel compartments. They're like all instruments of that sort. They work on rheostats based on a zero setting. By simply altering the setting upward, we arranged to have the instrument tell us there was radioactivity— when, of course, there wasn't any. We drew off a sample of the cooling water and sent it to the lab for analysis. Since the lab was run by the Libyans, they gave us the answer we wanted.''

''How about the inspectors and safeguards of the United Nations in Vienna?''

''We notified the International Atomic Energy Agency that we were shutting down the reactor to remove a faulty fuel charge. By mail, of course, to win a few days. As we had suspected they would, they sent out a team of inspectors to watch us make the change.''

''How did you convince them that something was really wrong with your fuel?''

''We didn't have to. We had the printouts from the faked meters which we then set back to their zero setting. We had the lab results. And the fuel itself was so radioactive, who would want to get near it?''

''And they didn't suspect that you were faking?''

"The only thing they got suspicious about was the fact that all three of the reactor's fuel charges went bad at the same time. You see, the fuel is loaded into three completely sealed-off compartments. But the fuel had all come from the same source, so it was conceivable. Barely, but conceivable."

"And how did you get the fuel rods out of the storage pond after they'd left their cameras there taking pictures every fifteen minutes?"

"The Libyans had worked that out. The cameras the IAEA use are Austrian-made, Psychotronics. The Libyans bought half a dozen of them through an intermediary. Each camera has two lenses, a wide-angle and a normal, and they are set to go off in a sequence. The Libyans listened to the IAEA's cameras with very sensitive stethoscopes until they had worked out the sequence. Then with their own cameras they shot the same scene the IAEA's cameras were shooting from exactly the same spot. They blew up big prints and placed them in front of the IAEA's cameras, so what those cameras were doing, in effect, was taking a picture of a picture."

"And so they took out the fuel rods at their leisure." Again Bertrand thought back to his conversation with his scientific adviser. "But how did they fool the inspectors when they came back to see if the rods were still there?"

"Quite simply. When they took the real fuel rods out they put dummy rods treated with cobalt 60 back into the pond. They give off the same bluish glow, the Czerinkon effect, that the real fuel rods do. And they give an identical reading on the gamma-ray detectors the IAEA inspectors put into the pond to check what's in there."

Bertrand could not suppress a glimmer of admiration for the Libyans' ingenuity. "How did they separate out the plutonium?" The hostility had left his voice now, replaced by a sympathy for the shattered man before him.

"I wasn't involved in that at all. I only saw the place where they did it once. It was in an agricultural substation fifteen miles up the seacoast from the plant. They had a set of designs for a small reprocessing plant they got in the United States. A company over there, Phillips Petroleum, circulated them in the sixties. They contained very detailed sketches and designs of all the components in the process. They had made shortcuts. Neglected quite a number of basic safety precautions. But the fact is, everything you need to build a plant like that is available on the world market. There is nothing that's required that's so exotic as to be unobtainable."

"Isn't all that terribly dangerous?" The director of the SDECE thought back to his young scientist's warning in the morning about radiation.

De Serre was suddenly distracted by the stench of the vomit on his dinner jacket, an acrid reminder of the nightmare through which he had just passed. "God, I've got to get out of these clothes," he said. "Look, they were volunteers, all of them. Palestinians. I shouldn't wish to write an insurance policy on their lives. In five, ten years . . ." De Serre shrugged. "But they got their pluto-nium."

"How many bombs would they be able to make with it?"

"They told me they were reprocessing two kilograms of pluto-nium a day. Enough for two bombs a week. That was back in June. Altogether, allowing for error, I should say they should have been able to get enough for forty bombs out of there."

Bertrand whistled softly, spilling as he did the ashes of his Da-vidoff. *Mon Dieu!* Could you recognize any of those people in a photograph?"

"Perhaps. The man I dealt with was a Palestinian, not a Libyan. Heavy fellow with a moustache. Spoke perfect French."

"Get out of those clothes," Bertrand ordered. "You're coming to the Boulevard Mortier with me."

The scientist staggered to his feet, vomit dripping from his filth-covered pants, and started for the door. "I'll go and change."

Bertrand followed him. "I trust," he said, "that in the circum-stances you won't mind if I accompany you."

There comes a time in every international crisis when the President of the United States feels the need to get away for a few moments from his formal circle of advisers, to isolate himself with the one or two intimates with whom he feels totally at ease, in whose judgment and candor his confidence is total. In the dark moments after Pearl Harbor, Franklin D. Roosevelt inevitably turned to the frail figure of Harry Hopkins. The voice that Jack Kennedy listened to in the White House corridors during the Cuban Missile Crisis was that of his brother Bobby. Now, in the aftermath of his disastrous phone call with Qaddafi, the President was alone with Jack Eastman, pacing slowly up and down the colonnaded terrace linking the West Wing to the Executive Mansion.

The afternoon sun was still warm, and all around them melting snowdrops pattered to the ground with the gentle rustle of a light rain. The President was silent, his hands thrust into his pocket. At the end of the colonnade, a Secret Service agent, arms folded across his chest, kept a discreet watch.

"You know, Jack," the President said finally, "I got the feeling we're like a guy who's got some obscure virus and none of the miracle drugs his doctor recommends seem to do anything for it." He stopped and looked across the White House gardens toward the Ellipse. Somewhere down there was the national Christmas tree he was supposed to light in a couple of hours, a reassuring annual demonstration of hope, an affirmation of the constancy of certain values his nation liked to think it stood for in good times and bad. Hope, it occurred to him, was in precious short supply at the moment.

He stopped and threw an arm around Eastman's shoulder. "Where do we go from here?"

Eastman had been waiting for the question. "Well, one place I don't think we go is back to him. You'd have to crawl. And despite what the doctors say, I don't think he's going to be reasoned out of this. Not after listening to him."

"Neither do I." The President withdrew his hand and ran it through his wavy hair. "That leaves us Begin, doesn't it?"

"Begin or those people in New York finding that damn thing."

The two men resumed their pacing.

"We offer Begin some kind of ironclad guarantee of his state inside the 'sixty-seven borders if he'll agree to get out of the West Bank. Get the Soviets to subscribe to it, which they certainly will. It's the only reasonable solution to that damn mess out there anyway." The President waited for his friend and adviser's reaction.

"It is." Eastman shook his head. "But in these circumstances? I just don't see Begin agreeing. Not unless you're prepared to pull out all the stops. Remember what General Ellis said last night? Are you ready to go in there and get those people out if he refuses? Or at least threaten to?"

Again the President was silent. The implications of what Eastman had just said were not pleasant to contemplate. But, he thought grimly, contemplating the thermonuclear destruction of New York was far worse.

"I've got no choice, Jack. I've got to go after him. Let's get back to the conference room."

William Webster of the FBI was just hanging up his phone when they returned.

"What's up?" Eastman asked.

"It was New York. There's a bomb up there all right. They just picked up traces of radioactivity around a house out in Queens where it was apparently hidden for a few hours last Friday."

By the standards of the city he administered, the office of the Mayor of New York was miniscule, smaller than that of many a secretary in the great glass sheaths of Wall Street and mid-Manhattan. Abe Stern sat in it now, staring at the oil of Fiorello La Guardia on the wall opposite him, fighting to control the anger and frustration surging through his nervous system. Just as the President was, he too was making a determined effort to put on a façade of normality. For the past thirty minutes it had consisted of talking to the City Hall press corps gathered like a swarm of angry hornets around his antique cherry-wood desk, trying to explain the logistics of snow removal. He saw with relief the last of the reporters disappear and ordered in his next visitor, the Manager of his Budget Bureau. "What do you want?" he snapped at the mild-mannered, bespectacled CPA.

"The Police Commissioner wants to mobilize his force for some kind of emergency, Your Honor."

"Well, let him."

"But," the Budget Manager protested nervously, "that means we'll have to pay them overtime."

"So what? Pay it." Stern was beside himself with exasperation.

"But, my goodness, do you realize what that will do to the budget?"

"I don't give a damn!" Stern was almost shouting. "Give the Commissioner what he asks for, for God's sake!"

"All right, all right," the intimidated accountant said, opening his briefcase, "but, in that case, I've got to have your signature on the authorization."

Stern grabbed the paper from his hand and stabbed at it with his pen, shaking his head in dismay. The last man on earth, he thought, the very last, will be a bureaucrat.

As the man left, Stern turned his back on him and looked out across the snow-covered lawn of City Hall down to the old Tweed Courthouse, an enduring monument to the potential for graft inherent in his office. I can't stand this anymore, he thought. He jabbed at one of the buttons on his telephone console. "Michael," he asked, "where the hell is that guy who was going to tell us how to evacuate this place?

"Tell him to wait," the Mayor ordered when he heard the answer. "I'm coming, too." In a flash, Stern was into the pantry beside his office—its refrigerator stocked with tomato juice, the only drink he consumed—down a flight of stairs and out of the building by his semisecret side entrance.

Five minutes later, he was being buckled into a helicopter on top of Police Plaza, Oglethorpe beside him, the Police Commissioner and Lieutenant Walsh in the back. Entranced, he watched as slowly his city took shape below him in pace with the chopper's thudding ascent into the afternoon sky. He could see the tight cluster of Chinatown, so closely woven together that it looked as if it had been constructed with Tinker Toys; the Fulton Fish Market and the brownish-gray wakes of the shipping along the East River; then Wall Street and Exchange Place, and all around them, reflecting back the glory of the afternoon sun, the proud glass-and-steel cylinders of lower Manhattan. This city's got so much going for it, Stern thought, so much energy, such strength and vitality. His eyes studied the rectangular canyons below, the yellow forms of the cabs clogging the streets, the scurrying figures of his people on the sidewalks, recklessly darting through traffic. Ahead, he caught a glimpse of a Staten Island ferry scuttling like a sand crab over the slate-gray surface of the harbor. It just wasn't possible, Abe Stern told himself, it wasn't possible that some distant fanatic would destroy all this. He blinked, feeling the sting in his eyes, hearing as he did the jabbering of the Civil Defense expert beside him interrupting his nightmare.

"The subways are apparently going to be a problem," Oglethorpe was remarking, "unless we can find a way to run the evacuation without telling people what's going on."

"Not tell people what's going on?" The Mayor started to shout and not just to make himself heard over the thump of the rotors.

"Are you crazy? You can't do anything in this town without telling people what's going on. I want to use those subways, I gotta tell the head of the Transit Workers his people got to do special shifts. 'Emergency?' he's going to say to me. 'What's the emergency?' And then he's going to say, 'Hey, listen, I gotta tell Vic Gottbaum and the Municipal Workers.' And Gottbaum's gonna say, 'Listen, I can't keep this from Al Shanker and the teachers.' "

The Police Commissioner leaned forward. "That's his problem, Abe. At that point we haven't got a train driver left in the city, you realize that?"

Stern spun angrily around to confront his Police Commissioner. He was about to yell something, then stopped himself. Instead, he turned back and crumpled dejectedly into his seat.

"Our only hope is a highway mode evacuation," Oglethorpe was looking down at the Battery. "But down here we've got some real problems. Only two lanes in the Holland and Brooklyn–Battery Tunnels, which are our best escape routes. We figure the best you can do is seven hundred fifty vehicles per lane hour, calculate five people to a vehicle, that's fifteen thousand people an hour." Oglethorpe stopped. "We've got about a million people down here to clear. It's going to be a terrible scene. You'll have to have awfully good police control. I mean, your officers will have to be ready to shoot the people who want to break the line and disrupt things."

Do that, Walsh thought grimly, and you'll have to shoot nine tenths of the people in the city. And some of them are going to shoot right back.

They were skimming up the Hudson now, passing midtown. "Up here we're in better shape," Oglethorpe offered hopefully. "We've got six lanes in the Lincoln Tunnel, nine on the George Washington Bridge and twelve between the Major Deegan and Bruckner Expressways. That would give us an outflow of about a hundred thousand people an hour." Oglethorpe was getting hoarse from shouting over the rotors; yet he plowed on, a determined slave to his facts and figures, to all those years down there in Washington making things work on the charts and computers. "We'll need plenty of police to handle the movement on the ramps. Helicopters to monitor the traffic flow."

Abe Stern wasn't listening anymore. He turned again in his seat to face the Police Commissioner. His old friend's face mirrored what he had expected to see, the reflection of his own despair.

"It isn't going to work, is it, Michael?"

"No, Abe, it's not." Bannion looked down at the rooftops of the tenements crowding the Upper West Side, the snow-filled sweep of the park. "Maybe thirty, forty years ago. A different time. A different city. Maybe we would have had the discipline then, I don't know. Now?" Sadly he shook his head. "Now, there's no way we can do it. We've all changed too much."

Oglethorpe, ignoring their exchange, prattled on about the need for good, disciplined crowd control, about the right system to manage the flow to the bridges.

"Oh, shut up!" Stern barked. The jolted bureaucrat blushed. "The whole thing is crazy. We're wasting our time. We're not going to evacuate this city. I'm going back to tell the President to forget it. We're stuck here and there's not a damn thing we can do about it." He leaned forward and gave a sharp jab to the pilot. "Turn this thing around," he ordered. "Take us back to the plaza."

The helicopter pivoted in a tight arc. As it did, the panorama of Manhattan Island below them seemed to tilt end on end for an instant, rising up to meet the horizon, a flashing insight, Abe Stern reflected, into the upside-down world they were living in.

On the surface the scene in the spacious sitting room six thousand eight hundred seventy-five miles from New York City was one of touching domestic tranquility. Menachem Begin's youngest daughter, Hassia, sat at the grand piano of his official residence entertaining her father with the crystalline notes of a Chopin étude. A menorah, two of its eight candle branches flickering, was set in the window. Begin himself had lit the candles just an hour earlier to mark the first night of Hanukkah, the Feast of Lights.

He was sitting now in a leather wing chair, legs crossed, chin resting in the cat's cradle of his folded fingers, apparently wholly absorbed in his daughter's music. In fact his mind was miles away, where it had been all day, on the crisis confronting his nation. His armed forces were on alert. Just before he sat down he had talked with the military governor of the West Bank and the embassy in Washington. The West Bank was quiet; if the Palestinians who were to benefit from Qaddafi's appalling initiative were aware of what was going on, they gave no indication of it. So, too, was

338

Washington. Nothing, the embassy reported, had leaked out to indicate to the United States's public the crisis at hand. Of even greater concern to the Israeli Prime Minister was the fact that the embassy's usually reliable sources inside the White House had revealed nothing of the debates in the government's inner councils.

His daughter finished her étude with a flourish. Begin rose, walked to the piano and kissed her gently on the forehead. As he did, his wife appeared in the doorway.

"Menachem," she announced, "the President of the United States is calling."

Hassia saw her father stiffen the way he often did when he was about to review a guard of honor, then march from the room. He settled into the office where he had taken the President's first call and listened in stolid silence to his proposal for a solution to the crisis. He would call an emergency joint session of Congress. The United States would offer Israel the ironclad guarantee of its nuclear umbrella inside the 1967 frontiers. The Chairman of the Central Committee had already agreed to associate the Soviet Union publicly and formally with the U.S. declaration. In return, the Israeli government would announce its immediate, unilateral decision to withdraw its forces, administration and settlements from the occupied territories and return them to Arab jurisdiction. Begin paled visibly listening to the President, but otherwise he appeared completely composed.

"In other words, Mr. President," he said when the American had finished, "you are asking me and my people to yield to a tyrant's blackmail."

"Mr. Begin," the President rejoined, "what I am asking you to do is to accept the only reasonable solution to the gravest international crisis the world has ever faced."

"The only reasonable solution was the one we were prevented from carrying out this morning by the Soviet Union—with, or without, your nation's complicity." Again the Jewish leader pronounced the words without heat, nothing in his manner indicating the interior storm shaking him.

"If that were a reasonable solution," the President replied, "I could—and would—have invoked it hours ago. But my first consideration in this crisis, Mr. Begin, is to save lives, the lives of six million innocent people in New York—and, indeed, the lives of two million equally innocent Libyans."

"But you are asking us to abandon the fundamentals of our national sovereignty in response to an action which is criminal, which is without precedent in history, which you yourself told me this morning jeopardizes the very foundations of world peace and international order."

"My proposal doesn't impinge on your nation's sovereignty, Mr. Begin." The Prime Minister could sense the American's exasperation. "Israel has no claims to sovereignty over the West Bank and it never has had. Those lands were given to the Arabs of Palestine by the United Nations in 1947 at the same time your people were given a state."

"I'm sorry, the United Nations did not give those lands, or any other lands, to the Jewish people." There was a confidence born of belief, of deep conviction, in the Israeli leader's voice. "Those lands were given to the Jewish people by the God of our forefathers, once and forever."

"Surely, Mr. Begin," the President protested, "you cannot as a responsible leader of the twentieth century, of the thermonuclear age, be pretending to order the world on the basis of a forty-century-old religious legend?"

Begin adjusted his tie and leaned back in his chair. "That legend, as you call it, has sustained us, nourished, preserved us, united as a distinct people, for four thousand years. However difficult it may be for you to comprehend, Mr. President, for a Jew to have the right to settle on this land, on any part of it, is as indispensable an attribute of his nation's sovereignty as an American's right to travel from New York to California."

"To settle on another people's land? Land that has been theirs for two thousand years? To deprive them of the very right of national existence for which your own people claimed and fought for so many generations? All that in the name of an event, a religious moment, which may, or may not, have ever taken place? Surely you can't be serious?"

"I have never been more serious. But what is at issue here is not those settlements you so oppose. They are just a handful of people, finally. They do nobody any harm. You are trying to force another nation to an act it refuses for moral reasons, for reasons which go to the core of its right to exist. Are we or are we not a sovereign land? If we are forced to crawl out of the West Bank before a totalitarian dictator—and need I remind you of our experience at the hands of such men?—you will turn us into slaves, destroy our belief in ourselves and our nationhood.''

"My proposal, Mr. Begin, offers your nation the very thing it has wanted so long, a firm guarantee of its survival. It will reinforce your national will, not weaken it." The younger man's slow, precise enunciation revealed to the Israeli how hard he was struggling to control his emotions.

"Guarantees of our survival, Mr. President? What faith do you think my people are going to have in your guarantees after they've seen that you, the one nation in the world that was supposed to be our friend, our ally, have coerced us into acting against our will, our interests, our very right to survive? Why—'' Begin hesitated to say what he was about to say but the intensity of his feelings was so deep he couldn't restrain himself—"it's as if Franklin Roosevelt had said to my people, 'Go to those camps. I'll guarantee Hitler's good behavior to you.' ''

The President's control over his impatience was slipping away again, his frustration and anger at being trapped in this seemingly hopeless dilemma beginning to tell on him. "Mr. Begin, I am not questioning Israel's right to survive. What I am questioning is Israel's right to continue a policy which is nothing other than a cold-blooded, calculating effort to annex another people's land. Those settlements of yours have no valid justification whatsoever—"

This time Begin interrupted him. "In another time, Mr. President, in another way, perhaps the future of those settlements could be discussed. But not like this. Not under this threat."

"Mr. Begin, the reason those settlements are there is because you put them there. Against our will. Against the Camp David agreement. If we are in this dreadful impasse today it is due to your stubborn persistence in carrying out a policy the whole world— and even a majority of your nation—condemned.''

"Whatever the feelings of the people of this country may be about those settlements, Mr. President, their feelings about their nation are unshakeable. And they will see in your demand, just as I do, an invasion of their national rights and sovereignty.''

This time there was a long pause. When the President resumed, his voice was suddenly resigned and weary. "I told you at the beginning of our conversation, Mr. Begin, that I believe this proposition is the only reasonable way out of this dilemma. Accept it, renounce your claims to the West Bank, and you will give your own nation peace and save the lives of six million New Yorkers." He paused, waiting for an answer that did not come. "But if you refuse," the President continued, "I am not going to see six million of my countrymen massacred because you will not rectify the consequences of a policy that has no basis in justice or political fact. It will be the most painful order I will ever have to give, Mr. Begin, but if you will not remove those settlements from the West Bank, then the armed forces of the United States will."

Begin paled and sank slowly back against his chair. So there it was, the naked threat of force he had expected from the moment this conversation had begun. A strange vision swept through his mind. He was a four-year-old boy in Lodz trembling at his window as a galloping mass of mounted Cossacks rampaged through his ghetto, wielding great staves like swords, lashing the heads and shoulders of any helpless Jews in their way, trampling their twitching bodies under their horses' thudding hoofs.

His voice was hoarse with sadness when he finally replied. "So we come to that, do we? The final act, the final, if I may say it, betrayal?" Begin sighed. "We live in a terrible world, Mr. President. All the values we counted on to guide us, all the precepts of world order, are disintegrating about us. Someone, some people must somehow find the courage to stop it. I had hoped and believed you and your people would, but I was wrong." The Israeli could almost sense the distant President's discomfiture at his words. "We are a democracy. I cannot reply to your demand—or threat —alone. Only my government can. I will call an emergency Cabinet meeting immediately."

Begin's first act after he had hung up was to ask his wife to bring him a glass of water. Trembling slightly, he took one of the pills his doctors had urged him to use in moments of stress.

In New York, winter's quick-falling dusk was dropping its silken shroud over the city. Already the four men crouched in the window, fieldglasses trained on the entrance of the Long Island Bar and Grill across the street, were beginning to have trouble distinguishing the features of the customers entering the bar.

"Shit," Angelo Rocchia moaned, "if the son of a bitch doesn't hurry up, we'll have to stuff Benny here in the back seat of a car

342

and use the old Kotex-box gimmick." The "Kotex-box gimmick" was a standard police tactic, putting an informer in a car with a box, into which eye slits had been cut, over his head. That way he could identify someone without giving away his own identity.

Benny the Fence, squatting at the window of his "store" between Angelo and Jack Rand, had no intention of getting involved in that. He looked at his watch. It was a few minutes before five. "He ought to be along any minute," he said. "He's usually in there by five."

"Somebody's ass is going to be in a sling if he doesn't turn up." It was the deputy director of the New York office of the FBI standing behind Rocchia, Rand and Benny. Harvey Hudson, the director of the office, had ordered him to take charge of the stakeout as soon as the emergency command post had been informed of Benny the Fence's story. Half a dozen other police officers and FBI men, one holding a line open to the command post, drifted in and out of the shadows of the Long Island Trading Company's anteroom. Benny's secretary sat at her desk, feet twitching to the Top Ten tunes coming from her transistor, totally bored by what was going on around her. Her employer's cooperation with the police had been total. The Arab who came each night to the bar across the street for a Seven-and-Seven had first established contact with Benny three weeks ago through the bartender. He had rented a snub-nosed .38 that he returned, unfired, the next day. Ten days ago he had told Benny he wanted plastic, a good fresh card, and some ID. The fence had sized the man up as a guy with dough. He'd asked for—and gotten—$250 for the papers, a price well above the going market rate. Then, last Wednesday, the Arab had asked him for a "tailor-made," a Friday-morning hit on a guy in his midthirties, medium height, not blond. For that he had sprung $500.

Benny's information had forced the directors of the search operation to make some fast decisions. It was unlikely that the Arab had picked up the truck himself. He looked like an intermediary, a buried sleeper with street contacts to whom someone who knew the right words had come for help. But he was clearly the only link to the man who had rented it. The FBI had wanted to bring in the bartender right away and grill him. Bannion and Feldman of the NYPD had objected strenuously. Benny and guys like the bartender made it a point not to know each other too well. Jump the

343

barman and you might let the word out that the bar was hot, scare away the Arab and wind up with no lead to the renter of the van. They had recommended the trap waiting in the street below, assuming the Arab would keep to his normal routine and show up for his evening drink.

Nothing down on Union Street would have indicated to the untrained eye that anything unusual was going on. Yet the neighborhood was alive with detectives and agents. The Con Ed FBI crew was still there busily tearing up the pavement. They had been reinforced by three real Con Ed men who knew how to operate a jackhammer. In relays, they'd begun to drift into the bar for a drink, and three of them in blue overalls sat by the bar now nursing Miller Lites. An Econoline van belonging to a Queens television repair shop was parked behind the bar. Four agents were inside staring out of its one-way windows, guarding the rear of the bar. The trio of blacks Angelo had spotted earlier were jiving now at Sixth and Union, blocking that escape route.

By five minutes after five, there was still no sign of the Arab. Suddenly behind him, Angelo heard Benny growl, "There he goes."

He pointed to a slender young man in a sheepskin jacket walking past the flashing red Budweiser sign into the bar. Rand rose. He was wearing an Army fatigue jacket, blue jeans and a turtleneck someone had found for him, looking, Angelo thought uncharitably, like a stockbroker ready to go slumming. He headed down the stairs. A minute later, Angelo followed him.

As soon as he opened the door of the bar he saw the Arab alone on a stool halfway down the counter sipping his Seven-and-Seven. Rand was two stools away. Angelo strolled casually down the bar until he was behind the Arab. Gently but firmly, he pressed the muzzle of his .38 to his back while, at the same time, with his left, he gave him a flash of the shield.

"Police," he said, "we want to talk to you."

The Arab twisted around to face him. Rand was already off his stool, his own arm discreetly drawn, blocking one way out. Three fellow FBI men in Con Ed overalls shifted into a half moon to seal off the other.

"Hey," gasped the Arab, "what's all this about?"

"We'll tell you downtown," Angelo said.

344

Outwardly, General Henri Bertrand appeared as composed as ever, the expression on his face set in the weary, inscrutable gaze for which he was so well known. Inwardly, he was seething with frustration. For almost an hour, Paul-Henri de Serre had been sitting at his Boulevard Mortier desk going through the SDECE's collection of photographs of Arab terrorists and scientists, trying to find a familiar face. He had found none.

The General had no doubts about the sincerity of his efforts. The man was ready to do anything to mitigate the consequences of what he had done in Libya. Bertrand was also sure, as a result of a few questions in his car en route to the office, that de Serre was innocent of any involvement in the death of his colleague Alain Prévost. That, like the manner in which the Libyans had set de Serre himself up, had to be the work of Qaddafi's secret service. The bastards, he reflected, are getting better. Maybe the KGB is training them. A point, it suddenly occurred to him, to run down when this was over.

He looked at his scientist. De Serre was completing his second run-through of the pictures. "Still no one that looks familiar?"

De Serre shook his head apologetically. "Nobody."

"Damn." The Gauloise in the corner of Bertrand's mouth wriggled as he inhaled. He was sure every photograph available was there on his desk. The CIA wouldn't have held out on him, not on this. His relations with Israel's Mossad were extremely close, as they had been for over thirty years. He was certain they would come up with everything they had. They could try to do an Identikit portrait of the Arab scientist, but Bertrand had little confidence in such portraits. They could tell you what a man didn't look like, that he didn't wear glasses or have a beard, but they were quite ineffectual when it came to providing a description of what he did look like.

Suddenly, the General stopped his measured pacing of the office and picked up his telephone. The Palestinian had spoken excellent French, hadn't he? Those most likely to hold something back in sensitive matters, he had learned long ago, were those usually closest to home. It took him several minutes to locate his friendly rival, Paul-Robert de Villeprieux, the director of France's internal-security agency, the DST.

"Tell me, *cher ami*," he asked when Villeprieux came to the phone at the Neuilly apartment in which he was dining with friends, "would your people be apt to have anything, anything at all, on Arabs, Palestinians probably, involved in nuclear matters, which just might not be available in my dossiers?"

The suspicion of a satisfied smile appeared on Bertrand's face at the long silence which greeted his question.

"I shall have to call you back on that, I'm afraid," Villeprieux finally replied.

"Don't bother," Bertrand said. "Just call the secretary general of the Élysée and ask for the President's authorization to send me whatever you have. Immediately."

Half an hour later two gendarmes from the DST's headquarters delivered another locked attaché case to Bertrand's office. It contained a thick envelope bearing a red wax seal and the legend "The contents of this envelope are not to be divulged without the express authorization of the President of the Republic or, in his absence from the country, the Minister of the Interior." Inside was the long-suppressed story of the Dajanis' unsuccessful effort to steal plutonium from Cadarache and their expulsion from France.

Bertrand handed Whalid Dajani's picture to de Serre. "Was this your man?"

The scientist paled. "Yes," he answered. "That's he."

Bertrand passed Kamal's photograph across the table. "How about him?"

De Serre studied the terrorist's picture closely. "Yes, I think he was one of the people I noticed at the reprocessing plant."

"And her?" Bertrand gave him Laila's picture.

De Serre shook his head. "No. There were never any women around."

Bertrand was already on his phone. "Open up a photo-facsimile line to Langley," he ordered, "and tell our friend Whitehead the photos of the people he is looking for are on their way to Washington."

Why the hell doesn't he hurry? Laila Dajani fumed. I stand out on this street like a Saudi prince in a synagogue. It was seven-thirty, and West Eighth Street swarmed with NYU students, shoppers, late-night bargain seekers. Finally, Laila saw Kamal drifting out of the pizza joint, his checkered cap jammed onto his head, his black leather jacket's collar turned up, a rectangular box of pizza under his arm. They fell into step and started down West Eighth, moving away from Fifth Avenue.

346

"Everything all right up there?" her brother asked.

Laila nodded. "Except Whalid is drinking again. He bought himself a bottle this morning."

"Let him drink. He can't do us any harm anymore." Kamal stared at the passersby on the sidewalk, the garishly lit shops, the odoriferous fast-food stores. His eyes caught those of an emaciated teenage whore lurking in the shadows at the top of the stoop of a brownstone. She glared at him. Kamal snorted.

A few minutes before he had had her for twenty-five dollars, brutally, quickly, mechanically. It was the kind of imprudence he should never have indulged in. But, he had told himself, it might be his last time, and he had slammed himself at the girl with savage anger until she had cried out in pain.

Why did you cry, child? he thought, looking at her now. After all, you'll be able to do it a few more times before you fry. He turned his eyes away, back to the passing crowd.

I loathe this street, Kamal reflected. I loathe these people. I loathe this city. It's not the Jews I hate, he suddenly realized. It's these people. All of them. Satiated. Smug. Indifferent. Lording it over the earth. He spat. Why do we all hate them so much, he wondered? The Baader-Meinhoff people he had known in Germany, his Italian friends, the Iranians, those strange dour Japanese he'd once trained with in Syria. What is in these people that makes us hate them so much? Were the Romans hated like them once?

"What are you going to do tonight?" he asked his sister.

"Nothing," she replied. "I took a room at the Hilton. I won't leave until I'm ready to come for you."

"Good." Kamal stopped. To his right was 74 West Eighth, a hardware store. "What time have you got?"

Laila checked her watch. "Seven-thirty-six."

"I'll meet you right here at one tomorrow. If you're not here I'll be back at one-ten, then one-twenty. If you don't show up by then, I'll go back. If they catch you, you've got to keep quiet until then." Kamal had stopped and glared intently at his sister. "For God's sake, if something should happen to the car and you show up late at the garage, be sure I know it's you. Because once I get back there I'll be ready to set it off at the first noise I hear."

He squeezed her hand. "*Ma salaam,*" he said. "All will be well, *insh' Allah.*"

Then he strode off alone, off to his last lonely vigil with his rats and his bomb in the midst of the people and the city he proposed to destroy.

"Come here, baby."

Enrico Diaz sprawled on his gold silk mattress like some Oriental nabob, his head and shoulders leaning against the black walls of his flat, his knees drawn up, legs spread apart, the soft satiny folds of his djellabah falling down to his bare ankles. He was flying, winging to a distant place on the coke he had snorted ten minutes ago, the blood surging in his brain as his mind fled through clear, crystal prisms of delight.

Two of his girls lolled in a corner of the pad, sharing the joint whose slightly rancid odor mingled with the Ceylonese incense burning in the bronze censors hanging from the walls. His third girl, Anita, squatted like a supplicant on the gold-covered mattress before Rico. She was a twenty-five-year-old Swede from northern Minnesota, a lanky raw-boned girl whose blond hair tumbled in unkempt strands to the small of her back. It was to her that Rico's command was addressed.

"Yeah, honey."

Anita snuggled forward toward the pimp. Her fleshy lips were fixed in the sullen pout everyone told her made her look like Marilyn Monroe. She was wearing skin-tight emerald disco pants Rico had bought her—albeit with her own earnings—and one of the strapless black lace bras she wore to work because she could snap it off with one deft gesture and flick it challengingly at her waiting clients.

"You know what your man did for you today?"

Anita shook her head.

"He buy you five years." Enrico drew out the number, lacing it with the Southern intonation he so despised.

"Hey, honey, you . . .?"

"Yeah. I seen a man, we got those charges dropped."

Anita was about to gush out her gratitude when Enrico sat bolt upright. His hands shot out and grabbed two fistfuls of the girl's hair. Brutally, her jerked her forward. She shrieked.

"Dumb cunt! I told you never to stiff no John, didn't I?"

"Rico, you're hurting," Anita whispered.

The pimp's response was to yank harder. "I don't want no cops sniffing around my women."

Rico dropped one of his hands, reached under the mattress and drew out a switchblade knife. Anita gagged with terror as he snapped the steel blade open. Before the petrified girl could move, he whipped it across her lips, keeping the blade a precise eighth of an inch above their pulpy surface. "I oughtta streak your lips."

A razor's slash down the lips was the pimp's traditional vengeance on a girl who has strayed. No surgeon, no matter how skilled his fingers, could fully repair the cut.

"But I ain't." Rico snapped the blade shut and tossed the knife over his shoulder. With tantalizing, lascivious slowness his free hand took the hem of his djellabah and inched it up his dark, muscular calves to his knees, then back down his thighs, revealing the dark cavern of his crotch and the slowly stiffening form of his member. While his left hand continued to hold the terrified Anita's head firmly in place, the right reached leisurely toward his snuffbox for a pinch of coke. With sensual, deliberate gestures he patted the white power around the tip of his organ, then once again grabbed Anita's head.

"Now," he announced, "you going to have a little talk with my friend down there. You going to tell him you sorry you gave old Rico so much trouble."

He pulled the girl forward, thrusting her head into his groin. Obediently, she bent to her task, long red fingernails dancing their way around his testicles as her slithering tongue licked at the coke.

He released her head and leaned back against the wall. "Yeahhh," he groaned in pleasure.

That was when the doorbell rang.

At the sight of the two men in old GI khakis and black berets standing on his doorstep, Rico went limp. The taller of the two jerked his head at the staircase. "*Vamonos,*" he said. "*Hay trabajo*—let's go, we've got work to do."

In Jerusalem, the carillon of the Church of the Holy Sepulcher tolled 2 A.M. Tuesday, March 15. Each resonant note was hurled across the old city by the winter wind sweeping the hills of

Judea. Eyes half closed in strain and sadness, Menachem Begin studied the warring members of his government assembled around him in his Cabinet Room. Just as he had foreseen it would, the President's threatening phone call had produced the bitterest, most acrimonious debate the room had ever known; worse than those that had preceded the 1967 war, more vindictive than the recriminations that had followed the 1973 conflict, more impassioned than those that had led to the raid on Entebbe.

While the heated words swirled around him, Begin silently reckoned up the balance of the fourteen men who shared with him the responsibility of governing their nation. As he had expected, the most vigorous reaction to the President's threat had come from Benny Ranan. The former paratrooper was on his feet now, waving his arms, urging a full and immediate mobilization of the Israeli Defense Forces to oppose any American intervention on their soil.

His most ardent supporter was Rabbi Orent of the religious parties. It was a strange but fitting union, the mystic believer and the indifferent atheist, the synagogue and the kibbutz, the man who loved the land because God had given it to his people and the man who cared for it because it could be made to bring forth good fruit. A lot of Israel's strength, Begin thought, was reflected in that alliance.

To his surprise, the most articulate advocate of a compromise with the Americans had been his Minister of the Interior, Yusi Nero, a man the Israeli public usually labeled a hawk. Seize the occasion to force from the Americans and the Soviets guarantees so ironclad their state could never again be menaced, he argued. That would allow them to begin reducing the crushing armament burden which would destroy their nation in the long run more surely than Qaddafi and his bomb.

Begin leaned forward, clearing his throat to get his ministers' attention. Despite all the tensions of the day he remained as cool and as poised as he had been at dawn when the President's first call came in, the clean white handkerchief folded in his suit coat pocket, the tie firmly knotted and precisely in place.

"I would like to remind all of you," he said, "of what is our fundamental responsibility to the nation and to history. We must remain united. Whenever we Jews have allowed our enemies—or our friends—to divide us, the result has been a disaster."

"My dear Menachem." It was Yadin, drawing quietly on his

pipe as he spoke. "It is all well and good to speak of unity now, but if we are confronted with this disaster it's because of a policy you insisted on following in total disregard of its effect on our unity. Taking Arab lands for these settlements—"

"Arab lands!" The voice of Rabbi Orent exploded through the room. The leader of the religious parties was as far removed from the traditional image of the pale, stoop-shouldered rabbinical student as it was possible to be. He was six three, a two-hundred-pound former discus thrower and paratroop captain who was an outspoken supporter of the Gush Emonim, the Block of the Faithful, the movement whose followers had defied their countrymen, the Arabs and most of the world by flinging up their settlements on the land seized by Israel from Jordan during the 1967 war. "Once and for all, let it be clearly understood that there is no such thing as Arab territory or Arab land here. This is the Land of Israel, the eternal heritage of our fathers. The Arabs who have dwelt upon it have done so by usurping our right. They have no more claim to it than a squatter has to the dwelling he has taken over while the owner is away!"

The words that Orent articulated with such passionate intensity reflected the ideas of the founder of the Gush Emonim. Ironically, it was not to Begin or Arik Sharon or Moshe Dayan or any of the other legendary figures of modern Israel that the settlers owed their loyalty, but to a man who, like Orent, was a rabbi. He was a frail ninety-year-old who might have been a survivor of the world that had disappeared forever into the gas chambers of Dachau and Auschwitz, a gentle Eastern European ghetto patriarch dispensing wisdom and cheer to his grandchildren at the end of the day. Rav Zvi Kook was anything but that. The wizened, bearded old man, barely five feet tall, was, however improbable, the heir to the mantle of militant Judaism, the successor to the vengeful warriors of the Old Testament in whose pages he had found the source and justification of the messianic vision that inflamed him and his followers.

Like most ideas capable of inspiring men to zealotry, his benefited from their great simplicity. God had chosen the Jewish people as His Elect to reveal His Nature and Works to mankind through prophecy. He had promised Abraham and the Children of Israel the land of Canaan as evidence of the bond between them. Just as a tree can bring forth fruit only when its roots are plunged into the soil that gives it life, so, Rav Kook taught, the Jewish people could realize their God-given destiny only when they were installed upon the land—all of it—that God had deeded them. Go forth and claim it, he had told his followers, as the instruments of God's Holy Will, the vehicles of His prophecy.

"Be not deceived," Orent intoned, waving a warning finger at Begin. "No Jew can renounce our claim to the land God deeded us. Our settlers went forth to nourish our land with their sweat and toil, but they will nourish it with their blood as well if anyone tries to take it from them."

Begin shuddered, both from the prospect of civil strife and from the implacable fanaticism in the rabbi's voice, a fanaticism he well knew he had done much to encourage. Sadly he turned to Yaacov Dorit, the commander of the Israeli Defense Forces. The Israeli leader had a genius for forcing his Cabinet to a decision by forcing it to confront, as starkly as he could, the issues before it. "General," he asked, "can we count on the Army to evacuate the settlements forcibly if it is ordered to do so?"

"Are you going to tell the Army why?"

Begin blinked, perplexed by Dorit's reply.

"Because if you do," the General went on, "they'll never do it. The Army reflects the majority of this country, and whatever the majority thinks about the settlements, it's not going to be in favor of manhandling—and maybe killing—Israelis for Qaddafi. Or even to save New York."

"And suppose we don't give them the real reason?" Begin inquired.

"Then they won't do it either."

Begin turned an infinitely sad regard to the men at the table. "You see, my friends, I do not believe we have the option of capitulating in front of Qaddafi's threat, even if we wanted to. We would destroy the nation in civil disorder and bloodshed if we did." As he spoke, he employed a revealing nervous reflex, twisting the frame of his glasses between his thumb and forefinger. "I will be accused of falling prey to the Massada complex for what I am about to say, but it is my sincere belief we have no choice. We must resist Qaddafi, and the Americans if it comes to it."

"The Americans are bluffing," Ranan growled. "I don't believe they've got the military capacity to come in here, and if they do we'll tear them to pieces."

Begin eyed him coolly. "I wish I shared your sentiments, Benny." He sighed. "Alas, I do not."

From the reception this kid is getting you'd have thought we were bringing in Yassir Arafat himself, Angelo Rocchia mused. The car that had sped the Arab he had arrested from the Long Island Bar and Grill to the cellar of Federal Plaza had pulled up in front of the direct elevator reserved for FBI use; two other cars each filled with agents had stopped just behind it. Their occupants, hands ready on concealed weapons, swarmed around them as protectively as Secret Service men shielding a President in a hostile crowd.

Angelo got his first good look at his quarry in the fluorescent glare of the elevator. He was in his late twenties, a pale, almost fragile figure with uncombed black hair and a thick drooping moustache that seemed somehow a pathetic boast for a virility he did not possess. Above all, he was a worried, perplexed young man; Angelo could almost smell the fear oozing from his glands like some malodorous secretion.

Everyone, Dewing, the Police Commissioner, Salisbury of the CIA, Hudson, the Chief of Detectives, was waiting for them when the doors slid open on the twenty-sixth floor. For just a second, after the Arab had been led away for a hasty arraignment, Angelo and Rand were celebrities.

"Good work," the Police Commissioner said in that mellow baritone he reserved for promotion ceremonies and Communion-breakfast speechmaking. "First break we've had all day."

As soon as he had been fingerprinted, photographed and arraigned, the Arab, who had given his name as Suleiman Kaddourri, was led into the FBI's interrogation room. The room was as far removed from the public's idea of what an interrogation center should look like as a Hamburger Heaven was from the Tour d'Argent. In fact, it resembled nothing quite so much as a middle-class suburban living room. Thick wall-to-wall carpeting blanketed the floor. The prisoner's chair was a comfortable deep-blue sofa covered with scatter cushions. In front of it was a coffee table with newspapers, cigarettes and a bubbling coffee maker. A pair of armchairs were ranged on the opposite side of the table for the FBI interrogators. The whole, carefully contrived atmosphere was, of course, a hoax designed to relax and disarm a prisoner. Every sound in the room, from the lighting of a match to the rustle of a piece of paper, was picked up and recorded by sensitive, noise-activated microphones in the walls. From behind two of the half-dozen watercolors on the walls, television cameras focused tightly on the prisoner's face. On one wall was a huge photomural of the skyline of New York. It concealed a one-way viewing window. Behind that window was the interrogation room's semidarkened control booth from which a dozen senior officials could see and hear everything that went on inside. Angelo's special status as the arresting officer won him entry to the booth. Fascinated, he studied the faces in the gloom around him.

"Hey, Chief," he whispered, gesturing to an unfamiliar figure in a white open-necked shirt whose collar was pressed down over the lapels of his blue suit, "who's the new girl in town?"

Feldman's eyes followed his glance. "Israeli intelligence," he answered. "Mossad."

In the interrogation room itself, the Arab, his handcuffs removed, was perched warily on the edge of the sofa. Frank Farrell, the Bureau's Palestinian expert, was pouring coffee as gaily, Angelo thought in disgust, as a waitress serving breakfast at a Howard Johnson's Motor Lodge. The second FBI agent in the room, Leo Shannon, a genial New York Irishman who specialized in interrogations and terrorist negotiations, reached into his pocket and laid a white card on the table. Angelo groaned.

"Would you believe it?" he said to the Chief of Detectives. "Guy wants to blow up some gas that's going to kill Christ knows how many people in this city, and they got to give him the fucking card?"

Feldman gave a resigned shrug of his shoulders. The "card" was the slip of paper all New York policemen and FBI agents carry bearing the warning to a prisoner of his civil rights based on the Supreme Court's *Miranda* decision. Shannon "gave" it to him by informing the Arab he could remain silent if he chose or refuse to talk except in the presence of a lawyer. Everyone in the control booth tensed. It was a critical moment. Their efforts to find Qaddafi's hydrogen bomb could come to a dead halt right here. If the man asked for a lawyer it might be hours before they could start to question him, hours more before they could make a deal with his lawyer to let him off in return for talking.

354

Whether from ignorance of the law or indifference, the Arab gave Shannon a halfhearted wave of his hand. He didn't need any lawyers, he said as the men in the booth sighed gratefully. He had nothing to say to anybody.

Behind Angelo, the door to the control booth opened. An agent in shirtsleeves stepped in, blinked a second in the shadows, then stepped over to Dewing. "We've got a sheet on him from the prints," he announced triumphantly.

The men in the booth tightened into a knot around the FBI's assistant director, forgetting for a moment the scene on the other side of the one-way glass. As soon as the Arab's fingerprints had been taken they had been sent to FBI headquarters in Washington, where the memory bank of the Bureau's IBM computer compared them with millions of prints taken from everyone arrested in the country during the past ten years. A second computer out at Langley put them into a CIA IBM containing all the fingerprints of Palestinian terrorists available to the world's intelligence agencies. That machine had registered "tilt" three minutes after ingesting the prints. It had identified them as belonging to Nabil Suleiman. He had been born in Bethlehem in 1951 and had been picked up and printed first by the Israelis after an antigovernment demonstration at Jerusalem's Arab College in 1969. In 1972 he had been arrested for possession of a firearm and given six months in jail. Released, he had disappeared for six months, an absence subsequently traced by Mossad to one of George Habbash's PFLP training camps in Lebanon. In 1975 he had been identified by an informer as one of two men who left a charge of explosives in a shopping basket in Jerusalem's Mahne Yehuda open-air market. Three elderly women had been killed and seventeen other people injured in the explosion. Since then he had vanished from sight.

"Did you run his prints past State and the INS?" Dewing asked as he compared the photograph attached to the file with the man in the interrogation booth.

"Yes, sir," the agent who had brought the file answered. "There's no record of a visa. He's an illegal."

Inside the interrogation room, the Arab was giving his address as the Century Hotel, 844 Atlantic Avenue, Brooklyn. "Get a couple of our cars down there right away," Hudson ordered, hearing his words. They were, for all practical purposes, the last the Arab intended to speak for some time. Overtaken by some shift in his

355

mood, he muttered, "I want a lawyer," to the two FBI men before him, then refused to speak any further.

Angelo studied the Arab. Scared, he mused, scared absolutely shitless. His failure with Benny the Fence in front of Rand still rankled. The young agent was in the shadows behind him, somehow more at ease in these corridors of officialdom than Angelo was.

Angelo leaned toward Feldman. "Chief," he whispered, "let me have ten minutes with him while they're running down a lawyer. After all, he's mine, isn't he?"

Five minutes later, Angelo settled into the chair opposite the Arab with a weary sigh and a complaint about the heat in the room. He took a sack of Planter's Peanuts out of his pocket and spilled a mound into his palm.

"Peanut, kid?" he asked. Closed up like an oyster, the detective thought, watching the Arab defiantly shake his head. Angelo tossed half the handful into his mouth and offered it again to the prisoner. "Go on. You don't need a lawyer to eat a peanut . . . Nabil."

He had held off on the name, then came down hard on it, his eyes fixed on the Arab's face as he pronounced it. He saw him start as though he had received a jolt of static electricity. Angelo sat back in his armchair and slowly chewed the rest of the peanuts, deliberately allowing the Arab time to reflect on the fact that his real identity was known. Finally, he cleaned his hands with a little clap and leaned forward.

"Kid, you know, different guys got different ways of operating." He used the same husky, confidential voice he had employed unsuccessfully with Benny. "Bureau's got their way. I got mine. Me, I say always level with a guy. Let him know where he's at."

"I don't want to talk," the Arab snarled.

"Talk?" Angelo laughed. "Who asked you to talk? Just listen." He settled back in his chair again. "Now, what we got you on here is receiving stolen goods. Bunch of plastic Benny Moscowitz got for you on consignment Friday a week for five hundred dollars." Angelo paused and gave the Arab a friendly smile. "By the way, kid, you paid too much. Two and a half's the going price."

He could have been a priest trying to talk a young husband out of a divorce. "You can figure that's one to three, depending on your sheet and the judge. Now, the matter of interest to us here is not that. It's where it went. Who you did it for."

356

"I said I didn't want to talk." There had been no softening in the Arab's defiant tone.

"Don't, kid. You don't have to. You heard what the card says." Reassurance dripped from Angelo's voice. He thoughtfully munched a couple of peanuts, then jerked his head toward the New York mural on the wall to his left. "See that?" he asked.

The Arab nodded.

"One-way window. They got about twenty guys back there watching us. Judges. Feds. Like that. Got a guy there in a white shirt's very interested in you." Angelo paused, letting the Arab's curiosity peak. "Comes from that Israeli outfit there, whatta they call it? Mossad." Again Angelo waited, pretending to chew a peanut, watching the Arab through half-closed eyes. The fear he was looking for was there all right.

"Now, this is how things stand, kid." His voice took on a matter-of-fact tone, as though he was totally disinterested in what he was about to say. "You're an illegal. We know that. Ran your fingerprints at the INS, and we know you never had no U.S. visa. Okay? We got this treaty with the Israelis. Extradite terrorists. Boom!" Angelo snapped his fingers. "Just like that. Guy's on his way down to the Federal Courthouse now for the papers. That Mossad fellow's got a plane waiting for you, just for you, out at JFK. They figure to have you on it by midnight."

Angelo could see how rapidly the Arab was blinking. Scared out of his mind, he thought. "Because we're going to hand you over. Got to. Have no choice. We got no reason to hold you. Not on some lousy charge of receiving stolen goods." He clapped his hands and brushed his trouser leg as though he was getting ready to go. "You don't want to talk to us. It's your right. Perfect right. But as a result we got no reason to hold on to you."

Angelo began to rise.

"Hey," the Arab said. "I don't understand."

"It's simple," Angelo explained. "You help us, we help you. You talk to us, we make you a material witness. Then we gotta keep you here. Can't extradite you anymore." He was on his feet now, tipping up on his toes, slowly stretching his joints. "You don't want to talk, what could we do? We gotta hand you over. It's the law.

"You know those Mossad guys out there better than I do. I mean, from what I hear they don't care too much for them little white cards and all.'' Angelo let a little smile flicker an instant at the edges of his mouth, relishing the tension in the man's face. ''Particularly when they got a chance to spend eight hours on an airplane all alone with a guy put a bomb in a shopping basket, killed three little old Jewish ladies, you know what I mean? I mean, how tender do you figure they're going to want to be with a guy like that?''

The Arab's face lightened as though a bright light had been switched on at the mention of the bomb in a basket. So, Angelo thought, you did it, you little creep.

''Hey,'' the Arab muttered, ''what do you want?''

Angelo settled slowly back into his interrogator's chair. He crossed his legs and delicately hitched up the crease of his trousers. ''Just a talk, kid. Just a little talk.''

Grace Knowland started impatiently at the sight of her son on the steps of the Seventh Regiment Armory in midtown Manhattan. It was after seven. He should have been inside already, changing for his match.

''Hey, Mom,'' he called down in a voice shrill with adolescent anger, ''the match is off.'' Grace strode up the steps and kissed his reluctantly offered cheek.

''What happened?''

''I don't know. They got some soldiers there and nobody can go in. They won't even let me go down to the locker rooms to get my racket so I can play Andy tomorrow.''

Grace winced. It had been that kind of a day, her trip to Washington wasted because the Mayor hadn't come back on the shuttle as usual, her fruitless efforts all afternoon to worm something about the South Bronx out of his press secretary, the rush to get here for her son's match only to find it had been canceled.

''I'll see what I can do about the racket, dear.''

She walked up to the military policeman at the door. ''What's going on? My son was supposed to play a tennis match here tonight.''

The soldier banged his black mittens together with a smack and stamped his boots in the cold. ''Lady, I don't know. All I know is I got orders to seal off the area to the public tonight. They got some kind of mobilization exercise going on in there.''

"Well, surely," Grace cajoled, "you can't imagine my son's going to disturb anybody just going down to the locker room to get his tennis racket?"

The soldier squirmed uncomfortably. "Listen, lady, what can I tell you? I got my orders. No unauthorized personnel in the area."

Grace felt a surge of anger rising inside her. "Who's in charge here?"

"The lieutenant. You want I get the lieutenant?"

The military policeman was back a few minutes later with a clean-shaven young officer in freshly pressed fatigues. He eyed Grace appreciatively.

"Tell me, Lieutenant." She covered the cutting edge of her question with a frosting of sweetness. "Just what is it that's going on here tonight that's so important a thirteen-year-old boy can't go down to the locker room to get his tennis racket?"

The officer laughed. "It's nothing, ma'am. Just some kind of snow-removal test they're running. A bunch of people trying to figure out how they can help the city the next time you get a big snowstorm. That's all."

My day, it suddenly occurred to Grace, may not be wholly wasted after all. "That's very interesting." Her handbag was open and she picked over its jumble for her press card. "I'm with *The New York Times* and it happens I'm very much into the problem of getting the snow off the streets of this city. I'd like to talk to the officer in charge of your test and find out what you're learning."

"I'm sorry, ma'am. I can't help you on that. I got nothing to do with the operation itself," the young lieutenant replied. "They just sent us up here from Dix last night to handle the security. Tell you what, ma'am, if your son'll describe where his racket is to me, I'll go down and try to find it and at the same time I'll tell them you want to speak to someone."

The officer was thumping the strings of Tommy's racket against the butt of his hand when he returned. "Hey," he said, "that's strung real light. You must be a good player." He turned to Grace. "They told me all inquiries about the operation are to be referred to Major McAndrews, First Armory PIO." He handed Grace a slip of paper. "Here's his phone number. If you come back to do a story," he mumbled shyly, "how about having a cup of coffee with a stranger in these parts?"

Grace smiled, noting his name, Daly, on the black-and-gold

swatch above the pocket of his field jacket. "Of course. If I come back, I'd be delighted."

Angelo was sitting back in his interrogator's chair, chewing an occasional peanut, as relaxed as though he were chatting with a fellow cop about the Giants' chances of making the NFL playoffs.

"Okay," he said to the Arab before him, "so you do the odd job for the Libyan embassy over at the United Nations. How do they get hold of you?"

"They leave a message at the bar."

"How do you fix your meets?"

"I add four to the day of the month and then go to the corner of that street and First Avenue. Like if it's the ninth, I go to Thirteenth and First."

Angelo nodded. "Always at the same time?"

"No. From one to five. I add an hour each time, then start over again."

"And you always meet the same contact?"

"Not always. I have a copy of *Newsweek* in my hand. They make the contact."

"Okay. So how did this one go?"

"The contact was a girl."

"You remember the day?"

The Arab hesitated. "It had to be Tuesday the first, because the meet was at Fifth Street."

"Remember what she looked like?"

"Pretty. Long brown hair. She was wearing a fur coat."

"An Arab?"

The prisoner shifted his regard from Angelo's eyes, ashamed of his betrayal. "Probably. But we spoke English."

"So what did she want?"

"Fresh cards. She told me to bring her fresh cards at ten the next morning."

"And you went to Benny?"

The Arab nodded his head.

"Then what happened?"

"I gave her the cards. She said. 'Come for a walk.' We go a few blocks and we stop at a camera store. She told me to go in and buy myself a camera."

"And you did?"

"I went to a bar first and practiced signing a few times."

"Then you got the camera?"

"Yeah." The Arab sighed, aware of how deeply he was involving himself in all this. "So she said, okay, it was good. She wanted more fresh cards and a driver's license for Friday morning, ten o'clock. For a guy in his midthirties. She gave me a thousand bucks. Friday the meet was over on Fourth Avenue, Brooklyn. She didn't show up. A guy came instead."

Angelo's irritation at Dewing's interruption of his interrogation was manifest. The FBI official walked authoritatively into the room, sat down in the chair beside his and took over the interrogation without even consulting him.

"Excuse me, Mr. Rocchia," he said, "but I thought our friend here might look at some photographs for us. They've just come in from overseas."

He passed the photo of Laila from the DST dossiers that Henri Bertrand had forwarded to the CIA barely twenty minutes earlier. "By any chance would this be the girl who contacted you?" he asked.

The Arab looked at the photograph, then at Angelo, wary and mistrustful of this intruder who had snapped the current developing between them. The detective, silently cursing Dewing, gave the Arab what he hoped was a particularly friendly smile.

"That's her."

Dewing passed Whalid's picture to him. "Was this the guy you got the plastic for?"

The Arab laid the photo on the coffee table, shaking his head.

"How about him?" Dewing passed Kamal's picture across the table.

The Arab studied it a moment, then looked up. "Yeah," he said. "that's him."

The sight of the half-dozen exhausted, haggard men sitting around the National Security Council conference room in their dinner jackets would have been comical if the reason behind it were not so potentially tragic. In a few moments, as part of their determined effort to conceal the crisis behind a façade of normality, they would join their wives in the Executive Mansion for cocktails in the Blue Room. Then, in the State Dining Room, they would dine off the Lincoln gold service the President's wife loved, at a banquet honoring the departing dean of Washington's diplomatic corps, the ambassador of Bolivia.

Jack Eastman began their session by noting that nothing in the evening newscasts gave any indication the press was onto the crisis.

"Slender satisfaction," the President remarked curtly and turned to the communication which had come in from the Israeli government while he had been changing his clothes. "I guess Begin leaves us no choice except to do it for him, does he?" The President's voice was gruff as he asked the question, but he was a highly emotional man, and, looking at him, Eastman sensed how deeply pained he was. "What are the chances they'll oppose our action?" he asked Bennington.

"More than fifty-fifty, I'm afraid, sir."

The President slouched uncomfortably in his chair, his forefingers picking at his lip, his head bowed as though in prayer. He had laid claim to this office because he'd promised his nation a kind of moral leadership he sensed it needed and wanted. Yet nothing had quite prepared him for the lonely agony the exercise of power could entail or for how complex issues that seemed simple from the outside became when you had to deal with them. "We're trapped between the fires of two fanatics, gentlemen. We can't allow six million Americans to die because of their rigidity. If it comes down to it, we'll have to act. Harold," he said to his Secretary of Defense, "I want the Rapid Deployment Force ready to move at an hour's notice." The Rapid Deployment Force was a composite body of Army, Marine, Air Force and Navy units assembled after the Iranian crisis for swift movement to anywhere on the globe in a crisis. "And Warren," he ordered his Deputy Secretary of State, "you get to Hussein and Assad in total secrecy and make sure we can use their airfields as staging areas if we have to."

He rose. His movements, Eastman observed, suddenly had the stilted, uncertain gestures of the elderly or the infirm. He had reached the door when Webster of the FBI called out, "Mr. President!"

The Missourian was holding his telephone in his hand, and his usually laconic features were alight with an excitement. "New York has made a positive identification of at least three of the

362

people involved in this. They'll have forty thousand people out looking for them at dawn!''

"Thank God!" Some of the color returned to the President's face, and for just an instant an intimation of the shy smile the world associated with him reappeared. ''Maybe now I'll be able to digest my dinner after all.''

As he was leaving the National Security Council conference room for the reception upstairs, the Secretary of Energy paused a moment, then turned and walked determinedly to a public phone booth in the West Wing basement.

The number Delbert Crandell dialed rang interminably before a young woman answered. Her voice became sullen the instant she recognized her caller. ''What happened to you last night? I waited up for you until four.''

"Never mind that.'' Crandell had no time to waste on explanations. "I've got something very important for you to do.''

The girl groaned and stirred in her bed, the rose satin sheets slipping off her naked breasts as she did. The litter, the charmless disorder, in Cindy Garrett's bedroom was an accurate reflection of the disorder in her life. She had come to Washington in 1976 from a small town near Mobile, Alabama, fleeing the stigma of a pregnancy brought on by the town's deputy sheriff. As a parting gift her former lover had landed her a job as a receptionist in the offices of an Alabama Congressman he had befriended in a hit-and-run investigation. Her employment had been abruptly terminated by his constituents' angry protests after Cindy had appeared nude in *Playboy* magazine's ''The Girls of Washington Revisited.'' Fortunately, a chance meeting with Crandell at a Georgetown cocktail party a few evenings later had opened the way to employment that was not only less demanding and better paid but, in Cindy's case, infinitely more suitable.

"What do you want?'' Wariness as thick as the wrinkle cream glistening under her eyes lurked behind her reply.

"I want you to drive up to New York right away. Go to the apartment and—''

"Ah cain't go to New York,'' Cindy squawked in protest.

"The hell you *cain't!*'' Crandell couldn't abide the red-clay accent that crept into Cindy's voice after a few bourbons or in her

363

unguarded moments. "You're going to do what I tell you to do. Get the car and get up there as fast as you can. You know the painting over the fireplace?"

"The icky one that looks like someone peed on it?"

"Yes." The "icky" one was a Jackson Pollock appraised by Crandell's insurance adjusters at $350,000. "And the one to the left of the television?"

"The one with those funny eyes?"

"Right." That was a Picasso. "Get those two and the gray one in the bedroom." Crandell did not need to identify his Modigliani further. "And bring them back down here. Just as fast as you can drive."

"Ah, honey, ah really have to—" Cindy began, hoping that coquetry might somehow spare her the ordeal her lover had just proposed.

"Shut up!" Crandell interrupted. "Just get your ass moving to New York." He hung up, then decided to make a second call, this one to his real-estate agent at Douglas Elliman in New York. Finally, relaxed for almost the first time since this crisis had begun, he hurried up the stairs to the Blue Room.

Harvey Hudson, the New York director of the FBI, listened with growing concern to his deputy's account of Grace Knowland's conversation at the Seventh Regiment Armory. "How can we be so unlucky?"

His aide nodded sympathetically and continued his report. "So she got all excited when the MP said 'snow removal.' She pulled out her press card and insisted on talking to somebody. They finally gave her the cutout number we're using to protect NEST. It's a dummy line that's supposed to go to First Armory PIO. Rings downstairs. She's on the line now, insisting on a briefing on our 'snow removal' exercise tomorrow morning."

Hudson clutched his head in dismay. "Can you imagine? Some fucking kid can't get a tennis racket and we risk blowing the whole operation to *The New York Times?*" He tugged at the ends of his red-and-yellow bow tie, dangling like wilting vines from each side of his shirt collar. He seemed to have shrunk physically from the strains of this terrible day, from the horror that had come with each hour that had gone by with Qaddafi's bomb undiscovered.

"Okay," he ordered. "You stuff somebody into an Army uniform and get him up to that armory tomorrow morning. Give that woman the goddamndest song-and-dance briefing on snow removal that anybody's ever heard. I don't care what the hell you tell her, but make it good. The one thing we don't need right now is to have *The New York Times* on our backs!''

In the Blue Room of the White House, a Marine Corps band struck up ''Hail to the Chief.'' Smiling warmly, his wife the rigorous one pace behind him that protocol prescribed, the President strode into the diplomatic reception. Admiringly, Jack Eastman watched the couple drift through the room, shaking hands, chatting, laughing politely at the Bulgarian ambassador's clumsy attempt at humor. Quite a performance, Eastman thought. You could fault the man for his infuriating tendency to vacillate, for his lack of personal warmth, but one thing you couldn't take away from him was his icy self-control, his stoic front in a crisis.

Eastman was about to sip his grapefruit juice when he felt a slight pressure at his elbow. It was his wife, late as usual. He bent down to kiss her, smelling as he did the alcohol on her breath.

''Darling,'' she whispered as he pulled away from her, ''I've got to talk to you. Alone.''

Eastman wanted to laugh. Talking privately to your wife at diplomatic receptions was a privilege not accorded to high government officials.

Sally had him by the arm. ''It's about Cathy.''

Her husband tensed, then followed as she threaded deftly through the room seeking out an empty corner by the bar. When she found it she turned to him almost angrily. ''She's home,'' she blurted.

''Home?'' Eastman was stunned. ''How come?''

''Because what you laid on me last night was too heavy, Jack.'' Sally Eastman's brief show of defiance had already passed and tears diluted her eyes. ''I'm a mother, not a soldier.''

''Sal—''

She turned at his word, moved to the bar and thrust her glass at a bartender. ''A vodka martini on the rocks,'' she ordered.

Eastman stepped behind her, fighting now to maintain his own composure. ''Sally,'' he hissed, ''you had no right to do that. No right at all.''

His wife turned around. The mascara was beginning to run a bit as the tears started to unravel the careful façade of her worn and tired face. She started to reply, but before she could, Eastman leaned and brushed his lips to her forehead. "But thank God you did," he whispered. "Dab up the eyes. We've got to go back to the party."

The battered Toyota slid silently past the deserted warehouses. Rico was in front, beside the driver. To his right, through the high wire fence wrapping the Bayonne docks, he could catch an occasional glimpse of the black sheen of the harbor and, in the distance, the gleaming lights of Manhattan.

"*Aquí.*"

The driver stopped and snapped off the headlights. They were in total darkness. The only sound the pimp could hear was the keening of the sea gulls down by the water's edge.

The three men left the car and walked down a long alley toward the rear of an abandoned loft. At the end of the alley, the leader rapped on a door. It opened, and from the darkness inside a flashlight's narrow beam trapped each face a brief instant in its glow.

"*Venga,*" a voice commanded.

As soon as he stepped into the loft, Rico knew why he was there. At one end a long wooden slab rested upon a pair of trestles. Five chairs were ranged behind it. A pair of kerosene lanterns were on the table, their flickering glow falling on two portraits on the wall, Che Guevara and the founder of the FALN.

The Puerto Rican movement was the only terrorist organization firmly implanted on the soil of the United States, and it had succeeded in maintaining its integrity there because of procedures as ruthless as the one about to begin. It was the trial of a traitor, and Rico noted to his intense relief that the accused was already in place, firmly bound and gagged, in a chair facing the trestle table.

Rico, as a senior member of the FALN, took his place in one of the judges' chairs. He tried to avoid looking at the accused, at his wildly moving eyes, at the veins bulging in his neck as he strained to articulate through his gag the defense he would not be permitted to make.

The trial, which was nothing more than a ritualized justification for murder, was brief. The accused was a police informer, brought up from Philadelphia to be "tried" in Bayonne because it would be easier to execute his sentence here. When the evidence had been heard, the man in the center of the table polled his fellow judges. One after another they intoned, "*Muerte.*"

No one suggested clemency. With the exception of a few people like Rico, the leadership of the FALN was composed of lower-middle-class intellectuals, second-rate history instructors and professional graduate students, and mercy was not a feeling that registered in the sterile reaches of their academic, revolutionary minds.

On the table in front of the chief judge was a Walther P38. Wordlessly, he passed it along the table to Rico. This too was a FALN ritual. To kill deliberately in cold blood on the orders of the organization was the ultimate proof of a man's loyalty.

Rico took the gun, got up and walked around the table. Trembling slightly, concentrating his eyes on a corner of the warehouse floor so that he did not have to look at his victim's head, he drew the pistol up, pushed off the safety, felt briefly for the soft flesh of the temple and pulled the trigger.

There was a sharp click.

Rico looked down to see the mocking laughter in his victim's eyes. Six men moved out of the shadows, thrust Rico into the chair, bound and gagged him.

"There is a traitor in this room," the chief judge announced in Spanish. "But it is not he."

This time there was no need for a trial. It had already taken place before Rico arrived. The chief judge took back the Walther and drew out the clip. Methodically, he filled it with 9mm. cartridges, then slapped it shut with the heel of his hand. He offered it to the figure who stepped from the shadows at the back of the loft. It was the man Rico had given to the FBI.

Noiselessly, the man walked around the table and placed the cold black barrel to Rico's temple. He stood there a moment. Then he pulled the trigger and blew Rico's brains halfway across the loft.

Angelo Rocchia stared from his office window, out across the darkened, snow-frosted rooftops of lower Manhattan, feeling as he did the heat burning up his throat. The Rolaids, he thought, cursing himself for ordering the *spaghetti al pesto,* where did I put the Rolaids?

He turned back to his desk and started to fumble through its drawers. There was little to distinguish his office from most of the others on the detectives' floor of Police Plaza. On his blotter was a desk set made of the shields that had marked his progress through the Department—and life. Hung from the walls were the obligatory career photos:Angelo graduating from the Police Academy, being congratulated on the four citations he had won by an assortment of commissioners, at the Columbian Society banquet the night he had been elected president of the Department's Italian-American fraternal association. There was a portrait of Maria and one of his late wife, the black felt mourning button he had worn religiously for a year now fixed to its silver frame.

He found his tube of Rolaids, popped one into his mouth and returned to the window, waiting anxiously for the relief it would bring. They said heart attacks sometimes started this way, with the burning in the gut and all. So many of the older guys were going that way, the guys he had come in with right after the war; what with the hours, the strain, the fear, the smoking, they said your chances were a lot worse than most people's.

He never should have eaten so much, but he wanted to take the kid out, show him Forlini's. He had made him stick around while he typed up their fives, the supplementary investigation reports, that left every NYPD investigation, even one as critical as this, inches deep in paper. A good detective, he'd kept reminding the kid, always keeps his paper up.

Shit, what did they want to know, these kids like Rand? he suddenly asked himself. Wanted to have it all right away, they did. Learning slowly, putting it all together the hard way, they had no time for that. You saw them all over the Department now, figured they already had all the answers, didn't have to pay their dues the way the older guys had, out there doing the horseshit jobs, getting down the routine, the routine, the routine until it was as much a part of you as your dandruff or your body odor, soaking up experience until certain things became such a natural reaction you didn't even think about them anymore.

Angelo could see Rand now sitting opposite him in Forlini's telling him how good the wine was, at the same time letting him know he didn't approve of throwing guys like the pickpocket against the wall. Already so sure of himself he was just a little patronizing to the older guy.

He started at the sound of the telephone, its jangle echoing through the deserted offices.

"Where have you been? I've been trying to get you all day."

Hearing her voice, Angelo slid happily into his desk chair. "I've been enjoying a typical New York detective's day. Looking for a needle in the haystack with a bunch of the boys."

"I called you this morning, but they said everybody was off at a meeting."

"Yeah. Got a lot of people on this." Angelo's voice was gruff, but the gruffness was as transparent as his office window. "I shoulda called you, Grace, but I wasn't certain . . ." He hesitated. "I mean after last night and all."

"I know. I thought a great deal about last night, too, Angelo. I've made up my mind. I'm going to keep the baby."

"Grace, you don't really mean that."

"Yes, I do."

"You want another kid that bad?"

"I do."

How can so much happen in twenty-four hours? Angelo wondered. How can things suddenly change so much? "Grace, if that —" he dabbed at the touch of dampness on his forehead—"if that's what you really, honestly want, I mean, what the hell, a detective first grade's pension doesn't go very far these days, but I wouldn't know what to do when I retire anyway. There was a guy a couple of months ago was talking to me about taking something in security over at American Express. What I mean is, Grace, if it's what you really want, I'll do the right thing by you, you know?"

"Angelo." She pronounced his name as tenderly as she sometimes did when they were lying beside each other in the darkness of his bedroom, but there was something distant there, too, and it wasn't just because they were speaking over the phone. "That's a wonderful thing to say and I'll never forget you for having said it." He could hear her slowly inhaling her cigarette. He'd been after her to give that up, except she'd never listened. "But that's not what I want, Angelo."

"What do you mean, that's not what you want?" He tried to conceal the hurt and surprise with the roughness of his voice.

"Angelo, I am not trying to force you to marry me. That's not why I'm doing this. I tried to tell you last night. I want a child, yes. But not another marriage."

"For Christ's sake, Grace, you're not going to try to bring up a kid just like that? All by yourself? Without a father?"

"I won't be the first woman in New York to do it, Angelo."

"Goddammit." Rage escaped Angelo like steam hissing from a ruptured heating duct. "Grace, you can't do this."

"Yes, I can, Angelo. The world has changed a lot, you know."

"And what about me? It's my child, too, after all. What am I supposed to do? Come around once a year, pat him on the cheek and say, 'Hey, kid, how you getting on? Old lady teaching you how to throw a forward pass and all?' "

"Angelo." She sounded so quiet, so determined, that the detective understood just how completely her mind was made up. "One of the reasons I want this child is because I hope he—or she—will have some of those qualities I love and admire so much in you. But I'm having it for myself, because I want it and I'm ready to accept the responsibilities that go with having it. Alone. Of course, if you want to see the child, there'll always be a place for you in his or her and my life."

"Thanks, Grace. Thanks a lot." As he pronounced the words, Angelo could feel the dull ache constricting his stomach. He was staring out through the windows to the city lights again. This time their edges were blurred and indistinct because Angelo Rocchia had just understood that the last love affair of his life was drawing to an end. "I'll call you someday and we can have a nice talk about it."

When they had hung up, he started to unfold his portable camp bed. Lieutenant Walsh's Office of Civil Preparedness had passed out a bunch of them during Friday's snow emergency and some of them had gotten lost—like the one that had happened to get lost behind Angelo's door. He had hung up his tie and taken off his cufflinks when he saw the night desk man, Terry Keegan, in his doorway.

"Sleeping in?" Keegan asked.

"Yeah. I got to be over to Hertz Rent-A-Truck at Fourth Avenue, Brooklyn, six-thirty tomorrow morning." That, Angelo reflected, was typical of a detective's life. Tonight you're a hero, tomorrow you're a hack, assigned to be an errand boy for the FBI forensic guys busting up the truck that got the barrels. "Christ, the older I get, the more I hate these early calls."

"Me too." Keegan laughed. "Like that ballbreaker they gave us back in 'fifty-two when we were just breaking in up at the Tenth Precinct. You remember that one?''

"Do I?'' Angelo laughed. It had been a hit and run, a leaving the scene, with the victim DOA. Every morning they had had to get out on the West Side Highway at six-thirty stopping cars in the bitter winter cold. "Excuse me, sir, do you go by this way every day? See anything that looked like an accident last Friday?'' A thousand cars they must have stopped.

"It was an out-of-town salesman, came in to his office every Friday, remember?'' Angelo said. "Come up with the kind of car because his brother-in-law had one just like it.''

"Yeah.'' Keegan smiled at the memory, its pain washed away by time. "And the guy walked on us anyway because his lawyer said the other guy died of a heart attack.''

Angelo was stretching, yawning. "All the work that went into that one horseshit collar.''

"You imagine the overtime we'd make if we had that kind of a case today?''

"Shit,'' Angelo sighed, "they never put that kind of effort into a case anymore.''

Keegan disappeared and Angelo stepped to the window for a last glimpse of his city. He thought of that barrel of gas someone had hidden somewhere out there. What kind of guy would do something like that? he wondered. Could he look at the pictures of the people he'd killed in the papers the next day? Could he stand to watch kids, parents, relatives crying their hearts out on television for the people he'd killed? He shook his head. So much had changed since he had come up, the world was so different now.

He turned out the light and lay down on his camp bed, letting the kaleidoscope of oncoming sleep tumble the images before his mind, of Grace looking up at him in Forlini's, of his reproachful young FBI partner, of a frightened Arab and a handsome young detective, his hair as black as the shadows of the night, stopping the cars on the West Side Highway so long ago.

PART VII

TUESDAY, DECEMBER 15:
6:30 A.M. TO 1:15 P.M.

"I have reached a decision."

THE PRESIDENT ALLOWED THE ICY JETS OF WATER to batter him, savoring the numbness their chill streams inflicted on his exhausted body. His shower stall adjacent to the Presidential bedroom suite was still referred to in the White House as "Lyndon Johnson's wake-up shower." The Texan had ordered it installed during the Vietnam War, cursing as he did the inability of the U.S. Army Corps of Engineers to force the water pressure high enough to satisfy him. The current Chief Executive had every reason to be thankful for its presence. He'd been living on black coffee and its periodic assaults for twenty-four hours. At 4:30 A.M. he had finally left the NSC conference room to return to the living quarters in the hopes of getting a couple of hours' sleep. His gesture had been futile.

Toweling himself dry, he reviewed for the hundredth time the terrifyingly few assets and options the United States possessed to meet Qaddafi's threat, hoping against all reason to discover somewhere in the recesses of his mind the one solution they had overlooked. Amin, Khomeini and now this man: zealots menacing the whole fragile balance of international conduct and behavior. And why? He couldn't help thinking of the words he had read trying to force sleep onto his racing mind last night, a fragment of Aeschylus he'd found in the *Wisdom of the Ages* he kept by his bedside:

> So in the Libyan fable it is told
> That once an eagle, stricken with a dart,
> Said when he saw the fashion of the shaft,
> With our own feathers, not by others' hands,
> Are we now smitten.

How prophetic, he told himself again. Because it is with our feathers that their arrows are made, all the arms, the science, the technology we in the West have thrust at Qaddafi and everyone else who wanted them in our gluttonous, uncontrollable appetite for energy and capital.

His mess steward had set his usual breakfast on his bedroom desk: coffee, grapefruit, two soft-boiled eggs and a slice of whole-wheat toast. He gulped the juice and the coffee and ignored the rest. He had no stomach for food this morning. Then he punched the remote-control panel that allowed him to watch, simultaneously, the three television sets at the foot of his bed. Listening to the opening sequences of *Good Morning America, The Today Show* and *The CBS Morning News*, he noted with relief that no hint of the crisis had leaked to the media—despite the notorious permeability of his capital.

Before going downstairs, he opened the door to his wife's bedroom and tiptoed to the bed where she lay crumpled in sleep. He bent down and kissed her, savoring as he did the comforting warmth of her sleeping body.

Her eyes blinked open. She reached for his hand. "Darling," she whispered, "are you all right?"

The President nodded grimly.

"Is there anything new?"

"Nothing. Absolutely nothing."

With his hand, she patted the sheets by the side of the bed. Gratefully almost, the Chief Executive sat down beside her. There was no one, not even Eastman, in whose wisdom and judgment the President had greater confidence. Half a dozen times since the crisis had begun, he had unburdened himself to her here in this bedroom or the sitting room next door, relieved in those intimate instants of the need of maintaining the stern, composed facade he felt forced to give to his advisers.

For a moment he was silent, his hands clasped between his knees, his shoulders slumping forward. Then he shuddered, depressed by the weight of his thoughts.

"What is it, my love?"

The President reached for his wife's hands. She could see, despite the dimness of her bedroom, the patina of tears in his eyes. She pressed his flesh to her. He began to tremble, ever so faintly, like the ground tremor provoked by a distant explosion.

"I'm afraid," he whispered. "My God, I'm so afraid it's going to go wrong."

376

His wife sat up and wordlessly slipped out from under her bed-covers. For an instant she sat beside him, a comforting arm thrown around his shoulders. Then, with her husband beside her, she turned and slipped to her knees. There, in his wife's darkened bedroom, his face in his hands, the President began a private, desperate prayer for the strength he would need in the hours ahead.

       In New York, it was 7:15 A.M. when Abe Stern, numb with exhaustion, sat down at the dining-room table in Gracie Mansion and began to poke at the scrambled eggs his housekeeper had set before him. Next to his plate was a one-page summary of the events of the last four hours. One word would have been sufficient —"nothing." Stern had returned at 3 A.M. to the Federal mansion that had sheltered New York's mayors since 1942. He might just as well have stayed downtown—like the President, he hadn't been able to sleep.

The discovery of traces of radiation, first out in Queens, then in the truck that had picked up the missing barrel, the knowledge that two Palestinians involved in Qaddafi's nuclear program had picked up the *Dionysos'* cargo, had shattered the one hope Stern had clung to all during the desperate hours of Monday, the illusion that somehow, maybe just somehow, the bomb wasn't there.

From the transistor beside him the WNYC *Travelers' Timetable* droned out early traffic advisories for the first commuters heading into his city. Stern sickened listening to them. Three million people heading into the city, perhaps to die, totally ignorant of the menace threatening them. That had led to the bitterest argument he had had with the President since the crisis had begun. Confronted with the certainty that there was a thermonuclear device in Manhattan, he had asked the White House at midnight for permission to seal off Manhattan to incoming traffic, close down every bridge, tunnel, and railroad line into the city.

The military had backed him up; barring New York's three million commuters from the city would have brought the potential American loss from the explosion of Qaddafi's bomb much closer to the even-tradeoff point at which the Libyan would lose the advantage he held. The President and the rest of the Crisis Committee had all opposed him. There was no way Manhattan Island could be cut off from the rest of the world in silence, and the risk that the implacable zealot in Tripoli would detonate his device as soon as he found out what was happening was too great to be acceptable. You could not, the President had argued once again, take the chance of condemning five million New Yorkers to death to save three million commuters. Everyone threatened by this terrifying end act of political terrorism would have to share the risks equally, the President had ruled.

And so right now, Abe Stern thought, in the cold morning air in Darien and Greenwich, White Plains and Red Bank, New Jersey, people were gathering in bus stations and along train platforms, or lingering over a cup of coffee as they waited for the honk of a carpool driver. Soon they would be flooding into New York over the railroads and bridges he had wanted to cut, innocently heading for another day's work and very possibly their deaths. He pushed his eggs away, unable to eat. Should I have agreed? he asked himself again. How the hell can a man decide where his obligations lie in such a horrible dilemma?

His thoughts were interrupted by the appearance of his wife in the doorway, her gaunt figure wrapped in the faded rose satin dressing gown she had bought at Abraham and Strauss fifteen years before.

"Why are you up so early?" he asked.

Wordlessly, she moved to the sideboard, poured herself a glass of orange juice from the pitcher there, and sat down beside him. "What's the matter? You didn't sleep last night."

"Nothing's the matter," Stern rejoined irritably. "I couldn't sleep, is all."

His wife pointed a reproachful finger toward his plate. "How come you're eating eggs for breakfast? You know Mort told you eggs were bad for your cholesterol."

"So what? What is he anyway, some kind of genius because he went to Harvard?" Stern thrust his knife angrily at the butter dish, cut a thick slab and spread it defiantly on a piece of toast he had no appetite to eat. "I get a heart attack, it's not going to be from eating eggs, believe me. What time's your plane?"

Ruth was due to leave, as she did every year at this time, to spend the holidays in Miami with their daughter and son-in-law. She'd planned her departure two weeks ago, and the knowledge that she, at least, would be spared, not by any violation of his trust but by fate, had made Abe Stern's anguish just a little easier to bear in the past few hours.

"I don't know if I'm going."

"What do you mean, not going?" There was an intimation of panic in the Mayor's astonished reply. "You got to go."

"Why are you in such a hurry I should leave town? You got a girl or something?"

"Ruth! Look at me! Thirty-two years we've been married. Have I ever done something like that to you? What girl would want me anyway? Get the plane."

Ruth poured herself a cup of black coffee and sipped it thoughtfully. She was a year younger than Abe, her hair thin and white now, clinging to her head like sad wisps of angel's beard left behind on an old Christmas tree abandoned in the back yard. "I was kidding, Abe. About the girl." Her dark eyes gazed at her husband over the rim of the coffee cup she held before her lips. "But something's wrong, Abe. You've got something on your mind. Must be a big problem."

Stern sighed. After so many years of marriage there were no secrets anymore. "Yeah," he answered, "I got a problem all right. But I can't tell you about it. Please, Ruth, get the plane. Go down to Miami—for me."

His wife got up and moved behind him, letting her arms hang down until she could cradle Stern's cheeks in her aged and arthritic fingers. "Don't tell me, Abe. It's all right. But, you got a problem, this is where I belong. Not in Miami."

Stern reached up and clasped her bony hands. Outside, through the dining-room windows, the first gleamings of dawn were reflected off the dark channel of Hell Gate, creeping across Ward's Island and onto the tenements of Queens.

How lovely it all is, the Mayor of New York reflected, his hands tightening around those of his wife, how lovely it is.

At the underground command post where Abe Stern had spent most of his sleepless night, the whole thrust of the mammoth search effort had now taken on a new dimension. All the manpower available was now concentrated on the most extensive manhunt any American city had ever known, the pursuit of Whalid, Kamal and Laila Dajani.

Al Feldman had been up all night coordinating the NYPD's contribution to the search. With three identified suspects in hand, the decision had been taken to throw the full resources of the 24,000-

man police force into the search. The Dajanis were being described, to keep the secret of the bomb, as cop killers. Right now in every station house, in every precinct in the five boroughs, the patrolmen coming onto the day shift were being handed photos of the Dajanis, part of the thousands printed overnight. The men coming off the night shift were put into civilian clothes, given photos and held on duty. The headquarters switchboard was ordering the men and women of the four-to-twelve to report to their precincts at 10 A.M. so that by midday every police officer in New York City would be out looking for the three Palestinians. Forget everything, they were being ordered: burglars, traffic and parking violations, purse snatchers, junkies, whores, fighting drunks. Just find some trace of the neighborhood in which the three alleged cop killers had last been seen.

Feldman had laid down basic guidelines for the search pattern, based on the conviction that no matter how hard they had tried to avoid it, the Dajanis would have had to come into contact with certain aspects of New York life. Every newsstand vendor, every druggist, every counterman, cashier and short-order cook at every hamburger joint, fast-food franchise, pancake house, soda fountain, pizza parlor and Hero sandwich shop in the city was to be shown the Dajanis' photos. So, too, were the owners, clerks, salesmen and checkout-counter operators of every food store in town from the crummiest mom-and-pop store in Sheepshead Bay to the biggest Grand Union supermarket in Queens. Pushcart operators selling soft drinks and sandwiches off the sidewalks were to be queried, the attendants in all the big public lavatories, in the city's Turkish baths.

The vice cops were all brought in and ordered to check the city's countless prostitutes, massage parlors, "contact" centers, fleabag hotels to see if the Dajanis had patronized any of them. A similar effort against the city's dope dealers was assigned to the Narcotics Squad.

Patrolmen were assigned to all the toll booths, inbound and outbound, at all the bridges and tunnels with orders to scrutinize the passengers of every car passing through them. The three thousand men of the Transit Police were fully mobilized and assigned to watch every turnstile and station entrance in the subway system. The muggers might have a field day in New York's subways this Tuesday, December 15, but the Dajanis would have no better than a fifty-fifty chance of using them without getting caught.

The thousands of FBI agents freed from the pier and personnel searches were assigned to cover every hotel, roominghouse and car-rental agency in the city. Others were assigned New York's real-estate agencies with orders to validate every lease that had been signed in the past six months, looking for the place where the bomb might be hidden. Still others were teamed with the crime-prevention specialists in each of the NYPD's precincts, telephoning contacts and names on each precinct's business index file for any indication from shopowners and small merchants of new, suspicious activities in their neighborhoods. FBI agents paired with NEST scientists with hand-held Geiger counters were instructed to comb methodically all the city's abandoned buildings.

There had been a bitter debate just before dawn over the potential use of the media. Feldman had urged giving the Dajanis' photos and the cop-killer cover story to the papers and television stations. That way they could have mobilized most of the city's population in the search. He had been overruled by Eastman in Washington. The National Security Assistant's mistrust of Qaddafi after the scanner incident was total; there was every chance one or all of the Dajanis were kamikaze volunteers baby-sitting the bomb, and the sight of their photos on television might cause them to panic and set it off.

Now, with his orders out, his plans set, the Chief had nothing to do but think and wait. For ten minutes he had been doing just that, sipping black coffee and trying to remember what he might have overlooked. Only by the greatest act of will was he able to keep himself from picking up the phone on his desk, calling his home out in Forest Hills and quietly but firmly telling his wife to get the hell out of there.

He was thinking about doing just that when he saw the Police Commissioner, red-eyed and exhausted, standing over him. I wonder how Bannion is dealing with this one, Feldman asked himself. The Commissioner had ostentatiously moved back to Manhattan from the Island after his appointment to "demonstrate a sense of solidarity with the people of New York." I'll bet, the Chief told himself maliciously, Marie Bannion's demonstrating her solidarity with the people of New York right now barrel-assing through Yonkers in an unmarked police car.

Then, looking into his Commissioner's blue eyes alight with the same fright he felt, Feldman was ashamed.

"What do you think, Chief?" Bannion asked. "Can we make it?"

Feldman took a swallow of his bitter black coffee and stared up at Bannion. For a moment he sat there looking at him, thinking, appraising both the situation and his answer. Why lie? the Chief told himself. Why con him or myself or anybody else?

"No, Commissioner," he answered, "not in the time we got left, no way."

Angry and frustrated, Angelo Rocchia stalked the huge parking area of the Hertz Rent-A-Truck agency at 354 Fourth Avenue, Brooklyn, its expanse filled with a motley collection of trucks painted not in the familiar Hertz yellow and blue but in the commercial colors of the agency's leasing clients: the Omaha Hotel Supply Company, Junior's Restaurant, Sabrett's Kosher Frankfurters, F. Rabinowitz Caterers.

It was already close to midmorning, and, as he had expected he was going to be, he was nothing more than a glorified gofer for the FBI forensic experts pulling apart the truck the Dajanis had used to pick up their load of barrels at the Brooklyn Army Terminal pier only a few blocks away. In fact, he wasn't even a gofer. The FBI men were so studiously absorbed in their work they had completely ignored him.

The truck was lying in a hundred pieces on the floor of one of the agency's three garages. It had been sealed off to its curious employees and turned into a miniature crime laboratory. Even Angelo had to admire the thoroughness of the FBI effort. Every one of the thirty-seven bumps, scrapes, indentations on the truck's body and fenders, some so small they were barely visible, had been circled in red. Spectrographic-analysis equipment had been flown up from Washington and set up to examine paint chips from each, hoping to find one that would reveal some clue as to where the truck had gone when the Dajanis had rented it on Friday. The young couple who had taken it out Saturday had been brought in and grilled to see if the Dajanis had left anything behind, a matchbox, a restaurant napkin or carton, a map, anything that might have suggested where they had been.

The tires had been pulled apart, every speck of dirt and grime impregnated in their treads vacuumed out and studied for the one peculiarity that might indicate a particular place in which the truck had been parked. The floor mat had been carefully vacuumed and the results studied in the search for a speck of soil from the Dajanis' shoes that might indicate the kind of ground over which they had been walking.

Nothing was too outlandish. The FBI had learned that painters had been working on Friday on the Willis Avenue Bridge linking the Bronx and upper Manhattan. They had gone over the van's roof with microscopes to see if even a speck of paint could be found there to establish that the truck had used that route into the city. Someone had been through the computers at the Parking Violations Bureau at Park Avenue South and Thirty-first looking for unpaid parking tickets. That was SOP in New York since the Son of Sam murders.

It was marvelous, Angelo thought, precise, scientific and marvelous; yet he knew very well that up until now the whole staggering FBI effort had revealed virtually nothing. The FBI had rapidly determined with photographs that the rental had indeed been made by Kamal and Whalid just before ten Friday morning. They had explained that they were going to move some furniture to a new apartment. That in itself indicated that someone had briefed them on rental procedures, because had they said they were going to make a pickup of commercial goods from the docks their stolen driver's license wouldn't have worked. They would have needed a commercial license. Their whole effort would have ended there. The desk clerk in the trailer that served as the renting office had remembered that Whalid had inquired about the load the Econoline van they'd been offered could carry and had seemed relieved to learn it could handle five thousand pounds with no problems.

They had left, according to the time automatically punched onto the rental agreement, at 9:57. Kamal had returned the truck, alone, at 6:17, after the rental office had closed. The only other precise thing they had on it was the time, 11:22, that the guard at the gate down on the pier had signed them out with their load on his dispatch sheet.

Angelo stared across Fourth Avenue to the kids playing in an open schoolyard, the red brick outline of Engine Company 23 and the spire of the Church of St. Thomas Aquinas. He knew this area. Forty, fifty years ago, the two- and three-story turn-of-the-century tenements had housed an Italian neighborhood, heavy Mob turf.

He was lost in his recollections when he heard a voice beside him hissing, "Hey, what are you guys looking for in there? A murderer?"

"Yeah," Angelo answered. He recognized the yardman who had checked in the van. "A murderer who hasn't got around to murdering anybody yet." Casually he draped a friendly arm around the man's shoulders. "Listen, let's just go through what happened last Friday night one more time."

"Hey." The man's irritation was evident. "I told them guys in there already. Friday this place"—he gestured at the cluttered yard—"was a goddamn ice-skating rink. What the hell am I going to do, waste my time talking to some guy checking in a van when I gotta clean this place up?"

Angelo resumed his pacing and his recollections. Suddenly he stopped. Snow and ice. It was a proven fact. You could look it up on the computer. Snowstorms were hell on the accident rate, particularly the first snowstorm of the year. And what, he asked himself, do Arabs know about driving on snow? They didn't know snow from shit.

The men waiting for the President in the NSC conference room were as exhausted as he was. A few had managed to catnap an hour or two in a chair; most were living on coffee and their dwindling reserves of nervous energy. As soon as he sat down, Eastman reviewed the one substantial development of the last two hours. The Chairman of the Central Committee had just sent a report from the Russian ambassador in Tripoli. On Soviet insistence he had pleaded with Qaddafi to resume negotiations with Washington. The Libyan had been absolutely unyielding.

"At least, for once we're getting some help from our Soviet friends," the President noted grimly. "What I'm interested in now is the status of the Rapid Deployment Force," he told Eastman. "Get the military in here."

Three major generals of the Army, the Air Force and the Marines appeared at Eastman's side at the summons of the buzzer. They were responsible for planning the forcible removal of the Israeli settlements from the West Bank. The Marine took charge of the briefing. The 82nd Airborne Division at Fort Bragg, North Carolina, and the Second Armored Brigade in Fort Hood, Texas, he reported, had been mobilized during the night. At dawn, men

384

and equipment had been loaded onto their waiting C-5As and were airborne now in twelve separate flights en route to Germany. The lead flight was already far out over the Atlantic Ocean.

The Marine stepped forward and pushed a button that lifted the covering from one of the television sets on the wall. On the screen was an image showing the position of the Sixth Fleet Marine Amphibious Force, two helicopter carriers and four attack transports. They were twenty nautical miles from the Lebanese seacoast, just northeast of Beirut.

"Mr. President," Admiral Fuller, the Chairman of the Joint Chiefs, said, "we've got some decisions to make right now. The first concerns those flights from Fort Bragg and Fort Hood. Do we keep them en route to their restaging bases in Germany or do we turn them back? The first flights are coming up to their stop-or-go line."

"We've received Chancellor Schmidt's clearance to use our fields in Germany for restaging and refueling," the Secretary of State reported. The President had expected Schmidt's approval, but it was still a formality which had to be honored.

"The second decision involves landing the Marines," Fuller said. "General, explain."

The Marine stepped to the television set and indicated the map of the Mediterranean shoreline that now appeared there. "We have three possible landing areas, Mr. President. Here in southern Lebanon at Tyre, north of Beirut at Junieh Bay where the Christian Separatist movement is centered or up in Latakia in Syria. Tyre is closest to the scene, but if the Israelis oppose us from the outset we'll have a grave problem giving our beachhead adequate air cover. Our current plan is to use the aircraft from the Sixth Fleet on a shuttle basis, putting them down at Jordanian airports to refuel."

"Mr. President." Again it was the Secretary of State. "We've discussed this with King Hussein and he has agreed to let us use his airfields and has promised absolute secrecy until our decision is taken."

"How about the units of the RDF?" the President asked. "Where would you propose to put them in?"

"The only feasible spot, sir, is Damascus," Admiral Fuller replied. "They've got the airfield facilities we'd need for our heavy equipment, and it's astride the ground communications to the West Bank."

"Has this been discussed with Assad?"

"No, sir," the Secretary of State answered. "We thought that had better wait for your go-ahead. We don't have the same confidential relationship with him that we have with the King. Although, in the circumstances, it's hardly likely he'll object.

"All right." The President sat forward in his chair. "Move the RDF units on to Germany. Hold them on alert status ready to go on to the Middle East as soon as we give the orders. Brief the ambassador in Damascus on the situation and what we'll want from Assad, but tell him not to contact him until he receives the order."

He glanced at the Marine Corps General. "Set your planning up to put your forces into Junieh Bay. They can count on a friendly reception there, and if we decide to go ahead with this, cutting down on casualties is going to be a lot more important than a few hours' time." He was pensive a moment, then turned to the Secretary of State. "Prepare a message to be sent to the Chairman on the red line to Moscow over my signature telling him what we're doing and why. Ask him to see that it's relayed to Qaddafi. Do the same thing via our chargé in Tripoli. We don't want Qaddafi to have any misconceptions about these moves that would lead him to act precipitously. And tell the Chairman we would welcome his putting maximum pressure on Qaddafi to at least extend his ultimatum."

"How about the Israelis, Mr. President?" the Secretary of State asked. "Shouldn't we tell them too? If they realize we're not bluffing they might be more amenable to the idea of getting those settlements out of there themselves and avoiding this whole ghastly mess."

"Sir," Admiral Fuller countered, "if we're going to have a showdown with them, I'd sure hate to tell them eight or ten hours ahead of time what we're going to do."

His words were followed by an awkward silence as everyone in the room waited for the President to reply.

"Don't worry, Admiral," he said firmly. "We don't have to tell them. They'll find out for themselves."

A pair of military policemen escorted Grace Knowland down the broad wooden staircase of New York's Seventh Regiment Armory toward a lean officer in khakis waiting at the foot of the stairs.

"Major McAndrews, First Army PIO," he said, his face radiant with the studied congeniality of a seasoned PR man. "We're certainly grateful to you for the interest you're taking in what we are doing here."

He led her along the basement corridor to a well-lit office. "This is Major Calhoun," he said, introducing her to a bespectacled man rising to greet her from behind his desk. "He's our operations officer."

The two men offered Grace a chair. "How do you like your coffee?" McAndrews asked jovially.

"Black. Straight up."

While McAndrews hurried off to get it, Calhoun casually put his feet on his desk, lit a cigarette and waved at the maps spread over his office walls.

"Basically," he began, "what we're doing here is having a look at the resources we have in the First Army area which can provide federal military relief assistance to New York in the event of natural disasters, such as the snowstorm you had here last week. Or a power failure or a hurricane. Essentially, we're making an inventory of our capabilities to provide rapid federal disaster assistance to the city."

The major got up, took a pointer and began to tick off on the maps the First Army's military installations.

"We begin with McGuire Air Force Base down here in New Jersey," he said. "They can handle Starlifters, but, of course, they're not much help in getting snow off the streets, are they?" The major laughed at his little joke and continued his well-rehearsed briefing. It had been carefully prepared at Federal Plaza and designed to last half an hour, long enough, the FBI had calculated, to exhaust the journalistic possibilities inherent in snow removal.

"Any questions?" he asked, concluding.

"Yes," Grace answered. "I'd like to go in and talk to your people actually working on the exercise."

The officer coughed nervously. "Well, that's a little bit difficult at the moment. They're all working, and since reaction time is an important factor in our calculations, we wouldn't want to interrupt them. It might skewer our results, so to speak. Tell you what I'll

387

do, though. If you come back at three tomorrow when we wind up, I'll see to it you have all the time with them you want."

"Exclusively?"

"No one else is in on it."

"Fair enough." Grace gave the officer a satisfied smile and closed the steno pad she had used for her notes.

McAndrews offered to escort her out of the armory. As they passed through the huge assembly area where her son played tennis, something odd struck her. A panel of rope netting, high enough to stop everything but the wildest of lobs, sealed off the tennis courts from the rest of the armory's main floor. There was nothing unusual about that. The net was always there to keep stray balls from bouncing around among the olive-drab vehicles of the National Guard unit that used the armory. Except this morning there were no olive-drab vehicles behind it, only half a dozen rented Avis, Hertz and Ryder trucks.

"What are all those rented trucks doing here?" she asked McAndrews. "Are they part of your exercise?"

"Yes," the Major answered. "We used them to bring some material in. Infrastructure support."

"Since when," Grace inquired, "is the Army so wealthy it can afford to go out and rent trucks with the taxpayers' money instead of using its own vehicles?"

Major McAndrews gave another nervous little laugh. "Well, ma'am, our military vehicles are pretty cumbersome to maneuver around crowded cities like Manhattan. They're apt to tie up traffic something fierce. So we use these rented trucks. To avoid inconveniencing the civilian population, so to speak." The FBI agent masquerading as an Army major smiled, immensely pleased by the nimbleness of his reply.

"I see." Grace offered him her hand. "Oh, by the way, there's a young MP lieutenant here named Daly who was very kind to my son last night. I promised I'd have a cup of coffee with him if I came back to do a story. Do you suppose someone could find him for me?"

"How many Hertz trucks you figure there are moving in New York on any given day?" Angelo Rocchia addressed his question to the young Irishman running the Fourth Avenue truck-rental agency.

388

"We're doing thirty-five to forty a day right here, and we got two other Brooklyn locations. You add in Manhattan, the Bronx, Queens. Man, I don't know. Four, five hundred at the least. Maybe more on a big day. Why?"

"Just wondering."

Angelo was sitting in the manager's cramped office. Through an interior window he could follow the activities of the FBI forensic people in the garage. They're doing everything they can with that truck, he thought, but I don't think you can count on it. Not unless we get more time to find this barrel of gas than I think we do. Before him was the steadily thickening accumulation of reports of the FBI's operation. One file was missing. Classified, the head of the FBI forensic team had told him.

What was so important in this that the government had to classify it, wouldn't let the people who had to find the barrel know what it was? Angelo grabbed a peanut from his pocket and flipped it into his mouth, pondering that, then once again the idea that had struck him a few minutes before in the yard popped into his head. Far out, he thought, really far out. Still, I got nothing to do here except wait for some son of a bitch from the FBI to ask me to run out for coffee. A bunch of telephone calls is all, he told himself. What else do I have to do?

He took out his notepad and picked up the telephone.

"First Precinct?" he asked. "Give me your I-24 man." The I-24 man was the precinct desk clerk, the officer in charge of the station-house blotter which recorded the daily flow of crimes in each of the seventy-two precincts of the New York Police Department from wife beatings and drunken brawls to murders.

"Hey," he said when he had identified himself. "Pull out your Sixty-one sheets for last Friday and tell me if you got any Sixty-ones on there for leaving the scene."

Grace Knowland smiled affectionately at the earnest young officer opposite her. They were sipping coffee on the stools of a Madison Avenue drugstore, the lieutenant shyly telling Grace about himself and just as shyly hinting at how much he'd like to see her again.

"Of course, I'm not really an MP," Lieutenant Daly said. "I'm infantry. This is temporary duty."

"Well, you were lucky to get it. It must be tremendous to be assigned to New York just like that."

"Not as tremendous as you'd think. I mean, they moved us here in such a hurry, we have to sleep on the floor in there in sleeping bags and live off cold C rations."

"What!" Grace's anger was that of a million mothers listening to their soldier sons' woes. "You mean the U.S. Army can afford to rent a bunch of Hertz and Avis trucks and leave them sitting around that armory all day long and they can't afford to give you boys a hot meal?"

"Oh, those aren't Army trucks."

"They're not?"

"No. It's the civilians running that exercise in there that use them."

"Civilians? Why should they want trucks like that to study snow removal?"

"Beats me. They have some kind of technical equipment they put in there. Then they go out and drive around for hours. Probably measuring something. Pollution, maybe."

Grace swallowed the last sips of her coffee, reflecting thoughtfully on his words. "Probably. Here." She reached for the check. "Let me have that. Damn!" she groaned, picking her loose change from her pocketbook. "I think I left my compact down in the major's office. Could you escort me back down to look for it?"

Ten minutes later she gave the young officer a friendly kiss on the cheek and ran down the armory steps, waving to a taxi moving up Park.

As she slipped into the back seat, she pulled out her notebook and scribbled a number on its cover. It was for that scrap of information, not a missing compact, that she had returned to the armory. The number was the New Jersey license of one of the rented Avis trucks parked on the armory floor.

Abe Stern surveyed the frightened and dismayed men around him at the underground command post below Foley Square as Quentin Dewing began their now hourly review of the situation. It was already 10:30 A.M. and the almost jubilant atmosphere that had accompanied the dispatch of thousands of New York police officers with their photographs of the three Dajanis onto the sidewalks of the city had disappeared as the minutes had ticked by without a single conclusive lead or sighting.

The Mayor tried hard to concentrate on the reports of the men at the conference table, but he couldn't. All he could think about were the people, the people for whose lives he was responsible walking on the streets above the command post, going into the courthouses, the subways, sitting in offices, in City Hall Park, up in the towers of the World Trade Center or the crowded flats of the Alfred E. Smith housing project. Down here they were going to live if that awful device, wherever it was, went off. They had provisions, real provisions, not the rotten and inedible protein crackers in the shelters. They would allow them to survive. Eventually, they would be able to crawl out of here into whatever satanic landscape was left on the ground above them.

What about the people up there? What, Abe Stern had kept asking himself, is my moral obligation to them? He had at his disposal a facility that was unique in the United States. It was called Line 1,000 and had originally been set up by John Lindsay in the hot and fearful summers of the sixties. It was a direct radio and television link from his desk at City Hall and his study at Gracie Mansion to the control desk of WNYC, the city's broadcasting station. On his order, the WNYC desk man would make three calls to the three primary Emergency Broadcasting System stations, WNBC, WCBS and WABC. All three stations on receiving that call would push an emergency alert button which set an alarm bell ringing in the control room of every radio and television station in the New York area. When it went off, those stations were required by law to interrupt their regular programming and request their audiences to stand by for an emergency message. Within two minutes of picking up Line 1,000 the Mayor's voice could be heard live on over one hundred radio and television stations. Not even the President could address his countrymen so rapidly in an emergency.

Perhaps, Abe Stern pondered, I should go on the air and tell the people to get out of the city any way they can. That idiot Oglethorpe they had sent up from Washington yesterday had said that panic, the classic fire-in-the-nightclub, everyone-rushes-for-the-door-and-no-one-gets-out kind of panic, might not be applicable to this situation. People tended to behave much better in great crises than you expected them to do. And even if Oglethorpe was wrong and there was pandemonium, at least, as he'd told the President yesterday, he'd have saved some lives.

His thoughts were interrupted by a babble of noise from the squawk box on the conference table. Since last night they had been linked by a direct line to the men and women trying to manage the crisis from the NSC conference room, and he recognized the President's voice inquiring anxiously about the progress of their search. He's counting on us, Stern thought, listening to the worried string of words pouring from the box. All that confident "Don't worry, Abe, we'll talk him out of it" business of yesterday had disappeared. Three times the Chief Executive reported that they had tried to reestablish contact with Qaddafi in the past hour. Nothing had worked; the Libyan remained adamant in his refusal to talk. The President sketched out the military preparations he had ordered for a forcible removal of the West Bank settlements if it came to that. Stern paled. He was anything but an ardent Zionist, but the prospect of his countrymen and the Israelis coming into conflict due to the diabolical plotting of this zealot in Libya sickened him. Still, he thought, if that's the price we have to pay to save this city, so be it.

Grace Knowland pushed open the doors of the New York Times Building and strode quickly up to the security guards barring the way to the elevators. As usual, the lobby of the most influential newspaper in the world was vibrant with an air of subdued purpose. From one wall, a marble bust of the *Times*'s founder, Adolph Ochs, surveyed the passing throng with grim, unsmiling mien, a reminder to all who entered its precincts of the high sense of purpose with which he had endowed his paper. The front page of Ochs's journal still bore his slogan, "All the news that's fit to print," and six million trees a year fell as a consequence of the determined efforts of the *Times*'s editors to honor his imperious command. From the reception rooms of the Kremlin to gossip culled in the locker rooms of Madison Square Garden, the seventy-two-page paper on sale in the vending machine opposite Ochs's bust this December morning contained more news, more statistics, more figures, more results, more interviews, more analysis and more commentary than any other newspaper in the world.

Grace's destination was the newsroom on the third floor. It

392

sprawled over an acre and a half, an area so vast that its editors had, on occasion, employed binoculars to keep track of their reporters' movements and loudspeakers to summon them from their desks. Today, the place looked more like the actuarial clerk's bullpen at Metropolitan Life than a set for *Front Page*. Diffused overhead lighting bathed the place in its sterile glow; chest-high partitions broke the area into a series of little mazes; there was enough fake-wood Formica around to equip half a dozen fast-food franchises, and, final assault on the sensibilities of the paper's old-time reporters, there was even carpeting on the floor.

Grace's first gesture was to telephone Avis's New York headquarters. She quickly obtained the information she wanted: the truck she had noted at the armory belonged to the company's New Brunswick, New Jersey, truck-rental agency. Catching the bureaucracy of New York City in the heedless expenditure of the taxpayers' money was one of her special pleasures, and from the instant she spotted the rental trucks lined up on the armory floor her reporter's instincts had told her that once again she had caught some government agency stupidly squandering the city's meager resources.

She picked up the phone again and dialed the New Brunswick agency, glancing around as she did to be sure no one was near enough to overhear her. What she was about to do was considered a sin at *The New York Times*—not a mortal sin, perhaps, but a good, solid, venial one.

"This is Desk Officer Lucia Harris of the New York State Police, Pauling Barracks," she told the girl who answered the phone. "We've had a motor-vehicle collision here involving one of your vehicles. The driver was DOA at Pauling General, and unfortunately he didn't have any ID on him. Can you give me the details on your rental agreement so we can run a trace on him?" She gave the girl the number of the truck.

"It'll take a moment. Shall I call you back?"

"That's all right. I'll hold."

A few minutes later the Avis girl was on the phone again. "His driver's license gives him as John McClintock, 104 Clear View Avenue, Las Vegas. It's Nevada license 432701-6, issued May 4, 1979. Valid until May 4, 1983."

Grace jotted the information down on her notepad. Why, in God's name, would anybody look for a snow-removal expert in

Las Vegas? She glanced at her watch. It was a few minutes past eleven, just after nine in Las Vegas. From directory assistance she got the telephone number of a John McClintock at the address on the agreement. His phone rang, unanswered, for a long time before a woman replied.

"May I speak to Mr. John McClintock, please?"

"I'm sorry. He's not here," the voice replied.

"I see. Is he in Las Vegas?"

The woman hesitated. "Who's calling? This is Mrs. McClintock."

"Oh," Grace answered quickly. "This is the First National City Bank in New York. We have a transfer here for him and I need his instructions on how to handle it. Could you tell me where I can reach him?"

"I'm afraid I can't." Mrs. McClintock replied. "He's out of town for a few days."

"Is there some number where I could contact him?"

This time there was a long pause before Mrs. McClintock answered. "Well, I don't think I'm really allowed to tell you that. He's away on government business. You'd better contact his office down at the Federal Building."

Grace thanked Mrs. McClintock and hung up, feeling, as she did, a nervous chill in her intestines, the first flow of her reporter's adrenalin warning her that something was very wrong with this story. A few minutes later, she was through to the Federal Building in Las Vegas.

"Q Section Safeguards, O'Reilly speaking," a voice answered when Grace got McClintock's extension. Safeguards, she asked herself, puzzled. Safeguards against what?

"Mr. McClintock, please."

"This is his desk, but he's out of town for a few days."

Grace gave a little giggle which, she hoped, would convince O'Reilly that he was dealing with a dumb woman. "Oh," she said, "what's he off safeguarding?"

"Who's calling?" The voice was chill and formal.

Again Grace invoked Citibank. "Can you tell me where I can reach him?"

"No, I can't. The nature of his business and his whereabouts are classified information."

Stunned, Grace set the telephone back in its socket. Why would

394

the U.S. government feel it had to make a snow-removal exercise in New York classified information? And bring in people from Las Vegas to work on it? My God, she realized, those trucks have nothing to do with snow removal! That's just a cover.

She thought of Angelo's phrase last night, "a typical detective's day, running around looking for a needle in a haystack." And the Mayor. Why had the President given him a Presidential jet to fly back to New York yesterday?

She called Angelo's office. There was no answer. She took out the secret NYPD telephone directory he had given her and frantically began to call, one after another, the offices of a dozen senior detectives. Not a single one answered.

Two minutes later, Grace was standing by the desk of Deputy Managing Editor Art Gelb. She waited until he had finished talking to another reporter, then leaned down to him. "Art," she whispered. "I've got something I've got to talk to you about right away. I think it may be very, very big."

There had been six "sixty-ones," crimes of leaving the scene of an accident, recorded on the daily crime sheets of the seventy-three precincts of the New York Police Department on Friday, December 11. Because of the snowstorm that number was, as Angelo had guessed it would be, well above the Department's daily average. One of the six was a serious case under active investigation. It involved an elderly black woman knocked over by a motorcyclist on the pedestrian crossing at Broadway and Cathedral Parkway and transported to St. Luke's Hospital with a broken hip. The five remaining cases all bore the same notation under the heading "Disposition": "Detective McCann is assigned to this case." To the outsider, he might well have appeared to be the busiest investigative officer in the New York Police Department.

He in fact did not exist. Detective McCann was the wastebasket. His name after each of those complaints indicated the sentiments of the NYPD toward such a minor crime as leaving the scene of an accident involving a scraped fender: a lot of paperwork for nothing.

Angelo had covered nineteen precincts and four of the recorded incidents when he called the Tenth Precinct in west midtown, the area in which he had conducted his early-morning hunt for a hit-and-run driver years before.

"Yeah, I got a Sixty-one here," the clerk replied. "Procter and Gamble salesman got his fender scraped."

"OK," Angelo said. "Read it to me."

"Complainant M-42 indicates that between the hours of one and two P.M., Friday, December 11, his motor vehicle, a 1978 Pontiac bearing New York number plate 349271 was parked in front of 149 West Thirty-seventh Street, and when he came out he observed the fender had a crease in it. Under his windshield an unknown person or persons had left a note stating: 'A yellow truck hit you and took off.' Complainant interviewed Friday, December 11, Tenth Precinct by Officer Natale. Detective McCann assigned to this case with request it be marked closed pending a further development, at which time proper and prompt police action will be taken."

Angelo couldn't resist a laugh at the Department's bureaucratese. "Tell me about that 'proper and prompt police action' you got in mind," he remarked. "That note really said a yellow truck?"

"Yeah."

"OK. Give me the salesman's name and address."

On the other side of the United States the first warm rays of sunshine glinted off the great green rolls of Pacific surf crashing onto the Santa Monica seashore. An early-morning jogger had just turned off the beach and headed up the cliff toward his seaside cottage. He was a hundred yards from his front door when he heard the clatter of his telephone.

Still panting, the West Coast correspondent of *The New York Times* grabbed the phone and instantly recognized the caller from the intense, confidential murmur rippling from his receiver. "I've got something very important for you," Art Gelb told him. "Get your stringer in Reno down to Las Vegas right away. There's a John McClintock who works in some kind of a safeguards section in the Federal Building on Highland Street there. I want your guy to find out urgently exactly what it is this guy McClintock does and call me back as soon as he's got it."

Angelo Rocchia eased the telephone back into its cradle, thinking hard as he did it. The Procter & Gamble salesman whose

396

fender had been scraped was out making his calls on the West Side of Manhattan, his office had just told Angelo. He wouldn't be phoning in before nightfall. There was no way to spot his car on the city's streets; the Cincinnati soapmakers had long ago abandoned the practice of branding their salesmen's vehicles with the company's familiar trademark of a smiling man in a crescent moon against a dark-blue field of stars.

The only suggestion the helpful office manager had been able to make was that if Angelo wanted to reach him in a hurry he call on De Pasquale's Hero Sandwich Bar on West Thirty-fifth just off Ninth Avenue. The salesmen working the West Side gathered there for coffee and Danish around eleven. He would probably be there, and if he wasn't someone who could pin down the neighborhood where he was working probably would be.

Four hundred Hertz trucks out there, Angelo thought, and how many yellow trucks on top of that? It was a very, very wild unscientific idea. He glanced into the garage at the busy array of FBI forensic experts. Not the kind of idea they were apt to appreciate. Almost reluctantly, he heaved his heavy frame from the Hertz manager's chair and stalked into the garage with his deceptively awkward gait.

It had been the salesman's rear left fender that had gotten the scrape, so it would probably have been the truck's right side that had done it. Angelo surveyed the pieces of the right side of the van lined against the wall of the garage, counting on them fourteen red circles, each one numbered, each representing a different bump or scrape. He picked up the sheaves of spectrographic analysis that corresponded to the numbers. Inconclusive, just as he had thought they'd be. They had identified positively traces of three brands of paint on the truck's right panels, two used by General Motors, one by Ford. Together, the models that employed those three brands of paint represented just over fifty-five percent of the cars on the highway. A lot of help, Angelo mused, a real lot of help.

"Something I can do for you, Detective?"

The speaker was the agent in charge of the forensic team. His words contained, the New Yorker noted, about as much warmth as those of a bank security guard questioning a teenage Puerto Rican loitering in his lobby.

"No," Angelo replied. "Just looking around."

"Well, why don't you wait out there in the manager's office

where you'll be more comfortable? We'll let you know if we've got anything for you.''

I'm about as welcome in here, Angelo thought, as an archbishop in an abortion mill. Was it because of those classified papers they'd pulled out of the files? Or just the feds' traditional mistrust of other law-enforcement agencies?

In a corner of the garage, he noted his young partner earnestly talking to one of his colleagues. He had barely gotten the time of day from him since they arrived. No one seems to want me around here, or anyplace else for that matter, he reflected bitterly, thinking back to his telephone conversation of the night before. He strolled over to Rand and tossed a conspiratorial arm over his shoulder like a coach who's about to send a tight end onto the field with a critical third downplay.

"Come here, kid?" he growled, edging him away from his fellow agents. There was no question of telling him what he really had in mind. The young agent was much too procedures-conscious for that. He'd say, "Have headquarters send out someone else," and that wasn't Angelo's idea at all. On the other hand, one thing you could probably count on Rand for was a sense of solidarity, the "We're all cops together, so don't rat to the boss" thing. He would lose Rand's respect, but why the hell should he care about that?

"Listen, kid," he whispered. "Cover for me for an hour or so, will you? Your guys got nothing for me and—" he winked at the FBI agent—"I got a little something over here, a little biscuit I haven't seen for a while. I'm going to just drop in and say hello to her."

Rand whitened in shock more than anger. "My God, Angelo, you can't do that! Don't you realize how desperately important it is to find this—" He was about to say "bomb" when he caught himself.

"This what?" Angelo asked. There it was again, this thing they kept dropping in front of him, then pulling away.

"The barrel of gas we're looking for."

"Tell me, kid, what's so secret about chlorine gas the government has to classify stuff on it? Or is it really chlorine gas they got in that barrel?"

"Of course it is."

For a second Angelo gazed at him, his eyes as appraising as they had been twenty-four hours earlier scrutinizing the dip in the front

398

seat of his car. Then he jerked his head toward the agent in charge. "Your friend over there wants somebody to run out for coffee and a Danish while I'm gone, tell him they got a diner just up the street. I got the very clear message that's all he figures a New York cop is good for anyway."

"Angelo." Rand was almost begging. "Going away like that is like . . ." The young man paused, trying to think of the worst example he could cite. "Like a soldier deserting his post in wartime."

The New Yorker snorted, squeezing the young agent's shoulders as he did. "Don't worry about it, kid. I'll see if she's got a friend for you."

Arthur Gelb paced his office in the third-floor newsroom of *The New York Times*. The deputy managing editor was a lanky, intense man, all kinetic energy and raw nerve ends, a man who kept his staff in a state of constant tension—some would have said terror—with a nonstop flow of ideas, suggestions and queries. Like the paper he so proudly represented, he was not so much a conservative as he was a man devoted to a certain notion of responsibility. Above all, he was dedicated to the proposition that if it hadn't happened in the pages of *The New York Times* it hadn't happened at all, and to his growing anger he sensed that something very important was happening in his city and the *Times* didn't know about it.

Gelb suddenly stopped his pacing. Rushing through the maze of the newsroom was one of the dozen men he had sent to scour the precincts to find out what was going on after Grace's whispered conversation. On his face Gelb could read that special sense of purpose always present on a young reporter's visage when he knows he's about to impress his editor.

"This is what's going on!" he gasped, out of breath, dropping the photos of the Dajanis onto Gelb's desk. "They're Palestinians. Cop killers. Everyone in town's out looking for them."

Gelb picked up the photographs one by one, studying each of the three in turn. "Who did they kill?"

"Two patrolmen in Chicago two weeks ago."

"Chicago?" Gelb frowned. Since when had New York's police been so devoted to their brethren in the Windy City? "Get Grace Knowland for me, will you? I want to make a phone call."

Gelb passed the three pictures to her when she entered his office. "These are your needle in the haystack. Three Palestinians that are supposed to have killed two cops out in Chicago two weeks ago. Except there hasn't been a cop killed in Chicago for three months. I just checked with the *Tribune*."

As Grace studied the pictures, Gelb picked up his phone and dialed Patricia McGuire, the Deputy Police Commissioner for Public Information. She took his call immediately. New York City officials didn't keep the *Times*'s deputy managing editor on hold.

"Patty, I want to know what the hell's going on. There's a fake snow-removal exercise up in the Seventh Regiment Armory that's got nothing to do with getting the snow off the streets. And half the cops in the city are out looking for three Palestinians who didn't do what you told them they did. What's going on, Patty? You've got something here, some kind of major Palestinian terrorist action, and I want to know what it is."

There was a long, pained silence when he had finished speaking.

"I'm sorry, Arthur," the woman answered. "I'm afraid I don't have the authority to answer your question. Are you in your office?"

"I am."

"I'll ask the Commissioner to call you right back."

The odor of salami, of garlic, of provolone, olive oil and fresh peppers swept over Angelo like a veil of incense as he stepped inside De Pasquale's Hero Sandwich Shop on West Thirty-fifth Street. The detective took a deep, approving breath, then surveyed the place: a lunch counter with a dozen red moleskin stools, half of them occupied; a few booths in back, a counterman slapping heros together in readiness for the lunch-hour rush, the heavy mama in black hovering protectively near the cash register. Leave it to the drummers, he thought, they always find the best joint in the neighborhood.

He stepped over to the woman, nodded at the flasks of Chianti behind her and asked her in his best Sicilian-accented Italian for a glass of Ruffino.

"*Bellisima signora,*" he said as she gave him the wine with an approving smile, "you know Mr. McKinney, the Procter and Gamble salesman?"

"Sure," the woman answered. "He'sa down there." She indicated a middle-aged man in a gabardine overcoat, a coffee and Danish before him, reading *The Wall Street Journal* in one of the booths.

Angelo strolled over to the man and, as discreetly as possible, gave him the shield. "Mind if I join you?"

"Not at all." The salesman wore horn-rimmed glasses, and his ash-blond hair was retreating back from his forehead with evident rapidity. He was neat and well dressed; almost too neat, it occurred to Angelo, for someone who had to spend his days wandering in and out of grocery stores.

McKinney relaxed when Angelo explained the reason he had looked him up. Despite their seemingly innocent calling, men like the Procter and Gamble salesman were aware of a lot of things; such as which Italian wholesaler on the West Side was, in fact, a Mafia front running collections and payoffs in the numbers operations the Mob forced small storeowners to conduct as part of their businesses. "Oh yes," he said, "well, really, I gave them everything I had on that in my accident report at the station house."

"I understand." Angelo nodded sympathetically, leaning closer to the salesman as he did, so that no one could eavesdrop on their conversation. "Look, we've got a very, very important investigation under way, and it's possible, just possible, that your accident might provide us with some very important clues. The note they left under your windshield wiper did say a *yellow* truck, you're absolutely sure of that?"

"Oh yes." McKinney's reply was quick and assured. "I even showed it to the officer at the station house."

"Right." Angelo sipped his wine. "Now, I want you to understand what I have here's got nothing to do with you, but it's very important I get the exact location of the accident and the exact time frame when it took place."

"Yes. But it's all there in the report."

"Sure. But I just want to be absolutely certain. Now, you're sure you parked it at one o'clock?"

"Positive. I picked up the one-o'clock news headlines on WCBS just before I got out of the car."

"Okay. And how long were you gone?"

"Let's see." McKinney frowned, trying to recollect. He bent down and took a black order book from the briefcase at his side.

"I made three calls," he said, flipping through its long white sheets. "The last one was the supermarket up on the corner. I don't sell them, they're handled by the office, so all I do there is just say hello to the manager, check my shelf facings, see what the competition is doing. In all, I wouldn't have been away from the car for more than half an hour, forty minutes."

Angelo made a few hasty jottings on the notepad he had taken from his pocket. "And the place you parked, 149 West Thirty-seventh? You're sure of that?"

"Oh yes, I wrote it down right away." The man blushed slightly.

Why is he lying to me? Angelo wondered. He obviously has nothing to do with this. Maybe he's trying to hide something. Probably was off screwing a biscuit on company time. Let's come around on him another way. He sat back, smiling. "I understand you live up there in White Plains?"

"Yes. Do you know it?"

"Yeah. Nice place. I used to think when the wife was still alive we ought to move up there. Get the fresh air and all. You married?"

"Yes. I have three children."

Angelo bestowed his most approving smile on the salesman and leaned toward him again. "Believe me, Mr. McKinney, when I tell you this has nothing to do with you at all. But I got to be sure of that location. You're sure you parked at 149 West Thirty-seventh?"

The Procter & Gamble salesman bristled with nervous irritation. "Yes, of course. Why are you going on so?"

"Because, Mr. McKinney, there is no way in the world you could have parked your car at 149 West Thirty-seventh Street last Friday, or any other day, for that matter. I drove by there coming up here. It's a warehouse garage for a courier outfit with three driveways facing on the street, and it's a very, very busy place. You couldn't leave a car there for five minutes without starting a riot."

McKinney went scarlet. His hands shook slightly. Angelo felt sorry for him, but the guy irritated him. Why was he lying, playing games like this? Had to be a biscuit. And when he found the dent in his fender, he got nervous. Figured when the company saw the address on his insurance declaration, they'd ask him what the hell he was doing there.

"Look, my friend, giving false information to the police is a very serious charge. Get you in a lot of trouble with your company. I don't want to make no problem for you, because I know you're a good, law-abiding citizen, but I have got to know where that car was hit."

McKinney looked up from the Formica tabletop. "Will this go anywhere?"

"Absolutely not. Don't worry about it. This is just between us. Where were you for real?"

"Down on Christopher Street."

"The yellow truck on the note? That's true?"

The dejected salesman nodded.

"And the time? Was it one o'clock?"

"No. I parked at eleven-thirty. I know because I listened to the first stock market report on the radio. I bought a hundred Teltron shares two weeks ago . . ."

Angelo wasn't listening. He was making some quick calculations. The Hertz truck leaves the pier at 11:22. If they took the Brooklyn–Battery Tunnel and came up the West Side it would take twenty, twenty-five minutes to get to Christopher Street.

"How long were you parked?"

The man's embarrassment was now manifest and intense. "Not long. There's a bar down there. I had to see the barman and leave a message for someone. Fifteen, twenty minutes at the most."

"Do you remember the street number where you parked?"

"No." McKinney shook his head. "But I could find it for you."

Michael Bannion, the Police Commissioner, paled reading the note an aide passed to him in the underground command post.

"What's the matter?" Harvey Hudson of the FBI demanded. "Don't tell me we've got some more bad news?"

"About the worse we could get." Bannion grimaced. "*The New York Times* is onto the story and I've got to find a way to get them off it."

No wonder this guy didn't want to let the office know where he got his fender dented, Angelo mused as his stupefied eyes absorbed the scene around his car. I'm really out of touch. I thought he was after a biscuit when it was really a beating he was looking for.

They were in the heart of the "rough trade" area of Greenwich Village, and the detective, sickened and fascinated, couldn't take his eyes off the scene on the sidewalks: young men in studded black leather Hell's Angels jackets and boots, chains dangling from their belts or swinging from their wrists, motorcycle caps and aviator glasses on their heads, characters out of a bad fifties movie. He'd heard about the scene at the headquarters. These guys were cruisers, looking for soft trade from Wall Street or uptown, guys in their Brooks Brothers suits who, for whatever sick reason, came down here at lunchtime to get beaten with chains and whips in the "reception rooms" installed in the abandoned piers across the street.

He glanced at McKinney, not knowing whether to feel contempt or pity for the man. What bizarre urge could drive a nice guy like that from White Plains into this sick jungle of sadism, perversion and violence?

"You're sure you're not going to report this to anyone?" The salesman's voice quavered as he formed the question.

"Don't worry," Angelo reassured him. "This is just going to be between you and me."

"It was right here." The salesman had turned his face away as he indicated a spot on the sidewalk along Christopher. "I went to have a drink there at the Badlands on the corner." His finger indicated a bar a few doors away. "I had to leave a message . . ." The salesman's voice cracked with shame and embarrassment. "I have a friend—"

"Forget it." Angelo curtly cut him off. "That doesn't interest me."

So they would have turned off West Street and headed up Christopher, the detective pondered. That means, if my theory about the truck is correct, this barrel of gas has got to be around here someplace. Between the river and Fifth—say, Broadway to be sure. Otherwise the Palestinians would have come in by the East Side, over the Brooklyn Bridge.

Angelo studied the cruisers lolling along the sidewalks. Regulars, most of them. There was a good chance one of them put the note under the windshield wiper. Get a dozen guys down here in a big hurry, start asking questions and you just might get the answer you were looking for. And then there was this guy's car. The dent was low, on the front fender, probably from a bumper.

"Mr. McKinney, believe me I'll see your office doesn't find out about this, but we're going to have to call them and tell them you won't be selling any more soap today. We gotta get this fender over to Brooklyn in a big hurry." He laughed. "You know, it may turn out to be a lucky thing you didn't get it fixed right away."

Michael Bannion's voice poured from Arthur Gelb's telephone with the resonance, the imperiousness, of a Wagnerian overture. "Mr. Gelb," he said, "forgive me for not getting back to you right away, but as you have correctly surmised we have what may be a very serious problem on our hands."

"I know," *The New York Times*'s impatient editor replied, crooking his phone in his elbow so that he was ready to take notes of their conversation. "What is it?"

"I am going to tell you something in the strictest confidence, Mr. Gelb, because I know you and the *Times* have the safety and well-being of the people of this city at heart just as I do. Those three Palestinians we're looking for have hidden a barrel of chlorine gas somewhere in the city. It is, as you know, a deadly substance and they're threatening to blow it up if certain of their political conditions aren't met."

Gelb whistled softly. "Jesus Christ! What are they asking for?"

"For the moment their demands have been rather vaguely stated, but they apparently involve those Israeli settlements in what used to be Jordan and the Arab section of Jerusalem." Gelb was already frantically making notes on a piece of copy paper, nodding excitedly to Grace Knowland as he did.

"I'm sure you can imagine the panic and chaos this would cause if the information got out to the public before we've been able to pin down more precisely the location of the barrel."

"I certainly can, Commissioner, but I also have no trouble imagining the menace this poses to the people of this city."

"Absolutely. Our problem is it would be sheer, utter madness to order the evacuation of Manhattan Island for one barrel of chlorine gas. That leaves us only one alternative, finding that barrel before the public learns it's here. And that's where we need your help,

405

Mr. Gelb. If this leaks to the public before we find it, there's going to be panic out there. I shudder to think of the hysteria that could overtake New York if this gets out.''

"I'm leveling with you, Mr. Gelb, and I've got to ask you for your help and cooperation in return. I know how you people feel up there about requests like this, but I've got to plead with you to hold off printing this until we can pin down the location of that barrel.''

Gelb interrupted him. 'How did that barrel get here, Commissioner?''

"Well, we're not one hundred percent certain.''

"Christ, you mean there's a barrel of chlorine gas in this city and your people aren't sure how the hell it got here?''

"Our suspicion is that it came in through the piers, in a shipment of heavy petroleum products. But, frankly, our concern is not how it got here but where it went.''

"Commissioner.'' Gelb was about to address himself to Bannion's demand when he stopped. "What about all those people up at the Seventh Regiment Armory with their rented vans? What have they got to do with this?''

"They're a federal unit looking for any telltale gas leakages that could give us an indication of where the barrel is. Now, I want to tell you, Mr. Gelb, we'll keep you informed on this. You have my word on it. But I beg you, for God's sake, hold off printing it until we've found the barrel.''

"I'm not authorized to make a commitment like that, Commissioner. That's up to Mr. Sulzberger and Mr. Rosenthal.''

"Well, I cannot stress enough just how important this is. I'll take it up with Mr. Sulzberger myself if you like.''

God help us, Bannion thought as he hung up, when they find out we've been lying to them.

Angelo Rocchia held the horn of the salesman's Pontiac down until its strident blare brought three shirtsleeved FBI agents scurrying out into the cold from their Hertz garage.

"Open those damn doors,'' the detective ordered, waving at the entrance of their improvised forensic laboratory. "I got a present for you.''

His reception was anything but warm. "A yellow truck,'' the

director who had earlier told him to wait out in the office muttered when Angelo outlined his theory. "That's all you're going on? Some guy with a yellow truck scraped his fender?"

"At least you know it wasn't an Avis truck hit him," Angelo replied. "You can do a spectrographic analysis to see if you can get a paint match-up. I'll get a bunch of guys and go back there to see if we can find the guy who left the note."

The lab director lapsed into silence studying the barely visible scrape on the Pontiac's fender. "Yeah," he said reluctantly. "It'll take some time. But I guess it's probably worth it."

When Angelo came back into the garage after calling in his request for a dozen plainclothesmen, the Bureau's experts were already at work. One of them was moving some kind of gray metallic scanner along the fender. Probably some high-intensity magnetic device, the detective thought. He must be trying to pull out any metallic scraps embedded in there. Curious, he squatted beside the man.

"What's that you got there?" he asked.

"Geiger counter."

"Geiger counter!"

"Checking to see if there's any lingering radiation on here."

Angelo's face whitened. He felt his thigh muscles sag and he teetered back on his heels so that he had to thrust a hand to the cold concrete floor to keep himself from falling over. Those lying bastards, he thought. So that's why they had those classified reports. They had this all the time and they didn't tell us. Lied to us, kept us deliberately in the dark.

He staggered to his feet. Rand was over by a workbench busily interrogating an FBI technician. He knew. Those bastards from South Dakota and Tacoma, Washington, in their skinny ties and their wash-and-dry suits, they told them, sure, because they're feds. But me, the guy whose city this is, the guy who's got his people here, me they don't trust. He was abreast of Rand now, and he struck the younger man's shoulder with such force he started to tumble forward.

"Cut the bullshit," Angelo snarled. "You and I got work to do."

He almost ran to his car, then, when they were inside, slammed the door shut with such a furious jolt Rand looked up perplexed.

"What's the matter?"

"You knew it all the time, didn't you?"

"Knew what, for God's sake?"

"You've been giving me a stroke like everybody else, haven't you? It isn't chlorine gas they got in that goddamn barrel. It's a fucking atomic bomb." Angelo turned his ignition key so hard he almost snapped it off in the lock, then jammed the car into gear.

"This is my own home, my own people and they don't trust me!" he roared. There was a world of feeling in his shout, of fear and rage, bitterness and humiliation, the savage, wounded pride of the stag at bay. "You, a half-ass kid out of a Louisiana law school, doesn't even have two years in the Bureau, they trust, but me, a guy with thirty years on his ticket, me they don't trust. All those fucking years and when they got something like this they still don't trust you!"

He stomped so hard on his accelerator, the car fishtailed forward over the rutted snow and ice, its spinning tires shrieking in protest. The yardman he had quizzed earlier looked on, amazed. Man, he thought, he never going to get where he going driving like that.

Three hours. With a glance at the clock in the NSC conference room, the President measured once again how imminent was the horror facing them. It was six minutes to noon. Exactly three hours and six minutes remained before the expiration of Qaddafi's ultimatum. Men cling to hopes in a crisis as a dying believer clings to his faith, and the President still strove to cling to his despite the remorseless, inexorable pressures wringing them from his soul. At least in the last great American crisis in Iran, the United States had not had to decide its actions in the face of an ultimatum, an ultimatum laid down by a man the President had no doubt was ready to wreak the nuclear holocaust on six million innocent people.

Suddenly he interrupted the desultory flow of conversation around him. He had had an idea. It wasn't much of an idea, but, in the situation, anything was worthwhile. "Jack," he told his National Security Assistant. "I want to talk to Abe Stern."

"Abe," he said when he got the Mayor on their tie line to New York, "the sands are running down. In a short while, a very short while, we are going to have to act, and once we do there will be no turning back."

"I understand, Mr. President," Stern replied. "What do you propose to do?"

"The advance elements of the Rapid Deployment Force are on the ground in Germany now, refueled and ready to move on to the Middle East. We received secret assurance from President Assad in Syria half an hour ago that they'll be allowed to land in Damascus. The Sixth Fleet Amphibious Marine Landing Force would land in Lebanon simultaneously with their arrival. The two would hook up, then move into the West Bank to clear out the settlements."

"The Israelis will fight, Mr. President."

"I know, Abe." The President's words came in a soft groan. "But I will make our very limited objectives clear to them, and the rest of the world, before we go in."

"It may not be enough, Mr. President. Don't forget, they have nuclear weapons, too."

"I think I know how we can contain that threat. I'll ask the Russians to make it clear to them what the consequences of their employing nuclear weapons would be. They might not believe that from us, but they'll believe it from them all right. Before we get to that, though, Abe, there's one other card we can play. You."

"Me?"

"You. Call Begin yourself, Abe. Plead with him. Try to make him see the madness in not pulling out of those settlements."

"Can I tell him you're ready to—"

"Abe," the President interrupted, "tell him anything you want. Just get him to agree to go on the air and announce that those damn settlements are coming out."

Angelo Rocchia parked his Corvette at 189 Christopher Street in approximately the same spot in which the Procter & Gamble salesman's car had been parked Friday morning. The detective was still seething with rage. He slumped against the car seat, a walkie-talkie in one hand, a detailed block-by-block map of the neighborhood he had gotten at the Sixth Precinct spread on his knees. Twenty men were already combing the area he had designated on that map, from the river on the west over to Hudson Street on the east, two blocks north and south, knocking on every door, calling on every shop, interrogating every passerby, trying to find the author of the note.

Angelo wondered how much time they had. They'd probably lie to you if you asked them about that, too, he thought bitterly. Suddenly, a terrible urge swept through him, a single desire so terrible he trembled with feeling: to clasp in his arms the one person in the world he had left, the frail figure he could talk to only with his eyes, to grab her, hug her misshapen body to his. And to get her as far away from this city as he could.

He was so lost in his recollections of her pathetic efforts to babble out the words of "O Little Town of Bethlehem" that he didn't see the plainclothesman draw up to the car. He was followed by a young man in his midtwenties, his legs in black denims so close-fitting they might have been a ballet dancer's tights, his bleached blond hair heaped high, Elvis Presley style, on his head. He had a copper-colored boxer on a leash. Angelo got out of the car.

"Would you repeat to Detective Rocchia here what you just told me?" the plainclothesman ordered.

"Oh yes, certainly, of course. I was walking Ashoka here, I have to walk him a lot, he needs the outdoors so, poor thing, he just can't *stand* being cooped up all day in my little flat, can you, darling?" The young man bent down to pat the animal as Angelo scowled. "And I was right over there." He gestured to the other side of the street. "And I heard this *awful* scraping noise. I looked up and I just saw this yellow truck starting up and going up Christopher Street. So I went across the street and I saw they'd scraped some poor man's fender—"

"And you left the note?"

"Yes."

"Was it a Hertz truck?"

"Oh, well," the young man was perplexed. "I don't know, it could have been, but it was going up the street and I didn't see that much. And trucks and me, well . . ."

"Terrific. You're a big help."

"Was there anybody else around here might have seen it?"

"Well, there were two of those simply ghastly cruiser types that hang out down here right there." He indicated a storefront almost adjacent to Angelo's Corvette.

"You know them?"

410

The young man blushed. "I have nothing to do with that type of person. They hang out across the street—" he gestured toward the river—"in that old pier there."

Angelo beckoned to Rand. "Come on," he growled. "We gotta find these two."

The President of the United States had been right. There had been no need to inform the Israelis about the U.S. military preparations to move into the West Bank. Israeli intelligence had discerned the basic outlines of the U.S. moves almost from the moment they began. A source inside the U.S. Rhine Main Air Force Base in Wiesbaden, Germany, had informed the embassy in Bonn of the arrival of the C-5As of the Rapid Deployment Force. Radar had picked up the movements of the Sixth Fleet's Marine Amphibious Force, and its ships had been kept under discreet aerial surveillance as they moved up the Lebanese seacoast toward Junieh Bay.

The most revealing and complete portrait of U.S. intentions, however, had been provided by a Mossad "asset" inside King Hussein's Amman Palace, a lieutenant colonel in the Royal Jordanian Air Force attached to the King's personal staff. Yusi Avidar, the intelligence chief whose secret call had alerted the CIA to Israel's plans for a preemptive strike at Libya, reviewed the information his agent had sent across the Allenby Bridge. Like their American counterparts, the Israelis had been in a quasi-permanent crisis session for over twenty-four hours; their nerves were strained, their tempers on edge.

"So, gentlemen," General Avidar concluded. "There is no question about it: the Americans are coming."

"Let's leak it to the world press right away," Benny Ranan suggested. "That will stop the Americans in their tracks. Public opinion will force the President to attack Qaddafi."

Yigal Yadin looked at the man, appalled. "Have you gone mad, Benny?" he asked. "If the Americans discover six million people in New York may get killed because of our settlements, there won't be a single American alive who won't back the President in coming in here and taking them out themselves."

"Damn it!" It was General Avidar. "Can't this nation ever acknowledge it was wrong? Are we going to another holocaust because we can't admit a mistake and pull them out ourselves, for God's sake?''

"Our mistake was not carrying through our strike on Libya yesterday," Ranan said.

Begin, calm as ever, turned to the intelligence chief. "The original mistake was in your intelligence service's failure to find out what this man was doing so that we could destroy him and his project before he got his bombs."

The General began to protest, but Begin cut him off with a wave of his hand. "I read the reports. You never took him seriously, even after we found the Pakistani connection. He didn't have the technological resources you maintained, the infrastructure. He was just a pompous boaster. He—"

An aide interrupted. "Excuse me," he said to the Prime Minister. "The Mayor of New York wants to speak to you urgently."

The spectacle sickened Angelo: the filthy, debris-littered old pier, the gloomy office, probably once the Customs shed, the man half naked cowering in the corner like some frightened animal, the two "cruisers" in leather jackets, one dangling a studded belt from his hand. The detective started to go into the dimness, then stopped, disgusted. Let them come to me, he thought.

"Hey, you," he barked at the cruiser with the belt, "come out here. I want to talk to you."

The youth edged sullenly toward the doorway and Angelo's bulky figure. "Hey, listen, what is this?" he protested. "He's a consenting adult, for Christ's sake. We got civil rights now, don't you know that?"

"Forget it," Angelo snarled. "I'm not interested in what you're doing in there. Friday your friend over here sees a yellow truck scrape a guy's Pontiac over there on Christopher Street. He says you saw it, too."

"Yeah," the young man replied. His sidekick was just behind him now, glaring hostilely over his shoulder, arrogantly whacking his belt in his palm. Their client was crouched in the recesses of the darkened office, hiding his head in his hands, sobbing, convinced, probably, that he was about to be arrested and his career ruined.

"So what?"

412

"I just want to know if you remember anything about the truck, is all."

"Hertz truck. One of them vans there. What about it?"

"You sure it was a Hertz truck?"

"Yeah, sure. It had them blue stripes on it."

Angelo took a Hertz sales brochure from his pocket. Pictured on it was the spectrum of Hertz trucks rented in the New York area. "Do you suppose you could show me which model it was?"

"Right here." The youth's forefinger stabbed at the photo of the Econoline van. Angelo glanced at Rand, then back at the youth.

"Thanks, kid," he said. "Give you a good-conduct medal one of these days."

He turned and, with Rand behind him, ran out of the pier, dodged across the West Street traffic and raced for his car.

As Angelo Rocchia scrambled into his Corvette, just twelve blocks away in front of a hardware store at 74 West Eighth Street another man slipped into the front seat of a car pausing at the curb. Kamal Dajani noted that his sister had on her blond wig. It changed her so completely that she looked, sitting there beside him, like a total stranger. No policeman, even one equipped with a picture of her, could identify her now, he thought with satisfaction.

She headed into MacDougal Street and then, through Waverly Place, over to Sixth Avenue, letting the car glide in and out of the traffic with a deft and gentle touch. At Fourteenth she moved into the outside lane, waiting to turn left, stopping as she did at the red light.

"Is everything all right?" she asked, her eyes fixed on the rearview mirror to see if they were being followed.

"Of course everything is all right."

"There's been no news on the radio."

"I know," Kamal replied, his own eyes scrutinizing the throngs rushing to beat the "Don't Walk" sign. "I have a transistor."

"You don't suppose there's any possibility the Americans won't agree, do you?"

Kamal remained silent, staring at the crowds thronging the sidewalks, at the Christmas decorations and the white slashes of the advertising banners promising "Clearance Sale: Everything Must Go" and "All Stock Reduced." Nothing there, he realized, to

413

indicate that anyone in this city even suspected the enormity of the threat under which they were living.

Nervously, Laila lit a cigarette, struggling to concentrate on her driving, painfully aware that this was not the moment to bang somebody's fender the way Kamal had done with his truck.

"How do you feel about it, Kamal?" she asked, stopping for another light.

"Feel about what?"

"About this, for God's sake! The bomb. About what's going to happen if the Americans don't agree. Don't you feel anything? Triumph or vengeance or remorse or something?"

"No, Laila, I don't feel a damn thing. I learned not to feel a long time ago."

He lapsed into his dour silence again, staring straight ahead toward the grayish stain of the Hudson. Then, almost as though his body had been struck by a muscle spasm, he sat up and turned to his sister.

"No," he said. "That was wrong. I do feel something. Hate. I used to think I was doing this for Palestine or the cause or Father or whatever. But I realized last night the real reason I'm doing it is because I hate these people and the world they made for us to live in with their television and their movies and their banks and their cars and their goddamn tourists in their white shirts and their straw hats and their cameras, climbing all over our monuments, running the world the way they wanted it run for the last thirty years—my thirty years!"

"My God!" His sister shuddered. "Why do you hate them so much?"

"Hatred doesn't need reasons, Laila," Kamal replied. "That's the trouble with people like you and Whalid. You always need reasons." Angrily, he grabbed at the map of New York on the seat. They were in the outgoing tide of traffic now, moving up the West Side of the city. "Don't go the way you did the last time," he ordered.

"Why?"

"Because I don't want to go through any toll gates in the city. If they're looking for us, that's where they'll be."

Of all the pleas and threats, boasts and arguments Menachem Begin had heard since the President's first telephone call,

414

none had moved him quite as much as that articulated by the Mayor of New York. Begin had met the Mayor twice—once on a visit to New York for a fund-raising banquet, later when the Mayor had brought a group of New York Zionists to visit Israel.

He was listening to the Mayor at his desk, staring at the exquisitely peaceful vista of the Judean hills, dark welts gilded with the ghostly patina of a full moon, under those December stars which once were to have promised mankind a better world in which to live. How do I respond to this man, he asked himself, how do I answer the unanswerable?

"Look, Mr. Begin," Stern was saying, "I'm pleading with you on behalf of every single man, woman and child in this city, Italian, Irish, black, Puerto Rican, whatever. But why do you think he put this bomb here and not in Los Angeles, or Chicago, or Washington? Because he knows there are three million Jews here, more than there are in Israel, that's why."

"Ah," Begin interrupted. "That is the essence of this terrible tragedy, Mr. Mayor. A tyrant has succeeded in pitting brother against brother, friend against friend, as Roman emperors once forced their captives to slaughter each other in the arenas for their entertainment."

"The essence of this tragedy, Mr. Begin," the Mayor's distant voice was tremulous with anger and concern, "is not that at all. It's your government's refusal to take a handful of Jewish people off land which belonged to us two thousand years ago and hasn't belonged to us since. And your mistake in putting them there in the first place."

"My dear friend," Begin pleaded with the Mayor, "please believe me when I tell you I share every one of your concerns, your fears, your angers. They have been ours since this terrible ordeal began. But what you and the President are talking about is not those settlements. It is the very life of this nation. You are asking us to commit national suicide by handing this land over to a people who are sworn to destroy us. Our people, Mr. Stern, that part of us which is here, were in the camps. We were on the road to Jerusalem in 1948. We were in Sinai in 1956. We were on the Golan in '67. We were on the canal in '73. Our sacrifices, our blood on those battlefields, gave a dignity to our existence—and yours as well. They also gave us the right to survive, Mr. Stern, and that is a right we cannot and will not surrender."

"Look, Mr. Begin, all that is fine, but no one is asking you to commit suicide. All we are asking you to do is get the hell off land that doesn't belong to you anyway. Let the poor Palestinians have their place in the sun, too. That's going to satisfy Qaddafi and it's going to save my people. We'll deal with Qaddafi afterwards, but I've got to save my people. That is the number-one priority, people. If I've learned nothing else in the hell of these hours, it's that. The people come first. The rest of it doesn't matter.''

"I'm sorry, Mr. Mayor." Begin had set his glasses on his desk and was rubbing the bridge of his nose in fatigue and strain. "But the rest does matter. The principles do count. If we destroy the principles by which we live through cowardice or expediency or fear or whatever reason, we will destroy the basis of our existence. For all its faults, we were bequeathed a civilized order by our fathers. Are we going to bequeath our children chaos and the jungle?''

A few doors away from the room in which Abe Stern was completing his telephone call to Jerusalem, the handful of men directing the search operation gathered around the FBI's Quentin Dewing's table for a hastily called conference. For the first time there was an undercurrent of hysteria in their gathering, the first stirrings of panic before the enormity of their failure. Their concerns were worsened by the calls coming every fifteen minutes now from the White House, frantic demands for news, making it painfully clear how close the center of government was to panic, too.

Dewing didn't even wait for everyone to sit down before he turned to Al Feldman. The Chief of Detectives looked terrible. His pallor was gray; his shirt stank with the stench of the nervous sweat that had soaked into it in the last thirty-six hours. His voice shook as he replied to Dewing's query about Angelo Rocchia. "He's as solid as anybody I got."

The Chief did not have to continue, because Angelo, followed by Rand, entered the room while he was still talking.

"Sit down," Dewing told the detective, pointing to a chair at the end of the table, "and tell us your story."

Angelo dropped onto the chair, unbuttoning his collar as he did. He was breathless, panting from his frantic drive downtown from Christopher Street, from the sprint from his car to Dewing's conference room. He had never been in this underground command post before, and the frenetic nervous energy exploding all around him, men running and shouting, doors slamming, phones ringing, radios crackling and Telexes stuttering, told him everything he needed to know about the gravity of the situation.

As quickly, as tersely as he could, he sketched the background of his idea, the story of the Procter & Gamble salesman, the relationship on which everything depended: the time the van had been clocked out of the Brooklyn pier by the security guard, the time required to drive from the pier to Christopher Street, his reasonably precise idea of when the salesman's car had been hit.

There was a huge map of Manhattan on the wall and he indicated Christopher Street on it, stabbing its way from the Hudson River toward the heart of Greenwich Village.

"If this was the van we're looking for, then reason has got to tell you the barrel is going to be somewhere in here, between Fourteenth on the north, Houston Street on the south, the river on the west, and Sixth Avenue or maybe Fifth on the east. Otherwise they'd have come up the East Side." He traced out the area with his fingertips as he spoke.

"*If* this is the truck we're looking for." The speaker was Dewing, his features tightened into a cold mask of concentration. "That's a big if." He turned to Harvey Hudson. "How many Hertz trucks did you say circulate in this city?"

"Roughly five hundred, Mr. Dewing."

"And how many of those are vans?"

"Over half."

Dewing's gaze went back to Angelo. "And you got onto this just because you told yourself Arabs don't know how to drive on snow?"

Angelo had already taken an intense dislike to the man. "Yes," he answered, making no effort to conceal the hostility in his voice. "That's right."

Dewing pondered the map behind the detective. "That's about a four- or five-mile trip, isn't it?"

Angelo looked over to Feldman, hoping for some sign of support, then nodded his agreement.

"The truck had two hundred and fifty miles on it when it came back in, didn't it?"

"So what? If you're carrying what they got in that barrel, the first thing you're going to want to do with it is get it to wherever the hell it's going. Then you're going to dump those other barrels out in Queens. Then maybe you're going to spend the afternoon driving up and down the Long Island Expressway to make things hard for the cops, how would I know?''

"Harvey," Dewing said, "when will we have that paint match-up?"

"In an hour."

The FBI assistant director grimaced. "That's an hour we haven't got. Chief," he asked Feldman, "what do you think about this? He's your man. Can we search that area house by house?"

"It's a big area." Feldman replied. "Couple hundred blocks in there. Goddamn rat's nest of a neighborhood, too. But what else have we got to go on?"

"You realize that if we're going to search that area in a hurry, we'll have to commit every single resource we have to the effort? There'll be nothing left for anything else."

The Chief looked at his wristwatch. "Do you see a better way to use the time we've got left?"

Dewing's mouth twitched in nervous indecision. It was an awful choice to have to make. "God help us if we're wrong," he said.

He was on the verge of ordering the search when Harvey Hudson interrupted. A yellow classified phone book was spread on his lap. "Just a minute, Mr. Dewing. Hertz has got a Rent-A-Truck agency located right up the street from where the accident took place. Must be vans going back and forth down there all the time."

There was an instant of stricken silence before Dewing exploded.

"Jesus Christ!" he shouted at Feldman. "You let this old buffoon of a detective come in here and get us within a hair of concentrating all our resources on one part of the city and he hasn't even checked this out? This solid guy of yours?"

Angelo was on his feet before the shocked Feldman could answer. He pulled his notebook from his pocket, flipped it open, ripped out a page, crumpled it in his fist and hurled it at Dewing. "Here, Mr. whatever the hell your fucking name is," he growled, "here's the record of the vans that went in and out of that station last Friday. One out at eight-seventeen in the morning and two back in the afternoon."

Angelo's neck twisted back in the strange jerking movement of a man leaving a barber's chair as he started to rebutton his shirt collar. He took a menacing step toward Dewing. "I may be an old buffoon, mister, but I'll tell you what you are. You're a fucking liar. You've been holding out on us from the beginning, haven't you? Sent us out there like blind men because you didn't trust us." Angelo thrust his finger at the startled Rand. "Him you trust, because he's one of you, comes from Washington. Me you don't trust. Those people up there on the streets, the ones this thing is going to wipe out, them you don't trust. What do you care? You're safe down here in this cellar. But them—"

"Rocchia!" It was Bannion's commanding voice, but Angelo's rage was too great to be checked now. He was towering over Dewing as twenty-four hours earlier he had towered over Benny the Fence. "Because it isn't chlorine gas in that barrel, is it? It's a fucking atomic bomb, going to clear this place out and them along with it. Ghettos?" He laughed harshly. "We're not going to have to worry about the ghettos anymore. The whole city will be one fucking ghetto after that thing goes off."

Angelo stopped, his chest heaving. He could feel the thudding of his heart racing to the fury he had just unleashed. "Well, I told you where you can find your bomb," he said, his voice finally under control. "Look there or not, I don't care, because as far as I'm concerned, I'm finished. You don't trust me, mister, well, fuck you. I don't trust you either."

Before any of the astonished men in the room could react, the detective had stridden past Dewing, opened the door and slammed it behind him.

"Al," the Police Commissioner ordered his Chief of Detectives. "Go after him, for Christ's sake! We can't have him running around the city shouting 'Atomic bomb' at the top of his lungs."

The President had introduced four newcomers into his exhausted circle of advisers in the National Security Council conference room: the Chairman of the Senate Foreign Relations Committee, the Majority and Minority Leaders of the Senate and the Speaker of the House of Representatives. He had been keeping the four men abreast of the developing crisis in secret briefings, but now that the awful moment of decision was at hand he wanted them associated with it.

One by one, the President had called on each of the men in the room to voice his opinion. At the far end of the table, the Secretary of State was summing up in his characteristically succinct manner what was their virtually unanimous recommendation.

"We cannot, Mr. President, allow six million Americans to die because another nation, however friendly, refuses to modify the consequences of a policy we have always opposed. Land the Marines and the Rapid Deployment Force. Associate the Soviets with our action to fix the Israelis in place. Inform Qaddafi of what we are doing and let him follow the action through his embassy in Damascus. That will save New York, and when we've defused that threat, then we can deal with him."

There was an undertone of coughs and of throats being cleared, a kind of chorus of approval at the Secretary's words. The President thanked him formally. Then he let his eyes sweep the faces around the table, studying each grim mien he saw there. "Harold," he said to his Secretary of Defense, "I think you're the one person we haven't heard from."

Harold Brown's elbows were resting on the table, his shoulders drooping as though he was crushed by the implications of what he was about to say. He was a nuclear physicist, one of that high priesthood that had nurtured and furthered for mankind the scourge and the blessing of the shattered atom. With growing alarm he had watched as the civilized world had drifted, indolent and uncaring, to this inevitable end when a zealot with a bomb could impose his will by the threat of violence so terrible it brooked no opposition.

"Mr. President." He took a deep breath as he began. "The last crisis I lived through in this room was the Iranian crisis, and the events of those days are still painfully embedded in my mind. This country needed friends badly in those days, Mr. President, and may I remind you we had only one, Israel. When the chips were down, it was they alone who were ready to stand with us. The Saudis and the Egyptians, perhaps, in their way. But, above all, it was the Israelis who answered the call.

"Our supposed allies the Germans, the French, when we needed them, when we asked them to stand up and be counted, they turned their backs. They were so concerned about their oil, they were prepared to see this nation humiliated and humbled, our diplomats executed, provided we did nothing to disturb the tranquil pattern

420

of their existence. Those are moments I cannot forget, Mr. President. Are we now to turn our arms on the one people who stood by us when we needed them? At the behest of a dictator who loathes us, our nation and everything we stand for?

"I share the feelings of everyone about those settlements, about the Israelis' intransigence on so many points. But what is at issue here transcends those settlements, Mr. President. There are moral issues that are beyond debate and discussion, and this is one of them. There is a point beyond which a nation, like a man, cannot go and still maintain its dignity and self-respect. I say we are at that point."

Silence, a silence of pain and anguish, stilled the room when Brown had finished. The President rose. He looked at the clock on the wall opposite.

"Thank you, gentlemen," he said. "I should like to meditate in the Rose Garden for a moment on what you have said."

Al Feldman caught up with Angelo a few feet from the exit of the command post. He threw his arms around the detective and tugged him to the guards' quarters in which he had laughed at the fake Civil Defense poster.

"Angelo," he murmured, sitting him down in the midst of a row of green metal lockers, their inside doors covered with *Playboy* centerfolds, "you were right. Those guys did lie to you. They had to." Patiently, the Chief explained the details of Qaddafi's threat. "Dewing didn't mean to blow up at you like that, but you got to understand the strain we're all living under."

Angelo looked into his boss's frightened eyes. "I'm sorry, Chief. It wasn't him. It's my fault. Some other things have been working on me the past couple of days."

"Where were you running off to?"

"The Kennedy Center. See the kid."

The Chief pulled a Camel from his battered pack, lit it and exhaled his first drag with a sympathetic sigh. Angelo's attachment to his mongoloid daughter was well known in the Division. "And get her out of here?"

"Yeah."

Feldman rose and placed a trembling hand on his detective's shoulder. He squeezed it tightly. "Okay, Angelo. Go get her. Anybody earned a ticket up to Connecticut, it's you. Just keep your mouth shut, okay? I'm going back in there and sell them on your idea, because I think you're right.

The two men walked to the exit side by side. Angelo reached for Feldman's hand. "Thanks, Chief," he said. Then he turned right, past the guards, toward the stairs and safety.

The men around Dewing's table were still debating Angelo's idea when Feldman slipped back into the room. He made a discreet gesture toward Bannion to indicate that the situation was contained, then eased back into his place. He was still attempting to pick up the threads of the argument when a plainclothesman entered the room and placed a slip of paper in front of him.

"Jesus Christ!" he roared as he read it. "Rocchia was right!"

He jumped from his chair and almost ran to the map of the city. "One of our vice cops just interrogated a teenage whore who works out of a brownstone right here." The startled men around him watched as he hammered the map. "At 27 West Eighth. She identified one of these three Arabs, the one they call Kamal, as one of her clients last night."

"Is she sure?" Bannion asked. "Those girls see a lot of traffic down there."

"Absolutely. Apparently he's a sadistic bastard, and he banged the life out of her while he was doing it." Feldman's gaze went back to the map. "That's almost at Fifth. Right in the corner of the area Rocchia gave us."

His words had a galvanic effect on the men in the room. Hudson felt like standing up and cheering. Bannion had the smile on his face of an Irish racetrack tout who has just had a hundred-to-one shot come in.

"Chief," Dewing asked, "how long would it take us to search out that area your man gave us?"

Feldman scrutinized the map. "We better push the search area east to Broadway to be sure." He paused, making his calculations. "Twelve hours. Give me twelve hours and we'll find the goddamn thing, I promise you."

But on this Tuesday, December 15, there were not twelve hours left. There were only two. For five agonizing mo-

422

ments, the men in the National Security Council conference room had sat in silence waiting for their leader's return. Only Jack Eastman had gone upstairs with him. He too, however, had left him at the Oval Office door. He had stood there watching as, all alone, the President had paced the driveway beyond, hands in his pockets, his head sunk almost into his chest, meditating, praying, doing whatever it was that great leaders must do in the unbearable loneliness of the exercise of power. He had not uttered a word to Eastman when he came back in.

Now he stood at the head of the table, his fists still thrust deep into his pockets, calm yet clearly resolute, trying to find just the words he wanted.

"Gentlemen," he said finally, his voice barely a whisper, "I have reached a decision. It is certainly the worst any man who has held my office has ever had to make, but I am deeply, unshakably convinced that it is the one I must make. I am for better or worse the President of two hundred and thirty million Americans, and however deeply concerned I am about the fate of New York City and all of its people, my responsibility is to all of this country and all of its people. We are confronted with what is, finally, an act of war against this nation. If we cower before that threat, if we bow to blackmail and agree to blackmail in turn one of this country's surest allies, we will abandon our birthright and condemn ourselves sooner or later to destruction as surely as the sun will set this night."

He paused to catch the breath for which he was straining. "It is now one o'clock. Qaddafi's ultimatum expires at three. Admiral Fuller, I want the Poseidon missiles on the Mediterranean submarines targeted on Libya. All of them. Do everything you can to minimize fallout from their explosion on Egypt and Tunisia.

"Mr. Peabody," he said to his Secretary of State, "prepare flash messages for the Chairmen of the CPs of the Soviet Union and China and for Mr. Begin, Giscard, Helmut Schmidt and Mrs. Thatcher, informing them of the reasons for our action. Make it clear to all of them that in this crisis we expect their full support. Release them coincidentally with our action."

He looked down the table to his ashen Chairman of the Joint Chiefs. The Admiral's fingertips trembled visibly on the tabletop.

"If by two-thirty our time we have not found and defused that bomb or Qaddafi has not agreed to extend his ultimatum, then, Admiral Fuller, you will destroy Libya with those missiles.''

"Why, Mr. Rocchia! What a pleasant surprise!'' The little nun of the Sisters of Saint Vincent de Paul looked at the detective in the hallway of the Kennedy Child Study Center on East Sixty-seventh Street with pleasure and amazement. "Whatever brings you here at this time of the day? Not bad news, I hope?''

"No, it's not that, Sister.'' Angelo shifted his weight from foot to foot in nervous embarrassment. "I got to take Maria away for a couple of days. To see some of the family up in Connecticut.''

"Well, really, Inspector, that's a very unusual procedure. I don't know if Mother Superior—''

Angelo interrupted. "It's urgent, Sister. This sister of my wife, she came East for two days. She's never met Maria.'' He glanced impatiently at his watch. "Look, I'm in a hurry here. Would you get her things together, please?''

"Can't you leave her for the rest of the afternoon at least?''

"No, Sister.'' The irritation was easing back into the detective's voice. "I told you I'm in a hurry.''

"All right,'' she said. "Why don't you wait by the playground window while I get her and her things?''

She took the detective into the center, to a bay window giving onto an interior playground. Every time Angelo looked through that window he felt tears rise in his eyes. It was a playground like any other in the city, seesaws and swings, a jungle gym and sandboxes. The children playing there now were a little younger than Maria, probably the class below hers. He watched them, his heart aching for them, sensing the agony in the distorted faces, the pain in their deformed mouths, the frustration raging in those little bodies against fingers that refused a mind's commands, at legs that tottered uncertainly with each effort at movement. He could read the passing spasms of sadness in those bright eyes, the silent barometer of their revolt against life's injustices. How often had he seen it in his own daughter's eyes?

The children inside had seen Angelo, and some of them gathered around in a semicircle beyond the window, gawking at him, bodies twitching under the impact of the gestures of curiosity and greeting they could not perform. He was going to be able to get Maria away, but they were going to stay. And from the moment he had sensed the frenzied, almost hysterical air in the command post he'd realized that this time maybe everything wasn't going to turn out all right like it did on television, catch the guy in the last two minutes and tune in next week for another episode. Maybe there was not going to be a next week for this town or for these kids.

Five minutes after she'd left, the nun returned, clutching Maria's hand in hers. Angelo was no longer by the playground window. She took Maria into the entry hall, but he wasn't there either. Impatiently, she went to the door onto Sixty-seventh Street and looked down to the place where he always parked, illegally, his Corvette. It was gone.

Far up into the dairy and timber country of northern Minnesota, just a few miles south of the Canadian border near the town of Great Falls, there is a small U.S. government reservation. Its gate is discreetly guarded by armed men identified as belonging to the Department of Forests and Fisheries, and the reservation itself consists of acres of gently rolling land, some wooded, some planted, some, apparently, intended as pasture land; all of it enclosed in a barbed-wire fence.

The guards are in fact employees of the Department of Defense, and those miles of barbed-wire fence are an enormous transmitting aerial servicing the radio from which the thermonuclear-missile-bearing submarines of the U.S. Navy are commanded. It is in a state of constant transmission employing low-frequency, extremely low-wave radio bands, well below 10 HRZ because such long waves are uniquely capable of penetrating water to the great depths at which the submarines lie. Each submarine on station on the ocean floor trails its own aerial, a thin strip of wire as long as the two-mile barbed-wire fence in northern Minnesota from which it receives its messages.

At exactly 1304, less than ninety seconds after the President had issued his order, two submarines, the U.S.S. *Henry Clay* and the U.S.S. *Daniel Webster,* one twenty miles southwest of Cyprus, the other buried in a deep ocean trough below Sicily, reacted to a modification in the constantly varied pattern emitted by the fence. The radio operator on each sub brought the signal, automatically decoded by the boat's computers, to his duty officer, who, in turn, delivered it to the submarine's captain.

The captains and the executive officers, employing matching

keys, unlocked their subs' war safes and took out preprogrammed IBM punch cards which they inserted into the computers that commanded each ship's sixteen Poseidon missiles. Those IBM cards bore all the data the submarines' firing mechanisms would need to launch their missiles and the fourteen warheads each contained onto the Libyan targets set out on them, with an accuracy so precise that none of them would fall more than a hundred feet from its selected impact point. That task completed, the officers, joined now by their gunnery officers, opened their firing control systems with ten rigorously defined fail-safe measures. Seconds later, at 1307, each submarine flashed a return message to Minnesota. "Missiles Armed and Targeted," it read. "Vessel in DEFCON [Defense Condition] Red." "DEFCON Red" was the highest alert posture of the U.S. armed forces, the conditions of readiness that indicated that a state of war was at hand.

At the same time that the submarines' messages were flashing through the ether, another message was arriving in the White House communications center over the twin Teleprinters linking it to the Pentagon's terminal of the red line to Moscow.

As always, the communication came in two languages, the first in the original Russian, the second in English as translated in Moscow by a Soviet linguist. In view of the urgency of the crisis, the President rushed into the communications center himself to follow the message as it came in. A State Department Russian expert was beside him, responsible for verifying the accuracy of the Soviet translation and for pointing out to the President any subtle nuances in meaning or language.

There was none in this case. The message was brief and to the point. Scanning it, the President felt his legs tremble. He placed a hand on the shoulder of the stunned State Department official at his side.

"Thank God!" he gasped.

In the New York command post six men were on the telephone at the same time, each shouting to make his voice heard over the din of the others. Bannion was in the process of commandeering the Sixth Precinct station house on the Lower West Side as a subheadquarters for the upcoming search effort. Feldman was beside him assembling the men and material they would require. A few chairs away the usually imperturbable Booth was roaring at the NEST's Seventh Regiment Armory headquarters, asking for every available man, scientist and detection device. Harvey Hudson was mobilizing a team of federal judges to issue a flood of search warrants that would justify entry into closed apartments, offices, buildings or the dwellings of civil-rights-conscious New Yorkers who would otherwise refuse to let a detective or an FBI agent past their front door.

So chaotic were the conditions in the room that, for a few seconds, no one heard the sound coming from the squawk box on the conference-room table. To his horror, Abe Stern suddenly realized the President was talking and not a person in the room was listening.

He grabbed the phone before him and told the switchboard to feed the President's call onto his line. "Mr. President," he apologized, "I'm sorry, but we're in a state of near-hysteria here. We think we've got a fix on where it is."

The President, still shaken by the events and decisions of the past twenty minutes, wasn't listening.

"Abe," he said, "I've just had the Soviets on the red line. They've forced Qaddafi to extend the deadline in his ultimatum by six hours—until nine o'clock tonight."

PART VIII

TUESDAY, DECEMBER 15:
1:11 P.M. TO 9:17 P.M.

"Ten-thirteen. Assist patrolman."

THE AREA IN WHICH THE MEN OF THE UNDER-
ground command post had decided Qaddafi's thermonuclear device had to be hidden consisted of a rectangular slice of the Lower
West Side of Manhattan. It covered the major part of Greenwich
Village, a jumble of 2,579 miles of streets, 25,000 buildings of every
description: brownstones, restored Federal homes, apartment
houses, co-ops, condos, converted lofts, rotting piers, abandoned
warehouses, small industries, garages, bars, restaurants, dives and
discos.

There were the collapsing piers along the Hudson where once,
in the twenties and thirties, luxury liners had berthed. There was
the Gansevoort Meat Market; a touch of Little Italy in the southern
area surrounding Bleecker and Carmine Streets; big middle-class
developments like Washington Square Village and the West Village
Houses; upper-middle-class apartments and homes north of Washington Square; the vast New York University complex around the
square. Close to the river there was a conglomeration of transient
businesses, repair shops, artisans' ateliers and the gay SM area
where the Procter & Gamble salesman had been visiting when his
fender was scraped. And, above all, from Seventh Avenue South
over to Broadway and from West Third up to West Eighth, there
was the tourist center of Greenwich Village with its nightclubs,
jazz joints, theaters, bars, cafés, restaurants, whores, dope ped-
dlers, hustlers, chess players, poets, con men, bums and tourists
by the thousands, a transient, storied area graced with one of the
highest crime rates in New York City.

Once again Quenton Dewing laid out the general approach for
the search, setting it up in a rigorously orderly fashion, like a
military operation. First he intended to send teams of NEST and
FBI men through the area. They would "walk" every building in
blue Con Edison overalls, surveying it from top to bottom, but

they wouldn't actually enter offices or apartments unless they hit a hot reading. Twenty-five of the FBI's New York agents and twenty-five detectives would be standing by as a strategic reserve, ready to rush out whenever they found radiation.

Following the NEST teams would come a slower, more methodical door-to-door, room-to-room search for the barrel. Three thousand FBI agents and all the NYPD's available plainclothesmen would be assigned to the task. Dewing's idea was to run them in teams of two, two teams to a building, so that there would be a backup in case of trouble. Because of the barrel's weight, they would limit their search to the first two floors in buildings with no elevators and would pay particular attention to garages and cellars. Bannion had turned up an idea to conceal what was happening from the public. One man would identify himself as a police officer, the other as an official of the gas company. Lieutenant Hogan's Office of Civil Preparedness delivered to the precinct hundreds of pencillike yellow Geiger counters—removed from the air-raid shelters—which the search officers could identify to the unsuspecting public as gas detectors.

One question remained to be decided: where to begin. Dewing, Hudson and Feldman gathered in front of a huge map of the area.

"I would say right off the bat," Feldman said, "that there are two places in there it won't be. The first's the meat market. Very law-abiding area, one of the lowest crime rates in the city." He bestowed an angelic smile on Dewing. "It's completely run by the Mob. And that tightly structured old Italian neighborhood. Unless these guys speak Arab with a big Italian accent, they'd set off alarm bells just walking down the street in there.

"Since we got an ID on this guy at Eighth near Fifth from that hooker," Feldman continued, "I'd say start around Washington Square. Then maybe move up, cover Eighth to Fourteenth and Broadway to Sixth Avenue. After that, work back toward the river.

"Except for one thing," the Chief concluded. "I'd get people into those piers right away. That's got to be the perfect place to hide something."

"All right," Dewing agreed. "We'll proceed on the basis you've outlined."

Feldman had just started back to the desk Dewing had assigned him when the familiar hulking figure drifted up beside him.

432

"What the hell are you doing here?" Feldman demanded. "I figured you'd be in New Haven by now."

Angelo shrugged. "Got anything for me to do?" he asked.

Laila Dajani drove down the quiet Spring Valley street to the house she had rented as a temporary hideaway for her brother and herself. It had belonged to an elderly widowed vice-president of the Chemical Bank who had died of cancer in October. His son and heir, who lived fifty miles away in Connecticut, had been delighted to rent it to Laila for a month during the holidays. As had been the case with the retired stockbroker from whom she had rented the house in Queens that they had used as a cover for their import firm, their transaction had been simple: a letter of agreement and two thousand dollars in cash, half for a month's rent, half as deposit.

Laila turned into the driveway and continued into the open garage, thinking again what perfect concealment the bland sameness of this street offered. Kamal did not agree. He paused a moment, leaving the garage to scrutinize the houses of their neighbors, each house set on its plot of a quarter of an acre.

"It's not good," he said. "Too many people."

Laila did not answer. She opened the front door and stepped inside. Whalid was in the den off the entry hall, sprawled on a sofa in his stockinged feet, a bottle of whiskey, a quarter of it gone, on the table beside him. She continued to the kitchen. It was littered with unwashed dishes left over from her brother's breakfast and supper. Tossed into the wastebasket was an empty bottle. So, she thought, that bottle in the den isn't his first.

Kamal was looking scornfully at Whalid's Johnnie Walker bottle when she returned to the study. "Taking care of your ulcer?" he asked his brother.

Whalid ignored him. "Why go on waiting around here? Why don't we get going now?" he asked.

"Because our orders are to wait here until the announcement is made or the bomb explodes."

"For God's sake, Kamal, don't be such a fool! That bomb's never going to explode."

"Never? Why not?" Kamal's blue eyes were chill and lusterless as they contemplated his brother.

433

"Because the Americans are going to agree. They haven't got any choice. You know that."

"There is only one thing I know for sure, my brother." Whalid squirmed uncomfortably listening to the flat, menacing tone of Kamal's voice. "That is that we have orders and I will see we follow them. All of us."

"We found it!"

The jubilant shout echoed through the silent chamber, as jarring, as discordant, as a shout in a library. The room in which it rang out was the operational center of the United States's ultrasecret communications intelligence agency, the National Security Agency in Fort Meade, Maryland.

The scores of men and women hunched over the blinking lights of individual computer terminals in the room were searching for what an Air Force colonel had earlier described to the President as the right snowflake in a blizzard, an electronic blizzard. Their computer terminals flashed out the distinctive print of every sound, phone call, radio message, Morse-code transmission moving in and out of the East Coast of the United States. They were being compared with the sounds captured by the U.S.S. *Allen* that had come out of Libya and had been relayed to the NSA's computers. From the instant Qaddafi agreed to extend his ultimatum, the search had been on for the signal the Agency was sure he would have had to send to reprogram the detonator of his bomb.

The man who had found it, a balding forty-two-year-old Ph.D. from MIT, leaped from his console. The signal was nothing more than a 1.2-second burst of noise, a string of zeroes and ones, the binary system of transmission in which all international communications, even those of the human voice, were made. But it matched up perfectly with a burst caught by the *Allen* coming from the Libyan seacoast a few miles from the Villa Pietri a few hundredths of a second before the NSA's scanners had intercepted it hurtling toward Manhattan.

The MIT scientist took his data to another computer bank and, employing triangulation and electronic devices, some so secret their existence was unknown outside of the NSA headquarters, wrested a vital secret from the overpopulated orbital plane of the

434

earth: he discovered which of the thousands of satellites littering the skies Qaddafi was using to transmit his signals.

By the time the Dajanis had settled into their upstate safe house, the search for their hidden bomb was already well under way. On the waterfront, the NEST and FBI teams sweeping the rotting piers protruding into the Hudson found rats, garbage, winos, the battered desks and upturned chairs of Customs officers who had once, in the heyday of those docks, swept through steamer trunks from Vuitton and matched leather baggage from Mark Cross. They found frightened stockbrokers from Pelham, aspiring lawyers from Sullivan and Cromwell, CPAs from Price Waterhouse, layout artists from Jackson, McGee, a fashion designer apprenticed to Charley Cole cowering in the shadows of the piers' "reception rooms," some nearly hysterical with fright; everything, in short, except a trace of the bomb for which they were searching.

Across town, progress was slower. The NEST-FBI teams in their Con Ed overalls were able to move quickly, but the door-to-door police follow-up was a nightmare. Dozens of apartments in the area were unoccupied at the time; owners away at work. The police could have used their battering rams on them, but that, Abe Stern and the Commissioner knew, would provoke unbelievable problems. They would have to station a precious policeman at every opened door to stand guard. Otherwise New York's litigious citizenry, Stern pointed out, would be certain to sue the city for millions in real or imagined losses—assuming there would be a city left for them to sue. At the police teams' recommendation, a list was made of all unoccupied apartments for a follow-up effort if the first full sweep of the search area failed to turn up Qaddafi's device.

And there were those determinedly civil-rights-conscious New Yorkers who were not going to let a police officer across their threshhold without a search warrant, even if he was ostensibly trying to save them from escaping gas. In that case, a call for a warrant went back to the Sixth Precinct. There a team of federal judges and U.S. attorneys ordered to duty by the President filled in the protesting citizen's name and address on a predrafted warrant and authorized entry by walkie-talkie.

At 156 Bleecker Street, a pair of detectives burst into a junkies' shooting gallery. Half a dozen addicts lay around the room on mattresses, some cooking up their next shot, others spaced out in the euphoria of an earlier hit. The detectives kicked over the junkies' cooker, smashed their hypodermic needles, flushed their dope down the toilet, then left, leaving the uncomprehending addicts to gape at the door slamming shut behind them. In three different places, search teams stumbled on burglars busting a flat. Having no time to waste on petty thievery, they ordered the astonished burglars to drop their loot and run for the front door.

At Quintana's Bar in the West Village, the sight of the agents' shield brought a shower of goodies onto the floor: knives, brass knuckles, pills, coke, pot, heroin; any piece of evidence that the collection of petty crooks in the bar wanted to get rid of before the shakedown they were sure was coming. The agents pocketed the knives, flushed away the pills and the pot, searched the cellar, then stalked out, leaving the bar's unsearched clients spluttering in rage. There were lovers whose coupling was interrupted or fights momentarily calmed, delinquent muggers routed out of stairwells. In a garret on Cornelia Street police found the decaying corpse of a suicide hanging from the rafter to which he had tied himself, and on Thompson Street the body of an elderly woman who had apparently died of the cold in her unheated flat.

The search turned up barrels of every description: old wine kegs, beer barrels, barrels of chemicals and motor oil, of old rags; even, in a cellar on Washington Place, three barrels of hoarded gasoline left from World War II. Every one had to be carefully, meticulously scrutinized and eliminated by NEST's scientists.

Each move made out on the streets was carefully, painstakingly logged at the Sixth Precinct on huge maps, on great sheets of photos now covering one whole wall of the station house. Feldman studied the stain of the area searched. It was like a glob of heavy liquid slowly, ever so slowly, spreading over the map. They were in a race between the tantalizing slowness of its advance and the clock, and for the moment, the despairing Chief of Detectives realized, the clock was winning.

In the NSC conference room, the same Air Force colonel who had briefed the President and his advisers shortly after Qaddafi's threat came in Sunday night stood once again before his charts. "The man has been extremely clever in his choice of a satellite to handle his transmission, Mr. President," he declared. "He's using an absolutely forgotten bird up there called Oscar. It was designed for amateur radio enthusiasts and put up by NASA. Quite frankly, once it was hung up there, everybody simply forgot about it. We don't even carry it in our classified listing of all the satellites currently in space."

The colonel cleared his throat in nervous acknowledgment of his service's shortcomings. "And I've also got to say that for his purposes it's the perfect bird. Since these ham radio operators it was designed for can't afford a lot of expensive equipment, there's a lot of power in its down leg back to earth. A relatively small receiver could pick up a coded communication like this with no trouble at all."

"Well, for God's sake, can't your Air Force blow that damn thing out of the sky with one of our missiles?" Crandell asked.

"Del, just a minute." Jack Eastman bridled at yet another of Crandell's proposals for instant, ill-thought-out action. "We have every reason to assume this bomb is programmed to detonate automatically if it doesn't receive a countersignal. Blow that thing out of the skies and how will Qaddafi stand it down if somehow we're able to convince him not to detonate it before his ultimatum expires?"

"Jack, when in hell are you going to wake up to the fact that the man is not going to compromise?"

The President interrupted his quarreling advisers with a weary wave of his hand. He turned to the Air Force colonel. "For the time being at least," he asked, "can you blanket all transmission out of that satellite? Shut it down completely?"

"Yes, sir."

"Then do it."

Mesmerized and uncomprehending, the three Dajanis sat in front of the television set in the den of their rented house in upstate New York. There were only minutes left, yet the screen before them contained no image of the President announcing a new Middle East settlement or a national emergency, no frenzied Mayor telling New Yorkers to flee their city, no humbled Menachem Begin proclaiming that his nation was withdrawing from East

437

Jerusalem and the West Bank. Instead, the screen flickered with the interminable images of a soap opera featuring a psychiatrist trapped in an adulterous relationship with a patient.

Laila was close to hysteria. "It's gone wrong!" she sniffled. "It hasn't worked. It's going to explode!"

Whalid set his half-filled whiskey glass on the TV set and put an arm around her shoulders. "They must be talking in secret. Who knows? Maybe he's going to extend the ultimatum." On the floor of the den was a blue metallic case, similar to the detonation case attached to Whalid's bomb except that it contained none of the protective devices the Japanese had built into the original. It too was connected to a slender needle rising almost invisibly above the TV antenna on the roof. "If he is, we'll find out soon enough."

"What time is it?" Kamal asked for the third time in five minutes.

"Four minutes to three," Whalid replied.

Kamal got up and walked to the window onto the quiet, deserted suburban street. "Maybe the Americans refused, after all. Will we hear it explode up here?" he asked his brother.

He was talking about an event that was going to cause the deaths of six million people, yet he put the question to Whalid as though he were asking him if they would be able to hear a door slam across the street.

"No," Whalid replied. "There might be a flash of light. Or if you were out in the street, you might feel the heat." There would be a cloud, the mushroom cloud. That we'd see." Whalid pointed to the window behind Kamal. "The weather's clear enough."

On the television set, the announcer droned a final tease about the next day's episode of the soap opera while an image of the sun setting to the throb of violins faded from the screen. It was replaced by that of a man marching past the shelves of a supermarket extolling the virtues of a can of spaghetti with real Italian-style meat sauce.

"Look!" Laila shrieked, pointing at the screen. "It's three o'clock and they're showing that! It's failed! It's gone all wrong!"

Kamal turned from the window. He studied their silent radio receiver, then the television set. "Calm yourself," he ordered his sister. "Do you have no dignity?" He turned and with his gliding walk stalked through the hall, out of the front door and onto the snow-covered lawn.

438

Whalid watched him through the window as Kamal marched slowly up and down, eyes fixed on the distant horizon, as purposeful, as determined, as a beast waiting by a water hole for a lesser animal to appear. The scientist glanced at his watch. Three minutes past three. If something had happened, the signal would have arrived on their radio by now.

Whalid Dajani shuddered, reached for the whiskey bottle and with a shaking hand poured a large dollop into his glass.

Laila remained on the couch, her knees drawn up to her chest in a trance of horror and ill-comprehension. There had never been any question this was going to happen. The logic of their act was irrefutable, overhwleming. It had been evident from the beginning that the Americans would have to give them what they wanted. Yet, clearly, they had not, and now they were paying the price that was never supposed to be paid.

Suddenly she sat up, her finger thrust at the television set. "Wait a minute," she cried. "That station is in New York and it's still on!"

"That's right."

It was Kamal standing in the doorway to the den. He looked at Laila, at his brother slumped in his chair, one hand on his whiskey glass on the table beside him, at their silent radio receiver. "It's seven minutes past three. We had no word of an extension of the ultimatum. Clearly, the bomb was meant to explode and did not. Why?"

Thirty-five miles away in New York City, the frightened men at the Sixth Precinct had one eye on the clock, the other on the stain spreading all too slowly over the map of the area they were searching. Al Feldman, at the center of the room, wanted to cry out in frustration. Why hadn't they found it? Why was it taking so long? Three times Washington had called on the direct line they had installed here, urging them to hurry, warning them that there would be no extension this time, that after nine o'clock there was nothing, only the void.

Up until now there had been no panic, no hysteria, nobody breaking down. That was because they still had time, and time was hope, tangible, palpable hope. But what was going to happen at six o'clock if they hadn't found it? At seven, at eight when there was

439

just one more hour remaining? Would they hold then? Or would they panic like the frightened animals they would be, rush to the door, stampede for cars, for the telephones, shriek the news of the coming disaster to friends and relatives? It would take only one or two people then to break and it would all collapse. One voice shouting "Fire!" in the dark and crowded theater. There would be a hundred voices screaming "Fire," Feldman realized, all of them in this building. We don't have six hours, the Chief suddenly understood. We probably don't even have five. At seven o'clock it will all be over. The news will break and five million human beings will become five million rabbits trying to run before the flames of a forest fire.

The cackle of the squawk box linking them to the NSC conference room in the White House interrupted his baleful meditation. "Any progress to report?" Jack Eastman's voice asked.

Normally Feldman honored the formality of the chain of command in a crisis as religiously as a priest guards the secrets of his confessional. Now, however, he leaned past the Commissioner and Dewing to address the squawk himself. "No, none," he answered, his voice so hoarse he could have been a perfect candidate for an antismoking commercial. "Is the President there?"

"Yes," came the familiar soft voice.

"Mr. President, this is Al Feldman, the Chief of Detectives up here. I have got to tell you, sir, there is no way we are going to find that bomb before nine o'clock tonight. Either you got to get us more time, Mr. President, or you got to tell the people what's happening. You can't let them die trapped up here like rats."

Kamal Dajani was perched on the imitation-mahogany cabinet of the now silent TV set, his arms folded, studying his brother with a steady, imperturbable gaze.

"What are you looking at me for?" Whalid took an anxious gulp of his whiskey. "Get yourself a drink. Celebrate. We won. The Israelis must be moving out of the West Bank right now. They'll probably announce it tonight."

Kamal remained as immobile as an actor caught in the concluding freeze frame of a police serial on the TV set his legs concealed.

Whalid lurched to his feet. "We got to get going." He looked at Laila. "Your things ready? We're going home. To Jerusalem."

440

He started toward the door. Kamal didn't budge. Whalid turned back to him. "What the hell is the matter with you?" he demanded. His face was flushed, his voice beginning to thicken under the impact of strain and whiskey.

"Why didn't the bomb go off, Whalid?"

"Kamal, you damn fool." Whalid swayed in the doorway like a sapling hit by a gust of wind. "Can't you understand anything? That bomb was never meant to go off. You knew that. Qaddafi knew that. It was just a threat, a way to right a wrong, to get us justice."

His brother glared at him with sullen probing eyes.

"And you wanted to be sure of that, did you?"

"The trouble with you, Kamal, is you're still back there in your training camp in Damascus playing with your chunks of plastic." Whalid was beginning to shout. "You thought this was going to be like ambushing a bus full of kids, or hijacking some people in a plane, didn't you? But this is five million people. We can't go home to Palestine over the bodies of five million innocent people, you damn fool! There has to be another way." Whalid grasped at the top of the sofa for support. "I didn't build a bomb to kill five million people. I built it to make us even with the rest of the world. The Jews have it. The Americans have it. The French have it. The Chinese have it. The Russians have it. The English have it. Now, thanks to me, we have it. And we're going to get our homes back with it. They must be finishing up their agreement right now. That's why we haven't heard anything."

"Oh no, Whalid. I don't believe that's why we haven't heard anything." The words were as soft, as gentle, as a kitten's purr. "I believe Qaddafi wanted that bomb to explode and the reason it didn't is you did something to it while we were up on the roof Sunday fixing the aerial. That's why you've been so relaxed since then. That's why you started to treat your ulcer with whiskey again, isn't it?"

Whalid was silent. His breath was coming in shortening bursts, an oil slick of nervous sweat beginning to clot the pores of his temple.

"You're a traitor. A drunk and a traitor!" Kamal rose, each of his limbs seeming to follow his action individually like the legs of a folding bridge table snapping out one by one. "What did you do, Whalid?"

Whalid stood immobile before his younger brother's advance. His lower jaw trembled slightly as he tried unsuccessfully to give sound to the words fear had trapped in his throat.

"What did you do, Whalid?"

Kamal's right hand flicked out like a rattlesnake's tongue. The calloused ridges below his little finger, the ridge of flesh that had chopped the life from Alain Prévost in the Bois de Boulogne, crashed against his brother's cheekbone. Whalid shrieked in pain as the bone cracked. His scream was choked off by the fingertips of Kamal's left hand driving a wedge into the recess of his solar plexus. The breath burst from Whalid's mouth as air explodes from a punctured balloon. He tottered backward, hit a chair, then crashed into the maple table the house's owner had once used as a desk. Dishes, his whiskey bottle, the framed portraits of the dead banker's grandchildren cascaded to the ground in a clatter of breaking glass and splintering wood.

"You know what's happening now because of you? The Americans are preparing to destroy Qaddafi. They're going to wipe him out because he's at their mercy, because of you, because of whatever you did to that bomb."

Whalid was choking, trying almost to bite the air in his effort to bring the breath back to his lungs. He gagged.

"I want to know what you did to it."

"No!"

Kamal's foot drove with crushing force into his brother's crotch. Whalid screamed in agony as the tip of Kamal's shoe crushed his testicles against the flesh of his groin.

"Kamal!" It was Laila. "For God's sake, stop it. He's your brother!"

"He's a traitor. He's a filthy dirty traitor!" Kamal's foot lashed out once more, a swift vicious stroke to the base of his brother's spine. "Tell me what you did to it, you bastard."

"No."

Again the foot smashed forward, this time into the kidneys of the figure crumpled in the fetal position on the floor.

"Tell me!"

Kamal hadn't seen his sister pick up the whiskey bottle. Yet, instinctively, he sensed the swish of air as it descended toward him. He moved forward enough, just enough, so that instead of smashing it against his skull she crashed it down onto the vertebrae

442

at the head of his spine. He buckled under the blow, then, off balance, stumbled back against the sofa.

Whalid rolled over, reaching for his pocket. He had his gun in his wavering, untrained hand as his brother flung himself at him. His first shot exploded just over Kamal's shoulder. There was no second. The fingers of Kamal's right hand, pressed together into a wedge of flesh and bone, smashed against his trachea just below his Adam's apple, forcing it backward against the bone of his neck until its delicate membranes snapped apart like elastic bands stretched beyond their breaking point.

A look of surprise melting swiftly into horror spread over Whalid's face. His mouth and jaws contorted in a grotesque and futile effort to inhale the air that would never again reach his lungs.

Kamal stood over him, rubbing the ridge of his right hand almost meditatively in his left palm. Laila was transfixed, her mouth agape with horror, still not quite comprehending what had happened.

"What did you do to him?" she gasped.

"What a traitor deserves. I killed him."

Kamal knelt down beside his brother. Whalid's face was grayish purple, his eyes bulging, whites protruding from their sockets, imploring them silently for some stay of the death he realized was overtaking him.

"It takes a couple of minutes for them to die," Kamal announced matter-of-factly. With a quick heave, he rolled his brother onto his stomach as a calloused vet might turn over the still-warm body of a dog. "I want the checklist."

He patted the hip pockets of Whalid's trousers. There was something hard in the left one. Kamal reached in and thrust the object he pulled out up to his sister. It was a thirty-minute BASF tape, and both of them recognized instantly the tiny red crescent in its upper right-hand corner.

"That's why it didn't go off. The bastard put another tape in there while we were up on the roof."

Furiously, Kamal rolled his brother back over onto his back again. His face was bluish purple now, the eyes slightly less protruding, the hysteria of a moment ago replaced by a fearing resignation to the death that was only seconds away. Kamal bent down and pressed his lips against his brother's ear, shouting to make sure his dying brain would record the message, would send the angry curse spinning around him as he stumbled toward the void.

"Your bomb is going to go off!" he yelled. "Because I'm going to set it off. You lost, traitor!"

Dorothy Burns had been about to leave for the Tuesday-afternoon tea of her Aquinas discussion group when she thought she heard a shot. Never, except on the television programs that comforted the lonely nights of her widowhood, had Dorothy heard a gunshot. Anxiously she rushed to her bedroom window and stared at the house next door. She was about to turn away again when she saw the man, almost pulling the woman behind him, burst from the front door and run to the garage. Then she saw the car back recklessly down the driveway and go careening off up the street.

Dorothy shuddered. Ever since poor Tom's boy had told her he had rented his father's house to foreigners for Christmas, she had wondered what kind of people they were. Was this the answer? There was only a second's hesitation before she picked up the phone.

"Operator," she said, "please get me the police."

Al Feldman's despairing plea for time had affected everyone in the NSC conference room from the President to the twenty-five-year-old Vassar girl responsible for keeping track of the classified documents flowing in and out of the chamber. It was as if the exhausted, desperate Chief of Detective's voice had suddenly incarnated for each man and woman in the room the five million New Yorkers whose lives were at risk because of the decision they had made. Bennington of the CIA was the first to break the stricken silence.

"Mr. President," he said. "I have a suggestion. It's a tactic that might allow us to convert the limited extension of his ultimatum into an indefinite one. Let's get Begin. Tell him we want to go ahead with our West Bank operation. Except it will be mutually agreed it's just a show to gain us time to let New York find the device. He'll certainly agree to that. Then we'll tell Qaddafi we're going in. Invite him to send observers from his embassy in Damascus along with our forces to verify that we really are doing it. Just landing and deploying our forces and moving them up to the West

444

Bank is going to take close to ten hours. If it comes to it, we can actually move in, fight a couple of sham battles with the Israelis. The important thing is, if we can get him to agree to this, then we, not Qaddafi, will be controlling the time element in the crisis.''

The President looked around the room, a first glimmer of hope registering in his face. ''Harold,'' he asked the Secretary of Defense, ''what do you think?''

''Mr. President, try it. With so much at stake, it's worth trying anything.''

A police car bearing two uniformed officers of the Spring Valley police screeched to a stop in front of Dorothy Burns's home three minutes after her call. Visibly excited, she confided to them what she had seen and heard.

''Probably been watching too many TV programs lately,'' the first officer whispered to his partner as they trudged through the snow to the house next door. When there was no answer at the front door, they circled the house looking for telltale signs of a forced entry. There were none. They returned to the front door and decided to give it a try. It was open.

The first officer drew his pistol and poked his head inside. ''Anybody home?'' he shouted.

Silence followed his cry. ''We'd better have a look,'' he said, advancing down the hallway. He paused at the door of the den and looked inside.

''Jesus Christ!'' he yelled back to his deputy. ''Get the State Police! The old lady wasn't kidding!''

An atmosphere as despairing, as hopeless, as that in the NSC conference room gripped Qaddafi's command post in the basement of the Villa Pietri. As always, even when he was in a crowded room, Qaddafi was alone, slouched at the head of the table, morose and withdrawn. The men around him murmured their exchanges in restrained little ripples of noise that would not intrude on their chieftain's silence.

The passing hours had brought to the Libyan and the men around him the growing certitude that their ghastly gamble was failing. Each understood full well what the consequences of failure would

445

be. As the time had passed with no sign of Israeli acquiescence to their demands, Qaddafi had withdrawn, spiritually, from their gathering. He was a man of dark and unpredictable moods, capable of temper tantrums so violent he could, literally, smash the furniture of his office and roll on the floor in rage. Once he had personally shaved the head of his Prime Minister, Salam Jalloud, because the latter had violated the puritanical standards of his revolution by consorting with bar girls in Rome. And there were his periodic retreats to the desert, pilgrimages to his past in which he sought in the austerity and loneliness of the sands the strength to confront a world he did not always choose to understand.

The dark, brooding eyes studied the men around him now. Like most revolutions, his had been nourished by the blood of its makers. Of the band of brothers that had overthrown Libya's King Idris in 1969, only Jalloud remained. The others were dead, disgraced or in exile, replaced by a new generation of followers of more certain loyalty and less menacing demeanor. Qaddafi pondered each face in turn. Which among them would remain loyal to the end of this trial? And which among them would be the first to raise the dagger, to accuse their leader of the dictator's unforgivable sin—failure?

A shout from the communications center next door interrupted his meditation. "*Ya sidi!*" a clerk cried. "It is the American airplane. The President wishes to talk to you. The Americans have accepted your terms!"

The men in the room let out a collective jubilant roar of triumph; they did, that is, with one exception—Qaddafi. He remained motionless and unsmiling, fixed in the position he had been in for hours. Finally he raised a finger.

"Tell the President this time I will talk to him," he intoned.

Three police cars of the New York State Police, C Troop, their red rooftop lights slowly revolving, lined the road in front of the house in which Whalid Dajani had been killed. An ambulance, its doors open, stood in the driveway. Across the street, a circle of neighbors and of kids who had interrupted their afternoon walk home from school looked on in shock and concern. Murder was not an everyday occurrence in the quiet byways of Spring Valley.

In the den, the police hovered around Whalid's body. The im-

446

pact of his errant bullet was circled in red on the wall. A finger-printing team was already dusting for prints while a trooper with a piece of chalk traced out the exact position of his corpse on the floor. Above him, a police photographer recorded the scene from every angle.

"Take his prints down at the morgue," the captain in charge of the investigation ordered, "and tell the coroner to run an autopsy on him." He looked at the broken fifth of Johnnie Walker on the floor, then cast a scornful glance at Whalid's corpse. "I'll bet he'll find enough alcohol in there to open a distillery. Come on," he said, squatting down beside the body, "let's see if he's got any ID on him."

While he started through Whalid's pants, another trooper picked up the suit coat. He pulled out Whalid's passport and flicked it open. "Hey, Charlie," he said to the captain, "he's a fucking Arab."

The captain held the passport photo up beside Whalid's face, still contorted by the agony of his dying struggle for air. He grunted, satisfied at the match-up, then went through its pages until he found what he was looking for: the entry stamp an INS officer at JFK had placed on it. "Poor bastard, didn't have time to do much Christmas shopping," he said, noting the date, December 9. "I'll go down to the car and call this in."

The captain, unaware of the emergency in New York, sauntered out of the house, stopping as he did to order the ambulance men to pick up the body. At the curb he lit a cigarette, then finally picked up the speaker of his car radio. "Okay," he said when his head-quarters replied. "I have the details on this stiff we got up here in Spring Valley.

Muammar al-Qaddafi listened impassively to the President's recital of his proposed U.S. movement into the West Bank. No such restraint fettered the men around him. They were already preparing to celebrate the enormity of the triumph their leader's gamble had won.

"Mr. President," the Libyan replied when the American had finished, "your terms are unacceptable."

His advisers looked at him aghast, but Qaddafi ignored them. "I do not intend to substitute an American occupation of my brothers' lands for an Israeli one. The terms of my letter were simple. I want Begin to renounce to the world and his people publicly and forever Israel's claims to our lands. And then I want the Israelis to leave immediately their settlements and East Jerusalem. There is no need to extend my ultimatum for that. All that I have asked can be accomplished in one hour. No more.''

As his interpreter began to translate his words, Qaddafi's circle of advisers erupted in protest. ''You can't do this,'' Jalloud protested. ''We've won. They're giving us what we want.''

Qaddafi smashed his fist into the table. ''Fool!'' he shouted. ''Have you no vision? It is a trick to lull us, to win time for them.''

The President was back on the Doomsday circuit again. He spoke very slowly this time, his tone as void of emotion as his adversary's had so often been. ''Mr. Qaddafi,'' he said, ''understand this, I beg you. There are, at this moment, thirty-two Poseidon missiles targeted on your nation. They can destroy every living creature on Libyan soil. I will give the order to fire those missiles, even if it means the destruction of the finest city on earth, if you have not agreed to extend your ultimatum and end this unacceptable attempt to blackmail another nation by eight o'clock tonight. I pray God, sir, you believe my words.''

The Libyan did not stir on hearing them. Nor did he choose to measure the horror and dismay they caused in the men around him as the finality of what they were heading to had registered on them.

''I cannot and I will not live in a world without justice for my brothers,'' he answered. ''I and my people are ready to die for the justice you deny us.''

His intelligence chief exploded at his words. ''No!'' he shouted. ''We are not. You have no right. You have no right to sacrifice us and our children, a whole nation, for this. You can't go through with it.''

Qaddafi did not look at the man when he replied. His dark unfathomable eyes were riveted to some distant vision whose outlines only they could perceive.

''I can, my brother,'' he whispered, ''and I have.''

As Qaddafi lapsed into an impenetrable silence, a third of the way around the world in the city he menaced three men stared at a map of Greenwich Village. Al Feldman had held Angelo

448

Rocchia and Jack Rand at his Sixth Precinct search headquarters as part of his mobile reserve.

"Something isn't right," he told them, studying the areas they had already searched. "We should have found the damn thing by now."

Angelo shuddered. "Christ," he said, "you don't suppose I could have been wrong, do you?"

He was interrupted by a shout to Feldman from across the room. "Hey, Chief," an officer called, "They want you on the amplifier to the other command post."

Among the underground headquarters' many communication circuits was a copy of the New York State Police's intelligence network, and Feldman's caller had just torn a routine all-points bulletin from its Teleprinter.

"Chief," he said, "they got a DOA up in Spring Valley. Suspected murder. The guy's an Arab and his ident is close to one of those guys we're looking for."

"Read it to me," Feldman ordered.

The officer read:

"1532 Code 71 Caucasian Male discovered DOA, 32 High Farms Road by Spring Valley PD. NYSP Troop C, McManus IC, dispatched. Victim's height approx. 5'10". Weight 185. ID given by Lebanese Passport 2346J1 issued Beirut November 22, 1979, as Ibrahim Abboud. Electronic Engineer born Beirut September 12, 1941. Entered USA JFK International Airport in December this year. Probable cause of death: violent assault. Hair: brown. Eyes: brown. Identifying marks or features: brown moustache. Tattoo inside right forearm of dagger, snake and heart."

"Tattoo! Jesus Christ, did you say tattoo?" Feldman was shouting with excitement. "Get me that file the French sent us last night," he screamed at Dewing. He rummaged through it until he found what he was looking for.

"That's him!" he screamed. Everyone in the crowded top floor of the Sixth Precinct froze at his shout. "That's one of the guys we're looking for!"

At almost the same moment, Art Gelb of the *Times* was accepting a collect call from Las Vegas.

"Mr. Gelb," came a distant and timid voice. "This is your Reno stringer. I'm sorry it took a while to get the information you wanted about that guy McClintock."

"Oh yeah, that guy in Safeguards out there. Some kind of chemical safeguards, I suppose."

"No, Mr. Gelb," the stringer replied. "He's assigned to one of those hush-hush government organizations that works in a restricted area out at McCarran Air Force Base. It's called NEST, for Nuclear Explosive Search Teams. They're meant to go out and look for hidden radioactive materials, stuff that might be stolen from a nuclear power plant. Eventually, even a hidden atomic bomb."

The stringer continued, but Gelb wasn't listening anymore. He had gone suddenly limp. Oh, my God, he thought, how they've lied to us!

The officer of the New York State Police Troop C in charge of investigating Whalid Dajani's murder raced toward his squad car.

"Hurry, Captain," his deputy shouted. "It's an emergency."

The captain grabbed the radio out of his hands, listened to Al Feldman a minute, then turned to his deputy. "Quick. Get that lady in there who saw them take off."

Flushed and excited by her sudden prominence, Dorothy Burns was bundled out of her house and down to the squad car by two burly state policemen. Miles away, bursting with strain and excitement, Dewing and Feldman interrogated her in the chaos and confusion of their Sixth Precinct search headquarters. They already had the time her call had been logged in by the Spring Valley police, 1532. From the overwrought woman they drew out two other vital pieces of information, a description of the man and woman she had seen running out of the house and the color of the car, dark green, in which they had raced off.

"It's the other two!" Feldman said, listening to her. "It's got to be." Bannion, Hudson and the CIA's Salisbury were gathered around the Chief's desk following the conversation. "Where the hell would they be racing off to?" Feldman asked the state trooper. "Are you near any big arterial highways up there?"

"Yeah," the trooper replied. "There's an entrance to the New York State Thruway about half a mile down the road."

"In the direction they were going?"

"Yup."

Feldman looked at the men around him. "That's it!" he shouted. "They're taking off! They're heading north before it explodes." He turned back to the squawk box which linked him to the squad car in Spring Valley.

"Captain," he yelled, "get a car up to the toll gates just as fast as you can drive! Try to get me a confirmation from the guys that collect the tolls that that's where they went."

The captain shouted an order. One of the three cars turned around and screeched off, its siren shrieking.

In New York, Feldman shouted for a map of New York State. A dozen cops ran through the building looking for one. Finally a patrolman rushed up with an old Esso road map he had found in the glove compartment of his car. Hastily, Feldman spread the map on his desk.

"They must be going north, right?" He checked his watch. "We know they took off thirty-seven minutes ago. They couldn't have done more than fifty miles in that time." He made a quick calculation, then jabbed the map north of Kingston. "They've got to be between Spring Valley and here. We've got to seal off that Thruway right away. Get police cars to close off every exit ramp. Have the State Police throw up roadblocks at Newburgh and Kingston. Flood the highway with cars. Stop every green vehicle they see. We've got to take these bastards!"

Abe Rosenthal, the executive editor of *The New York Times,* stared at his deputy managing editor. The usually volatile, animated Gelb had a face on him as grim as a Florentine death mask.

"What the hell is the matter with you, Art?" Rosenthal asked. "Are you sick or something?"

Gelb closed Rosenthal's office door to be sure that no one could overhear him, then repeated what his Las Vegas stringer had said. This time, it was Rosenthal who paled. He was a disheveled roly-poly man in his late fifties, sometimes described by his subordinates behind his back as a rumpled teddy bear. The description was inept. There was no Winnie-the-Pooh geniality in Abe Rosenthal. Without a word to Gelb he picked up his phone and called Police Plaza.

"I don't give a damn where he is or what he's doing," he snarled at the Police Commissioner's harassed detective-secretary. "I want to talk to him immediately and I'll hold on here until you get him."

It took several minutes to patch the call through the improvised lines to the Sixth Precinct, then to get Michael Bannion into a quiet corner away from the distress and turmoil of the search center.

Rosenthal wasted no time in chitchat when he heard the Commissioner's voice. "I understand you told one of my editors your people are out looking for a barrel of chlorine gas hidden in this city, Commissioner?"

"Yes, sir, that's right, Mr. Rosenthal, and I can't tell you how much we'd appreciate your help at the *Times* in keeping this from the public until we've been able to locate and neutralize it."

"Hidden by some Palestinian terrorists, I understand?"

"That is correct." Despite the strain under which he had been living, Bannion's baritone was as resonant, as commanding as ever.

"Commissioner, you're a goddamn liar. There's an atomic bomb in that barrel. There are thousands, maybe houndreds of thousands, of people in this city at risk and you're refusing to tell them their lives are in danger. You don't expect *The New York Times* to go along with that, do you? To stand by silent, after we've been lied to, knowing that thousands of the people we serve are threatened with death?"

A stunned silence followed his words. At the Sixth Precinct, Bannion had clapped his hand over the mouthpiece of his phone. He was waving frantically at an aide. "Get Washington!" he shouted. "Get the President! The secret's out!"

"I don't believe it! Repeat that again," Al Feldman roared at the squawk box on his desk.

"One of the toll-gate attendants at the Thruway entry up here just identified your Arabs," replied the irritated state trooper up in Spring Valley. "But he said they were heading south toward the city, not north."

By now a dozen men were around Feldman's desk, all listening. "You absolutely certain of that? He's sure it was them? Going *south?*"

452

"Of course, damn it. The guy only collects southbound tolls."
The knot of people around the Chief returned his astonished air.
"They broke a five-dollar bill, and when he gave them back the
change he saw the broad was crying."

"Why?" Dewing demanded. "Why in hell would they be coming
back to the city when they know it's about to be destroyed?"

"Because for some reason they've got to get to that bomb,"
Feldman replied. "That's what it's got to be. They're heading for
the bomb."

"Sweet Mother of Christ!" Bannion hammered his forehead
with the heel of his hand. "If they left Spring Valley at three-thirty
they might be here by now."

The Police Commissioner almost knocked Dewing over lunging
for the squawk box. "Patch me through to SPRINT!" he shouted.
"SPRINT" was an acronym for Special Police Radio Inquiry Network, the multimillion-dollar core of the Department's Communication Division that sprawled over two floors of Police Plaza and
processed nineteen thousand calls a day on the 911 police emergency phone number.

"I want every available radio motor patrol unit, detective cruiser
and emergency service truck routed to the Sixth Precinct immediately. Set up an airtight cordon. Fourteenth from the Hudson to
Broadway, Broadway down to Houston, West Houston back to
the river. Block off every street into the area with cars. I want
every vehicle and pedestrian trying to enter the area stopped and
all identities verified. Two of those three Palestinians we're looking
for are going to try to get in there." Bannion stopped, flushed with
excitement.

"Jim," he told the captain running the center, "tell the precincts
to get every available patrolman onto that cordon right away. Tell
the West Side precincts to concentrate their men on Fourteenth
Street, East Side and Queens on Broadway, downtown and Brooklyn on Houston. Have the barrier shop break out every sawhorse
they've got. Move, Jim, move!"

Bannion pulled a handkerchief from his pocket and mopped his
face. It didn't occur to him for the moment to check his decisions
with Dewing and the FBI. This was his city. Only speed was going
to save it, and he wasn't going to waste time arguing with anybody.

"Mr. Mayor," he shouted. By the time Abe Stern was at his side
he had the Fire Commissioner on the phone. "Tim," he ordered,

"get all your midtown apparatus onto the line Fourteenth–Broadway–West Houston immediately. Let my people use that equipment to block access to the area."

There was a pause while the Fire Commissioner protested Bannion's peremptory order. Even on their level, New York firemen regard their colleagues in the Police Department as warmly as a group of South Bronx juvenile delinquents might look on an assembly of Wall Street stockbrokers.

"Don't fucking argue!" Bannion roared. "Do it! Here's the Mayor." He turned to Abe Stern and pointed at the squawk box. "Tell him!" he commanded his superior.

Stern had barely finished confirming his order when Bannion had cut that call and placed another, this one to his Deputy Commissioner for Public Information. "Patty," he said, "in about two minutes you're going to be swamped with calls from the media. Feed them the chlorine-gas cover story."

Seven floors below the Deputy Commissioner's offices in Police Plaza, Bannion's first orders were already being put into effect. The SPRINT complex was broken up into five radio rooms, one for each of the city's five boroughs. In each, a dozen radio dispatchers controlled all the police cars in the boroughs from televisionlike computer consoles rigged to a keyboard. Through them, they knew what each of their cars was doing, whether its driver was having a cup of coffee or bringing in a murderer, and by flicking a couple of keys they could call and reassign every car in their command.

Almost in synchronization with the flicking of those keys, the undulating wail of police sirens began to rise from every corner of the city as patrol cars wheeled about and started their dash for the Village. Seconds later, their high-pitched chorus was joined by the deep *wonk-wonk* of the city's fire apparatus converging on the police line. Within minutes, all Manhattan Island echoed to those vibrant bellows. The red lights of the oncoming police cars cascaded in the evening darkness down all the great arterial avenues: Ninth, Seventh, Broadway, Fifth. Stunned traffic policemen at the city's major intersections barely had time to block traffic so that one car could scream past when the next came thundering down on them. From the sidewalks, New Yorkers, usually inured to such spectacles, looked on amazed.

SPRINT's current-situation desk routed the incoming cars into position as they neared the area, slotting them into it block by block so that it was gradually sealed off like a water tap being twisted shut. Two or four cars were assigned to each intersection depending on its size. They parked abreast of each lane of traffic, lights flashing. One officer leaped out to reroute the traffic. The other rushed to the sidewalks to start checking the pedestrian flow. In commandeered taxicabs and police trucks, other policemen descended on the area from around Manhattan. Ten minutes after Bannion's orders had been issued Police Department trucks were dropping off at each intersection the gray wooden sawhorses marked "POLICE LINE—DO NOT CROSS" that the NYPD used for traffic control.

The resulting traffic jams were monstrous; so, too, were the outraged protests of people being screened before they were allowed into their neighborhood. And, at 5:17, for the first time, the story went public. WABC-TV interrupted a rerun of *Batman* with a flash from its newsroom. Unmade-up and clearly rushed before the cameras, Bill Beutel, the anchorman of the station's Eyewitness News Team, told his city, "A police emergency is in progress in the Greenwich Village area, where," he reported, "Palestinian terrorists are alleged to have hidden a barrel of deadly chlorine gas."

Ten minutes later, Patricia McGuire appeared before the media's cameras at Police Plaza, announcing the cordon in the Village area and the hunt for the gas, and assuring the public that the city's police authorities had the matter well in hand.

Arthur Sulzberger, the publisher of *The New York Times,* stood by the window of his office on the fourteenth floor of the Times Building and pondered, horrified, the President's words. From the canyon of Forty-third Street below came the snarl of traffic, tailgates clanging shut, the rasp of impatient taxis' horns, a few distant roars of anger; the vibrant cacophony of the city, his city, the city that his family and his family's paper had served for over a century.

He ran a nervous hand through his curly black hair, as closely cut almost as it had been when he served in the Marine Corps. There was an awesome responsiblity to his office as publisher of the paper that considered itself the conscience of America: a responsibility Sulzberger felt every bit as intensely as the President of the United States felt the burden of his office. What were his responsibilities now, he asked himself, what were the obligations of the *Times* to the city, to the nation now?

He turned from the window back to his massive walnut desk and his surprisingly modest office, its walls decorated with *Times* artifacts, historic front pages and stern and sober oils of the father and grandfather who had preceded him in this room.

The door opened. "They're here, Mr. Sulzberger," his secretary announced, and she showed Abe Rosenthal, Art Gelb, Grace Knowland and Myron Pick, an assistant managing editor, into the room.

Rosenthal was still seething with anger at the Police Commissioner for having dared to lie to *The New York Times,* for concealing from the citizens of the city the terrible threat that menaced them.

"Can you imagine, Punch," he said, referring to the publisher by the nickname that had followed him from childhood, "an atomic bomb in this city that could kill ten, twenty thousand people and they don't say a word to anybody?"

Sulzberger was seated now, his hands folded before him as though in prayer, his lips pressed against the knuckle of his left index finger. His head moved slowly back and forth as he listened to his senior editor. "It's not an atomic bomb, Abe. And it's not ten thousand people. It's the whole city."

As they listened in growing horror, he recounted the details of the pleading telephone call he had just received from the President. "Needless to say, he begged us not to use this information."

He looked at each of his employees. Despite the vastness of his enterprise, he knew them all personally. "That's not all he asked us, I'm afraid." His remote, melancholy eyes looked at each face in turn. "He's also asked us to restrict this information to those of us who already know about it. To tell absolutely no one else. No one."

Grace Knowland's hand went instinctively to her mouth to stifle the gasp forming there. Tommy, she thought, where is he?

"My God, I can't believe it!" It was Myron Pick. "He expects us to just sit here and wait to be thermonuclearized? Not even to warn our families?"

"Precisely." Sulzberger, whose own wife and child were only a few blocks away, reiterated Qaddafi's injunction to secrecy and his warning that he would detonate his device instantly if an evacuation was begun.

"Why the hell should we?" Pick demanded. "Just because the President tells us to? How do we know he's telling the truth? Presidents have lied to us. And why the hell should his judgment on what to do in this situation be any better than ours just because seventy million people voted for him in an election?"

"Myron." The publisher studied his agitated editor. "Forget about the President. Forget about Qaddafi. Forget about everything except one thing: what is the responsibility of *The New York Times* to the people of this city?"

"Well, I think it's clear. Publish just as fast as we can. Warn the people that this city is threatened with destruction and tell them to save themselves any way they can."

"Jesus, Myron, you can't possibly mean that!" Grace Knowland said.

"I certainly do. We've got it. Our obligation is to publish it. Doesn't experience teach us that nothing is gained when we hold back the truth? Look at the Bay of Pigs."

The *Times* had had the story of the Bay of Pigs invasion and the CIA's involvement in it but had effectively squelched it on the urging of President Kennedy. Later, both the paper and the President regretted the decision, realizing that the story's publication might have prevented a national disaster.

"For Christ's sake, Myron, this isn't the Bay of Pigs. We're talking about doing something that might cost millions of lives. Yours and mine included."

Both Grace and Pick were on their feet shouting furiously at each other.

"We're talking about the rights and obligations of this paper," Pick roared. "I say it's our right and duty to warn the people of this city what's about to happen to them."

"Who the hell do you think you are to put yourself over the President? Why do you have some God-given right to do whatever you see fit just because you're a newspaper editor? To risk people's lives for some principle?" Grace was beginning to sob in anguish and concern. "Like those horrible people out there in Wisconsin who published the secret of the hydrogen bomb. Now a million people in this city, including my son, may die just because they had to make a point about their goddamn freedom of the press."

"We have no proof Qaddafi got his hydrogen-bomb secrets from those papers," Pick shouted back at her.

"Well, he damn well didn't get it sitting out in the desert medi-tating!"

"Quiet, both of you. Sit down." Sulzberger was on his feet. Usually his voice retained, despite the authority that was his, a kind of youthful timidity, but there were no traces of it present at the moment. "Neither one of you is addressing the problem. Art," he said, turning to Gelb, "what do you think?"

"It seems to me that the U.S. government has no convincing plan that can save this city beyond some vague hope for a miracle of some sort. I mean the only response the government seems to have been able to put together is flooding the Village with FBI agents and detectives."

Abe Rosenthal looked morosely at his friend and associate. "Maybe the problem, Art, is there isn't any other response."

"Then," Gelb said, "maybe our obligation is to say to the peo-ple, 'Get out of the city any way you can.' So there'd be chaos in the street, but maybe a couple of million people would make it. At least the *Times* would have saved them."

"And killed how many others?" Rosenthal peered at Gelb through his outsized dark-framed glasses. "Let's get a couple of points straight here. First, if we feel our responsibility to the people of this city is to warn them about what might happen so they can run for the hills, then there is absolutely no question of holding it to publish an extra of the *Times*. Punch"—he turned to the pub-lisher—"has got to pick up the phone right now and give it to the television networks.

"That would mean we're voting to shout 'Fire!' in the crowded theater, because to let the news out like that, with no warning or preparation, will start a panic that is surely going to kill a million people, bomb or no bomb."

Rosenthal got up. He was in his shirtsleeves, his tie undone, the untidy roll of fat he never managed to control despite all his spo-radic efforts at dieting spilling over the top of his trousers. He seemed to be clawing at the air with his fingertips as he strode nervously about the room. "The second thing is, nobody has elected *The New York Times* to be the government of the United States. We're supposed to monitor the government's decisions, not make them. Okay, Presidents have lied to us, but I don't think this one is lying, not about this. He's made a decision, and millions of lives are involved with it, including our own. I think we have to go with him." He stopped. "Anyhow, it's your decision, Punch."

The publisher turned away from his four employees and stepped again to the window. Already the gray pallor of evening hung upon the city. He had made many a hard decision in this room, the decision to defy Richard Nixon and publish the Pentagon Papers, to overrule his editors and hold the secret of the Glomar Explorer at the request of the CIA. None of them had compared even remotely in their importance to this one.

Finally he walked around to the front of his desk. "My dear friends—" he choked as he articulated the words—"our responsibility, it seems to me, our ultimate responsibility, is to the people of this city. If breaking the secret is going to put their lives in jeopardy, then it seems to me we must keep the secret and accept all the consequences of our act by ourselves—by ourselves alone."

Sulzberger thrust his fists into the pockets of his gray flannel suit. "The President says the ultimatum expires at nine o'clock. I intend to stay here in this office until then. I leave it to the rest of you to follow the dictates of your consciences. If you want to leave, go ahead. Just do it quietly. You have my solemn promise the matter will never be mentioned between us again.

"Otherwise, I'm afraid there's nothing to do except to go on preparing tomorrow's paper—and pray we'll be alive to publish it."

Kamal had insisted they take a different route into the city in the unlikely event they had been seen on their trip up to Spring Valley, and Laila had chosen to come down the East Side along the FDR Drive after crossing the Third Avenue Bridge to avoid the tolls on the Triboro. Since leaving, they had barely spoken. Fingers clenched to the steering wheel, her eyes full of tears, still in a state of quasi-shock from the horrible scene she had witnessed, Laila drove like a robot. Only fear and the memories of her dead father had prevented her from spinning the car off into a roadside ditch and trying to somehow flee her demented brother. Exhausted, her nerves shattered, she was resigned to fate, to carrying this enterprise through to the end she had never believed possible.

Kamal sat beside her in silence, listening to the radio. It said nothing. He studied the flow of traffic moving out of the city, the lights on Roosevelt Island and Queens beyond. Everything seemed perfectly normal. Even the distant wail of the sirens was a part of the city's daily landscape. His eyes studied the green rectangle of the United Nations Building, the towers of light and glass beyond it, a technological universe that by now should have been reduced to a lifeless slag heap. The people in the buildings above, in the traffic enveloping their car, were alive while at this instant, perhaps, in Libya or Palestine or both, Arabs, his brothers, were dying, helpless once again before their enemies because his brother had been a traitor.

Suddenly, seized by an uncontrollable rage, he hammered the dashboard with his fist. Failure, failure, failure, he raged; failure eats at us like maggots in a corpse. We are always the joke, the poor fools whose plans go astray.

He tapped the chest of his leather jacket, reassuring himself for the hundredth time that the checklist was there. Introduce the code to reopen the case, he thought. Switch the tapes. Punch 636 to start the right cassette with the firing instruction. One minute, no more. Ahead of them he saw the highway sign "15TH STREET—EXIT FOR 14TH STREET." He tapped Laila's arm.

"This is it, remember?"

"How's it going?"

Angelo Rocchia didn't have to look up from the charts on which he was following the progress of the search in the crowded streets around Sheridan Square to recognize the voice. The Mayor's gruff yet slightly high-pitched way of speaking always reminded Angelo of the time when he was a kid and Fiorello La Guardia used to read the funny papers over the radio on Sunday mornings during the newspaper strike.

"Not good, Your Honor. Too many buildings. Too few guys. Too little time," Angelo commented grimly.

Abe Stern shook his head in dismayed agreement. He put his chunky hand on Angelo's shoulder. "We took a big chance on you, my friend. I hope to God you were right."

As he wandered off, hands behind his back, head bowed in concern, his words "We took a big chance on you" kept coming back

460

to Angelo like one of those Hindu phrases the kids kept repeating to themselves—except in their case they were supposed to bring you peace.

Every time they cross out another street on that map without finding the barrel, the detective realized, there's another pair of eyes in this room on me.

Where did I go wrong, he asked himself yet again, where, where? The FBI lab in Brooklyn had called in the results of their analysis of the salesman's fender. The paint match-up checked. There was the whore. They had found two countermen in a pizza joint four doors down from the broad's brownstone who recognized the guy. Everything checked. So why hadn't they found it?

He walked back to the desk he and Rand had been assigned, concentrating so intently he banged his thigh on the sharp edge of a filing cabinet along his path. As he sat down on the desk, rubbing his leg in pain and frustration, he turned to his young partner. "What the hell did we do wrong, kid? What do they teach you to do down there in Quantico in a case like this?"

"Angelo," Rand replied in what he meant to be a quiet, comforting manner, "in Quantico they teach us to always go by the book, but you don't seem to believe much in the book."

Angelo gave his shoulders a despairing toss. "There are times to go by the book, times to forget it. Problem is knowing when to do which." Wearily, he rubbed his eyes in the palm of his hand. "My book says when something doesn't work, you go back to square one and start all over again. Try to find out where you went wrong."

"Mine does, too."

Angelo rubbed his still-aching leg, studying the crowded room, the strained faces trying to conceal their fear, listening to the strangely subdued voices of the men working the radios, the phones, consulting the pictures and the chart on the wall. It had all seemed so logical, so straightforward when he was down there in the underground command post. Was it really possible this bomb was somewhere else, uptown, and they were all looking for it down here because he'd made a mistake? He stopped himself. There were things it was better not to think about.

"Square one is back where that guy's car was hit, right?"

Rand grunted his agreement as Angelo was getting to his feet.

"I'm going to ask Feldman to let us out of here for ten minutes. Let's go back there and walk through this one more time."

Kamal saw the flashing red lights first, just after they passed Irving Place, coming up to Union Square. "Slow down," he ordered.

A fine, cold drizzle had begun to fall, half snow and half rain, and he leaned forward to peer through the blur of the windshield at the crowd in the square ahead. He could see half a dozen squad cars and two ladder trucks drawn up in a sort of crescent. The gray wooden barriers were out, and police and people were spilling into the square. Traffic police were waving cars away from Thirteenth Street and University Place, heading them onto Fourteenth.

"Stay well over to the right, so that no one gets a look at you," he commanded his sister. "Maybe it's a fire." The choked-up traffic edged slowly west on Fourteenth Street toward Fifth Avenue. Near the corner, the crowds thickened. For a moment Kamal thought of lowering the window and asking what was happening. No, he told himself. With my accent, it's too dangerous. Then, as they drew up to the intersection with Fifth, he understood. Two more fire trucks and a police car were drawn up in a line across Fifth from curb to curb, completely sealing off the avenue to traffic.

"They know where it is," he said to Laila. His words came in that flat, mechanical manner of his, but inside the black unreasoning rage he had felt on the FDR Drive engulfed him once more. We have failed, he thought, we have failed again.

Laila inched the car along toward Sixth Avenue. It too was blocked off on the south side by police cars.

"It's all over, Kamal," she said. "We've got to get out. When they find Whalid they'll know who we are. Then they'll have police looking for us at every border crossing into Canada."

Kamal said nothing. He was sitting rigidly upright, his back not even touching the seat of the car, staring straight ahead, tears of fury and frustration coursing down his cheeks.

Laila turned north on Sixth. Better get away from this traffic, she thought. She had driven two blocks when she felt Kamal's hand squeeze her forearm so tightly she gave a little yelp of pain.

462

"Stop," he said. "I'm getting out."

"Kamal, you're crazy!"

This time she screamed in pain at the pressure on her arm.

"Stop, I said. I'm going in on foot."

He had opened the door before the car even came to a halt. "Go north," he told her, "as fast as you can drive. At least one of us will get home." He slid out, slammed the door shut and leaped to the sidewalk.

For a second, Laila was too stunned to react. She watched in the rearview mirror as he started back down the avenue in the rain, head low, the checkered cap pulled down, his collar turned up to conceal his face. He'll never make it, she told herself. For an instant she considered putting the car in reverse, going back down the avenue after him, to urge him to flee with her. Instead she jammed the gear lever into drive. One simple thought had over-powered her, like the rush of a powerful anesthetic. It was an almost demoniacal desire to get away, to survive, to get as far away from this city as fast as she could.

Barely fifteen blocks from Laila's speeding car, Angelo had once again stopped in front of the location at which the Procter & Gamble salesman's fender had been scraped. Unaware of the chlorine-gas threat or indifferent to it, the leather jackets prowled the sidewalk in search of their willing preys. Angelo looked at them scornfully, thinking with satisfaction for just an instant of the impact a bomb would have on this neighborhood. Then he turned his gaze back up the street.

If you were going into the Village with a truck, Christopher's the way you'd go. A big, open street. You wanted to come into town lower down, you'd take Houston; farther uptown, Fourteenth.

"It's simple, isn't it, kid?" he said, ostensibly to Rand, in fact to himself.

"Maybe too simple."

Angelo let the car begin to drift slowly up the street. The two men scrutinized the façades along their way, looking for some-thing, they were not sure what, searching for one flaw in their apparently faultless logic.

The man they were looking for was stalking through the rain up Seventh Avenue, sealed off from the bomb he wanted to detonate by the police lines on Fourteenth Street. Kamal had realized that the police were looking for someone. He'd walked down to a point across the street from their lines and seen the way they were checking everyone crossing their barricades. Was it him? Was it because of the one shot his brother had been able to get off before Kamal killed him?

He should never have left the garage. That was why we failed, he thought, we wanted too much to live. How could he get back in now? A disguise of some kind, but what kind? And where would he find it? Or should he just have the courage to pick a crowded street and take his chances?

Behind him, Kamal heard a siren's wail. Instinctively, he drew away from the curb and pulled up his jacket collar. It was not a police car that swept by him, but an ambulance, the lights glowing in its van. As it reached the corner of Nineteenth, he could see its taillights flare bright red. The ambulance slowed, turned, then accelerated again, racing off into the rain and the dark.

Kamal watched it, frozen on the sidewalk. Then he broke into a run, his feet driving forward as fast as he could move them, racing for the corner, for the fading white form of the ambulance.

Angelo and Rand idled at the stop light at Christopher and Greenwich Streets, still scrutinizing in silence the street around them. Suddenly, Rand laid his hand on Angelo's arm.

"Angelo," he said. "Look." His free hand waved excitedly toward the white arrow hanging from the stop light.

The older man glanced at him appreciatively. "Yeah," Angelo mumbled. "One way. How about that?" He began talking to himself. "Suppose they weren't going over toward the center of the Village. Suppose they turned east onto Christopher because they wanted to double back, get onto a westbound street like Charles. Or Barrow. And being real clever guys they hike all the way over there to Eighth to get their pizza pies to throw us off just in case somebody saw them. In that case, our mistake was beginning our search over there in the center of the Village instead of down here."

He glanced at the bars on the street corners, the brick rear wall of Saint Luke's School. The area, Angelo knew, hadn't been searched yet. "Jesus Christ, kid," he said, "you know you could just be right. That could just be it." He shot the car through the intersection as the light changed. "We gotta get back there and convince them to flood a hundred guys down here to comb this place out."

The sharp clap of Kamal's running feet rang up from the pavement of Nineteenth Street. He ran fast, elbows digging, breathing through his mouth in steady gulps as he had been trained to do in the camps, his eyes, all his attention, concentrated on the white vehicle, a light blinking from its roof, on the other side of Eighth Avenue.

His hat flew off. He igorned it, ignored the stares of the people crossing Eighth Avenue. He'd take his chances on being recognized now. Success was too close not to be grasped in one final, furious lunge. He slowed down as he drew up to the ambulance. The rear doors were open and its stretcher was gone. Trotting by the brightly lit entrance hall of the tenement at 362 where the ambulance was parked, Kamal could see a gaggle of curious neighbors on the landing, peering from their doorways at the blue-coated figure of the ambulance driver easing the front end of the stretcher down the stairs.

He sprinted for the ambulance, slammed its rear doors shut and leaped into the driver's seat. The engine was running. The siren, he thought, where's the siren? I've got to have the siren to make it work. Frantically, his eyes swept the dashboard looking for the unfamiliar knob of the instrument that would guarantee his passage through the police lines.

Behind him, he heard angry shouts. He glanced in the sideview mirror. The blue-jacketed ambulance driver was running toward him, gesticulating wildly. On the tenement doorstep the intern in white had the end of the stretcher in one hand, a bottle of intravenous solution held over his dying patient in the other, a look of total disbelief affixed to his face. The siren, Kamal almost screamed out loud, where's the siren? He turned. The attendant was only a few yards away, ready to leap for the door. No time left to look. Kamal threw the ambulance into gear and raced down the street. As he did, he heared the outraged ambulance driver shouting to a spectator, "Get nine-eleven!"

Kamal turned left at Ninth Avenue, finding at last the red knob that activated the ambulance's siren. Sweating profusely, he rushed down Ninth to Fourteenth Street, then started to swing across the traffic toward the blockaded entry to Hudson Street. As he did, he almost screamed with joy at the sight before his rain-spattered windshield. A patrolman leaped into his squad car and pulled it out of line, opening a hole in the police cordon through which a second policeman was frantically waving him.

I made it, he thought, shooting through the gap in the cars, I'm inside!

Angelo, less than ten blocks away, was so concentrated on what he was going to say at the Sixth Precinct that he barely heard the dispatcher on his radio: "West Midtown and Lower Manhattan cars. Just stolen in vicinity 362 West Nineteenth Street, St. Vincent's Ambulance Number 435, white with orange side markings."

The driver of the ambulance, struggling for breath, ran up to the police barrier at Eighth Avenue and Fourteenth Street. Knowing the bureaucracy of his employers at the Emergency Medical Service, he had decided that the only way to save his dying patient was to run back to the hospital for a second ambulance himself.

"Hey," one of the patrolmen at the barricade called out to him, "where the hell do you think you're going?"

"Son of a bitch!" the driver exploded, gesturing at the police all around. "Where the fuck were all you guys when my bus got stolen?"

"Oh, yeah," the cop said. "We got that on the radio. That was your ambulance? You see the guy?"

"Yeah, I seen him. Almost had my hands on him."

"Come here a second," the cop said, leading the driver to one of the patrol cars in the cordon. He handed him Kamal's picture. "He look like this?"

"Yeah, that's him."

"Christ!" The patrolman leaned into the car and grabbed the speaker of his radio. "Central," he shouted. "This is Car Six Able, Fourteenth and Eighth. I have the complainant on the stolen Saint Vinny's ambulance and he indicates the man who stole his ambulance may be the subject we're looking for."

466

Angelo heard the call as he was preparing to park his car at the Sixth Precinct station house on West Tenth Street. This time the words registered instantly on his mind. "Shit!" he exclaimed. "He's inside!"

Damn it, he thought, why didn't I think of that? I figured it was some drunk, some kid getting himself a ten-dollar ride. The guy must have known the cops would wave the ambulance through. Who'd figure?

"Where are you going?" Rand asked as Angelo spun his car into the broad alley paralleling the Sixth Precinct station house.

"To Charles and then Barrow to run a fast check on your idea!"

He rocketed along Charles leaning on his horn all the way. It was a quiet, mixed street of tenements, garages, private homes, a sidewalk café, trailing off as it neared the river into lofts, garages and half-empty warehouses. Crossing Greenwich Street, Angelo gasped. Parked down almost at the end of the street, close to the river's edge, its interior lights still burning, he could see the white bulk of an ambulance. As soon as he saw it, Angelo switched off his headlights so that the car could glide silently up behind the ambulance. He picked out its orange stripes and, in the glow of its interior lights, he could read the words "St. Vincent's Hospital" and its number, 435, on its white rear doors.

"It's him!" he whispered to Rand. The ambulance was parked in front of a kind of a warehouse-loft, three stories high, a double garage fronting onto the street. The garage doors were closed, but beside them a door into the building was ajar. "He's in there."

He grabbed his radio mike, squinting as he did to read the numbers on the building across the street. He was proud of the fact he still had twenty-twenty vision and, as he liked to joke, could read upside down particularly well—so that he could read the papers on a guy's desk.

"Ten-thirteen," he called, "199 Charles. By the river." There may have been an atomic bomb in New York, but Angelo knew that nothing was going to get help to the scene quicker than that "Assist patrolman" call. "The suspect we're looking for is here," he added.

"Come on, kid," he said. "If he's fooling around with a bomb that can blow up half the city in there, we can't wait for help. We got to take him ourselves." He gestured to the half-open door. "You stay there and give me backup."

The street was silent and deserted. Off in the distance, Rand and

Angelo could hear the rising wail of sirens, probably the first cars responding to their 10-13. They slipped out of the car, leaving its doors open to minimize noise, and headed for the warehouse. Its door gave onto a long, dingy corridor. At the far end they could see a flickering, uneven glow of light falling against the wall. Probably, Angelo guessed, a flashlight moving in a room just off the corridor. He pointed to it.

"There he is," he whispered.

He peered down the corridor. He couldn't see a thing, just the wavering light in the distance, and barely, just barely, he thought he heard noise at the end of the corridor. He stepped inside, moving quickly as he did behind the half-open door so that he was concealed by the shadow it cast and not silhouetted by the lights of the street outside. The detective stared down the corridor ahead of him. It was perhaps twenty-five, thirty feet long, but to Angelo it seemed interminable. He took a half-breath and slowly, deliberately, began to work his way along its length.

Inside, Kamal Dajani squatted behind the black cylindrical form of his brother's bomb on the loading ramp at the back of the garage. He spread his checklist onto the cement floor beside the blue metallic case containing the bomb's firing mechanisms. Methodically, in the glare of his flashlight, he reviewed exactly what he had to do to reopen the case. First he had to punch the INIT button. When the green light glowed "IDENTIFICATION," he would tap "OIC2" on the keyboard. Then, when the word "CORRECT" appeared he could tap the code 2F47 which would allow him to open the case and switch cassettes.

He rubbed his hands nervously, feeling the sweat greasing his palms, thinking. Maybe he should just take the chance of kicking it, of doing something violent to the box to trigger its protective devices. Kamal was too distrusting for that. Suppose his brother had somehow altered those systems? Then he might damage the entire package. There was no question of failing now. He glanced at his codes again and turned to the box.

Outside, Angelo was working his way, careful step by careful step, down the corridor. The trick was to listen for street noises outside, like the rumble of a passing truck, and use them as cover for your moves. Trouble was, this was such a quiet neighborhood that it seemed to Angelo the only thing he could hear in the darkness was the thump of his racing heart. He remembered what they had told him at the physical about the high blood pressure and how the heart attacks come at times like this from sudden stress. Not now, he begged some ill-defined deity, not now.

Somewhere up in the darkness he heard a dog bark. Oh shit, he thought, not that. Don't let there be a dog around here. He stopped to listen for voices to see if more than one person were in there. He heard none. For a second he considered what his moves should be when he reached the door, now ten feet away. The guy in there had killed his own brother a couple of hours ago. And that thing he had could blow the whole Village away. You wouldn't want to just tap on the door and say, "Hello—police," at a time like this.

He resumed his advance. His pistol was pointing down, his finger outside the trigger guard. It was hard to see there, but he could whip it up and get off a fast hip shot if he had to. It was a heavy-barreled Smith and Wesson .38 because Angelo knew well the longer the barrel, the more accuracy you got. And it was a very impressive weapon if you ever had to face off anybody.

Inside, the word "CORRECT" gleamed in the reading window of the bomb's control case. Kamal tapped on the keyboard the code to open the case, then removed the blank thirty-minute BASF tape his brother had placed inside. He picked up the original tape bearing its firing instructions for the bomb preprogrammed in Tripoli. As he did, a strange, incongruous memory overwhelmed him. It took him back several years to a windswept plateau above Damascus. His squad of fedayeen, out on a training mission, had stumbled on a bird's nest filled with newborn birdlings. The squad leader had placed one in each of his recruits' hands. Crush them, he ordered, crush them with one swift, brutal gesture. That, he had explained, was how a fedayee had to learn to stifle his emotions: coldly, completely, at the first stirrings of life.

It was a lesson Kamal Dajani had never forgotten. He could almost feel once again in his palm the slick pulp of the life he had snuffed out that day as slowly, deliberately, he fitted the original tape back into its sprockets in the detonation case.

Angelo was at the door. He froze. Outside, the wail of sirens was drawing closer. He cursed himself. Why didn't I tell them to come in silently? They'll scare the guy. He inched forward and peeped inside. He could see a man's head, bent over, and there it was right in front of him, the barrel they were all looking for, a

469

long black object in the shadows. Despite his efforts to keep himself under control, he trembled sighting it.

He could barely see the figure behind its dark form. The guy was down there on his hands and knees working. All he was giving him was a head shot. And there was the barrel. You'd have to aim high so you didn't hit that. The thing to do, Angelo understood, was to try to move him away from the barrel, then hold him away from it until help came up.

Angelo eased himself flat against the wall inside the doorway to narrow the angle of the return shot the guy could fire at him. Slowly he drew up his gun, pressing it to the wall for support. Angelo was no gun buff, you'd never find him out at a shooting range Sunday afternoons like some guys, but he was a good reliable shot, in the nineties when he shot for the record twice a year at the police range up at Rodman's Neck. He took his half-breath, then roared the stock phrase that was drilled into every police officer in the city: "Police—don't move!"

Kamal was so concentrated on the bomb's detonation box that Angelo's shout took him completely by surprise. Instinctively, he dove to the floor behind the barrel. Angelo fired.

He missed. The shot went high, just over the barrel. Kamal's flashlight, jarred from his hand in his sudden fall, rolled down the loading ramp and tumbled with a thud onto the floor, two feet below. He reached for his own weapon, a Browning 9mm. fifteen-shot automatic. As he was falling, he had glimpsed the American in the doorway. Kamal stretched until he could peer around the end of the barrel at the vague outline of the doorway. Swiftly, he sent a burst of fire tearing into the darkness toward the door, a pattern of six shots stitching it up and down.

Angelo wasn't there. He was sprawled flat on the floor, his eyes clenched in fright, listening to the rounds roar past his head, then the whir of the ricochets bouncing around the doorway. He had dropped to the floor the instant he fired his first round, reacting without thinking, changing his stance from the one Kamal had seen at the instant he looked up in response to his shout.

He tried to lie still, his face pressed against the damp concrete, hoping the guy would think he'd killed him and make another move. Outside he heard footsteps racing down the corridor, then Rand's voice shouting, "Angelo, Angelo, are you okay?"

In the street outside, two parked cars and the first Emergency

Service truck screeched to a halt. The Emergency Service men, giants in helmets and bulletproof vests, leaped out, grabbing their shotguns from the long green boxes in the van of their truck, throwing shells of double-O buck into them as they charged for the door.

"Who's in there?" they shouted at the first patrolman who had reached the scene.

"Two of our guys," he answered. "Big guy in a gray topcoat, a guy in a gabardine raincoat."

At the end of the corridor, Rand was drawing up to the doorway. Again Angelo could hear him shouting, "Angelo, are you okay?"

Don't move into that doorway, kid! Angelo wanted to scream the warning. He lay there forcing himself into the floor, listening for the first warning rustle, watching for the first movement behind the barrel.

"You all right?"

For Christ's sake, kid. It was as though Angelo was trying to shriek his thought to Rand by mental telepathy across the wall separating them: Don't step into that fucking doorway!

"Angelo!"

Lying in the cement and filth, Angelo heard the two quick steps. Then everything happened at once: the head rising behind the barrel, the automatic banging away in the dark, five quick shots tearing over his head as he raised the Smith and Wesson in both hands and fired. The head behind the barrel jerked up, then tumbled backward. From behind him, Angelo heard a strange voice shouting, "Police—don't move!" A burst of light from the Emergency Service lanterns flooded the room, and with it came the terrible boom of exploding shotgun barrels, two of them riddling Kamal Dajani's body with double-O buckshot.

Angelo rolled over, limp with fear and spent emotion. He staggered to one knee. Rand was just behind him, crumpled against the back wall of the corridor where the force of Dajani's bullets had hurled his body. The detective lurched to him. "Get an ambulance!" he yelled. "Get an ambulance!"

He knelt down beside Rand. One of Kamal's shots had torn into his face just below the nose, turning his handsome features into a mush of blood and bone. Two other shots had hit him in the upper body, and blood oozed over his shirt, his jacket and his raincoat. Angelo cupped an arm behind Rand's neck and lifted the bloody, unrecognizable face toward his, realizing as he did that they wouldn't be needing an ambulance for Jack Rand. He pressed the lifeless head against his chest like a mother consoling a weeping child, only it was he who was weeping.

"How could I tell you, kid?" he cried. "Why couldn't you figure it out? Why did you have to go by that goddamn book?"

Two Emergency Service men rushed into the room, stepping over Angelo and Rand's body as they did. One had a Geiger counter. He ran it along the barrel, then looked aghast at his readings.

"Christ!" he exclaimed. "Where are the scientists?"

The scientists were already there, alerted by Angelo's first call, racing down the hall, John Booth at their head. The burly nuclear physicist saw the blue firing case and almost toppled an Emergency Service man leaping away from it.

"Who was here when this happened?"

An Emergency Service lieutenant pointed to Angelo.

"What was he doing?" Booth asked, indicating Kamal's corpse. "Was he right next to that blue box?"

He gave a grateful sigh at Angelo's reply. His first concern had been that the case was protected by a proximity detector that will trigger an automatic response if someone approaches it.

"Okay," he said to the Emergency Service officer. "Two men on the door. Everybody else out."

With Jack Delaney, his mountain-climbing friend from the Livermore Laboratories, Booth squatted down on the floor beside the blue box. He saw the word "CORRECT" glowing on its screen. The dead terrorist, he realized, had been trying either to open the box or to give his computer new instructions. He scrutinized the olive-drab plugs linking the case to the aerial and the bomb. He understood instantly there was no question of disconnecting them.

"What do you think, Jack?" Delaney was an expert on firing mechanisms. "Do we try to get in there with the laser cannon?"

"Suppose it's pressurized with inert gas."

Booth nodded thoughtfully. That was a classic technique. Stuff the thing with helium or azote to protect it. If the case was opened and the gas started to escape, a gauge detected the drop in pressure and triggered the firing mechanism.

"We'll punch a pinhole in it first. Go down to a hundredth of a millimeter and take a reading for escaping gas. If there's any in there we'll melt the plastic around the hole with the laser and seal it back up."

"It's a risk," Delaney said, "but we could try it."

A special NEST truck packed with sophisticated defusing devices accompanied Booth's teams every time they went into action. Over a dozen times, his anonymous beige van had been flown by Booth's aircraft from Las Vegas to some menaced U.S. city. Never before, however, had he and his fellow scientists had to use the equipment it contained.

Delaney and his two aides rushed in the truck's high-powered laser gun with its independent power supply and set it up on the floor beside the case. Booth sprawled flat on his stomach, aiming the gun at the flank of the case like a kid in a shooting gallery taking aim at a target. He marked with a speck of white paint the point at which he intended to punch a hole in the case, so that Delaney could install just below it his gas-detection device.

Booth took a breath and held it to still the nervous fluttering of his hands. He pressed the gun's button and sent at the case one powerful jolt of light energy thinner than a pin but powerful enough to cut through the wall of a steel safe. Delaney's eyes were fixed on the gas detector. The two men waited, not speaking, for thirty, forty-five seconds.

"It's clean," Delaney said finally.

Booth exuded an enormous sigh of relief and altered the firing mechanism of the gun to expand his beam. Employing it like a remotely controlled knife, he sliced four cuts two inches long in the form of a square into the case's side wall. Delaney crept over and inserted a razor-thin scalpel into the top cuts. As delicately as a brain surgeon cutting a tumor from a vital nerve, he tugged on it until the plastic plaque tumbled to the ground.

Booth crawled over and with a high-intensity light peered into the transistored jungle of wiring inside. "My God," he gasped, "how did the Libyans ever get access to something like this?"

Toward the rear of the case he spotted a pair of wires, one red, one blue. They were thicker than the wires running into the heart of the box from the keyboard. The positive and negative lead from the power supply, he realized. They could slice them with the laser. He hesitated. No, he cautioned himself. Suppose it's set to detonate if there's a sudden drop in the current?

He returned to his slow, thoughtful study of the case's interior. There was only one way to do it: burn out the computer's memory bank. You could try to do it with an electromagnetic burst. Or flood it with ultraviolet rays.

Booth rolled over on his back, away from the case. He and Delaney weighed the alternatives. This was not something about which you would want to make a mistake.

"Ultraviolet," Delaney said finally. "There might be some sensing device in there to pick up an electromagnetic beam."

Again they sent to the truck outside for their specialized equipment. Carefully, Booth aligned the objective of the ray's beamcaster on a clump of plaques of resin covered with a forest of wires, the microprocessor chips that stored the computer's memory. The two Emergency Service men guarding the door watched, their feelings a mixture of terror and fascination.

Finally Booth pulled back. "Jack!" he ordered. "You doublecheck that alignment."

Delaney looked along the objective's line of fire, studying its projected path intently. The transfixed Emergency Service men watched in horrified silence.

"Okay," he said finally. "I think we've got it."

Booth activated the machine. For fifteen interminable seconds there was not a sound in the room. Then suddenly a *beep-beep-beep* came from the case. It was faint and shrill, but to the tense men in the garage it sounded like a roar of gunfire.

"Jesus, Mary and Joseph!" shrieked one of the Emergency Service men, furiously blessing himself. "It's going off!"

Booth rolled over, the release of tension so great he broke into hysterical laughter.

"It's not going to do anything anymore. It's all over!" he roared. "The computer's gone crazy." Now he knew there was not even a million-in-one chance it could find its firing instructions.

Outside, the crowds, attracted by the shooting, by the dozen police vehicles cluttering Charles Street, were already pushing up against the police lines, gawking, exchanging excited speculation on what had happened. The media were there, the TV stations with the trucks setting up their cameras and their lights right in front of the warehouse doors, ready to record the statement

Patricia McGuire, the Deputy Commissioner for Public Information, was completing in the front seat of the Commissioner's car.

A police ambulance pulled away from the curb, and four patrolmen opened a path in the crowd so that it could get out to West Street. It contained the bodies of Jack Rand and Kamal Dajani, riding off side by side on their last journey, to the police morgue.

Angelo slumped against the side of one of the Emergency Service trucks. He was pale and panting, hyperventilating, skirting along the edge of hysteria where tears and laughter are inextricably mingled. Over and over again he thought of Rand. What could I have done, he kept asking himself, how could I have kept him out of that doorway?

A young black patrolman came up to him, eyes sparkling with admiration. "Hey," he said, "terrific job. Hear you really blew that prick away."

Angelo looked at him blankly, thinking as he did of the other body riding off to the morgue beside Rand. It had been the first time in thirty years as a New York police officer that he had to kill someone in the line of duty.

Bannion pushed through the circle of admirers around the detective and clapped him heartily on the shoulder. "Great work," he enthused. "Wonderful. You'll get a citation for this. I'm going to try to swing you Chief of the Telegraph Bureau. Get you inspector's money for what you did."

The officer in charge of the Emergency Service Squad joined them. "Excuse me, Commissioner," he said, "but shouldn't we put some of those yellow-and-black radiation warning signs around the area?"

Twenty feet away, in the circle of television lights, the three men could hear the Deputy Commissioner for Public Information reading her prepared text for the press: " . . . explosive charge attached to the barrel of chlorine gas has now been deactivated. The barrel will shortly be transported in a bomb-disposal vehicle to the explosives range at Rodman's Neck for further analysis and ultimate disposal."

The Commissioner turned back to the Emergency Squad officer.

"No," he replied. "Just put out the usual 'Crime Scene' signs."

Every fiber of Laila Dajani's being was concentrated on the concrete ribbon of the Saw Mill River Parkway slipping past the wheels of her car. It was as if it was only now, in this final determined flight, that she had mastered the injunction of her terror master, Carlos: don't think. Instead of the doubt and hesitation that had plagued her for days, her mind was focused on one simple, overwhelming desire: to survive, to get to Canada, to Vancouver and home.

So intent was she on her driving that she did not see the blinking red lights or hear the first burst of the siren. When she finally saw the yellow New York State Police car moving up behind her in her rearview mirror, she did not hesitate. Somehow they had found her, traced the car. But she was not going to let the Americans catch her, not now. She drove the accelerator to the floor.

Behind her, the New York State policeman saw her car bound forward. His instructions were strict. In a case like this you didn't play the macadam cowboy, try to force the fleeing car off the road like they did in the movies. You kept the fleeing car in sight while you called in help. He reached for his radio.

Laila saw her speedometer register 90, 95, 100, 110. She held the accelerator on the floorboard, trying to squeeze a few last thrusts of force from her car's straining engine. The police car had dropped back a bit, now its red lights perhaps half a mile behind her. A little bit more, she thought, and she could risk leaving the highway, trying to lose him somehow in the open country.

Her mind was so wrapped up in her flight that she did not see the black stain of ice spreading like an ink blot from the shoulder of the highway, the surface glistening faintly in the path of her headlights. For just an instant as her front wheels hit it, she sensed a gentle, almost euphoric sense of helplessness as the car went into a skid. Then she hit the guard rail. The car flipped like a toy, somersaulted into the southbound lane and crashed upside down. The cascade of sparks from steel scraping concrete that drifted up as it skidded over the highway found in seconds the spillings of her ruptured gas tank.

By the time the state trooper reached the site, the car was an orange ball of flame, too hot to approach. Through their gusting swirls, he caught a quick glimpse of Laila's corpse, a black stick figure in an orange fog.

"Christ!" said a passerby beside him. "Just like those guys used to burn themselves over in 'nam."

476

The trooper shook his head. "Crazy broad," he said wonderingly. "Whatever got into her? All I had her for on the radar was seven miles over the limit."

The first instinctive reaction of most of the relieved and exhausted men in the NSC conference room at the news that the bomb had been found and defused was to urge the President to launch the missiles targeted on Libya in the nuclear submarines in the Mediterranean. It was only 6:30 P.M. Eastern Standard Time, two and a half hours before the extension of Qaddafi's ultimatum was due to expire, and he would not be expecting an attack.

The President overruled his advisers. The two million Libyans the U.S. rockets would destroy would, he argued, be as innocent victims as the citizens of New York would have been.

The Israelis, Bennington pointed out, would do it anyway. No, the President argued, they would not. Their urge to do so would be swiftly tempered by the sobering realization that Qaddafi now had deployed along his eastern frontier a string of missiles capable of causing untold destruction in Israel if an attack was launched on his country. For both Israel and Libya, a day of cold realism was dawning: their mutual possession of the weapons of mass destruction promised them no happier a salvation than possession of those weapons had offered the U.S. and the U.S.S.R. for three decades —the prospect of mutual suicide.

"But for God's sake, Mr. President," the CIA chief protested, "we're not going to let him get away with this?"

"No," the President replied, "we are not."

For Muammar al-Qaddafi and the knot of men around him in the Villa Pietri, the two-and-a-half-hour wait for the expiration of their ultimatum was a slow descent toward hell, toward the growing certainty that the gamble had failed, that they and two million of their countrymen would shortly die to pay for the error of their leader whose unbending fanaticism they had been all too ready to follow.

As the minutes rolled by after nine with nothing happening, no rockets streaking toward their shores over the radar screen, their fear and resignation turned to incomprehension. So great had the tension become that the terse message from Washington informing them the bomb had been found and defused was greeted with relief and even, by some, with satisfaction.

Two minutes later, the radio operator returned bearing a second message, marked for the eyes only of the Libyan dictator. Qaddafi paled slightly reading it. Whom was it from? The CIA? The Mossad?

He looked at the men around him, recalling their growing bitterness and disillusionment as the failure of his scheme had become evident. What did it matter whom it was from? The answer was probably here, somewhere in this circle of faces ringing him, jailing him in the consequences of his act.

He rose and left the room, headed up to the villa and down the path to the sea. For a long time he stood there by the water's edge. Then he turned away to face inland, toward the distant solitude of his desert. As he did, the paper he clasped in his hand, the paper his radio clerk had handed him a few minutes before, dropped to the ground. The wind picked it up and sent it scurrying along the beach, until gradually it disappeared from sight. It bore just fifteen words, a prophetic message from the fourth chapter of the Koran:

Wheresoever ye shall be, death will overtake you,
even though you be in lofty towers.